JURASSIC WORLD™

The
EVOLUTION of
Claire

JURASSIC WORLD™

The EVOLUTION of Claire

TESS SHARPE

RANDOM HOUSE 🏠 NEW YORK

© 2018 Universal Studios. Jurassic World, Jurassic Park and all related marks and logos are trademarks and copyrights of Universal Studios and Amblin Entertainment, Inc.

Jacket art used under license from Shutterstock.com and iStock.com
Jacket art by Shane Rebenschied
Jacket design by Megan McLaughlin

All rights reserved. Published in the United States by Random House Children's Books, a division of Penguin Random House LLC, New York.

Random House and the colophon are registered trademarks of Penguin Random House LLC.

Visit us on the web! GetUnderlined.com
Educators and librarians, for a variety of teaching tools, visit us at RHTeachersLibrarians.com

Library of Congress Cataloging-in-Publication Data is available upon request.
ISBN 978-0-525-58072-0 (hardcover) — ISBN 978-0-525-58138-3 (lib. bdg.) —
ISBN 978-0-525-58073-7 (ebook)

Printed in the United States of America
10 9 8 7 6 5 4 3 2 1

First Edition

Random House Children's Books supports the First Amendment and celebrates the right to read.

For my husband, who put up with an entire winter of me talking about nothing but dinosaurs and gleefully tramping through the forest pretending to be a T. rex.

Rawwwrrrr (translation: I love you and I like you).

PROLOGUE

The thing about running scared? You can't run forever.

I thought about trying. After the . . . incident, as soon as the boys and Karen were safe at home, I went on autopilot. Survival of the fittest and all that.

If there's one thing I am good at, it's surviving.

I see now that we have that in common, them and me. I'm still standing despite everything, and they returned from extinction. Sheer human hubris mixed with our desire to know, our thirst to see, and our greed to exploit brought them back here—and where does that leave us? What does that make us? God? Predator?

Or prey?

Survival is written in their DNA, but I worry it's being written out of ours. In our spot at the top of the food chain, we've grown so complacent. So content. So very destructive.

I dream about it every night. The screech of the paddock door as it rose; my fingers gripping that flare so tight they cramped.

Counting in my head, waiting for her to show herself, I'd never felt that kind of fear. *One Mississippi, two Mississippi, three Miss—*

Sometimes I wake up screaming. My neighbors are going to hate me, and I haven't even had a chance to meet them yet.

She made me come back, my sister. Karen doesn't play the family card often, but her boys almost got eaten by dinosaurs, so she gets whatever she wants. Forever. Because I will *never* be able to make it up to her or the boys.

I want you home, Claire. Safe, with us. Far away from all the chaos. I'm begging you.

It was more running, but this time I was running from the inevitable government investigations and the conspiracy theories online . . . and the death that's haunted all the dreams I've had since we left the island.

I took it—the escape hatch my sister offered me. I just didn't think about how it would feel once I finally stopped running.

Now I have a half-unpacked apartment and an empty fridge and scars in places my hands can't reach. But early Monday morning, I'm up and I'm awake and I'm determined.

I unpack boxes of clothes as my coffee brews. The fuzzy pre-dawn light creeps through the French doors as I hang up shirts and chiffon skirts, pushing the skirts to the side because I won't be needing them now. I could spend the entire day in sweatpants if I wanted. It should be appealing, shouldn't it? But there's something in me that craves clean white lines and feather-light silk and hair swinging straight and neat, because that was the old normal. Now . . .

Some new kind of normal needs to be found.

My fingers brush over a wooden box under another stack of hanging clothes, and my breath catches because I thought I'd lost it long ago. I don't even remember packing it.

I lift it out. The box itself was a gift from Simon Masrani to mark my first year working for him. I'd kept all the mementos from my internship in it.

Eyes burning, I set the box down on my bed. My intern badge is on top of the pile of trinkets inside. I forgot how long my hair was back then. There's a notebook below the badge, the corners frayed. The spine cracks as I open it. A thistle—a spiky purple flower whose color is almost as vibrant now as it was the day Justin gave it to me—is pressed between the pages, and when I see it, and the handwriting—not mine, *his*—defining the genus and species, I snap the notebook shut. My heart picks up like I've been running, like I'm back there, like I'm nineteen again, because some wounds go so deep there are no marks. Just pain.

I close my eyes and breathe in deep. *Control.*

When I open them, I turn my focus back to the box. There are postcards from Karen at the bottom, and when I lift the stack to leaf through them, I see one last thing inside.

I smile as I pick it up. The pin was carved out of amber into the shape of a cicada, the bug's long wings and spiky legs graceful, if you appreciate that sort of thing.

I do. Or I did, once upon a time.

I lift the pin to the light filtering in from the window, and it shines through the insect's golden wings and the arched carvings on its exoskeleton.

Maybe that's the way to a new normal: finding that girl I once was again, the one who loved animals fiercely and stubbornly fought for what she believed in. The one who loved organization and color-coding, but who wore bug pins and her hair loose and took flowers from boys with dark eyes and smiles that made me think of hope.

That girl . . . I wanted things beyond me. I ended up sacrificing things I couldn't even fathom. But as I turn the pin in my fingers, the sun catching the amber, glowing through the wings, I think about it.

At nineteen, over one summer, I became something new. Someone different. I don't think it was bad. Or good. I think it was both.

I think it was survival.

And like I said, if there's one thing I'm good at, it's surviving.

1

"Did you *color-code* your boxes?" Regina asks.

I look up from taping the last one. "Of course. That way I know where everything is."

Our dorm room is a study in opposites. My side is completely packed up, the bed stripped, the sheets and blankets tucked away in their labeled yellow boxes. My posters—matted prints of extinct plants and animals—are already wrapped and in their blue box. Everything on my checklist is crossed off—I'm ready to go.

On her side, Regina's got half-folded bins and boxes strewn across the floor, Degas prints hanging askew on the wall, and a massive collection of eighteenth-century French literature still stacked underneath the bed.

My roommate shakes her head, walking over to her half-made bed and throwing herself on it. "Dearing, you're one of a kind. And to think that the first time we met, I wasn't so sure about you. Especially when I opened the mini-fridge and saw that box of crickets."

"You were so freaked out." I snicker at the memory.

"What was I supposed to think? You had *bugs* in our fridge!"

"Well, yeah. What else would Sally eat?"

"And then there was that time you had your lizard on that snail-and-spinach diet . . . ," Regina continues.

"Switching up a blue-tongued skink's protein sources is important. *You* wouldn't want to eat the same thing all the time, would you? That'd be boring."

Regina gets up and walks over to the aquarium, where Sally is hanging out on her favorite rock. "You're lucky you're so cute, Sally Ride." She grins when my lizard flicks her tongue out. Regina has this thing where she insists on calling Sally by her full name, ever since she figured out I named her after the astronaut. She's funny like that.

"Speaking of bugs . . ." She goes over to her fringed bag, digs around, and pulls out a small box. "I have a present for you. I may have had to put up with crickets and snails this year, but you had to deal with my repeated snooze-button smashing and night-owl tendencies."

"Plus that gross-smelling tea you love," I add.

"It's good for you!"

"It smells like the Grim Reaper opened a perfumery," I tell her, taking the proffered jewelry box. I open it, and a smile breaks across my face when I see what's inside: a cicada pin, carved out of amber. "Regina," I say, pulling it out. "You didn't!"

"I remembered you were looking at it when we were at Riverter's Vintage last time," she says. "It's not a cricket, but I thought it was fitting."

"You're so sweet." I reach over and hug her. "Thank you. I love it. And I've loved being your roommate. Not everyone would've been so cool with the lizard. I know she's not the most conventional pet."

"You're not the most conventional person, Claire."

"Neither are you," I say, making her laugh. "I have a present for you, too." I grab her gift from behind one of my boxes. The edges of the bright red houndstooth wrapping paper are perfectly lined up, the tape smooth and nearly invisible, the edges of the ribbons curled just so.

"This is so pretty I hate to open it," Regina says, right before she tears into it like she's five. Of course. The book inside is an old copy of Rumi's *Masnavi.*

"Is this the Nicholson translation from the 1930s?" she squeals. "The one Professor Gillian was talking about in class?"

I nod. "She helped me find it from a used bookstore in Oregon," I say.

"Thank you. This is awesome! Especially considering your aversion to poetry and all things emotional in verse."

I groan. Professor Gillian's Poetry 101 was harder than molecular biology. "I would've failed without your help."

"Oh, you would have been fine," Regina says. "That last paper you did was good."

As usual, she's being nice. Every essay I wrote for that class—every poem I analyzed—I felt completely out of my league. Like I was just scraping along the surface of something that everyone else was diving deep beneath. And no matter what I did, I couldn't quite slip under with everyone and *get it.*

It was hard. I like school. I'm *great* at it. Struggling with a class—struggling with anything—isn't what I do. But with Regina's help, I managed to kind of muddle through.

"I don't know how you do all that literature analysis stuff day in and day out," I confess.

"Well, I couldn't do all the political analysis stuff you're working on, or go to law school so I can lobby to protect animals, so I guess we're even," Regina replies. "You are all about the long game, Claire. I appreciate that. I so don't have that kind of patience."

I smile. She's right; what I wanted, it's a long game. I realized a long time ago that in order to create real change for animals—from domestic pets to wildlife to farm animals—you need to have a lot of money, or a lot of power. Laws that could—and should—protect animals more aren't being championed the way they should be.

All it takes is one person, determined to rise, to get enough power to give a voice to the voiceless.

Politics make so much more sense to me than Rumi's talk of gardens that aren't actually gardens and love that runs so true you're shattered when it ends. Politics are about what you want, who you know, how you manipulate, and what you control. The climb to get the kind of power to make laws and pass bills and create *real* change—that path is clear to me.

It's the path I've chosen, and nothing will get in my way. I won't let it.

There's a knock on our door, and I go answer it. My big sister's standing there grinning, her blond hair in an intricate braid down her back.

"Karen, hi!"

We hug. She smells like home, like the cinnamon candles our mom lights in the evening and the barest whiff of smoke from the backyard fire pit. When we were little, we roasted marshmallows and hot dogs on long sticks over the big bonfires our dad built. Now Dad does the same thing with my nephew, Zach.

Karen looks over my shoulder, still holding me. "Did you actually color-code your moving boxes?" she asks. "Claire . . . honestly!"

Regina cackles from her bed. "I like your sister, Dearing." She waves. "I'm Regina."

"Karen," my sister says, finally letting go of me. "It's nice to meet you. Claire's been so busy this year we've barely seen her, and getting her on the phone has been nearly impossible."

It's a pointed comment. Mom's obviously been complaining to her. She watches Zach while Karen's at work, and Karen and her husband live just across town from my parents. So she's close. And I'm . . . not anymore.

I've gone home only a few times this year, and it's not enough for Mom. Dad probably feels the same, but he's kept it to himself.

"I needed to get good grades," I protest.

"I know," Karen says, reaching out and squeezing my hand. "And you did great, didn't you?"

I nod. My GPA is perfect—partly thanks to Regina saving my butt in that poetry class. But even as Karen turns to ask Regina about her summer plans, I feel guilty at my sister's reminder of how I've neglected my family this year. The last time she sent me a picture of Zach, I was startled at how big he'd grown.

I want to go back more often, I really do. But money is always so tight, and I don't have a car, and taking the bus turns the six-hour drive into fourteen. And then Professor Broadhurst offered to be my mentor, and that also meant managing her office hours once a week. I've tried to explain what a big deal it is to be chosen as a freshman, but I don't think my parents quite get it.

There's a lot my parents never quite get. They try. They're wonderful. I love them. But there's something in me that wants more than a little family in a little house with a quiet little life. And I've never figured out a way to say that without sounding mean or scornful.

I am grateful. For our little house and the lovely childhood I had. For my parents and for Karen and for the chance to be an aunt.

But I'm different. I want things they don't. Control. Change. Power. I want a bigger life. One far from here. One that's never boring. One that's always a challenge. One where I fix problems and always have the answer.

I see a climb ahead of me, a long, rough road with hazards and hills . . . but it's not defeating and it's not scary—it's exciting.

Driven is what people call girls like me to our faces.

Bossy is what people call girls like me behind our backs. Like it's a bad thing.

Someday, they won't be able to say it's like a bad thing.

Because someday, I'll be the boss.

2

When Regina's parents show up about fifteen minutes after Karen, they take one look at my roommate's still-unpacked boxes and shake their heads.

"I tried!" Regina says, her dark brows rising the way they do when she lies about stealing my last bag of pretzels. "But my French final was intense, and I needed to argue with the know-it-all in my class afterward about the second-to-last question."

I snort. The "know-it-all" in her French class was as into her as she was into him, but they were both in total denial. They got coffee six times over the last semester to conjugate verbs or something, and after each encounter, Regina came back to our dorm with this little kick in her step and a rant on her lips about whatever they'd debated that day and how he was so very wrong and why in the world did she let him draw her into these conversations.

"We're going to take you to lunch and then we'll help you

deal with this," Regina's father says. "We'll be downstairs waiting, sweetie. Claire, it was nice to see you."

"We should get your stuff in the truck," Karen tells me as Regina's parents leave. "We've got a drive ahead of us."

I turn to Regina, worried I'm going to tear up or something. I have friends, of course, but when I moved to college, it was different. I've only ever shared a room with Karen, and that was forever ago and I *have* to love her, even when she's being annoying, because she's my sister. Living with a completely random stranger sounded like a recipe for disaster. But what could've been awful turned out to be the best thing ever. Without Regina, I probably would've spent all my time in the library instead of just a lot of it.

"Call me when you get home," Regina says, hugging me. "We'll make a plan for our off-campus apartment next semester. And I want to hear about your internship."

"And I want to hear all about France," I say. Regina's planned her own internship overseas.

"I'll take a ton of pictures," she promises, eyes shining at the prospect. Then she turns around. "I should go before my dad gets annoyed. Have a great summer, Claire!"

"I'll call you."

"Bye."

We hug again, and after Regina leaves, Karen looks at me over a stack of boxes. "It's nice you two got so close," my sister says. "I spent my first year away from home getting sexiled by my roommate."

"You got even in the end, if I remember correctly," I say.

My sister smiles, a sly, smug grin that snakes across her face. "You helped," she says.

"It was one fox, one time," I say, remembering. "His paw was broken, and your place was closest to the field I found him in. He just needed to stay for a few hours, until the wildlife rehab lady made it there. I don't know why she freaked out so much."

"I've never heard someone scream so loud over a cute little fox," Karen says. "He didn't even look rabid." She shakes her head. "City girls."

"Because we're so roughneck," I say, laughing. We grew up on the outskirts of our town, in a little house on two flat acres at the edge of a white beech grove. That land was Dad's pride and joy. He kept bees and fixed trucks in the detached garage and devotedly pruned the apple trees he'd planted when Karen and I were born.

"We're more countrified than little Miss Beverly Hills was," Karen points out.

She turns back to the boxes, pursing her lips. "Okay. I've got Dad's truck, as promised. And I've got tie-downs and a tarp, and I cleared out a space for Sally's travel terrarium in the cab."

"And I've got an old blanket to wrap up the big aquarium for transport," I add.

"Then I think we're good to go," Karen says briskly. "Now, do you want to bribe some boys to move the boxes, or should we do it ourselves in the name of independence and whatnot?"

I laugh. My sister's humor has always been a little deceptive. People look at her and think one thing . . . but once you get to know her, there's a dark, sarcastic streak that she lets out only when she's comfortable. It's one of my favorite things about her. She owns half of the contents of a Sephora store *and* she'll go to war for you, using her wits, her words, and her fists. And she'll win without breaking a nail, because she's the kind of strong that people underestimate.

"I took a weight-lifting class last semester to fulfill one of my GE requirements," I say. "And I know you have superior upper-body strength with all the yoga and baby wearing and toddler chasing. So I think we'll be okay."

Karen grabs the nearest box. White label. Books and files, because I've kept a printed copy of each paper I wrote this year. Plus all the hard copies of my class notes. I type them all out, just in case I lose a notebook. Not that I ever have. That would be a nightmare.

I hold the door open for her, grabbing a box under each arm, and we make our way to the elevator. Karen raises an eyebrow and punches the down arrow. "If you and Dad start lifting weights in the garage together, I'm going to get you matching father-daughter sweatbands that say *Big Bear* and *Little Bear*," she teases.

"Don't you dare." I wince, and she laughs in that way that tells me that's *exactly* what I'm getting for Christmas.

My dad's old Ford F-150 in the college parking lot is a familiar sight, mud flaps and rusty red paint that's slowly faded to pink through the years. He's rebuilt that thing time and time again. . . . He jokes about Zach inheriting it someday.

It takes us about an hour to squeeze everything in. Sally comes last. I transfer her to her little travel carrier, and she skitters around in the cork bark spread across the bottom. After we fit her aquarium into the cab, I bring her down to the truck.

"It's okay," I say as I set her down on the bench seat. Karen jumps into the truck and closes the door.

"I can't believe you sacrificed your precious purse space for Sally. I'm touched." I nod at Karen's purse. It's not a mom purse. I mean, it is, because she's a mom. And it's full of all those endless secrets and supplies all moms seem to have somehow. But it's enormous and black and sleek, and looks like it could be used to bludgeon someone. I like it because it reminds me of her, is kind of representative of her. My sister's layers. How she's one thing on the outside, how she has all these roles, but on the inside, there's so much more.

"I would only put my purse on the dirty floor for you and your lizard," Karen says, putting the key in the ignition. She pauses.

"Ready?" she asks.

I nod.

She looks at me expectantly.

"What?" I ask.

"You don't want to . . . I dunno, take a moment or something? This is goodbye for now. Your first year. Your college experience!"

"I'm good," I say.

Karen sighs like I've disappointed her as she pulls out of the parking lot and heads toward the highway. I hate this feeling, like I've done something wrong because I'm not really sentimental. Karen and my mom, they like to savor stuff and reminisce, put together scrapbooks . . . they have all these little traditions that are really important to them.

Meanwhile, I'm over here. It's not like I don't enjoy remembering things. I remember everything! But school is done for the year. I've said goodbye to the important people. I'll see them again in a few months.

Now I get to focus on the summer. On my internship.

Just the thought of it sends a twirl of excitement through me, like a red ribbon dancing in the wind. I've applied to six. The long shot, an internship in DC, fell through when they changed their age requirement at the last minute. But they asked me to keep them in mind when I turn twenty. Professor Broadhurst said that's a good sign.

That leaves the remaining five. I've heard from four—and was accepted to all of them. But I've put off choosing until the very last minute. All because I haven't heard from that final one.

"Tell me about the rest of your year," Karen says as we hit the highway, merging behind a semi and settling into the long drive home. "I know about your classes and about Regina and your friends, but what about dating? Was there anyone interesting this year?"

It's funny that she says *anyone interesting* instead of *anyone special*. It's a careful distinction, really. Like she knows that interesting is my kind of special.

"Not really," I say. "I went on a few dates with this guy one of my friends set me up with, but it kind of turned into a mess."

Karen frowns, glancing over at me, immediately in concerned mode. "What do you mean?"

Heat crawls up my face at the memory. "I thought he was okay at first. But then he started making all these snide comments about how I decorated my dorm, and he was really weird about Sally. I get it if reptiles aren't your thing or even if they creep you out, but he was the type of guy who'd never admit that a little lizard scared him. So I told him I didn't think we should spend any more time together."

"That's fair," Karen says.

"Well, I thought so," I say. "He apparently didn't, because he blew up at me and showed up at my dorm and said all this stuff about how I was cold-blooded, just like my creepy lizard. Apparently, he was just hanging around to sleep with me, and I messed with his plans."

"Um, *excuse me?*" My big sister's fingers clench the steering wheel in outrage. "What's this guy's name? I think he and I need to have a talk."

I roll my eyes. "It's fine, Karen. Regina came into our room just as he was finishing his rant, so she had my back. She took Sally out of her tank and just stood there scratching her head and staring at him. It made him so nervous, he bolted. Now he goes in the other direction whenever he sees us on campus."

Karen laughs. "What a jerk," she says. "Claire-bear, you know what he said isn't true, right?"

I nod, pasting an encouraging smile on my face, and it seems to reassure her, because she turns her attention back to the road.

Jackson's comment stung, though. It felt strange at the time because I'd been the one trying to get him out of my life, and I shouldn't have cared what he thought. It took me a minute to realize he was trying to chip away at me, like he'd been doing the entire time. He was just being more obvious about it because I took control of a situation I didn't like and ended it.

I guess I'm not supposed to do that. I'm supposed to sit back and smile while he implies I'm not a "proper girl." Proper girls have cats or dogs instead of lizards named after astronauts. Proper girls don't have creepy artwork on the walls, or childish little toy dinosaurs marching across their desks. . . .

I roll my shoulders back, like I can shake off that flash of humiliated heat still alive inside me.

Some boys suck.

"How's everything at home?" I ask. "Did you figure out what kindergarten to send Zach to?"

"We're still trying to decide if he should go to school near our house or by Mom and Dad's so she can pick him up after school when I can't get there," Karen says. "But with everything, I'm kind of leaning toward Pine Grove, near our house."

Her tone is casual, but my brain trips over the first part. "What do you mean, 'with everything'?" I ask.

Immediately, the air in the truck changes. My sister licks her lips and her hands tighten around the steering wheel as she hyper-focuses on the road. She's got her "oh crap" face on. She's trying to figure out how to lie to me and she's not going to be fast enough because she's *never* fast enough. She's a terrible liar.

"What's going on?" I demand.

"I really didn't want to get into this your first night back," Karen says . . . more like warns.

My stomach drops.

"Are they breaking up?" I whisper.

Karen's eyes stay fixed on the road. "Mom and Dad are having some problems," she says quietly. And I know that the fact she even admits that means it's bad.

It's my turn to stare out the window, biting the inside of my cheek hard to keep from tearing up. Now I feel even guiltier that I didn't go home as much. That I didn't even notice things were strained. Had they been pretending for me, when I did manage to visit?

"They're trying counseling," Karen continues. "That's a good sign."

"Yeah," I say.

"Dad didn't want you to know," Karen says. "He doesn't want it to affect your decision about your internships. He knows how much your plans for this summer mean to you and your future."

"And Mom?" I ask.

"Mom didn't even want *me* to know," Karen sighs, neatly sidestepping my question. "You can't let on that you know! They'll both kill me. But I really think now that they're in counseling, they'll get to a better place. That's why I didn't want to tell you. I don't think this is anywhere close to the end. They just need to reconnect. To remember what they loved about each other. It'll be fine."

Optimism is something I don't have in common with my sister. But I give her a tight smile and nod, saying, "Yeah, of course," even though I feel like I've been punched in the stomach and I'm running divorce statistics in my head like a mathematician.

It's not like I didn't notice that my parents haven't been getting along. It's been a rough few years. Dad made an investment that fell through and money was so tight they couldn't put anything toward my college, and I know Dad feels like it's his fault. And when Grandma passed away, it was so hard on Mom, because she took care of her that entire last year. That's who Mom is. A care-taker. She takes care of everyone.

But no one takes care of her. And as soon as the thought occurs to me, a guilty, crawling heat fills me.

I don't take care of her. Karen does. Karen is always there to help, even though she has a family of her own.

Karen's the good daughter. And I'm . . .

I'm the one who's already dreaming about leaving, and I'm still a few hours away from home.

I stare out the window at the blurring trees and buildings, trying to ignore the growing pit in my stomach at the thought of my parents not working things out.

Karen and I drive for a good three hours before we stop at a drive-through and grab some food. Then we get back on the road, my strawberry-and-chocolate milkshake sweating in the cup holder, Karen eating fries with one hand while steering with the other.

"So . . . no romantic prospects worthy of your time," she says, clearly not wanting to discuss the bombshell she's dropped on me. "What about your internships?"

I take a sip of milkshake, wondering if I should prod her more about our parents. But when I look at her closely, I can see how tired she is. How long has she been holding on to this burden of knowing without me? Being the youngest is a pain in the butt sometimes. Even after you grow up, people treat you like a baby.

I decide to let it go. For now.

"I've been accepted by five of the six places I applied to," I say. "Four law firms and one internship with a Ninth Circuit judge."

"That's amazing!" Karen says as we pass the sign that says NORTHAMPTON 240 MILES. "What about the sixth place?"

"I haven't heard back from them yet," I explain. "The deadline is tomorrow, actually. So it's totally not going to happen."

"Yet . . . you've been waiting out the deadline before you accepted the others," Karen says, cluing in immediately. You can never sneak anything past a big sister.

"I had to. It's with the Masrani Corporation."

Karen's eyes widen. "As in Simon Masrani, the billionaire? The dinosaur guy?"

I nod, kind of amused at hearing Mr. Masrani described as "the dinosaur guy."

"He's just started this internship program called Bright Minds. It's for the 'best and brightest' in the country." I shake my head, looking out the window. "Like I said, the deadline has basically passed now. So it'll be one of the law firms or the judge, I guess." I try not to sound too disappointed. Getting my hopes up about it isn't rational, but I think I did, just a little.

"Well, at least you won't be stuck at home with Mom and Dad and me and Zach for the whole summer," Karen says.

My cheeks do a fast burn. You probably can't even see my freckles, I'm so red. "I didn't mean it like that," I mutter.

"I know," Karen sighs. "Mom just misses you. She thinks you're going to graduate from college, go off, and never come back."

The idea of a life full of big cities and influential people just a click away on my phone is too appealing to protest. I am a lot of things, but I always try to be honest. Especially with Karen.

"I'll come back" is all I say, the silent *sometimes* at the end practically filling the car.

"I understand why you want to go," Karen says gently, looking over at me. "It's just . . ."

"You came back home," I finish, because that's the truth. Karen set a precedent. After college, she came back home, got her job, and married Pete, her husband. They have dinner with my parents every Sunday, and my mom gets to see her every day when she picks up Zach at their house after work.

"I never planned on staying away," Karen says, and now she's being the honest one. It's the fundamental difference between us: Karen is built to stay.

And I am built to run. Not away, but forward. And running forward means sometimes leaving things—people—behind.

There's a long pause, like neither of us knows what to say. Like the past year I've spent away has roughened parts of us up, so we don't quite fit like we used to.

"You know what? Let's play Dad's wishing game." She nods at the napkin next to Sally's terrarium. "Take that and write down the internship you really want on it. I don't care if the acceptance deadline's tomorrow. Then—"

"Fold it thirteen times and toss it into the fire," I finish for her. I've tossed dozens of pieces of folded-up paper into backyard bonfires through the years, the wishes sailing off into the air with smoke and sparks. "Okay, but there's no fire."

"We'll improvise," Karen says. "Think about it and then write it down. We've got time."

I roll my eyes hard at her, but inside, I'm smiling as I take the napkin and grab a pen out of my bag. As Karen drives down the highway, the cars and trucks around us blurring as they rush by, I tap the pen against my mouth and think.

A practical person would choose one of the sure things. The judge would be the smartest choice. It would look great on my resume and would help with law school. Same with the law firms—they're all top practices in the fields I'm most interested in. Professor Broadhurst really came through with her connections and letters of recommendation.

But there's another side of me, the reckless side, that's all about wonder and discovery, that wants something else.

There's always been this thirst in me . . . this desire for adventure that comes only with the kind of risks I rarely take. I talk myself out of dangerous things more often than I do them. I was the designated driver and walker-home of my girlfriends more than I was drinking this year. I absolutely refused to go bungee jumping with Regina during spring break, and I can't remember the last time I skipped a day of sunscreen.

Careful Claire—that's me.

What would happen if I weren't so careful? Just once?

Who could I be?

What could I do?

I look down at Sally. Half buried in cork bark, her eyes narrowed, she looks decidedly annoyed that I've disrupted her day like this. I've had her since I was eight. When I was little, she was kind of my only friend, apart from Karen. Things got better when I made it to high school, but for a long time, Sally was the holder of all my secrets, all my hopes, all my dreams. She's the reason I let Professor Broadhurst talk me into applying for the Bright Minds internship, even though I have nowhere near the pedigree to get that kind of attention.

The Masrani Corporation has taken Dr. John Hammond's revolutionary work and put it into action. To be a part of that, even if it means a summer of getting the scientists' coffee—which, let's face it, is probably what the internship is about—would be the ultimate opportunity. It would mean interacting with amazing creatures that only a handful of people have ever seen up close. A monumental chance to do historic work that could benefit the world—the kind of opportunity that shouldn't exist, because really, dinosaurs shouldn't exist.

But now they do.

When they announced Dr. Hammond's breakthroughs after the photos of the first dinosaurs surfaced, I was twelve. Some people called it a nightmare, especially when news got out about what happened with Dr. Hammond's first park, the one that never opened.

But for me, it was like a dream. It still is. It's the impossible fantasy and the wild frontier of scientific innovation. It's the chance to re-create the past and forge it into the future . . . to experience the very start of something enormous—the beginning of a new cycle of evolution itself.

How could anyone pass that up?

So I write down the reckless, impractical path—*Bright Minds*. I bite my lip, making sure Karen isn't looking at what I'm writing, before I scribble at the bottom of the napkin: *Let Mom and Dad find their way back to each other.*

I fold the napkin thirteen times, just like Dad taught us. Karen glances at me out of the corner of her eye, but she doesn't say anything as I tuck the little square into my pocket.

An hour later, we pull into a rest stop. After we're done using the facilities, Karen digs a lighter out of the glove box (because Dad is *always* prepared), and we sit down at one of the cement picnic tables.

I take the folded napkin out of my jeans and hold it up as Karen flicks the lighter. The square catches fire, and I drop it onto the table, watching the flame curl around the paper, burning the ink—and my wish—to smoke.

"Are you gonna tell me which one you wrote down?" Karen asks.

I bite my lip, looking down at the gray and black curls of ash. I blow gently, and they break apart, skittering off the table and up into the air like a swarm of mosquitoes.

"The Bright Minds project," I blurt out, not even able to meet her eyes when I say it, because I'm embarrassed to, when it's so out of reach. "It's stupid. They have, like, twelve hours left to let me know. The acceptance letters probably went out weeks ago."

But there's a light in my sister's eyes that makes the skin on the back of my neck prickle. And then she's smiling in a way that's pure "I told you so," and a frantic kind of hope rises inside me, like an animal scratching at the door in a snowstorm.

"They did, actually, get sent out weeks ago," Karen says. "There must have been a holdup at the post office, because this just arrived at Mom and Dad's before I left to get you."

Karen reaches into her purse and pulls out an envelope.

A *big* envelope.

The kind of big envelope that acceptances and welcome letters come in.

My heart's thudding.

She slides it across the picnic table. It's flipped over, the address side down, and the first thing I see is the seal on the flap.

Bloodred. A T. rex pressed into the wax.

My fingers close around the envelope, and the future I've always wanted is finally in my grasp.

3

When Karen and I finally get home, the sun's sinking behind the hills. It's weird, or maybe it's not, that I feel kind of nervous as we turn onto our street.

Mom's waiting on the porch before we even pull into the driveway, and she hugs me a long time, stroking my hair. Dad comes out from the back, beaming when he sees me, and Earhart, my dog, is right behind him, her tail wagging so fast it's almost a blur.

I hug Dad. "It's good to see you, sweetie," he says. "The drive went okay?"

"The drive was good," I say. I bend down so I'm eye level with Earhart, rubbing between her ears as she closes her eyes.

She's a mutt but clearly has some Lab and Rottweiler in her. She's not just named after the pilot—she has this scar on her left ear that's in the shape of a heart. She also has the cutest little eyebrows, and when she came into the rescue I volunteered at in high school, I knew she was supposed to be with me. She was so scared when she first arrived, any noise she wasn't used to would send her into shaking fits. Sometimes, at the rescue, you'd get the full story of a dog, because they were taken out of abusive situations or because someone had to surrender their animal for whatever reason and bringing them to the rescue was the best thing they could do. But with Earhart, we had no idea about her past, so earning her trust took time. She'd been found wandering down the highway with a bad case of mange and her right eye terribly infected, probably from a tangle with another dog. The vets who worked with the rescue had to remove her eye, but other than a few depth perception issues, it's never seemed to bother her.

While Earhart loves me, her *real* true love is Sally. As soon as she sees the travel terrarium in my hands, her ears prick up, her tail whipping back and forth. I laugh. "Yep, I brought your buddy home," I tell her, and Earhart licks the plastic outside of the terrarium enthusiastically.

Sally flicks her tongue out, unperturbed by the sloppy drool.

My dad shakes his head. "That dog," he says, grinning.

I pat Earhart on her head one more time for getting up.

"Your dad's been grilling all day," Mom says as we go inside. "And I made that herb bread you love."

"Sounds great," I say as Earhart scampers in front of me, spinning in circles, trying to keep her eyes on Sally.

"I'm going to call Pete," Karen says. "He'll bring Zach over."

"I'm gonna put Sally upstairs, then I'll come out," I say.

When Karen gets back and we sit down for dinner, I watch my parents closely for any sign of trouble, but they seem fine. Dad's a little distracted helping Zach cut his chicken, and Mom's focused on me, especially when I tell the table I got the Bright Minds internship. I can tell by the way her lips flatten just *so* that she isn't thrilled.

Karen and I break out the bubble machine from the garage after dinner, and we play bubble tag in the backyard with Zach, who rolls around in the grass and shrieks with laughter every time a bubble bursts in between his hands. Earhart barks delightedly every time he does it. It's nice to be home.

But it's also kind of strange, after Karen and Pete leave with a sleepy Zach and I put my boxes in the garage instead of my room and toss a suitcase on the bed. Like I don't quite fit in this space anymore. Earhart's the only thing in it that feels like mine. She curls up on the rug next to my bed, and in minutes, she's snoring blissfully.

I guess that'll make one of us.

My mom's kept my room the same. She did that with Karen's room too. Until she got married. I didn't want her to do that with mine, so when I left for school I told her she should turn it into a sewing room. She makes these beautiful quilts, and she should have the space for her sewing machine and all her supplies instead of the corner of the living room she has now. But she kept saying I'd need my room when I came home to visit. And then, of course, I didn't, except for Thanksgiving and Christmas.

I press my palms against my eyes, trying to drive away the guilt.

When Karen gave me the envelope, I was so happy. But now that I'm here, alone in my room, I've already begun making a pros-and-cons list in my head. All this change the past few years . . . it obviously messed with my parents. And now that I know they've been having problems, I'm suddenly questioning things. Do I really want to go so far away, leave my family when there's a crisis?

But what could I do if I stay? My parents don't even want me to know they're having trouble. Am I supposed to stay here and pretend I don't know? Because that would be awful.

Am I supposed to go and trust they'll work it out?

I let out a long breath and turn off my bedside lamp, plunging the room into darkness. I stare up at the intricate solar system I created on my ceiling in eighth grade. I spent so many hours looking up at these glowing stick-on constellations in high school, studying hard and waiting to get away to college. And now I'm right back here, looking up at the stars and waiting to get somewhere else.

If I stay, I'll regret it. That's the truth. I'll lose momentum and fall behind. I'd catch up, because I always find a way, but it would be hard. I would hate it.

But I also hate that I don't want to stay. I hate that it isn't an easy choice, like it was for Karen. Her ambitions fit into staying. But mine never have.

Being ambitious is like being consumed. Like something's gnawing at me. Sometimes the desire fades, but other times it's so intense, I'm afraid it'll burst through my skin, all gnashing teeth and feral hunger. I think it should scare me, because it's a part of me that's hard to tame. It's a part of me that grows every day. The more I learn, the more I see, and the more I see, the more I want.

The next morning, I get up early. I step over a snoozing Earhart, careful not to wake her. The house is quiet. It's Saturday, and Dad is not a morning person.

But Mom is. When I go downstairs, she's already in the kitchen, cup of coffee in hand.

I walk over to the pot and pour myself a cup, and I see her raise an eyebrow.

"You know I was sneaking coffee all through high school," I say, and her mouth twitches like she wants to laugh, but it goes against the Disapproving Mom Code.

She sits down at our kitchen table—Dad built that, too, out of reclaimed barn wood. It's old and just a little rustic, and it reminds me of him more than anything else in this house. I can tell by the way Mom tilts her head that she wants me to sit down across from her. That she wants to talk.

You know that dreadful kind of anticipation you have when one of your parents is getting ready to break something to you? It feels like when you're hurrying down a flight of stairs and take the last step, and it's just . . . not there. Your stomach drops and you realize you miscalculated, but it takes a moment for your body and your brain to line up. It seems to last forever, that moment, and you're just falling, falling, in this long, horrible drop that feels endless.

I *hate* that feeling.

Is she going to tell me they're getting a divorce? Was Karen wrong? Has counseling not worked?

I'm white-knuckling my coffee cup as I sit down across from her, thinking maybe I should've added sugar to get through this. Normally I drink it black, just like she does.

Surely Dad would be here if she was going to tell me they were splitting up. And Karen. They'd tell us together. Right?

This must be about something else. I remember how she got progressively quieter last night every time Bright Minds was mentioned.

Of course. She wants to talk me out of taking it. I feel more relieved than I should.

She smiles gently at me, in that fond way that has me bracing myself. My mom loves me. I just don't think she really *gets* me. My dad and I have more in common. We're quieter, stubborn; we like to observe.

Mom and Karen have things in common. They're both creative and artistic; they go to that ceramics studio on Fourth Street and paint bowls and plates. I have a soap dish Mom painted with little girls picking daisies painted on it. It's beautiful. Every time I look at it, I'm reminded that she loves me, but there's just this . . . space between the two of us. We're somehow out of sync, and we never quite seem to line up in the same place at the same time, with anything close to the same ideas.

I'm not creative in the way they are. I'm not artistic, and I *cannot* go with the flow or whatever.

I am scientific. I am methodical. I like to fix things. And I'm determined enough to do it. To find the problem and pull it out from the roots so it doesn't return.

My mother is determined in a very different way. She's sweet and caring and wants everyone to get along. Conflict is one of her big no-nos. There used to be a list of them on the kitchen chalkboard when Karen and I were little.

But life's *about* conflict, isn't it? History is. Evolution is.

And right now, in our little kitchen, conflict has arrived at the door. I invited it in, my desire for more getting the better of me.

"I wanted to talk to you about this internship," Mom says. She's being *so* careful, I think she's maybe as nervous as I am right now.

"Okay," I say, trying to keep my voice level.

"I am incredibly proud of you for being chosen for Bright Minds," Mom continues. "But you're going to wait, aren't you, until you get news about the rest of your applications?"

"Of course," I say.

I don't know why I don't tell her right away that I've already been accepted to the other internships. That if I don't call in to one of the law firms by Monday, I'll have missed my opportunity. It's not like me to leave things to the last minute. But I had to wait out the Bright Minds deadline.

And here I am. Even now, my fingers tremble at the thought of that red wax seal.

Mom lets out a noise I'm not sure she's aware of, this tiny sigh of relief that makes my stomach twist. "I'm glad to hear you're going to consider all your options," she says, like that's not exactly what I've been doing.

Frustration snaps in my chest like silk in the wind. I made pros-and-cons spreadsheets last winter when I chose which internships to apply for. I have pros-and-cons lists from last night, even, because I am never not thorough. But my mother thinks I need to consider all my options.

"Most people would say that turning down Bright Minds and

a chance to work with Simon Masrani would be a big mistake," I blurt out.

"I'm not telling you to turn down anything," she says quickly. "And . . . I am not most people. I'm your mother."

Did Karen feel like this on her first summer home from college? This weird teeter-totter of having spent a year finally being the ruler of her own life, but staying in her childhood bedroom again, under our mother's hand-stitched quilts—and under her thumb. Not quite a child, but not quite an adult in her eyes. She still feels the need to tell me what to think.

But I've *never* needed to be told what to think. She should know that by now.

This dance Mom and I are doing—I don't like it. I don't dance. Literally or metaphorically. And I'm not going to dance around this. Misleading her is no use. Springing it on her right before I leave would cause an even bigger mess.

"I've heard from all the internships," I say. "I've gotten acceptances from every place I applied. I'm going to need to decide very soon, and right now, I'm leaning toward Bright Minds." I try for a casual tone but completely fail at keeping the edge out of my voice.

She bites her lip. It's such a familiar sight—I do it; so does Karen—that it makes me ache. I don't want to worry or disappoint her. But I think I'm going to have to.

"Tell me why," she says.

I open my mouth to protest that I don't need to justify it, when she hurries on: "Honey, if you want me to be okay with you flying off to an island in the middle of nowhere to interact with *dinosaurs* that a now-deceased billionaire doctor created out of amber or mosquitoes or something, then I need you to help me understand.

"You've always been so focused," she continued. "So . . . intense. That's not a bad thing," she added hastily, catching the look on my face. "But even as a little girl, your drive . . ." She sounds almost bewildered in her admiration, and it shouldn't hurt, but maybe it does a little. "It's amazed me, all these years. You did so much good in high school working with the rescue, and now you've got your pick of internships. I know you love animals. But dinosaurs . . . they're a little different from working at a pet rescue."

I wanted to laugh at the understatement. She was trying so hard and not getting anywhere, because she didn't understand the draw of Isla Nublar. She wouldn't make the choice I wanted to.

"Wouldn't interning for a law firm or the judge be a better choice if you want to get into politics?" she asked. "Dinosaurs aren't going to help you get to Congress."

"The Senate, Mom," I correct her.

"Right," she said.

Like I said, my mom is sweet. She really believes I can somehow become a senator—as a woman with no pedigree, no family connections, no money—out of nowhere.

But I know better. Money is influence. Money is power.

And Simon Masrani has a lot of money. He has connections all over the world, in hundreds of different industries. He has the ear of important people. If I play this right, impress him, in fifteen years, when I'm mounting my first political campaign, he may very well be my first donor, and lead me to many more.

A kingmaker—that's the kind of man Masrani is. He's brought

true royalty back into the animal kingdom to show the world. After the island is open to the public, there will be *nothing* that man can't do. If he invested just a sliver of his fortune and influence into changing certain laws, the world could be a better place for all of us—human, dinosaur, and any other animal.

If I tell this to my mom, she'll get a look on her face I don't want to see. A look that's flat-out *concerned* because I shouldn't think that way . . . I shouldn't be so calculating.

But when you're a girl with no name, no money, and no connections, you've got to seize every opportunity that comes your way. And this is the biggest one I will ever get.

"Bright Minds is a once-in-a-lifetime thing," I explain. "Especially because this will be the only intern group on board *before* the park opens."

"That's what worries me," my mother says.

"I don't think they'd be bringing in interns if they hadn't worked out all the problems," I say with a smile. "They don't want to get sued before opening."

I don't want to remind her of the first park—the one that never opened. She'll just freak out even more.

"This is just one summer," I continue. "I can always get a legal internship next year. And the year after that, I'll qualify for the internship with the DC fixers I *really* wanted, which I'm not old enough for now."

"So . . . this internship . . . this is your way of cutting loose," Mom says, her eyebrows drawn together like I'm a bunch of scraps she needs to piece into a crazy quilt but hasn't figured out how. "This is you having fun."

"I'd have fun at all these internships," I say. "But *this* . . . Mom, only twelve people in the entire world get chosen for this. That's . . ." I'm smiling just at the thought. "I will never get another chance like this," I finally whisper, afraid to say it out loud, because it's true.

Mom taps her fingers against her lips, that puzzled look still on her face. "Are you going to talk to Professor Broadhurst about it?" she asks.

"I emailed her last night."

"She'll probably want you to take it, won't she?" Mom asks tentatively.

"She's the one who encouraged me to apply," I say.

Mom sighs, staring into her coffee cup like it holds the right answer I can't seem to give her. Upstairs, I hear the shower turn on—Dad's awake.

"Karen will be here to drop off Zach soon for breakfast. We'll talk about this later," Mom says, like she thinks this isn't over.

"Okay," I say, even though I know it is.

My mind is made up. Maybe it's selfish. Maybe it's reckless. But it's what I want.

When I go upstairs to my room to change, I write an email accepting the Bright Minds internship. And as I hear the front door open and my nephew calling for Grandma, I press send before I go to join my family.

4

"I cannot believe you got accepted to Bright Minds!" Regina shrieks over the phone.

I close my eyes, her excitement making me feel normal for the first time since I left college three days ago. "I can't believe it either. I only applied because Professor Broadhurst insisted."

"Aren't you glad she did now?" Regina asks, laughing. "What did she say when you told her?"

"She sent me the nicest email," I say. "She said she's really proud of me."

"Of course she is! This is an *achievement*," Regina crows. In the background, I can hear an automated voice saying something about baggage claim.

"Are you at the airport?" I ask. "I thought your flight was next week."

"It was, but turns out the literary magazine needs me a week earlier, so I'm heading out tonight."

"Are you nervous?" I ask.

"Are you?" she shoots back.

"Completely," I confess, lying down on my bed and staring up at my star system.

"You'll be great."

"*We'll* be great." Her confidence feels so good, it's contagious.

"Maybe you'll fall for a handsome dinosaur trainer on the island," Regina says.

"Who needs boys when you have a Brachiosaurus?"

Regina laughs so hard she snorts. "Okay, I just found my gate and I really need to pee before my flight, so I'm going to go. International calls will cost a fortune, so email me instead, okay?"

"Got it. Have a good flight."

"Give the dinosaurs a kiss for me!" Regina says with absolutely no trace of irony, which makes me shake my head and laugh as I hang up.

There's a knock on my bedroom door, and Karen peeks her head in. Earhart trails after her as she enters. "Hey," she says.

"I thought you were picking up Zach after dinner," I say, looking at the clock on my wall. It's only noon.

"My final meeting of the day canceled, so I thought I'd come by."

"Mom took Zach to the library."

"So I saw." Karen nudges me, and I scoot over so she can lie down next to me. Earhart looks hopefully at us with her one eye, like she expects me to let her up on the bed.

"You know you're not allowed!" I tell her, and she tilts her head, like she's hoping I'll change my mind. I pat her on the head instead, which seems to content her. She finally lies down on the floor, resting her chin on her paws.

"Mom told me you accepted Bright Minds," Karen says. "You'll be leaving in just a few days?"

I press my lips together so tight I'm afraid they'll just disappear into my face.

My sister sighs. "You know she's proud of you. She's just . . . a worrier."

"I need to do this," I say, unable to look at her when I say it, my eyes fixed on the arc and twists of stars across the ceiling. "I need to go there. I just . . . I have this *feeling*."

My cheeks flush at going so metaphysical on her. It's not like me. But it's the truth.

Discovering that dinosaurs existed was pretty much *the* event of my childhood. It was for everyone. There was so much mystery around their existence for the first few years, and then Dr. Hammond's death added even more questions.

Even Mr. Masrani's announcement of his plans to open a park had been shrouded in mystery. The man had a flair for drama. It started when packages containing amber-handled archaeological tools—the kind that paleontologists use to dig up bones—began arriving. At first, it was journalists, social media influencers, actors, pop stars, the leading professors and minds of the world. Then, as the buzz began to start, the tools began arriving at random people's doorsteps across the world. Everyone starting talking about it because it was so weird—and the selection of people who got the tools was so broad and varied. The tools came with no note, just a simple card that had the profile of a T. rex skeleton stamped upon it.

Two more packages arrived for the lucky recipients over the next few weeks. It became this status thing to post about them. Everyone was trying to trace the company that sent them, but no one could figure it out. The second package contained a compass; carved on the back was that same T. rex stamp.

When the third and final package arrived, it caused a sensation. Each person's box had three clues—a jagged tooth, a curled piece of parchment with the sketch of a gate in spidery ink, and an old-fashioned-looking key, one clearly not made to unlock anything. The speculation this caused throughout the world was unparalleled. What did these objects mean? Did they relate to each other? Was this just some elaborate prank?

The first person to discover how to activate the boxes was a farmer's son in Bolivia. After he disassembled the wooden box the trinkets were sent in, he noticed a strange indentation in the top of the lid and placed his key inside. Once he posted his discovery on YouTube, people across the globe were inserting their key in the notch, activating a hidden hologram chip embedded in the key's handle. This beamed a message. Two silver words. One date.

They're coming.

May 30, 2005

By the time Mr. Masrani held his press conference the next day, the entire world was buzzing about the possibility of a new park and a chance to get close to the dinosaurs. Both of the islands had been restricted for so long, it was the only thing anyone could talk about. It's one of those things you compare notes on with other people: Where were you when Masrani announced Jurassic World?

Ever since Mr. Masrani announced he was going to develop and protect Isla Nublar and bring Dr. Hammond's research full circle, I've felt drawn to it. To the work, to the island, to the innovation and refuge this next step presented. Isla Nublar is a sanctuary. A place where science makes miracles happen.

But it's not just that.

I think . . .

I think it's the fact that it's an island of outsiders. Occupied by people who push dreams to the very edge of human limits and animals that should not exist but do.

Sometimes I feel that way. Like my shoulders are rubbed raw from people's expectations. Like I should not be, but I am. I persist, even if they don't like it.

Just like the dinosaurs.

If I tell Karen that I feel a kinship to dinosaurs, of all things, she's going to . . . well, I don't even know.

"I'm not surprised you want to do this," Karen says, saving me from my struggle to articulate. "You spent, like, a year chasing me around the backyard pretending to be a T. rex when the news came out."

"I was a little kid!" But I laugh when I see the warm smile on her face. I knock my shoulder into hers gently.

"I told Mom I was going to take you to lunch and shopping," Karen says. "So let's go do that."

I make a face. "Do I have to go shopping?"

"Look, it'll get you out of the house. And the internship people must've sent you a list of things you need, right?"

She was right. The packet had a list. I would need about a

gallon of sunscreen. I definitely wouldn't be able to fit that in my carry-on.

"Okay, fine." I stand up and grab the list out of the envelope on my desk. "But no window-shopping."

Karen rolls her eyes, sliding off my bed and heading toward the door. "That's half the fun."

"You take forever," I complain. "Come on, Earhart." I snap my fingers and she follows us as we make our way downstairs. I leave her in the living room with her basket of toys and special memory-foam dog bed that Dad bought her.

I finally get a good look at the list after we get into Karen's car and get on the highway. It's pretty detailed, organized in neat columns. There's even a list of shots I need to get.

"Do you really need to get new shots and immunizations?" Karen asks, glancing over at it. "I guess we wouldn't want you to get dinosaur flu."

"There is no dinosaur flu," I scoff.

"Well, what if you get bit by a mosquito and catch scurvy?"

"You mean malaria," I correct her. "Scurvy is what the sailors got because their diets were low in vitamin C. And yes, I'm going to need to get some new shots." I shrug, trying not to think about it because I *hate* needles.

Karen clucks her tongue like a mother hen. "You'll do great. Just don't look at the needle when they do it. That's what I told Zach when he needed to get his shots."

I shake my head. That makes it even worse. I have to look. Exert some kind of control over the process. Even though it always makes my stomach swoop in the most horrible way. "It'll be fine," I say.

"What else do you need to get?" Karen nods toward the list as she switches lanes, getting ready to take the exit for the mall.

"Basic stuff. Water bottles, bug spray, work gloves. And I should get some cargo shorts."

Karen shudders, her fashion sense obviously offended.

"It's not my fault every clothing designer in the world decided to stop putting pockets in dresses," I say. "And I can't even fit my hand in half of the pockets of the jeans they make for us."

"Okay, I agree with you there," Karen says as she takes the exit. "Pocket space is abysmal. Though I don't think tromping around the dinosaur pens or fields or whatever they are in a dress is the best idea. What if you trip and moon the dinosaurs?"

The mental image is so absurd and embarrassing that the laughter just bursts out of me. "I'll have to add new underwear to my list of things to buy," I say between giggles, and that sets *her* off, and by the time we pull into the mall parking lot, my eyes are wet, and Karen's cheeks are bright red from snickering.

"Where to first?" I ask my sister, because I have no delusions: This is one of Karen's domains. She's in charge here.

"Sephora," she says. "Then we'll get your . . ." She lets out a long sigh. "Cargo shorts."

"If it makes you feel better, I'll get them in blue or purple or something instead of khaki," I say.

"Touching," Karen says, quirking her mouth. "Come on."

Sephora is vaguely terrifying. The lighting is so good, and the women working the counters and floating around wear supersharp eyeliner, and it's all kind of intimidating. Karen walks down the aisles with purpose. She knows exactly what she wants. She looks the way I feel walking into a classroom, ready for an exam. But here . . .

That outsider feeling grows.

"I think you need a new lipstick," Karen says, looking up at me from the line of colorful tubes, her glance assessing.

"I don't need lipstick. I'm probably going to be down in a lab or walking around in the sun all summer."

"Hmmm." Karen purses her lips. "You're right. You need a lipstick *and* a moisturizing lip balm with a high SPF. And something for your hair, because it's going to freak out in all that humidity. Ooh, and a good facial spray too."

"Just make sure it's cruelty free," I say, before I kind of tune her out for a second, because when Karen gets started on beauty stuff, she'll go on for a long time. There's a red lipstick at the very end of the row where she's standing. It draws my eye, the bright pop of color like a crooked finger, beckoning me.

Regina was always trying to get me to wear bright lipstick. I have half a dozen glosses and lipsticks in the same shade of muted pink, and she'd paw through my stuff as we got ready to go out and say, *Dearing, you need to embrace the bold sometimes.*

"That'd look good on you," Karen says, catching me picking up the lipstick.

"It'll clash with my hair."

"The right red won't," Karen says, plucking it out of my hands before I can put it back and adding it to the little basket looped around her wrist. "Now let's go find the sunscreen."

By the time we get across the mall to the sporting goods store, Karen's got three bags full of stuff and the eternal devotion of one of the Sephora clerks because she agreed to call in a favor for her to the most popular stylist in town. My sister is one of those people who seems to just know *everyone*. And they all seem to owe her a favor. It's kind of like she's queen of the moms.

At the sporting goods store I load up on extra-strength bug spray and get a set of those snap-and-shake glow tubes. They're not on my list, but the Girl Scout in me is sifting through all the information I picked up in my troop—and what Dad taught me when we went camping. Isla Nublar's terrain and geography will be different from anything I've ever experienced—maybe from anything *anyone*'s ever experienced. How many different habitats did Masrani build—or is he still building—on the island? I can't wait to find out.

"I think you should get some of that," Karen says, looking up from her phone to point at the row of bear repellent cans on the shelf next to the bug spray.

"Because there's no dinosaur repellent?"

"It's better than nothing."

"You and Mom both have a totally wrong idea of what's going to be going on during my internship." I shake my head, grabbing the smallest can of bear spray to appease her. "I'm not going to be running wild with the dinosaurs. I'll be getting coffee and taking notes and probably transcribing really boring dictation about the calorie content of the Brachiosauruses' lunch."

"But a part of you absolutely wants to run wild with the dinosaurs, admit it," Karen says.

"That would require having a death wish," I say primly, sidestepping the question and walking down the aisle. There's a glass case in front of us, a selection of pocketknives gleaming in black velvet boxes.

"Ooh, this one has a pearl handle," Karen says. "Could we look at this one?" she asks the guy behind the counter.

"Karen, I don't need a knife," I say, but I have to admit, it's pretty. "I couldn't take it in my carry-on."

"You're bringing more than your carry-on," Karen says. "See if the weight of it feels good."

I take the knife and flip it open. The handle is smooth and cool against my skin, the blade shining and sharp.

Mom gave each of us a Swiss Army knife when we left home. Mine even has a little pen in it. I always carry it with me, but it's the tiniest version. The small blade is useful in a pinch, but it isn't a weapon.

This knife is something that could hack through vines and branches, shave bark off trees finely enough for fire starters, and cut through rope like butter. Useful. Practical.

And really shiny. The mother-of-pearl handle sparkles iridescent in the light. It reminds me of the old Formica table my grandparents had.

"We'll buy it," Karen says to the clerk, who smiles and takes the knife away to box it up for us. "It's my treat." She turns to look at me. "I know taking this internship is kind of out of your comfort zone. I'm really proud of you for choosing to do something you feel so passionate about versus the more practical law firm route. You've always loved animals so much, I figured you'd become a vet when you were little."

It's an offhand comment, and she's distracted almost immediately by the clerk calling her over to ring up the purchase. But it sticks with me, roots me to my spot for a moment.

There was a time when I thought I'd become a vet too. Before I got Earhart, even before I started working at the rescue, I learned how cruel people could be to animals. When I was twelve, a man who owned the empty, run-down warehouse down the street from school started keeping a dog, a scrubby Pyrenees mix with sweet eyes, on a five-foot chain to guard the yard. Day and night, that dog had no one and no space to roam. Just a crude shelter under an old rusted-out truck bed and enough food and water to keep Animal Control from creating trouble.

To the man who owned that property, the dog was a tool, not a living being. That man didn't care that the dog suffered in the summer and almost froze in the winter. He didn't care that he couldn't exercise. All he cared about was the dog scaring off squatters. And if the dog died? Well, he could always get another.

I had to do something. So I went to the library and I read up on all the laws and I made a plan. I bought disposable cameras with my allowance and I took pictures of the dog each day. I filled a notebook with daily observations. On weekends, Dad drove me over so I could keep track of the dog then, too.

He was chained too far in the yard for me to touch. So instead,

I talked to him a lot. He'd always stare at me, riveted, like he craved any kind of contact he could get.

It took patience. It took time. But finally, there were two weeks where the warehouse owner didn't show up to give the dog water or food. And I was able to prove it with my logs and my photos, and Animal Control finally took the dog away from him. My mom had arranged for the rescue I started working for in high school to take him, and he got to go live with a family out on a farm in Maine. They still send me pictures of him at Christmas. His name is Roo now. He looks like a totally different dog. No more sad eyes. Every photo I get, he's smiling.

It took six months to get Animal Control to do something. Every few weeks, I would call them, and I would hear it in the workers' voices: that they understood how frustrated I was, that they knew it was unfair, that they agreed with me.

Their hands were tied. The law was the law.

I decided that I would grow up to be the kind of woman who could make laws and enact the kind of sweeping change that was needed. I've never wavered from that choice, and I've never regretted it.

But I know I'll have to sacrifice for it. I can feel myself teetering on the brink of that point with each decision I make lately. I'm swaying back and forth along an edge, and I know the fall will be hard. I only pray that it'll leave me bruised, not broken.

But I learned one thing from saving Roo: even if you're broken, you can always be put back together.

5

My dad is the one who drives me to the airport. Mom . . . if she'd
come with us, I think she might not have let me go. Mom hugged
me a long time on the porch while Earhart knocked against our
legs, whining, because she's always been sensitive to other people's
moods. When Mom finally pulled back, she cupped my face in her
palms and stared at me like she was trying to memorize the moment, burning the lines of my face, every freckle, every strand of
red hair, into her memory.

"It's gonna be okay, Mama," I said, and it was all for her, because
I didn't need any reassurance.

She cried as Dad pulled the truck out of the driveway. And now
Dad and I are an hour into the four-hour drive to the airport. This
whole last week, he hasn't said *anything* about what he thinks about
all this.

I'm kind of afraid to ask.

My dad is someone who likes to fix things, too. Trucks, washing machines, tractors—anything mechanical. He built me a telescope when I was twelve. It's still in the back shed, and I take it out every winter, to track the stars in the night sky.

But he likes things that are solid and real, things he can hold in his hands, see with his eyes. He once told me he never saw the point in asking *What if?*

But that's the only thing that ever truly quieted my mind . . . to ask myself that. Over and over. About so many things.

I mean, that's the reason I'm in a truck right now, my arm aching from all the vaccinations I had to get. It's the reason I'm heading to the airport, getting on a plane, and then going to an island full of the kind of wonder most of us couldn't dream up.

But Dr. Hammond did. He asked *What if?*

If you ask yourself enough questions, the right one might lead you down a rarefied path . . . the kind that leaves your names in the history books.

One Christmas I got this book about historical women. Stories about women like Ada Lovelace and Ida B. Wells and Phyllis Wheatley. I was just starting to understand that the history books . . . the science texts I loved so . . . they weren't as full of women who changed the world as they should be. So I loved this book. It was proof, but it was also a lesson.

We have to work so much harder, because we're underestimated and undervalued and dismissed. And it sucks. It's just harder for girls. And there are so many different kinds of girls, and that means there are lots of different *kinds* of hard. Even though it's hard, I have it easier than a lot of girls. I've gotten opportunities that others more qualified didn't even get considered for because they're not as feminine or they speak uncomfortable truths or they're not the "right" color.

Sometimes the unfairness of it swamps me—it's one of those things that should be staggering but isn't. Because it's the way it is. We chip away at it the best we can and hope to pull up others along with us, until there are enough of us to force real change.

"What are you thinking about, sweetie?" my dad asks.

I look from the window to him. "Just . . . history," I say.

"You excited about your trip?"

"I don't think that's a big enough word," I answer, and he smiles.

"You're going to impress them all," he says, with the kind of surety that comes only from being my father.

"I hope so," I reply, wishing I had the kind of faith in myself that he has in me.

"I *know* so," he says. "From the very start, Claire-bear, I knew you were destined for big things. Great things. This is just the start for you."

What if the start for me means the end of everything else that's safe and familiar and *home,* though? That's the what-if that keeps spinning in my head. I try to push it down, but it's hard. Especially now that I know my parents are having problems.

I look at my father out of the corner of my eye, wondering what he'd do if I asked him, if I let him know that I know. But I push down that urge too. I remind myself that my father likes to fix things. That means he'll find a way to fix whatever's broken in their marriage.

Right?

When we get to the airport and to the security check-in, Dad does the same thing Mom did on the porch: he hugs me for a long time and cups my face with his palms, his eyes shining with pride.

"Remember to follow all the orders the adults give you," he says. "And if you somehow get lost on that island, think back to Girl Scouts and all our camping trips, okay?"

"Sun rises in the east, sets in the west," I remark, and it makes him smile. "I won't get lost," I assure him. "It's an entire theme park. It's not like all wild jungle. And the parts that are, there's fences and signs everywhere, I'm sure."

"Still, I want you to keep water on you, and a knife, and . . . use the buddy system. Make friends and stick with them, and if you get in trouble . . ."

"I won't. And Karen already had me pack the bear repellent she bought me."

"That was smart of your sister," he says. "Okay. I don't want to make you late." He smiles again, but it's tighter this time, like he's trying not to worry. "Go show them what you're made of, Claire," he says. "You'll blow them all away."

I hug him one more time before going through the line for international travel. After I finally get through security, I walk away toward my gate and I don't look back. I don't have to. I know he's still standing there. He'll stand there long after he loses sight of me. Because that's what good fathers do.

I got to the airport early—of course. But the check-in for

international travel took longer than I expected, and by the time I find my gate, passengers are already starting to board. Tucking my blanket scarf a little tighter around my neck and making sure the cicada pin is still secure, I get in line behind an older man and woman. I pull my boarding pass out of my blue canvas satchel and hand it to the attendant, who scans it and nods me on.

I have to stow my carry-on a few aisles away from my seat, but I have everything I need in my bag. I sit in my window seat and unhook the pin from my blanket scarf, letting the ends fall free. I rearrange the soft plaid cashmere—a sixteenth-birthday present from Karen—around my shoulders. Out of my bag, I pull a bottle of water, a granola bar, and my travel pillow. I flip the tray table down and grab my latest read and my science magazines, a thick stack that I'm going to spend the *entire* plane ride catching up on. I can't wait.

As the passengers take their seats, I leaf through the *Journal of Avocational Paleontology*. The flight attendants are checking the overhead bins, getting ready to give the all clear, when I hear someone calling, "Wait, wait! I'm coming!"

I look up from my magazine—and from the fascinating article about the discovery of the fossil *Pneumodesmus newmeni*—to see who's so late.

"Sorry!" I hear his apology before I see him. He hands off his suitcase to the flight attendant to stow below and turns. He's a cute white boy, with floppy dark hair and neat black-framed glasses, which are slipping down his long nose. When he pauses in front of the empty seat next to me, I look up to meet his blue eyes.

"Hey," he says, sitting down next to me. "I'm Justin. I solemnly promise not to man-spread my legs all over the place and give you no room."

Startled, I laugh. He smiles back. My stomach does that swooping thing that's all about smart, cute boys and a fizzy kind of connection.

"I'm Claire," I say.

"Nice to meet you." He smiles again and then turns his attention to his bag, giving me some breathing room in case I don't want to talk.

It's nice—respectful—and I appreciate it, because as the flight attendants secure the plane and the Fasten Seat Belts light goes on, my stomach drops for reasons that have nothing to do with Justin's smile.

It's not really the plane itself that gets to me. It's the being-up-high part. I *hate* heights.

As soon as I got into my seat, I'd closed the shade on the window firmly because looking out the window makes me all kinds of panicky. As we taxi onto the runway, I breathe in and out slowly through my nose, and it takes me a few minutes to realize that my seatmate is doing the same thing.

He doesn't like flying either.

When he tenses up as we lift off, I feel a flash of familiarity—it almost distracts me from the way my own heart's thumping in my chest like an animal slamming against a cage.

As we're climbing into the sky, we hit a rough patch. The plane rocks back and forth, and I suck in a sharp breath. A hand closes around mine tight, and as the plane levels out, I look down at the same time he does.

"Sorry," he says, snatching his hand away. "Sorry," he repeats, meeting my eyes. "I get really nervous flying, but I didn't mean to invade your space."

"It's okay." I smile. "I don't like flying either."

"Some trips make it worth it, though," he says.

"We can agree on that, too," I say. My magazines and book slip off the tray table as the plane encounters some turbulence, and he bends down and scoops them up for me.

"Thanks," I say when he hands them back.

"Reading about the Bone Wars, huh?" he asks, nodding to the book.

"I am," I say.

During the late 1800s, there was a time when fossils were in high regard. Fossil hunting and discovering new species created a scientific war between two prominent collectors, Edward Cope and Othniel Marsh. Their egotistical competitiveness led them to discover more than 120 new species—but during their pursuit, they also destroyed smaller fossils and dig sites so the other wouldn't discover them, wrote deceptive scientific papers, and even named and renamed the same species over and over again.

They were scientists, yes, but they were shady—to the max.

"So, whose side do you fall on?" Justin asks me. "The wealthy, connected Edward Cope or the poorer, better educated Marsh?"

"Neither," I say, and I see a flicker of surprise in his face. "This isn't a cut-and-dried situation like Edison and Tesla," I say. "There's a clear villain in the AC/DC war, right?"

"Edison," he says instantly, and I feel relieved, because it *may* have been a bit of a test. You never want to be attracted to a guy who takes Edison's side in the AC/DC war.

"With Cope and Marsh . . . they're *both* kind of terrible people. Marsh totally screwed over Chief Red Cloud and the Sioux people by promising them payment for digging on their lands. He also said he'd speak on their behalf to the government. But he ended up skipping out on them in the dead of the night—without paying, and right before an attack!" The thought of it makes me feel sick.

"I didn't know that," Justin says, his eyebrows snapping together. "That's horrifying. He shouldn't be lauded the way he is if he contributed to the suffering and death of indigenous people."

I agree," I say. "It's disgusting. Both he and Cope laid waste to sacred lands in their scientific pursuits. It'll never be okay, what they did, how they treated those lands and the tribes. Cope was a huge exploiter too. He's the one who played the long game and kept detailed journals for *years* about his enemy's every move. When Marsh got a cushy government job, Cope publicly accused him of plagiarism and all sorts of other shadowy activity and destroyed his reputation. And, in an ultimate act of scientific rivalry, Cope had his head *preserved* after he died, issuing a challenge to Marsh to have *his* brain pickled and measured too so they could face off in the Big Brain competition—because back then, brain size was thought to be the measure of intelligence."

"Now, I *did* know that," Justin says. He shakes his head. "Can you imagine having that fierce a rivalry with someone?"

"Science," I say. "It makes some of us a little . . . intense."

"But they still made massive contributions to our understanding of the past," Justin points out. "Over a hundred and twenty species, and Marsh discovered some of the most famous ones."

"But do their contributions erase their misdeeds? The hurt they caused?" I ask. "That's the question, isn't it, outside of the fascination of such a heated rivalry. When discovery—advancement—comes at a cost, where do you draw the line? Marsh hurt entire tribes while promising to help them. Both men destroyed smaller fossils so the other wouldn't identify them—who knows if they got rid of fossils that we'll never find again? So how much did they hold science back? As much as they moved it forward?"

He tilts his head, looking at me, his eyes sparking beneath his glasses. Heat crawls across my cheeks as I realize I've been talking *a lot*.

"You're not a science student, are you?" he asks.

"Poli-sci," I admit. "I just like paleontology."

His eyes crinkle, and it's like drinking champagne; I can feel the fizziness to the tips of my toes. "So, you're a bleeding heart," he says, but it doesn't sound like a criticism . . . almost like a question.

"I'm someone who likes the scales to be balanced," I say. "It seems like a lot of the time, the bad guys don't just win, they get extra rewards."

"Hmmm," he says.

"And what about you?" I ask. "Are *you* a bleeding heart?"

"I'm a business major," he says, with a self-deprecating grin.

"Oh, so you're a capitalist—no heart at all. I thought you said you were on *Tesla's* side of the AC/DC war," I add lightly, hoping he'll know it's a joke.

To my relief, he laughs. "A good businessperson would've

recognized Tesla's value. You get better results from your employees when you empower them . . . or at least, that's what my mom says. I went into business because of her. She started a vegan cosmetics company when I was a kid. It was cool, seeing her fill a spot in the market that was needed. Plus, that's how I got into chemistry."

"Seriously?" I ask.

"Ivy Rose Cosmetics . . . ever heard of it?' he asks.

"I have a bunch of their lip glosses."

"That's Mom," Justin says proudly. "She started out in my grandma's basement, and now her stuff is stocked in hundreds of stores."

"That's so cool," I say. "Do you want to go work for her after college?"

"Oh God, no," he says. "Her company's great, but she'd hover and I'd get all smothered."

"My mother likes to hover too."

"It's the mom talent, I swear," he says. "It's weird, right, coming home after being away at school?" he asks. "I was only back for a few weeks before I had to leave again, but the entire time, I felt like I was in a *Twilight Zone* episode where everyone was treating me like I was a child, but I knew I was an adult."

"My mom tried to stuff me with food every day," I say. "That's how she shows her love."

"I wouldn't have minded that," he says as the flight attendant comes to take our drink orders.

After a few more hours, the lights dim and I take my eye mask out of my satchel and settle my pillow against the shuttered window. As I drift off, I can hear Justin's gentle breathing and the soft ding of the call button somewhere up the aisle. The next thing I know, someone's tapping me gently on the shoulder.

"Claire?"

I push the mask off my face, smoothing my plane-head with one hand as I squint in the light.

"We're getting ready to land," Justin says. His glasses are crooked on his nose, and I have the most absurd urge to reach out and straighten them. But I keep my hands to myself.

"Thanks," I say, pushing my stuff into my bag and running my hand through my hair one more time. Our descent is smooth, but it doesn't matter; it makes that familiar fear rock inside me like we're being tossed back and forth in the air. This time, Justin doesn't grab my hand, but I almost wish he would.

Getting off the plane, as always, is a hassle, and I lose sight of him in the hustle, but he catches up with me at the top of the escalators.

"It was really nice talking to you," he says. "I hope you have a good trip."

"You too," I say. "Thanks for listening to me ramble on about science. It was nice. I don't get to do that a lot."

"It was fun," he says. "I like the way you think."

In my pocket, my phone beeps. I need to call my mom to let her know I've landed. I also need to find a bathroom and get a handle on my hair situation. I can already feel it getting staticky from the humidity.

"Anyway, I should get going," I say. "Enjoy your travels."

He heads down the escalator and I duck into the bathroom. My hair's all clumpy and wilting like a cut flower on a hot day. I pull it into a quick, messy bun and spray my face with some of the aloe-rose face mist Karen insisted I buy at Sephora. To my amusement, I realize that it's from Justin's mom's company, Ivy Rose.

He was so cute. I like how he talked, not just about science, but about his mom. He looks up to her and he doesn't care who knows it. That's . . . unusual, in my experience with guys. Not that I really have a lot.

I wash my hands and finish up in the bathroom before going to baggage claim and grabbing my suitcase. According to my itinerary, a shuttle should be waiting at the airport to take the interns to the ferry. And then we'll be off to the island.

This is it. My fingers are sweaty around the handle of my suitcase, and not just because of the heat. I'm nervous.

I think about what my dad said, about showing them what I'm made of. I want to. More than anything. But will I be good enough?

I step into the arrivals area, looking for a sign with my name on it. *There.* A short woman with curly hair is talking to a guy with his back to me, and she's holding a sign that says BRIGHT MINDS INTERNS.

Resisting the urge to break into a flat-out run, I make my way over to her. "Hi," I say. "I'm Claire Dearing. I'm one of the interns."

At my name, the guy the woman had been talking to turns, and once again my eyes meet those blue ones behind the glasses.

Justin's mouth curls up. "I should've known a girl who knows so much about the Bone Wars would be going to Isla Nublar."

I can't stop the answering smile blooming across my face,

because my heart's beating in that thrilling way I've never felt directed at another person—just at my own discoveries.

"Looks like you and I can continue our debate, then," I manage to say.

"I mean, we're gonna have what Cope and Marsh never had—real, live specimens!" he says. "Imagine what we might discover."

And there it is again, that thrilling, heart-thumping kind of excitement, like I'm on the edge of a cliff, about to dive into endless blue.

Just imagine.

6

"Claire Dearing," says the woman, looking down at her list. "Perfect! Then I've finally got you all. I'm Jessica. I'm Ms. Jamison's assistant. She runs Bright Minds for Mr. Masrani. You'll be meeting her on the ferry, which is where we're headed now. Do you have all your luggage, you two?"

Justin and I nod.

"Then let's go," she says, leading us through the lobby. "We don't want to keep the boat waiting. As it is, we'll be arriving after nightfall. You'll have to wait until morning to get the full experience."

"How many species are on the island right now?" Justin asks as we go through the double doors onto the sidewalk, where taxis, shuttles, and cars are bustling away from and up to the curb.

"Five different herbivore species have been integrated into their on-island habitats," Jessica says, leading us down the sidewalk to a black van with a sleek silver logo stamped on the door.

I can't help but notice she makes no mention of the carnivores, even though we all know there are a few living on the island. Will we be allowed to see them? Or would it be considered too great a risk?

"We have a herd of Triceratops," Jessica continue. "Four Brachiosauruses, over a dozen Parasaurolophuses, six young, Ankylosaurses, and several Gallimimuses in-habitat currently, but we plan on opening next year with a total of eight species. You're arriving at an exciting time. We're still building parts of the park, so your intern group will be kind of stand-ins for our first guests. You get to see everything before anyone else does."

She grabs the handle of the van door and slides it open. Inside are a guy and a girl with the same big eyes and dark hair, though the girl's is streaked purple and green.

"Tanya, Eric, this is Justin Hendricks and Claire Dearing," Jessica says. "We're going to head to the docks now, so everyone strap in!" She gets into the passenger seat up front, and the driver starts the van and pulls into the flow of traffic.

"Hi," I say, flashing a smile as I buckle myself in next to the girl.

"Oh my gosh, I'm so relieved there's another girl," Tanya says.

"I told you," Eric says, and Tanya rolls her eyes at him in a way that convinces me that they're brother and sister. Twins, maybe?

"That's how it is with STEM-focused programs," Tanya says. "You know guys are going to outnumber the girls. Can you say *boys' club*?"

I like her immediately. And to be honest, I'm also a little intimidated. This girl is *cool*. I'm about as far from cool as you can get.

"Maybe because the intern director's a woman, there'll be more equality," I say.

"Good point," Tanya says, hefting her bag from the floor onto the seat between us. It has buttons all over the straps—I see one with a woman symbol, another that says *Love Is Love,* and another that says *FEMINIST* in bold pink letters.

Like I said: *so* much cooler than me.

"Want a granola bar?" she asks, holding one out. "I hate plane food, so I packed a ton."

"Thanks," I say, and she hands one to her brother and Justin.

"So, what's your thing?" she asks as we weave through late-afternoon rush hour.

"My thing?" I frown.

"Your focus. What are you into?" Tanya explains. "I'm studying botany. I cannot *wait* to get my hands on the plant hybrids they've created for the dinosaurs. Can you even imagine the calorie-rich plant sources they've had to come up with to satisfy the herbivores?" Her eyes shine at the prospect. "My brother over there," she jerks her thumb at Eric, "is an AV club geek. I think his camera is attached to his face sometimes."

"Hey," Eric protests, but he shrugs, like it's true. Sure enough, I peek over the back of our seat and see that he's got a digital camera in his lap.

"I'm majoring in political science," I say.

"So you wanna be a lawyer?" Tanya asks.

I shake my head. "I don't want to stop there," I explain. "I want to go into politics so I can advocate for animal rights."

"What, like, Senator Dearing, so you can help shape laws and bills?" Tanya asks, and nervousness stirs in my chest. Is she making fun of me?

"Yeah," I say cautiously. "Exactly like that."

"That's *awesome*," Tanya says, with the same enthusiasm as she has for calorie-rich plant sources, and relief uncurls in me like a cat in front of a fire. "You could be president someday."

I laugh at the thought. "I wish!"

"You never know. What about you, Justin?" Tanya asks.

"I'm studying business," he says. "Boring, I know."

"Nah," Eric says. "Jurassic World's a business."

"That's what I'm really interested in," Justin says, his face growing animated as he warms to the subject. "This is a *huge* business undertaking, on top of being innovative science. It's like business-major catnip to get to see it all while it's still being put together."

"I guess it's cool that we all get different things out of the same internship," Eric says, his eyes still fixed on his camera.

Tanya purses her lips. "My brother is perpetually unimpressed," she says. "He'll probably see a Brachiosaurus and say *cool.*"

"Seeing a Brachiosaurus *will* be cool."

"All that I ask is that you try to embrace the awesome," Tanya says, and Justin turns to shoot me an amused look at the sibling bickering, which I return. "And I don't mean awesome as in cool. I mean awesome as in *there are dinosaurs,* Eric!"

Eric laughs. His front teeth are crooked, but the effect is charming, a little roguish. "I will try to be as impressed as possible, just for you, Sis."

"You two are twins, aren't you?" Justin asks.

"I'm three minutes older," Tanya says.

Eric snorts. "And she'll never let me forget it."

"Here we are, everyone!" Jessica says, her chipper voice breaking through the twins' back-and-forth. We pull to a stop in front of a long series of docks, the water beyond them an endless stretch of gray-blue. As we get out of the van, we see smaller boats—fishing boats with the catch of the day—pulling into the harbor. The air smells sharp, like we've already left land behind, no trace of the city remaining, just salt and water and the nameless scent of the wind.

Jessica leads us down one of the docks, water and fish splashing across the wooden boards. I breathe through my mouth and look away from the fishes' empty eyes, because a dead fish is always a bit creepy.

"Watch out!"

I look up, and so does Tanya, who's beside me. A net full of fish is suspended above us—and then it's not. The rope breaks, I grab Tanya's wrist and yank her backward with me, and fish rain down onto the dock, right where we were walking.

"Ick," Tanya says as fish jump around our ankles. She backs off, shaking her foot. "Thanks for the save, Claire."

Someone snickers behind us. I look over my shoulder and see a tall guy with a shock of blond hair so pale it's almost white, his hands in his pockets and a lanyard around his neck that says *Bright Minds*.

"Ms. Jamison sent me to see if you'd arrived, Jessica," he says.

"Oh, Wyatt!" She smiles at the boy. "It's nice to see you. I just had a meeting with your father the other day. He's very proud of you."

"Mr. Masrani keeps Dad busy," Wyatt says with a slick grin.

"Well, they both are working hard on the launch," she says. "Anyway, we're finally all here! Kids, this is Wyatt, another intern.

You'll be able to meet everyone else on the boat, so let's go! Just . . . avoid the fish." She steps gingerly over the mackerels and the rest of us skirt the squirming pile. Tanya and I shoot apologetic looks at the fisherman, who looks relieved that he didn't brain us with a ton of fish.

The ferry taking us to the island is a large one. I can see jeeps and crates of supplies strapped to the top deck.

"I bet ships going near the island are monitored more closely than ever now," I say as Justin steps onboard ahead of me.

"It's amazing no photos have leaked yet," he agrees. "The first ones from the park are going to be worth a fortune."

"You really are all about business," Tanya comments from behind us, and Justin grins.

"Guilty," he says as he heads toward the cabin, where Jessica's gesturing us to join her.

"That guy looks like a really handsome superhero's naive idea of a good secret identity," Tanya comments when he's out of earshot.

My ears burn, because the description perfectly captures his good-looking geekiness. Like he doesn't really want to stand out, but he does.

"Totally not my type," Tanya continues. "But you should go for it, Claire."

I shake my head, partly for her, but also as a reminder to myself. "I think I'm gonna try to focus on the work this summer, you know?"

"Totally get it." Tanya peers toward the windows, where we can see the rest of the interns gathering. "This is a huge deal. I'm really nervous."

"It's a lot of pressure," I agree. "I don't want to screw it up."

"Me neither," she says. "But I've got your back, okay?"

"And I've got yours," I reply, happy that I've made a friend so fast.

"The botanist and the politician-to-be," Tanya says. "We'd make a weird sitcom."

"It'd run for five episodes, then get yanked," I say, and her dimples flash as she smiles.

"My brother will be wondering where I am," she says. "You ready?"

I take a deep breath as the ferry horn blows and we pull away from the dock. I brace my knees at the movement and then nod. "Let's do it."

There are more than a dozen people inside the ferry's great room, where a buffet-style dinner has been set out. And I realize it isn't just interns being ferried to the island. There are vet techs, trainers, scientists, all sorts of people who probably live and work on the island already.

Tanya wanders off to find her brother, and I get into line behind a tall woman dressed in green khaki. She's engaged in an animated conversation with the guy next to her about the effectiveness of playing music to dinosaur eggs.

"But, Gregory, here's the thing: different species seem to respond to different music," she's saying. "I can play classical to the Brachiosauruses, but the Triceratops prefer jazz. They get agitated otherwise. My current theory is that they interpret the music as a heartbeat—maybe a mother's heartbeat—and that's why the response is different."

"Gotta agree with the Triceratops," says a voice in my ear. "Jazz all the way."

I almost drop my plate. I'm so absorbed in the conversation that I didn't notice Justin.

"Sorry," he says, flipping open one of the chafing dishes and spooning rice onto his plate. "Didn't mean to scare you."

"It's okay," I say, helping myself to some chicken from one of the dishes. It smells spicy, with grilled lemon slices layered over the pieces. I load up my plate and grab some napkins and utensils.

"I'll get our drinks if you promise to share some of those napkins," Justin says, nodding to the stack in my hands.

"Deal," I say. He gets two lemonades and we head to a table in the corner, where Tanya and Eric are seated with a petite Latina and the boy with white-blond hair—Wyatt—who laughed at Tanya and me when the fish almost flattened us.

"Hi, everyone," Justin says as we sit down across from each other. He nudges the glass to me, and I hand over half of my napkins—a deal is a deal, after all. "I'm Justin," he says to the girl.

"Ronnie," says the girl.

"I'm Claire."

Ronnie holds her hand out, and I take it. She shakes it firmly. She's got the kind of strong biceps that make me think I *really* should be hitting the gym.

"I'm relieved to see more girls," Ronnie says.

"That's what I said!" Tanya laughs.

"There's, what, twelve of us interns?" Ronnie asks. She peers over the heads of the people seated at the tables. "Did they do half and half, because that's so cool if they did."

"I'm always outnumbered in my science classes," Tanya says. "But look." She nods toward a group of women wearing lanyards that identify them as scientists. "Masrani's obviously hired a lot of us."

"I don't know why that's such a big deal," mutters Wyatt. The other guys frown at him—even Eric, who teased his sister about being excited earlier.

Ronnie fixes him with a look. "It is a big deal," she says, slowly and precisely. No room for argument.

I take a bite of my chicken. It's delicious, bursting with lemon and chili.

"Ronnie, what's your thing?" Tanya asks, like she asked me in the van. "I'm a botanist. Claire's gonna be president and save all the animals someday. Justin will run a hopefully *not* evil corporation." Justin laughs. "And my brother'll be winning Oscars for his documentaries. What about you?"

"West Point," Ronnie says, a deep note of pride in her voice. "I'll be starting after this summer."

Justin lets out an impressed whistle.

"That's a big deal," I say. No wonder her biceps are so enviable.

"That's, like, the *biggest* boys' club," Tanya says, which makes Ronnie crack a smile for the first time.

"I come from a military family," she says. "I'm really excited about starting in the fall. Though"—her smile widens at Tanya—"it does suck I can't do cool stuff to my hair like yours."

"I bet green and purple hair is *way* against regulations," Tanya says.

"Doesn't keep a girl from wanting it," Ronnie admits.

"A true sacrifice," Wyatt drawls, the words dripping with sarcasm.

"Dude, don't be an ass about military service," Eric says, glaring at him.

Wyatt shrugs, like he isn't bothered by being called out. "Sorry, I just think some girls just try too hard. Dye your hair whatever crazy color you want, but don't expect guys to like it. We like more natural women. And if you're blessed with *naturally* bright hair . . ." He smiles at me.

I blink, momentarily shocked by how rude he is. And then heat lights my face—not out of embarrassment, but out of anger. The redhead thing, guys can be all sorts of gross about it. And I'm not going to let him get away with being so mean to Tanya.

"Did you just insult Tanya *and* try to pit me against her by basically implying I'm better because I don't dye my hair?" I demand. I look to the other girls, whose eyes are dancing. I feel strong with Ronnie and Tanya by my side. "Did this guy just 'you're not like other girls' me?"

"I think he did," Tanya says, practically shaking with suppressed laughter.

Wyatt shifts in his seat. "I just gave my opinion. Some helpful advice."

"News flash, Wyatt," Ronnie says. "Your opinion sucks. And no one needs your advice."

"You do realize we don't do our hair for you or any guy?" Tanya

All I can see is dark gray shimmers and foam chopped up by our journey through the water. And then, in the distance, there it is—a dark shadow.

"Is that it?" Eric asks, raising his camera to his eye. He fiddles with the lens. "Oh, wow."

Emerging from the mist, the mountains and valleys grow clearer the closer we draw to the island. I grab the ship's railing, staring out into the night. It's so big. I knew it would be—it would *have* to be—but the reality of it, seeing it . . .

I don't have words for it.

When the ferry pulls into the dock and the scrape of the gangplank against wood fills the air, I grab my gear and fall in line behind the others. And when I take that first step, off the boat and onto her soil, Isla Nublar, this place of possibility, of greatness . . . I discover I do have words for it.

It's like finding home. At last.

7

At the docks, four jeeps are lined up waiting for us, headlights shining on the road ahead. I hop into one with Tanya and Justin and Eric. We are goggle-eyed, and our heads whip back and forth, trying to take in the shadowy terrain as we zip through the jungle toward the park's enormous gates.

The gates, at least, we can see; they're illuminated by the flickering light from torches fixed to the towering posts flanking the doors. The gate's so tall that I feel like I'll get a crick in my neck trying to see the top.

"Holy crap," Tanya says, hushed, next to me as the gates suddenly swing open, smooth as butter, not even a creak. "When I saw fuzzy drone footage that leaked last year, I *thought* I saw the gates, but look! They modeled the entrance after Hammond's original gates. I bet they used the first park's specs and everything!"

"The visuals are amazing," Eric mutters, almost to himself, as he stays fixed to the viewfinder, his camera sweeping the scene.

"We could get online and compare the specs to see," Justin says. "Though I'm never sure if those 'leaked' plans from the original park that hit online a while back are actually legitimate."

"The concept art and Dr. Hammond's models of the park were released, though, remember?" I say.

"I . . . may have a replica of one of those models," Justin admits.

"No way! How did you get one?" I ask.

"I made it," he says. "It took forever."

Well, that's adorable. I don't say that, though. I just smile as Tanya says, "That's impressive. I'd love to see pictures."

Our convoy of jeeps makes its way into the park, and the gates swing closed behind us. It's like we're all eight years old again, going to the natural science museum for the first time, our noses glued to the windows. As we peer out from the glass into the dark, even though Justin's so close his shoulder brushes mine, I barely have time to feel fluttery, because there might be *dinosaurs* out there.

But all we can see is the beam of the headlights on the paved road and out the windows. It's all a blur of dark jungle. Trees and plants; some I could probably identify in the light, others I probably couldn't—because they died out long ago and have been resurrected, much like the creatures who will live in their shelter.

After a few minutes, the jeeps take a right at a sign that says LODGING.

"Do you think they keep it unlit because of the animals?" Tanya asks.

"Maybe they just haven't installed all the lights yet," I suggest. "They're still in the process of building some stuff. I don't think all the habitats are done yet. I read about the aviary for the Pteranodons being built—apparently Masrani had to invent a new polymer strong enough to withstand strikes from their beaks."

"That is so hard-core," Tanya says in admiration.

"And expensive," Justin adds. "Masrani can turn around and sell that polymer, though, for other purposes. The research it took to make it will be paid for long before he puts it to use."

"Plus, it's built-in advertising," Tanya snickers. "Dino-proof—a new safety standard!"

We laugh as we pull in at the back of a tall building—the service entrance.

"Kids! Come on!" Jessica peeks her head into the jeep, beckoning.

Once she has the dozen of us assembled, she starts handing out packets. "You'll all be staying on the fourth floor of the hotel, which has been designated for the Bright Minds interns. Room assignments are right there on your packets."

I break my packet open and see *Roommate: Tanya Skye*.

"Looks like you're stuck with me," Tanya says when I point it out to her. "You don't snore, do you?"

"Nope," I say.

"Oh good." She smiles. "I promise not to hog the outlets too much."

Eric, who's come to stand next to her, snorts. "I'll believe that when I see it," he says.

"You haven't shared a room with me for years," Tanya scoffs. "The only boy, so he gets his own room. Meanwhile, I have to share with our little sister."

"Oh, admit it, you love your blanket-fort tea parties with Victory," Eric teases as Jessica leads us into the hotel.

"Her name's Victory Skye?" I ask. "That's like a superhero name."

Tanya nods. "She has some health problems. They began before she was born, so my parents wanted to give her a head start with a strong name."

"That's really sweet," I say. "I'm sorry she's been sick."

"Thanks." Tanya smiles, and it's not like her big, careless smiles. It's tight, strained. I feel a flash of worry for her, because it changes her face. Is her sister really sick? I can't imagine what I would do if that were Karen. When she got her appendix out, leaving her in the hospital overnight . . . Mom, Dad, and I going home without her felt so wrong, even though everything turned out fine.

We take the elevator up to the fourth floor with the group of interns, and we walk down the hall—a long corridor with the spots for paintings freshly marked in blue painter's tape on the bare walls.

Tanya and I find our room, and we both hesitate outside it, unsure what to do.

"Everyone, we'll meet in the lobby tomorrow morning at eight a.m.," Jessica calls across the hall. "Everything's in your packet, along with a map. We'll have our orientation breakfast, and then you'll be going on a tour of the park! So get some sleep now—you've got a big day tomorrow."

"Night," I call, waving at Justin across the hall.

"Night, Claire. Night, Tanya."

"Night, Justin. Thanks for the defense earlier at dinner with Wyatt."

He shrugs. "No problem. That guy's a jerk," he says.

"Still . . . ," Tanya goes on. "I appreciate it. So does Claire."

My cheeks burn, but I nod, because it's true.

Tanya and I go into our room, and it's fancy . . . like, hotel-room fancy, which makes sense since we're in the park's hotel. The bedroom is all polished, sleek wood paneling and has two full-sized beds side by side. There's a tablet resting on each one, and when I pick up the tech, I can't keep from letting out an excited squeal.

"They gave us the NuTech tablet?!" Tanya gasps, picking hers up. "These aren't even on the market yet! I've only seen rumors of the leaked specs online!"

"I cannot believe this. . . ." I press the on button and the screen flashes *Hello, Claire* at me.

"Bio-IDed already! My brother is probably jumping on the bed for joy right now," Tanya says, going over to her luggage. "He loves his gadgets."

My own suitcases are next to my bed, and for the next half hour we lose ourselves in unpacking. When we're done I'm exhausted, but I manage to take a shower and send a quick email to reassure my parents and Karen. I see that Karen's already sent me a photo—of Earhart sitting on my bed with a bone and Sally right next to her, eating a cricket. The subject line is: *Talk about predator and prey!*

I smile, shaking my head. It's nice to see them.

I drift off, thinking about Earhart and Sally. The last thing I remember is the sound of Tanya's rain machine, and when I wake, it's the first thing I hear.

I get up, bouncing a little as I quietly walk over to the windows at the far side of the room. Tanya's still asleep. I step out onto the balcony.

The sun's starting to rise, and the fuzzy gray light turns pink before my eyes. The lagoon the hotel overlooks sparkles as the beams hit them. My gaze traces the water, but I don't think this lagoon is doubling as a holding tank. Apparently, Masrani has plans to introduce amphibious creatures into the park, but he probably doesn't have a tank *this* close to the hotel.

The thought sends a shiver through me. The sea still holds some of our world's greatest undiscovered secrets. And the preparation that would have to go into housing and caring for even the smaller water creatures would be enormous.

I lean against the balcony railing, looking out at the park as it starts to wake up.

There's a giant crane positioned to the right, dangling pieces of what looks like a monorail track half assembled high above the water. Will it run through the entire park? You'd be able to see everything and never have to leave your seat.

Across the water lies a series of buildings. I squint in the rapidly spreading sunlight, trying to make out any signs, but it's too far. Those must be the shops and restaurants. . . . At the center is a pyramid-shaped building that looks almost like a miniature volcano.

My eye is drawn to a nondescript gray building set beyond the others, away from the main thoroughfare, lodged deep in the slope of the mountain behind it.

That's where the magic happens. Where the science is. The command center. The beating heart of Jurassic World.

"Morning," Tanya mumbles behind me, coming to stand by my side. "This is . . . *Wow*. Will the monorail travel through the entire park?"

"I think so," I say.

"Too bad construction isn't done yet," she says. "It'd be neat to be one of the first people to ride it." Her alarm clock goes off, and she looks over her shoulder and groans. "Guess we should get ready. You want to shower first?"

"Go ahead," I tell her. "I want to check my email, make sure my parents know I got here okay."

She disappears into the bathroom, and as I hear the water turn on and her start to sing, I open my laptop. Mom's written me back, signing it from both her and Dad—that's a good sign about them, right?

Karen, probably tapped out from wrestling Zach into his bath, sent just a short note: *So glad you got there safe. Sally is doing great. Zach is taking his job of remembering when feeding time is (and don't worry, I'm doing the actual feeding) very seriously. Dad took Earhart to the dog park for over two hours yesterday and he's talking about taking her fishing. Don't worry about your pets. Focus on your internship! NOW GO HAVE FUN!!*

I pick up my tablet from the bedside table and tap through it, getting a feel for how it works. Our itinerary for today springs up on the calendar page, and I check the time—we're due down for breakfast in forty minutes.

Tanya finishes up and I jump in the shower, making sure to slather myself with sunscreen after I get out and dry off. I shove a tube of it in my bag for later.

"I'm starving," Tanya says as we grab our stuff and head out of the room.

"I need about a gallon of coffee." We walk down the hallway to the elevators and press the down button.

"Hopefully they have good tea here," Tanya says. "But if they don't, I'm prepared." She pats her fringed black bag. "In this coffee drinker's world, I'll go to any extremes to get my tea."

"How did you survive freshman year without coffee?" I ask, baffled, as we take the elevator down and step out into the lobby. The hotel isn't full, but there are signs of life all over, from the people manning the desks up front to the workers hanging the antique lithographs featuring different dinosaurs.

Tanya waves when she spots Ronnie standing near the stairs. "Some tea has more caffeine than coffee!"

I shake my head solemnly. "Not the same," I insist.

"Morning," Ronnie calls, walking up to us. "Is your room as nice as ours?"

"Did you check out the balcony?" Tanya asks. "And the tablets!"

"They're spoiling us," Ronnie says with a grin.

We follow the Bright Minds signs to one of the conference rooms, where a breakfast buffet is set out. There's a big WELCOME, BRIGHT MINDS INTERNS! banner strung across the front of the room, and the smell of sausage and pancakes makes my stomach rumble.

The three of us load up our plates and take a table up front as more people trickle in. Eric and Justin join us, along with a handsome black boy who introduces himself as Art, Justin's roommate.

"I got stuck with Wyatt as my roommate," Eric says as he sits down next to his sister.

"Uh-oh," Tanya says.

He shoots her a look, and it's like watching a silent conversation going on. Twin-speak.

"I told him to leave us alone," Eric adds finally.

"Is that the guy with the light blond hair?" Art asks.

Ronnie nods. "He was being really gross at dinner last night."

"I drove over on the shuttle with him," Art says. "He would not stop talking about his dad. I guess he's on the board of directors of one of Masrani's companies or something."

"What would guys like that do without nepotism?" Ronnie mutters, and I snort, almost coughing up my orange juice.

"Where do you think we're going to start our tour?" Eric asks, taking a bite of toast. "Other than wanting to see the herbivores in person, I want to check out the command room. They've got to have thousands of cameras on this island."

"I want to see the greenhouses!" Tanya says immediately. "I hope they've built them already. Plus all the fauna. Are the dinosaurs affecting the local seabird population? What about rodents and other small indigenous animals? Do the dinosaurs wipe them out? Or do they adapt?"

"Evolution in action," Art says, nodding along with her. "I want to talk to the vets who have been treating the dinosaurs."

"Art's going to be a vet," Justin adds.

"Oh, that's cool," I say. "Like pets, or like wild animals, or . . . ?"

"My focus is on the larger predators in the wild and on conservation," Art says.

"Oh, you and Claire should talk, then," Tanya says. "She's an animal rights activist."

"More like a wannabe politician," I say.

"Working the system from the inside?" Art suggests, and I nod. "Cool. I'll have to bug you for a favor once I have my own sanctuary."

I grin.

"This must be really amazing for a vet," Eric says. "You can't get fieldwork like this anywhere else."

"It's mind-blowing," Art says. "A whole new frontier."

"Can they even, like, build an MRI machine big enough for a dinosaur?" Tanya muses. "Does an ultrasound even work with their hides?" She frowns. "Is *hides* even the right word? Scales? Skin? Armor?"

"Hides is probably the best, broadest term," Ronnie says thoughtfully. "And they might have invented a different ultrasound machine. One big or strong enough, maybe?"

"Can you imagine spreading that ultrasound jelly stuff on an Ankylosaurus?" Tanya asks.

"She might smash you with her tail," Justin says. "One wrong needle-prick and you could be crushed to dino dust."

"The vets here, they're creating an entirely new subset of medicine," Art says. "What they're doing is the kind of dangerous our field's barely even touched. But the stuff that's being discovered about these creatures now will end up in scientific texts and history books."

"And I'm gonna have *all* of it on camera," Eric says, tapping his trusty Nikon next to him.

"I'm surprised they let you bring that," Justin comments.

"I had to sign a bunch of forms," Eric explains. "But apparently, they want as much authentic footage of the life of the interns as possible. It's part of my job here. My footage is gonna end up in some cheesy training video, I bet. But it'll *look* great."

Everyone around the table laughs.

"What about you, Ronnie?" Art asks. "What do you want to see the most?"

"I want to talk to the trainers who've been working with the herbivores," Ronnie says. "Jessica was telling me that a lot of them are ex-military. And I'm with Eric: I want to see the command room. The security surrounding this place is the best in the world. Masrani's spared no cost. I heard there are metal alloys he's using on some of the enclosures that even the government doesn't have access to."

"You heard right," says a voice behind us. "Nice to see the rumor mill is always churning." The group of us whirl, almost as one, to see a tall Indian man with wavy hair and a lavender tie knotted expertly around his neck. It's the man himself. We've all seen photos. We've all dreamed of having the kind of power he has. Of creating the kind of change he has.

Ronnie flushes. "Mr. Masrani!" She leaps to her feet, her military background in every line of her body as she snaps to attention. "I didn't mean any offense, sir."

"None taken," Mr. Masrani says with a wide smile. "You are Veronica Torres, is that right?"

Ronnie nods. "Ronnie, sir."

"Ronnie, then. I am very pleased you chose us this summer,"

Mr. Masrani says. He looks over at the rest of our group. "All of you. Art. Claire. Eric. Tanya. Justin. I know you had your pick of internships. We are glad to have you here." His eyes focus on someone—Beverly—waving at him from the front of the conference room. "And now duty calls." He shoots us a final smile before going to join her.

"I can't believe he knew my name," Ronnie says, sitting down in her seat.

"I can't believe he knew *all* our names," I say, letting out a nervous laugh on the last few words.

"Interns, attention up here!" Beverly, the intern director, is standing at the front of the room, waiting to get our attention. "Mr. Masrani has arrived. He'd like to give a little speech."

Instantly, the murmur at the tables goes silent as he walks up to the front.

"Good morning, and welcome!" he says. "This is a special day for me. You twelve are the first young people to set foot in Jurassic World. My very first intern class." He beams at us like a proud father. "You each have been chosen for your unique talent and intelligence. I don't have to tell you you're the best of the best—the fact that you are in this room *means* you are. Because I choose only the very best to work on my island." He scans the room, his intense gaze fixing on each of us in turn.

"There is still much to be done at Jurassic World. Each of you will be integral to the success of this summer. We are just nine months from opening, and five herbivore species have been integrated into their island habitats, but more will be arriving this summer from Isla Sorna, our secondary location. Access to our carnivores—the T. rex, and Dilophosaurus—is restricted until the trainers working with you deem you ready to observe them. But there are Compsognathuses who do move throughout the park, eating droppings, dead animals, and interns who don't keep to their curfews."

His smile flashes and a wave of laughter ripples through the room.

"Kidding, of course," he continues. "It's not just Compsognathuses I want you to keep an eye out for. Construction is ongoing all over, so always be aware of your surroundings. And most importantly: I want you to learn. Ask questions. Voice your ideas, no matter how silly or inconsequential you may think they are. Soak up everything you can with those beautiful sponges that are your young, curious minds. This is a chance of a lifetime. Now, if we're all done eating, let's go! And make the most of it!"

We get up, grabbing our bags and tablets, and follow him like a trail of excited ducklings following their parent. I have to clench my fists to keep my hands from shaking, mostly with anticipation, but also a hint of fear.

Sometimes you have those moments that are almost prophetic, when you know, without a doubt, that what happens next will change everything.

I guess I just never realized how much *changing everything* would cost in the end.

8

"The monorail will travel through much of the park," Mr. Masrani explains as we leave the hotel and walk up to the fleet of jeeps waiting for us. "But since it's not fully operational yet, we'll be taking the service roads." He flashes another smile, taking in our excited faces. "You'll be getting access that even some of my employees don't have," he says. "We'll start with the outdoor tour because I don't want the anticipation to kill you. You want to see the dinosaurs, correct?"

"Hell, yeah!" bursts out an excited intern behind us. The rest of us laugh nervously, and then louder when Mr. Masrani doesn't look offended; in fact, he seems delighted—as excited to show us his park as we are to be here.

"That's what I thought," he said. "We'll break for lunch, and then I'll be taking you to see our lab. But I think we'll start in the Gyrosphere Valley."

"Wait—the Gyrospheres are *real*?" Justin asks. "They aren't just a rumor?"

"Ah, you probably saw the papers. Some sneaky patent clerk snapped a photo of the Gyrosphere technology when it was filed," Mr. Masrani says.

Justin laughs. "Guilty," he says. "I've got a news alert set up for all things relating to the park."

Mr. Masrani leans forward conspiratorially. "So do I," he says. "I've got to keep ahead of the leakers! They're always trying to sneak their way onto my island with their drones and their photographers and their many, many bribes. Some buzz is good for a business, but too much will spoil some surprises I'm not willing to divulge."

"You've got to guard those trade secrets closely," Justin says.

"Indeed. But there's no point in keeping the secret of the Gyrospheres from all of you, since one of the interns' tasks is to test-drive them through certain terrains to calibrate their sensors."

"We're talking about the rolling hamster-ball things, right?" Tanya whispers under her breath to me after Justin and Mr. Masrani are out of earshot.

I nod.

"Are we sure they're safe?" Ronnie asks, raising a skeptical eyebrow.

"I guess we'll see," I say as the three of us girls load into the jeep. I see Justin and Eric jump into the one in front of us—with Mr. Masrani. Justin's going to love getting face time with him, and instead of feeling jealous, I'm glad for him.

I never expected to like everyone so much. In most of my

classes in school, everyone competes against each other. And everyone wanted to be Professor Broadhurst's assistant, so when I was chosen . . . well, I've never been really popular, and that certainly didn't help. I had Regina and my friends outside of my major, but in class, it could be lonely. And I worried it would be like that here, but it's totally different.

I think this is what belonging feels like. It's kind of scary. I've never really felt like I belonged anywhere . . . or with anybody.

"I'm Bertie," says the woman at the wheel, smiling at us in the rearview. She has an accent—I think it's South African—and dark curly hair cropped close to her head. "Everyone buckled up?"

We nod.

Instead of pulling onto the main road—which must lead to the main street, with its stores and restaurants, all still under construction—the jeeps turn onto a narrower road leading away from the hotel, cutting through the hollows and shadows of the jungle. When I look up out the window, I can barely see the blue sky above, the trees are so thick. The air is humid—my tank top is already sticking to my back, and I'm glad I pinned my braids up around my head before I left.

"Can we roll the windows down?" I ask, and Bertie nods.

I do so, letting the fresh air blow in—along with the scent of the jungle. It's sharp and wet, wild and green, fetid and fresh . . . like life and death all at once. A vibrant contradiction.

"Is that a waterfall?" Tanya asks as we drive past the thundering sound of water, the falls shielded by the thickets of trees. There seems to be a huge variety of plant species. I can identify a few ferns and the palm trees, but a lot of the lush green tangle surrounding us is a mystery to me.

"Yup," says Bertie. "There are five on the island. Three will be accessible to guests once we open."

"Mermaid goals," Tanya says with a grin, making Ronnie and me laugh. "Ooh, look!" She points out the window at a tree that looks like it was created by someone who's never seen a tree before. "Monkey puzzle trees! *Araucaria araucana*. They were a major food source in the Mesozoic period."

"Good eye," Bertie says approvingly. "Are you the botany student?"

"That's me." Tanya nods. "How did you know?"

"We're briefed on all the interns we'll be working with," Bertie explains. "I work with the young herbivores, preparing them for integration into the habitats. You'll be working with my team this week. Today you'll just be observing, but by the end of your stay, you'll be able to work with the very young herbivores—under our supervision, of course."

"So you're a trainer?" Ronnie asks eagerly.

"Head trainer," Bertie says.

Ronnie's eyes widen. "You're in charge?"

"That's right," Bertie replies with a grin. "I run a team of twelve, and we handle the herbivores in the park. There's another team of caretakers that deal with the carnivores we have onsite, but a majority of them are still working on Isla Sorna."

"What's the difference between a trainer and a caretaker?" I ask.

"Well, with the carnivores, training is more of a wild theory than an actual practice yet," Bertie explains. "Working with the herbivores like my team does is mostly about acclimation and encouraging natural behavior that's already ingrained in the animals. They want to graze, roam and run, sun themselves at the watering hole, and spend time with their herds. You can be up close to the herbivores in ways you can't with the carnivores, and if you can't get close…that makes working with an animal a lot trickier. Working with the carnivores is a lot of observation right now. It's going to take a special person—and a really brave one—to crack the carnivore code when it comes to real connection and training. I hope I'm around to see it." We fall quiet.

"Do you ever work with the T. rex?" Ronnie asks the question we're all wondering.

"I'm in charge of her Thursday feedings," Bertie says. "Once the park opens, we'll have more carnivore caretakers on Nublar, so my T. rex time will probably get cut down."

"Is she terrifying?" Tanya asks.

"She's beautiful," Bertie says. "They all are."

"She was here at the start," I say. "That's the rumor, at least."

"That's right," Bertie says. "She's one of the older dinosaurs; she lived in the original park."

"Is it mostly older dinosaurs here? Do the younger ones stay on Sorna until they're ready to come here?" I ask.

"We actually have quite a few young dinosaurs," Bertie says, and it doesn't escape my notice that she sidesteps my question about Isla Sorna, which somehow seems even *more* mysterious than Isla Nublar. I wonder if it'll ever be open to the public—probably not. I know it was the place where Dr. Hammond raised his first dinosaurs, but the real question is: What goes on there now that Mr.

Masrani owns it? Is it just the place to raise the dinosaurs? Or is it more?

"We like to integrate the young dinosaurs one at a time, especially a protective herd genus like the Triceratops. But we've had great success with each addition to the herd. Now if we can just get our teenage Brachiosaurus to completely stop playing with the Gyrospheres . . ." She shakes her head ruefully.

"She's *playing* with the Gyrospheres?" I ask, feeling even more nervous. And they want us to ride in them? No way!

"Just the empty ones. And we're working on some very successful distraction techniques," Bertie assures us. "I think we've almost broken her of the habit. She's very . . . spirited, our Pearl."

"Is that her name?" Ronnie asks.

"Our Brachiosauruses are Agnes, Olive, Dot, and Pearl," Bertie said. "Dot and Pearl are the younger of the four."

I can't stop the giggle that explodes from my throat. "They sound like a knitting circle of elderly ladies," I say.

"That was the theme we were going for," Bertie says with a smile.

"Do you get to name them?" Tanya asks.

"We take suggestions on a theme for each new species, then vote as a team," Bertie answers.

She turns onto a gravel road, and about a mile farther down, the lush press of trees and foliage that is the jungle suddenly opens into wide, rolling grasslands dotted with trees with long, reaching branches that create both shade and sustenance. The other three jeeps are already parked near a perimeter fence, and Bertie pulls up next to them.

"Thanks for answering all our questions, Bertie," Ronnie says as we get out.

"Any time, girls," she says. "See you later. I've got to go join my team." She jerks her thumb toward the enormous truck that's parked about half a mile down the road. The fence stretches as far as I can see, caging the beautiful valley in—and presumably, the dinosaurs, too.

But I don't see them anywhere. My palms are sweaty with anticipation as I get out and stare into the distance, searching.

"Where are they?" Tanya asks, shading her eyes with her hand and peering out across the meadow.

We walk toward the fence, joining Justin, Art, and Eric, who are standing together near the top of the hill. Eric's looking at everything through his lens, and his sister peeks over his shoulder. "You see anything on zoom?" she asks.

"Not yet," Eric says. "I got some great footage on the drive in, though. I'll show it to you later."

"Interns! Don't wander off!" Beverly calls, waving at us.

We go to join her and the rest of our group. Mr. Masrani has walked down to where the trainers are gathered. And then we hear it: a rumble—like a lowing noise—breaks through the air.

It's coming from the truck.

Our heads whip toward the sound, and the hairs on the back of my arms rise as I realize—there's a real, live dinosaur in there.

Beverly and Jessica both smile indulgently at our awestruck expressions. "That's right," Beverly says. "You'll be observing the introduction of one of the Triceratops to the herd today. She'll be the youngest member, bringing us to a total of sixteen Triceratops in the park."

"Can we go down there?" Art asks. I can almost feel him vibrating with excitement next to me.

Beverly shakes her head. "We'll be observing from up there." She turns and points to a vista overlooking the sprawling valley below. There's a flat pad, dotted with flags to outline whatever they're planning on building up there—maybe an observation deck, or a place to launch the Gyrospheres?

Beverly leads us briskly up to the overlook, and my thighs protest at the steep incline in the muggy heat. Ronnie takes the hill like it's nothing, and I remember at breakfast this morning she said she'd gotten up early to work out in the gym. I so do not have that discipline, even though I really loved the weight-lifting class I took last semester.

We make it to the top, and the view of the valley spread out beneath us is stunning. There are a lot more trees beyond the particular set of hills, and when I step up on one of the rocks with the binoculars Beverly and Jessica hand out, I can see a large body of water beyond the trees. Suddenly, all I want in the world is to see a dinosaur playing in the water. When I was little, one of my books about dinosaurs had a drawing of herbivores gathered around a watering hole, and I always loved the idea of them all hanging out together, splashing.

I turn my attention back to the immediate action. The truck parked below is a flatbed with an immense steel container. From this vantage point, we can see it has holes punched in the top.

The cables securing the container to the flatbed tremble as

more lowing fills the air. It's unlike any sound I've ever heard, but I can tell one thing: she's scared. It makes my stomach tight. I'd be scared too. Herded into a truck, moved in the dark, alone, not knowing what happens next, all these strange smells and sounds.

But soon she'll be free. With her own kind for the first time, free to explore the hills and lakes, where she belongs.

Back home.

"I think we're ready!" Mr. Masrani says, walking up to join us at the vista point. "Keep your eyes on Bertie, everyone." He points to her, and she strides up to the edge of the fence, her hands fitted around her mouth. She takes a deep breath and lets out a deep lowing sound just like the one coming from the truck—she's making dinosaur calls, like some people make bird calls.

"She's . . . she's calling them," Art whispers as his eyes scan the horizon.

Bertie steps back, gesturing to the trainers who've situated themselves on either side of the container. The section of the fence with an electrified gate swings open, and the truck backs up into the space. The trainers on the truck jump down to set up the ramp, and Bertie takes their place next to the container. She's standing near the container, talking—to the Triceratops inside.

I'm so focused on Bertie that I don't see until Tanya jabs me in the shoulder. "Claire, look!"

I raise my binoculars to look where she's pointing, right where the tree line thickens along the edge of the valley. Three Triceratops, peeking out through the trees, answering Bertie's call.

They're breathtaking. Earth-shattering. Life-changing.

And they're *enormous*. Bigger than I even imagined, even though . . . I *knew*. I've seen the fossils and the reconstructed skeletons and all the documentaries.

Intellectually, I knew.

But *emotionally*? I had no idea. Nothing can compare to seeing them, right then, right there, in the flesh, their strange, ancient voices carried on the wind. Tears prick at my eyes, to my embarrassment. Normally, I'd be mortified, but there are *dinosaurs* creeping out of the trees and into full view, so at this moment, I do not care about tears or shame or anything else.

My eyes trace over their bumpy gray hides, the famed frill surrounding their massive heads, the curve of their horns—what must they feel like? Smooth? Rough?—and the slow, almost sleepy way they move, lumbering, curious, but cautious as they spot the humans at the edge of the fence.

Do they recognize the trainers? Do they have favorites? Can you even *imagine* being a dinosaur's favorite? Obviously, you don't want them to like you too much because that might lead to being squashed affectionately, but to work with them, to form a real bond with them . . . that must be *everything*.

I glance to my right, and I realize Art's eyes are bright, and Tanya's mascara is streaked down her face as she sniffles. Justin just looks stunned, and for once, Eric's not peering through the camera lens, but looking right at them. Ronnie's stock-still, like she's frozen, not out of fear, but wonder.

So it's not only me, then. I feel relieved.

The three Triceratops stop their journey and come to rest in what is the hollow of the valley, the low point that's protected by sloping hills on three sides, leaving them a view of the gate where the trainers have finished setting up the ramp. They're just watching now, waiting. Like we are.

"What do you think?" Masrani asks, and I glance up at him, realizing he's looking at us the way we're looking at the dinosaurs. Like *we're* the fascinating ones.

"It's . . . it's . . ." Justin just shakes his head, like he can't quite form words.

The light in Mr. Masrani's eyes deepens. This is where he gets his joy, I realize as I turn back to the grasslands. This place, it's as much of a haven for him as it is for the dinosaurs. And being able to share your greatest joy with people who appreciate it . . . that's a rare gift, isn't it?

"It looks like it's Curie, Johnson, and Hypatia who have come to greet our newest addition," Mr. Masrani says, turning his attention back to the valley.

"Like Marie Curie and Katherine Johnson?" I ask without thinking. I can barely tear my eyes away from the dinosaurs. How does Masrani tell them apart? Aside from whatever trackers they're wearing, they must have subtle markings or behaviors.

"Good catch, Claire," Mr. Masrani says. "The trainers get creative with naming. And competitive!" He chuckles. "I once tried to suggest a theme for the Ankylosauruses, and they absolutely tore me apart!"

"Sir, with all due respect, I don't think naming the Ankylosauruses after the highest mountains in the world was exactly what they were going for," Beverly says with a smile. "Didn't they end up naming all of them after famous women warriors?"

"Yes," Mr. Masrani sighs. "Better than my idea by far, I know. But I would love to name a dinosaur Everest. It was my first big climb. I remember it like it was yesterday."

"Maybe one of the flying dinosaurs," Art suggests. "It'd be fitting."

Mr. Masrani nods approvingly. "I like the way you think," he says. The comm in his hand crackles, and we hear Bertie's voice say, "We're ready to release her, boss. With your go-ahead."

Mr. Masrani looks around at all of us. "Ready?" he asks, grinning like a kid in a candy store.

We nod.

"You're good to go, Bertie. Let's introduce Lovelace to her new home and family," Mr. Masrani says.

The metallic scrape of a chain being drawn up fills my ears, followed by the rattle of the container door opening, and then something different: not lowing, no, it's *stomping*. The sound thunders through my head as I focus the binoculars on the grass in front of the container, and the Triceratops—Lovelace, Masrani called her—practically bounds out of the container like a restless dog who's been riding in a car too long.

Laughter ripples through our group as Lovelace gives a full body shake, her frill rippling as she wiggles her butt a few times extra for good measure. Her tail slashes back and forth through the grass as she looks around. Then she goes still—she must have caught sight of the three older dinosaurs waiting for her. For a second, she seems to shrink, and Tanya says, "Aw, look, she's shy!" as Lovelace looks back at the container—and the trainers, who are backing out through the gate and swinging it shut. Only Bertie remains inside the fenced area, and my stomach tightens, because she doesn't look nervous or intimidated at all, even though she's right out there in the open with them. She's probably the bravest person I've ever met.

I focus my binoculars on Bertie. She looks *so* small near Lovelace. She's saying something to her, a wide, encouraging smile on her face. She gestures toward the valley, saying something again, and Lovelace looks back at the other dinosaurs. The one I think is Hypatia seems more concerned with the tree branch she's chomping on than the new dinosaur in her presence—maybe she's the oldest and has seen it all?—but Curie and Johnson are alert, watching Lovelace with interest.

"Look how stubby her horns are compared to the others," Art points out. "The theory's always been that their horns grow and might even curve with age. Now we'll be able to find out if it's true."

"So she's a teenager?" Tanya asks.

"Or the dinosaur equivalent," Art replies.

"It's like she's the new kid in school!" Tanya says, and Art laughs at her comparison. "I hope she finds a best friend."

"And a dinosaur girlfriend," Ronnie adds as Tanya grins.

"Maybe she'll meet a sweet Ankylosaurus to go to the dance with," Art says.

"Now, that would be something to see," Justin laughs. "A dinosaur prom." He shoots me a smile that makes me bite my lip, my stomach doing that twisty, warm thing.

"Imagine how big the queen's crown would need to be," Ronnie says, and someone snorts behind me, and I don't even have to turn around to know it's Wyatt. I just roll my eyes. That guy doesn't know how to have any fun.

"Look, she's going for it!" Art calls out, and we all snap our binoculars back to the valley.

He's right. Bertie's pep talk obviously did the trick, because Lovelace is moving forward, across the sloping meadow toward Curie, Johnson, and Hypatia, who's finally abandoned her tree snack in favor of watching their new addition.

The trainer slips out of the enclosure and rejoins her team on the other side to watch all their hard work in action.

Lovelace breaks into a run, and a new, excited kind of lowing fills the valley. I gasp as Curie breaks free from her little trio and rambles up to meet the younger dinosaur with her own noisy greeting. The two rub frills together, Curie's eyes closing in joy as Lovelace continues with the cow noises, like it's been *forever* since they talked.

"Oh my gosh," I hear Ronnie say, and then I see them too—the rest of the herd, emerging from the trees. A dozen Triceratops, some so big they must top out at twenty-five thousand pounds. They trek across the grass, surrounding Lovelace and Curie, who are still tangled together like old friends. Their greetings and stomping fill the air, and chills ripple through me as I watch them welcome their sister home.

9

They practically have to drag all of us away from the valley, even after the herd disappears into the trees, seeking shade from the sun beating down as it hits noon.

"Could we stay just a little longer?" Eric suggests. "The footage I'm getting is amazing. When they rubbed frills . . . I got it all!"

"I promise, you'll all get more time with the animals later this week," Jessica assures us as Mr. Masrani and Beverly lead our group back to the jeeps. "Including some Gyrosphere time!"

"Away from Pearl, the Gyrosphere-happy Brachiosaurus, I hope," I whisper under my breath.

"There's a Gyrosphere-happy Brachiosaurus?" Justin asks, catching up with me.

"Apparently, she thinks they're toys," I say, and it makes him laugh, that real, full-bodied kind of laugh that I shouldn't feel proud for causing, but I do, just a little.

"I wonder what the trainers are doing to distract her," he says.

"Mr. Masrani said the Gyrospheres have all sorts of tech to keep you upright at all times, but wouldn't a few good swats from a Brachiosaurus make guests start barfing all over?"

"Maybe they'll distract her with some different toys," I say as Jessica waves us into one of the jeeps. To my displeasure, I see that Wyatt's already sitting in it. I hesitate because I don't want to sit next to him, and Justin says, "Here, I can sit in the middle, Claire," all smoothly, like he's read my mind.

It's such a little gesture, but the fact that he even noticed makes my throat tighten as he shoots me a reassuring smile.

"So . . . toys for the dinosaurs," he begins, ignoring Wyatt completely as our driver—not Bertie, but one of her teammates—starts the jeep. Luckily, Wyatt falls into conversation with the other intern in the backseat and ignores us.

"What do you think?" Justin goes on. "Possible?"

"That'd need to be some really durable material to make dinosaur toys," I say. "But it's so neat that they play. I feel stupid, but I never really thought about them being so social and frisky before Bertie mentioned it to us on the drive. We always think of them as fearsome, don't we? Monumental and dangerous and scary, never playful."

"Well, young dinosaurs aren't exactly something we've had access to," Justin points out. "If I were in charge of the really little ones, I'd put up an online feed of them, twenty-four seven. Like some animal shelters do with their litters of kittens or puppies, you know? Think of all the free advertising."

The idea's so cute, I almost can't stand it. An online baby dinosaur feed? Someone sign me up.

"That would be adorable," I say. "You should suggest that to Mr. Masrani. And I mean that. Not just because I selfishly want that in my life."

"You're totally transparent, Dearing," he drawls sarcastically, making me smile even wider.

"Wasn't it amazing today?" I ask, unable to keep my voice from dropping to a hush, like the experience was sacred or something.

"I think I made myself look like an idiot in front of Masrani," Justin says, shaking his head. "Hopefully the excuse of being swept up in the whole moment will work."

"You did not make yourself look like an idiot," I assure him, because he's furrowing his brow. "Mr. Masrani seems pretty delighted at how into this all of us are. He's not going to fault you for being kind of speechless after seeing a herd of Triceratops for the first time! I felt like I wanted to cry . . . it was so much like a dream."

I can practically *feel* Wyatt rolling his eyes next to us. I try not to let the flash of annoyance overtake me. I refuse to let him ruin my day, especially this day.

Instead of going back to the hotel, we drive across the water that surrounds the resort area of the park and head onto Main Street. At least, that's what the sign we pass says: MAIN STREET UNDER CONSTRUCTION.

The contrast between the half-built storefronts and the wild jungle and mountains beyond should be startling. It should clash, but it doesn't. Not here, in this place that is just as much about the future as it is about the past. Just as much about science as it is about nature. Isla Nublar is a place of opposites, really. It's home to humans and dinosaurs. Carnivores and herbivores. Predator and prey. They'll live alongside each other—maybe not always aware of each other in their separate habitats, so it won't be exactly like when they ruled the land—but they will coexist. Thrive. And we will learn. About them. From them.

The jeep slows down to let three construction workers in helmets cross the street in front of us. The street stretches across the inlet's entire shoreline, which separates Main Street from the resort area of the island.

There's a bustle of activity on Main Street, silver-helmeted men and women working on buildings, installing streetlights, and hanging signs.

"Starbucks really *is* everywhere," I say, pointing at the coffee-shop-to-be that we pass.

"Never deny people their coffee," Justin says. "That's just Business 101."

We pull up in front of the building I spotted from my balcony this morning. Not the command center, but the one that almost resembled a volcano. As we get out, I see the sign that says SAMSUNG INNOVATION CENTER.

"Seriously? Wow," I say.

"Too far for you?" Justin asks.

"I mean, come on. They couldn't name it after Dr. Hammond? They had to go with corporate sponsorship?"

"I bet Samsung's funding a lot of great programs for their partnership," he says. "That's what's important, right?"

"Well, now I feel like a sad sack who doesn't like education," I say, making him laugh.

"You're just an idealist," he says, and I smile. I like that he gets it.

"Lunch is inside today," our driver says. "Just go straight in."

"Thanks," Justin and I say as we get out. Tanya and Eric are waiting for us at the bottom of the steps.

"Art and Ronnie already went in," Tanya says. "Did you see this building? It's wild. I hope it glows red at night."

"Maybe you can suggest it," her brother says. "Check it out." He nudges her, and she bends down to look at his camera's screen. "Oh wow," she says. "Look, he slow-moed Lovelace's gallop toward the herd."

We gather around to watch, Justin's hand brushing against mine as we bend down to look. He doesn't seem to notice—maybe I'm just reading too much into it. I focus instead on Eric's footage and Lovelace's joyful romp with her new family.

"You've got a really good eye, Eric," Justin says after the footage ends and we head up the steps of the educational center.

"Thanks," Eric says. "I love capturing the moment . . . and moments like these—well, this is the stuff film was made for." We all nod in agreement.

We step inside. It's quiet; no one's around. The room holds a lot of large objects draped with dropcloths, what looks like a help desk in the back, a console to my right, and several big screens on the wall, but nothing else. It seems like they're getting ready to paint everything—canvas sheets everywhere.

I frown. "Hello?" I call, walking forward, Justin right behind me.

It leaps at me—or at least, for a second, I *think* the Raptor is leaping at me. I shriek, Justin lets out a startled yell, and the twins behind me shout. Justin and I both stumble backward at the same time, knocking hard into each other, and the moment my *Run, run, oh my God, why aren't you running?* instinct kicks in, I finally register that the figure in front of me is see-through.

A hologram.

I burst out laughing, and one by one, as they realize, my friends follow, until all of us are cracking up. I'm hanging on to Justin, weak in the knees, and he's hanging on to me just as tight, and we're *sobbing* with laughter as the hologram Raptor tilts her head at us.

The twins have the same laugh—this funny belly laugh that reaches the high ceilings of the center's lobby—and Justin's laugh is deep, like his voice, like his eyes. Their voices tangle with mine in the air, and I feel it again—this sense of home, of belonging.

"I thought we were dead," I say, wiping my eyes as I finally let go of Justin.

"My entire body was just . . . *AHHH!*" Tanya giggles. "Wow." She walks up to the hologram, studying it with a rapt expression. "This is so cool." She reaches out, and her hand goes through the Raptor.

"Interns!" Jessica's now-familiar refrain breaks through our fading laughter. "We're over here. Come along."

Tanya walks through the Raptor hologram, but I can't bring myself to do it. I know it's silly, but I walk around it instead, following her as the boys bring up the rear. Jessica leads us out to an observation deck that overlooks the wilds of the island. I can see the command center from here, the sunlight winking off the windows. Tables have been set up on the deck, and there are little place cards at each plate. Assigned seating?

"Once a week, you'll be getting face time with members of the senior staff," Jessica explains. "Eric, you're over there, with some of our command center staff. Tanya, you're with the head of our botany team. Claire and Justin, you'll be dining with Mr. Masrani today."

I gulp, trying not to look like a deer in the headlights as I follow Justin over to the table where Mr. Masrani is waiting for us.

He gets up when he sees us. "Please, sit," he says. "How do you like the look of the educational center?"

"Your hologram technology is awesome," I say, and Mr. Masrani's teeth flash in a quick smile.

"Appropriately scary?" he asks.

"Sure to trigger anyone's fight-or-flight instinct," I say, praying I'm not coming off as too glib.

"It's a fine line to tread," Mr. Masrani says. "I don't want to terrify anyone—too much, at least."

"Maybe a Brachiosaurus hologram instead of a Raptor?' I suggest, trying to ignore the voice in my head that says I'm overstepping.

Luckily, he doesn't look bothered at all. "Maybe we'll immortalize our girl Pearl in hologram next," he says.

"Bertie was telling me how spirited she is," I say.

Masrani nods. "That she is."

"Do you spend a lot of time with the dinosaurs, sir?" Justin asks.

"I'm afraid my work keeps me very busy," Mr. Masrani says. "But since we're less than a year from opening, I do find myself spending more and more time here. Which I don't mind in the least."

"Do you have any projections yet for attendance?"

"Ah, the business major starts to come out." Mr. Masrani smiles. "This is why I chose you. Your personal essay reminded me of myself at your age."

Justin's ears turn bright red at such a compliment, and I have to bite the inside of my lip to not smile at how cute it is and embarrass him further.

"I'm really grateful to be here, sir," he says.

"Projections for our first quarter are very strong," Mr. Masrani says, signaling for a server to pour our drinks. There are little menus on each plate, with a selection of tapas and entrees to choose from. "While we plan on making small batches of tickets available starting six months before we open, I'll also be introducing several lotteries with all-expenses-paid trips because ticket scalping will be rampant the first year especially. Everyone deserves a chance to experience this place."

"I saw on Main Street you've already partnered with some big names," Justin says. "All the comforts of home."

"With the wonder of the unknown," Masrani adds. "That is our goal. With what you've seen so far, do you think we're accomplishing it, Claire?"

I'm taking a sip of water and I almost cough, because I wasn't expecting him to ask me that. I set my glass down. "I think this park is one of the most incredible feats ever accomplished," I say, because it's the truth. "This isn't just about one kind of science. It's not just about advances in paleontology or animal behavior or biology or the myriad of other fields. This affects everything. It changes everything. Things discovered here could change the world."

"And that's what you're interested in doing, is it not?" Mr. Masrani asks. "You want to change the world."

"I want to help make the world better for more than just the humans," I say. I've never said that out loud before, and it feels strange to say it here, on a fancy deck, with my soda in a crystal wineglass and a billionaire in front of me. Like I'm in a movie or something. But it's the truth. It's what I want. And so often, we're told that what we want doesn't matter. So we never even voice it, let alone ask for it or demand it.

I don't want to let myself be crushed like that. Not when I can try to climb, even if it's a precarious path.

"A noble goal," Mr. Masrani says. "Though politics is a ruthless game."

"Maybe I'm a ruthless girl," I say.

It's out my mouth before I can think, a truth that's not so pretty. It startles him, I can tell. His eyes widen, and for a second, I'm afraid he's going to laugh at me. But instead, he steeples his fingers, staring at me over them. "What you are is a surprise, Claire Dearing," he says. "Your resume is stacked with accomplishments. But you chose a very different direction with your personal essay. It intrigued me. And now that I've met you, I'm even more intrigued."

My cheeks heat up. I want to wriggle in my seat. Is he going to blurt out what my essay was about, here and now? But my worries are immediately swept away, because Beverly's hurrying up to him.

"Simon, I have Dr. Wu on the line," she says. "He has some concerns about the intern visit later?"

Mr. Masrani sighs. "Excuse me for a moment," he says, getting up and walking away with her.

I let out a breath and look up to see Justin staring at me.

"What?" I ask.

"You're kind of a badass," he says. "*'Maybe I'm a ruthless girl'*?"

There go my stupid cheeks again. "Shut up," I mutter. "It just kind of came out."

"No, really, that was impressive," he says. "You took him by surprise. Guys like that . . . they're not surprised easily. They've seen everything, they've done everything. Masrani *really* has, now that he has Isla Nublar. So when you surprise them, they take notice. I think you won major points."

"It's not about that," I say, and he shoots me an "Are you kidding?" look, all quirked eyebrows and those glasses slipping down his nose. "Okay, fine. I am a bottomless pool of ambition and I *really* want to impress him. Satisfied?"

"Only if you let me join you in that bottomless pool, because it sounds . . . *intriguing*," Justin says.

I don't even fight my smile. He is really not helping me with the whole not-liking-him thing.

"You're not going to tell me what was in your personal essay, are you?" he asks. "You're just going to let me sit here and stew, wondering what you wrote about that hooked Simon Masrani?"

"Would you tell me about yours?" I ask.

"Sure," he says, totally ruining my argument and my defense with one easy shrug. Guys. Honestly.

"That is not fair," I complain, and he laughs, fiddling with his glasses as he turns his attention to the menu.

The waiter comes over to take our orders while Masrani is still talking with Beverly, but before our food arrives, he returns, apologizing for the delay.

"Are we still going to be able to see the labs?" Justin asks.

"Of course," Mr. Masrani says as the servers deliver our food. I ordered the flatbread pizza, and with the gooey cheese and bright, tart sauce, it's like biting into heaven.

Masrani and Justin are talking about ROI and franchise agreements, and I just listen for a while until Justin excuses himself to go to the restroom.

"I wouldn't have revealed the subject of your essay," Mr. Masrani says when Justin is out of earshot. "Not in front of your peers. I value my interns' privacy."

"I appreciate that," I say.

"There are many reasons why I could have chosen you for this program, Claire," he goes on. "You are accomplished, you come highly recommended, and you are obviously brilliant. But it wasn't any of those things that drew me to your application. Political science majors aren't what we generally look for, you know."

"But you chose me," I say, confused.

"Because of your essay," Mr. Masrani says, and I shift in my seat, feeling exposed all of a sudden. Like I'm five and I'm back at that tap recital I bungled, where I forgot my solo and just froze on the stage in my top hat, everyone looking at me.

I don't know what to say, really. I knew there was a chance he'd read the intern essays. I guess I just never thought he'd be so *involved* with us. That I'd be sitting here with this man I admire so much, this man who knows so much about me.

Because that essay . . . that was the closest to pure *me* I'll ever get. It was the easiest and hardest thing I've ever done. It was like taking my searching heart out of my chest and mailing it in the essay's stead.

"Everyone else took the essay question as a challenge to explain some part of their past," Mr. Masrani continues. "But you . . . you wrote about the future. Not just your future. *The* future. But in looking outward instead of inward, you ended up revealing much to me about yourself and how you think."

Detail a significant challenge and solution.

That was the essay prompt. It was so vague and broad, I remember Regina laughed about it when I showed her. But now, looking across the table at Masrani, I realize that it was vague on purpose.

He wanted to see what we're made of. What we focus on. Past mistakes or future ones.

I've accidentally passed some test I didn't realize I was taking. And now I have his attention. The back of my neck prickles at the thought, because I know how important this is. If he thinks I'm smart or unique . . . Justin's right, that's *huge*.

"I am interested in how you think, Claire. You are someone who wants to build a better world. And so do I. This island is part of that. It is an indulgence, on one hand, of course. A man and his dinosaurs." His eyes sweep down, self-deprecation in them. "But I have built a whole new world. Piece by piece. 'An ultimate, never-ending, always-nurturing challenge. A chance to start anew.' It is a true gift."

My cheeks turn red, because he's quoting my essay back to me. Simon Masrani is quoting me *to* me, and I don't even know what to say in response. Thankfully, Justin saves me from stammering out something ridiculous by coming back just then, and Mr. Masrani changes the subject to some of the other attractions in the park that he wants to show us, like the river curving through the valley where the herbivores live, down which visitors will be able to take a guided kayak tour.

After we finish lunch, Mr. Masrani accompanies all of us to the true heart of Jurassic World: the command center. But instead of getting to see the state-of-the-art tracking systems and monitoring tech upstairs, we take a freight elevator down so many floors, I'm sure we're underground by the time the elevator doors open to reveal what seems like acres of glass and stainless steel.

The lab. My heart kicks against my rib cage as I breathe in the air. I can practically *smell* the science . . . or maybe that's the frog parts they're using to splice missing DNA strands.

A man with black hair and cheekbones that could slice through all the glass walls around him comes striding out of the sterile lab space and into the entryway. He raises an eyebrow at Masrani.

"I told you, I don't have time for interns today," he says. "I've been brought a very interesting amber specimen with multiple DNA profiles."

"Dr. Wu, I must insist," Mr. Masrani says. "I promise you, my interns will not disturb anything. I'm sure they'd love to see this specimen."

"Are you *the* Dr. Wu?" Tanya blurts out from behind me. "The one who worked with Dr. Hammond? You were at the original park?"

"Indeed," Dr. Wu says.

The excited murmur that breaks out among us makes him purse his lips. "I would really prefer to get back to my work," he says. "The potential of this specimen . . ."

"Fifteen minutes," Beverly suggests, or rather, insists, a determined smile on her lips. "The interns need to get a feel for the lab, Dr. Wu. They will be doing rotations in here."

"Interns break things," Dr. Wu protests, shaking his head in dismay at the thought.

"I promise not to break anything," Tanya says.

"Me too!" Art adds, craning to look over Dr. Wu's shoulder at the lab equipment visible behind those oh-so-tempting glass doors.

"They all promise they will try very hard not to break anything," Mr. Masrani says, amused. "And if anything *does* get broken, we can replace it."

"You can't replace a sixty-five-million-year-old piece of amber," Dr. Wu points out reluctantly, but it's obvious he's given up.

"We'll keep them away from that, if it eases your mind," Mr. Masrani says.

"Fine," Dr. Wu says, stepping aside. "Don't touch *anything*."

And with that in mind, we walk into the lab, where the real magic happens.

10

The lab is intimidating. A huge complex of large, open rooms connected by a twisting hallway, it's all sleek stainless-steel tables, glass walls, bright recessed lighting, and state-of-the-art 3-D imaging, electron microscopes, scanners, and other tech with higher definition than anything on the market. I'm on edge because of Dr. Wu's lack of enthusiasm, so I keep my elbows tucked in as we pass through a room of a dozen scientists working with old-school equipment: test tubes and beakers. In the next room, techs work at banks of monitors—some display images of dinosaurs; others show DNA strands.

"Perhaps they can at least see the amber specimen?" Beverly suggests to Dr. Wu, who's leading us through the complicated maze. Everything is open, the huge rooms divided only by glass and screens, so you can see *everything* going on. Which makes sense—in a place like this, doing such varied, cutting-edge research, the scientists would need to share their work with each other constantly. This is the kind of environment where a biologist or veterinarian might stumble across something that could help the chemists synthesize new drugs or even cures—a true fusion of scientific disciplines. The work being done here . . . it's like nothing else in the world. And you can feel it in the air, see it in the faces of the techs as we pass through the rooms.

Every day, the chance to make history and cause true change is at their fingertips.

"Fine, but they need to stay *outside* the retrieval room," Dr. Wu says. "It's a sterile space."

He comes to a stop outside a room with frosted glass walls. Justin kind of frowns at me, and I'm wondering how we're supposed to see anything too, until Dr. Wu presses his hand against a scanner and the glass suddenly turns clear.

"Whoa, cool!" Eric says. "Can you do that again so I can get it on camera?"

"No." Dr. Wu shoots Masrani a look. "You let him bring a *camera* into my lab?" he asks, like Eric's dragged in a putrefied corpse.

"He's getting footage for the intern program," Mr. Masrani says patiently. "All the footage belongs to the company. And technically, it is *my* lab."

Dr. Wu's raised eyebrow says it all. It may be Mr. Masrani's lab, but it's Dr. Wu's kingdom. And rightfully so. Would any of this exist without him? Doubtful. Dr. Wu knew Dr. Hammond. He was at the original park, and I want to ask *so* many questions about it, but I have a feeling that would single me out in a bad way.

In the years since the original park, Dr. Wu has continued with the science—developed it, improved it, and honed it. And now here we all are, just months away from making an impossible dream come true—a dream that many scientists, Dr. Wu foremost among them, have dedicated their lives to fostering.

"Don't touch the glass," Dr. Wu instructs us, stepping back from the window so we have a full view of the three scientists grouped around a large piece of amber. I can see some dark specks on the shard of fossilized sap—those are the *real* treasure. The mosquitoes, fossilized millennia ago, with their final meal of dinosaur blood filling their tiny bellies. The precious DNA in that blood served as the building block for this monumental project and this place—the key to all of this greatness. All because Dr. Hammond wondered, *What if fossilized mosquitos have dinosaur DNA in their stomachs?* And then he went and found out. Proved his hypothesis and returned the dinosaurs to the earth.

That is the power of asking yourself *what if?*

"We long ago acquired the DNA profiles of our eight premiere species, of course," Dr. Wu says. "But we must constantly search for more species." He points at the monitor behind the scientists. "Those are our top ten most wanted species at the moment."

"What's a Baryonyx?" Ronnie asks in a low voice next to me as we look at the list.

"It's a theropod," I whisper back. "Huge claw on the front finger." I curl my own finger in imitation. "*Baryonyx* means 'heavy claw.'"

"Literal. I like it," Ronnie says right before Art asks, "Dr. Wu, are you using the same tools to retrieve the DNA as you used with Dr. Hammond?"

"We've streamlined the process some since Hammond's day,"

Dr. Wu acknowledges, and I hear a note of sadness in his voice when he mentions Dr. Hammond's name. "But the real difference between then and now is in how we approach the DNA sequencing—and how we fill in the missing DNA strands and adjust certain other factors. Now." He folds his arms and looks at us. "Can you tell me why we've adjusted our methods? Starting with you." He nods at Justin.

"Um, aesthetics?" Justin asks, sounding nervous to be put on the spot. "I know that some of the dinosaurs—what we think they looked like isn't totally accurate. Certain fossils suggest that some even had feathers, right? Some fiddling with the DNA is necessary to bring them more in line with what we've always been taught they look like?"

"That's a reason," Dr. Wu acknowledges with a nod. "You." He points to Tanya. "Same question."

"Physical adaptation to the modern environment," Tanya says. "Studies suggest they existed in a world where O_2 levels were much higher. So without human interference, those Triceratops we saw yesterday wouldn't be able to romp around—if they could exist at all, they'd be out of breath all the time. Plus, we're dealing with dangerously high carbon emissions and a warming climate. All these factors have to be taken into consideration."

"Indeed," Dr. Wu says before turning to Ronnie. "And you?"

"Security," Ronnie answers in a firm voice, and she seems like the only one in our group who isn't totally intimidated by Dr. Wu. "Temperament is key to success—the dinosaurs here must be docile and able to adjust to a constant and varied human presence—the staff, scientists, and the public. Which is why I hope you haven't spliced any hippo DNA into the Tricer-atops. Those guys are mean."

That gets a ghost of a smile from Dr. Wu. "I agree that adding hippo DNA would be a bad idea," he says. He turns and fixes me with an intent look. "You—what do you think?"

I try to tamp down my nervousness. I'm no science student, and a lot of the people around me are, which just feeds into the whole imposter syndrome. But I've gotta come up with something.

"Nature always finds a way," I say.

Dr. Wu quirks an eyebrow. "Explain."

"You make them all female so they won't reproduce. But nature always finds a way. So do women, generally. Though with us, it's more just battering against society than fighting nature's forces. But here, with dinosaurs, you must constantly keep one step ahead of nature. Because they'll evolve, no matter how many choices you make, or how many different DNA strands you splice into theirs. Evolution is what the beginning and the end have in common. You lose sight of that and none of this will matter, because we'll be the ones going extinct."

He's quiet for a moment, and I'm worried I've offended him, but instead, he just nods thoughtfully and turns back to Masrani. My fellow interns crowd together at the window just as the scientists working on the amber start drilling. I lean in, but I'm still close enough to Dr. Wu and Masrani that I can catch their conversation. I'm not actively trying to eavesdrop, but I can't help hearing Dr. Wu say, "The one with the camera is no use to me. And the business major doesn't belong in my labs."

"Justin is majoring in business, yes, but he's a chem minor," Mr.

Masrani explains over the sound of the drill. The scientists have slowed it to a crawl as the tip nears the first mosquito.

"Key word being *minor*." Dr. Wu waves this away like it's an insult. "I'll take the girl who talked about the changing environment and O$_2$ levels. And the redhead has *some* foresight, at least, so I'll take her, too. I suppose these interns *might* be better than the train-wreck first batch."

I can't stop myself from looking over at them, because I thought Beverly said we were the first batch of interns.

"That is a *huge* needle," says Ronnie, and my eyes return to the scientists, who have pulled the drill out of the amber and are inserting a long needle. We watch with bated breath as the needle makes its way into what's left of the mosquito's body—that scientist's hands have to be *so* steady. I'd be too nervous to do it. My hands would shake and I'd screw it up and at the end, instead of potential dinosaur DNA in that glass syringe, there'd be fossilized bug guts spilled all over.

Because the scientists are standing in the way, none of us can see if they got it. But then a voice over the speaker near the finger-print scanner says, "Retrieval from specimen successful, Dr. Wu."

"Very good, Jamie," Dr. Wu says with a rare smile. "Let me know when you've retrieved specimens B through D, and we'll start the identification process."

The look he gives Beverly is cutting. "I believe my free time is up," he says, and it's not a question.

Beverly presses her lips together. "We'll talk about intern rotations at the staff meeting?"

"I'm looking forward to it," Dr. Wu replies, his tone saying the exact opposite.

"Thank you, Dr. Wu!" Tanya calls cheerfully as Beverly ushers us out of the lab. He doesn't turn around. He's already heading into the amber room, his face intent, his focus back on the important work.

We take the elevator back up to the lobby, and Beverly turns to us, smiling. "It's almost three o'clock, so you have free time until dinner. There are jeeps outside you can drive, and there's a map on your tablets that shows the areas you're allowed in without supervision. You can go swim in the resort area or visit the arboretum and public greenhouses—*not* the research ones—and our media center in the hotel is stocked with all sorts of games and movies. Any questions? Okay, then, we'll see you at dinner."

The twins, Ronnie, Art, and Justin hang back with me to figure out what we want to do.

"I need to hit the gym before I have my call with my family," Ronnie says. "So I'm gonna go back to the hotel."

"I'll drive back with you, then," Art says. "I could do with a run before dinner."

"I want to go see the greenhouses," Tanya says.

"That sounds fun," I say. "I'll come with you."

So Ronnie and Art head back to the hotel, and the twins and Justin and I load up in a jeep with Eric and Tanya in the back. Justin's driving, and I'm up front beside him.

I open my tablet to the map Beverly mentioned. There are areas in green and areas in red—pretty straightforward, really. I tap the greenhouse icon, and a cartoon DNA strand pops up in the corner of my screen. It bops back and forth, a little bubble appearing above its googly eyes: *Hi! I'm Mr. DNA. Do you need directions to the greenhouses?*

I tap *Yes,* and Mr. DNA bounces across the map. *Take a right in .5 miles.*

I navigate as Justin drives us to the greenhouse. Mr. DNA's directions get us there faster than I expected. Tanya bounds out of the car, much the way Lovelace emerged from the container into the valley. The rest of us follow her almost as eagerly. It feels a little intimidating and thrilling to be on our own here like this.

The series of glass-walled buildings in front of us are not your traditional greenhouses. They're geodesic domes, enormous ones that look like they belong in some futuristic alien world. The sunlight glints off their transparent surface, and we pass a sign that identifies the material not as glass, but as the same plastic polymer invented to create the aviary designed to hold the Pteranodons.

The greenhouses and the arboretum that lies beyond them are completely finished—there's no trace of construction anywhere, just lots and lots of hard work. Laying the foundation for this monumental project must have started as soon as Masrani began work on the island.

"I'm in love!" Tanya declares, running up the stairs of the biggest dome. "If there are Hügelkultur beds inside, I'm gonna die!"

"What is a Hügelkultur bed?" I ask Eric as Tanya disappears into the greenhouse. "Or should I just ask her?"

Eric's eyes widen. "Don't," he says. "It's a German gardening method, but if you get her started, she'll *never* stop talking your ear off about what goes into making fertile soil."

Justin laughs, grabbing the door and opening it for us. Inside the dome, it's like we've stepped into another universe: a hotter, muggy, colorful future where nature reigns. The curved walls and triangular pieces that make up the dome and the filtered green light shining on us are soothing, creating a space that wraps us in a kind of primal ease. I can imagine lying down on one of the benches scattered along the paths among the specimen garden beds and just closing my eyes, letting the sun and the scents and the sound of trickling water carry me off.

Tanya is nowhere to be seen—she's already disappeared into the flora—and I take a second because there is so much to look at. Palm trees loom over the greenhouse door, tied down to twist their trunks into an arch, and the raised beds that circle the floor inside the dome are exploding in a color riot of exotic flowers.

"Eric!" Tanya's voice calls. She sounds far away—this dome is *enormous*. "I found the carnivorous plants!"

Eric grins. "See you two later," he says, pulling his camera out of his bag and jogging down the aisle, looking for his twin.

Justin and I walk farther into the greenhouse. I hear other voices too now, and we turn the corner around an array of ferns to see Wyatt standing there with a girl with long black hair and a turned-up nose who reminds me of a pixie.

They're looking at the orchids grouped on the potting table ahead, and the girl laughs when the sprinklers turn on automatically, startling her. A fine mist floats over the orchids.

"Hi!" she says, catching sight of us down the way.

"Hey," I call back. "Amanda, right? The marine biology major?"

She nods. "You're Claire and . . . Justin?"

"Yeah."

"Wyatt's been indulging my flower obsession," Amanda says, smiling widely. Wyatt looks smug.

"The orchids are beautiful," Justin says.

"I'm obsessed," Amanda says, turning back to them and angling her tablet so she can take more pictures as Wyatt hangs back. He probably doesn't want Justin to embarrass him in front of the girl he's flirting with. Hopefully, Amanda will see through his gross negging approach. Why do guys *ever* think that'll work?

I put my own tablet away, pulling out my notebook instead because I want to write down the names of the ferns before I forget.

"Look at you, all analog," Justin says, smiling.

"Gotta love the classics," I say. "The tablet's great, but I remember things so much better when I write them down. Typing's just never been the same."

"I get it. I'm the geek who records all his classes and notes," Justin admits.

"No way, you're the guy in the front with the recorder?"

"Yup," he says. "I'm a total auditory learner."

"Kinesthetic, obviously," I say, tucking my pen behind my ear. I can see his eyes catch the movement. Turning pink is so not in my plans, but it's going to happen if he keeps looking at me like that.

"Hey." I lower my voice, hoping Amanda and Wyatt can't overhear. "Since you're an auditory learner, did you catch that weird thing Dr. Wu said in the lab?"

His brow furrows under his hair. "What weird thing?"

"After I answered his question in the lab, I heard him tell Masrani that maybe this intern batch wouldn't be as useless as 'the train-wreck first batch.' But . . . we're the first Bright Minds interns. So what did he mean?"

"I was focused on the amber; I didn't hear them," he says. "Maybe Dr. Wu was talking about his lab interns? But that doesn't make sense, since he would've picked those."

Someone snorts next to us. Justin grits his teeth, pushing his glasses up his nose before he turns and levels Wyatt with a look. "You've got something to contribute, Wyatt?" he asks.

"I guess you two aren't as keyed in to the rumors about Jurassic World as you thought," Wyatt says.

"What rumors?" Amanda asks. "Do you have gossip, Wyatt? Tell!"

Wyatt looks around at each of us, a superior expression on his face. "I thought everyone who researched Bright Minds would've stumbled across the stories about the phantom interns."

What is he talking about? Justin glances at me like he regrets even engaging Wyatt.

"Phantom interns? What do you mean?" I ask, even though I know that's *exactly* what he wants me to ask.

"There was another group of Bright Minds interns before us," Wyatt says. "The program wasn't called Bright Minds back then. They probably changed the name after the incident." He examines a spotted orchid carefully, like it's way more interesting than the story he clearly wants to tell.

"So you're saying there are like, intern ghosts?" I ask, unable to keep the incredulity out of my voice. Is he for real?

"They're called the phantom interns because all evidence of the program disappeared," Wyatt says. "Not because they're ghosts."

"Why would they do that?" Justin asks.

"Why do you think?" Wyatt asks. "Because something happened in that group during their time here. Something bad enough to cover up."

"No way!" Amanda says. "Are you sure?"

"Is this another one of the 'They're feeding people to the dinosaurs' rumors?" Justin asks. "You spending some time on the conspiracy theory websites, Wyatt? I thought your dad worked for Masrani. Why are you stirring things up?"

"I'm just answering your questions," Wyatt says. "And I didn't say anything about feeding people to dinosaurs. This goes way deeper than that."

I can't tell if he's just spinning a story or if he's serious. He's acting all dramatic and supercilious, and it's getting on my nerves. I can hear the twins talking near the carnivorous plants on the other side of the greenhouse, and I'm tempted to go over there and leave this nonsense behind. But what if there's something to his weird story?

"After the initial boundaries of the park were built, they began transporting some of the Brachiosauruses over from Isla Sorna. The interns—the program that would become Bright Minds— were brought here to help the staff with integrating them into their Nublar habitats."

"Okay," Justin says. "Every company uses interns. Was the scandal that they weren't paid?" Sarcasm drips off his words, and Amanda giggles, which makes Wyatt turn red. I have to bite my lip to keep from laughing too, because we all know our futures include lots of unpaid internships for a chance to break into our fields. It sucks.

"They were a month or two into the work when there was a storm," Wyatt says. "It was so bad it fried the main electrical grid, and the backup generators were overloaded—everyone had to evacuate."

"Still not seeing a reason for a cover-up," Justin says, sounding bored.

It's petty, but I enjoy how much it seems to annoy Wyatt that he can't ruffle or one-up Justin.

"There's a reason. A big one. In the rush to evacuate, they left someone behind. A girl intern." Wyatt says, with enough relish to send chills down my body, especially when I really think about it.

A storm. Chaos in the evacuation. Maybe you're out of radio contact and don't even know it's happening. Maybe you go back for something precious. And then when you rush to the rendezvous point . . . the boat is already gone. And you're alone.

Well, not exactly alone. But that would add to the terror: the dinosaurs your only company in a brutal, battering storm, the power grid out, leaving you so very vulnerable.

A primal kind of terror would take over. *Run. Hide. Survive.* Because sure, they're herbivores, but one misstep and you're squished, the dinosaur version of roadkill. They wouldn't even notice.

"That's gotta be an urban myth or something," Amanda says, but her mouth twists, her curiosity piqued.

"You can't believe these rumors," Justin scoffs. "If an intern had died in the storm, or gotten left behind and then died, we wouldn't be here right now. Jurassic World wouldn't be here. The intern's parents would have gone to the authorities. We would have seen the headline everywhere. Masrani would have been sued, and the insurance revoked."

"I thought you were a business major," Wyatt says snidely. "Ever heard of bribes? InGen certainly has. That's how they covered up the original park in the nineties. Ian Malcom was made out to be a pariah because he wouldn't play their game."

"Which would mean that they probably learned their lesson, since it got out eventually anyway. And it's not the nineties anymore. Ian Malcom didn't have a camera phone. There's technology that would make it even easier to be a whistleblower now—and to have the proof to back it up. You're talking about a massive cover-up," I point out. "Dozens of nondisclosure agreements would need to be signed. You'd have to keep not only all the interns quiet, but their families and the staff."

"Issuing dozens of NDAs is a normal day for someone like Masrani," Wyatt says.

"Sure," I say, because as much as I hate to admit it, he has a point. We had to sign NDAs as part of our contract. "But you're telling me somehow the bigwigs of Jurassic World managed to hush up parents whose child they lost because of the park's incompetence? What did they do, fake her death some other way? Are you kidding me? Come on."

"Money is a powerful motivator," Wyatt says, like he can't wait until he can exert that kind of power over people.

It makes my stomach churn like a boat navigating choppy waters. I want to make real change, but not at the cost of hurting people. Wyatt seems to thrive on the idea of winning at all costs, and I know better than to think like that. Some costs are too high.

"But her parents . . . ," I stress. If I never came back from this island, I can't even imagine the hell my parents would unleash on Mr. Masrani and every other person—or dinosaur—they could get their hands on. So the idea that some parents let themselves get paid off and kept their daughter's involvement—and death—quiet just doesn't compute.

"Don't be so naive, Claire," Wyatt says. "That makes no difference."

"To some people, it does," Justin says.

"I'd think you'd be well versed in parental abandonment," Wyatt says. "Mr. Ivy Rose. I read your mom's *Forbes* magazine interview. She talked about raising you on her own. She seems . . . plucky." Only he could make that sound like an insult.

"Wyatt! That's really mean," Amanda says, frowning at him.

Wyatt's words are designed to be a barb, but Justin doesn't even flinch. "Wyatt, if you'd actually understood what my mom was saying in that interview, you'd see that I had the parent I needed. Not everyone comes from a nuclear family. I can't believe I have to say this, but get with the times. You act like you wish it was the nineteen fifties again."

"It's not a good look," I add, making Wyatt's mouth flatten.

Justin turns to me. "You ready to check out the corpse flower Tanya was talking about on the ride over, Claire? Or do you want to hear more about the phantom interns?"

"Yeah, let's go find the twins," I say. "Amanda, do you want to come with us?"

Amanda bites her lip, looking back and forth between us and Wyatt. His comment to Justin has definitely put her on guard. "I'll be fine," she says finally.

"Come on over to our table at dinner if you want," I offer.

"I'd like that. I'll see you then."

"I wish Eric didn't have to room with that guy," Justin says under his breath as we walk away toward the other side of the greenhouse.

"Yeah, but Eric can hold his own," I say as we turn the corner and the carnivorous plants come into view, but the twins are nowhere to be seen. Considering how much Tanya was talking about the corpse flower on the way over, she's probably run off to find it if it isn't in this particular dome.

"Did they go outside?" I ask, standing on my toes to peer over the impressive array of Venus flytraps set along one of the potting benches. Something tickles my forehead, and Justin's dimples flash as I look up, a bright purple flower—more like a thistle, really, with spiky looking purple petals tightly clustered together—brushing against my head. I try to move forward, and that's when I realize it's caught in one of the pins holding my braids up.

"Please tell me it's not carnivorous and about to eat my hair," I say, holding very still as the thought occurs to me.

"It's just a flower," he assures me. "Wait a second, let me," Justin says, stepping close.

I'm concentrating so hard on not turning pink—and failing so hard—as his fingers brush against my hair. It shouldn't send this rush through me, like jumping off a cliff or running down a hill full speed, but it does. And it just gets worse when he snaps the stem of the flower where it's caught in my pin and holds it out to me.

"The purple's pretty with your hair," he says . . . and what do you *say* to something like that? Especially when he's *looking* at you like that? Greenhouses aren't particularly romantic, but the sun's shining through the dome's triangles, and sure, the Venus flytraps are stirring hungrily below us, but it kind of adds to the moment, and all I can see, for a second, is him, holding the flower.

He says, "Can I?" and he waits for me to nod before he plucks the pen out from its place behind my ear and tucks the flower there instead. The pads of his fingers are rough—callused from what, I don't know—against my skin, and it's all fluttery inside my stomach. I don't quite know what I want and I think he knows that, because he just smiles and steps back. "Let's hope it's not some rare prehistoric bloom," he says.

"It's *Cirsium vulgare,* common thistle flower," says Tanya, and I whirl around to see my friend smiling wickedly at me, like she knows *exactly* how many butterflies are in my stomach right now. "I don't think the botanists will be chasing you down with their pitchforks anytime soon."

"Oh good, because those pitchforks we saw on the way in looked nasty," Justin says.

"Come on, Eric's waiting for us outside," Tanya says. "I found the corpse flower!"

"If it smells as bad as they say it does, I'm calling first dibs on the shower when we get back to our room," I say, but I follow her, Justin right beside me.

11

After dinner, by the time we get back to our room, my eyes are starting to ache. My brain feels swollen, like so much has happened today that there's not enough room to hold it all in. I keep replaying everything over and over in my head . . . that moment Lovelace joined her herd, and how happy it sounded, greeting her.

"I'm going to go hang out with Amanda and Ronnie before curfew," Tanya says. "Wanna come?"

"I think I'm gonna call it a night," I say. "I want to write in my journal while everything's still fresh."

"I wish I had the discipline to journal," Tanya sighs. "Your memoirs are going to be so much more detailed than mine!"

Her confidence, it's infectious. I love that she just assumes someday we'll be writing memoirs; that someday, we'll be important enough for people to want to read them.

"Okay." She grabs her bag and tablet. "We'll be in Ronnie's room, if you change your mind."

"Thanks," I say.

After she leaves, I settle down with my notebook. I spend over an hour journaling, writing down everything I can remember about today—how I felt, what was said, what I learned, and the questions all that brought up. Because there are a million questions whirling in my head. When we arrived, I had this idea that this was a place of answers. And it is.

But it's also a place of questions.

When I'm done journaling, I take the thistle flower that Justin tucked behind my ear in the greenhouse and press it between two of the pages. I stack a few of my books on top of it, and for good measure add the amber dinosaur egg paperweight that was on the desk. I'll leave it for a few days, and when I open it up, the flower will be pressed and dried perfectly, and I can fix it to the page with some glue. A little reminder of a big day.

I set my notebook on the bedside table, knocking my row of colored pens onto the ground in the process.

"Shoot."

I get out of bed and scoop them up, but the green one's missing. Green is for notes about the herbivores. Red is for carnivores. Blue is for my journal entries. Purple is miscellaneous, and I even use the pink sometimes. To doodle. In the scribbles section of my notebook. Because I am not going to draw in the margins or outside of that section designated for scribbles. Organization is key. I absolutely cannot lose my green pen—my notes will be in chaos!

I get down on my hands and knees to peer under the bed. The pen's rolled all the way to the wall, and there's no way I can move this heavy wood bed frame on my own. Hoping Tanya doesn't come back unexpectedly, I wriggle under the bed. I have to crawl all the way under to grab the pen, and just as I'm awkwardly scooting backward, trying not to bump my head, I realize the lining of the box spring is torn and there's something tucked inside. I reach in, searching, and my fingers brush against something smooth and cool—a notebook. I grab it and inch my way out from under the bed. My hair's all staticky once I stand up, the pen clutched in one hand, the notebook in the other.

After I return my pen to its place on the end table, I sit cross-legged on the bed and open the notebook. It's your basic black Moleskine, but the spine is cracked and worn, like it's been opened over and over, and the edges of the paper are yellowed just a little.

Did Tanya hide this? I don't want to read her diary.

I open it to check, looking at just the inside flap, and see a messy scrawl that says *Property of Iz.*

So not Tanya's. Then whose? Did the notebook belong to someone who stayed in this room before us? A scientist or trainer, maybe?

I flip through it and see that every page is filled with cramped handwriting and intricate pen-and-ink drawings. There are dinosaurs, mountains, a waterfall, even what looks like a map of the island, scattered with red X's. I turn back to the first page and start reading.

1/15

I threw up the entire ferry ride over. Great start, right?
I almost missed it when we came upon the island,
but I dragged myself up to the deck, determined to

witness the moment.

The sun was just rising, and when it hit the mountains, I could hear them roaring a greeting. Fanciful, absurd, and not possible, but I swear ...

They put us to work as soon as our boots hit the dock. I was still queasy as we drove along the dirt roads—apparently asphalt's getting poured in a few months—but everything faded away when they brought us to their enclosure.

It's just two of them. That seems so ridiculous. Just two of them. Just two dinosaurs. They have names. Agnes and Olive. The names fit them. That seems so ridiculous too ... or does it? What did I think? That living beings wouldn't have personalities just because they're prehistoric?

I'm not making any sense. I'm overwhelmed. I'm probably dehydrated. I'll write more later. I just ...

They have names.

"Claire."

Someone's shaking me awake. I jerk up and see the notebook on the floor, where it must have fallen when I nodded off. "What time is it?" I ask Tanya.

"Seven," she says. "Breakfast's in an hour. I'm sorry I didn't wake you up sooner; I thought you set an alarm."

"It's okay." I pick up Iz's—Is it someone's initials? A nickname?—notebook and put it under my own on the bedside table. "I was tired, I guess. I'll get ready fast."

"Our tablets say we're due back in the valley with the trainers and the Triceratops," Tanya calls as I hurry to the bathroom and turn on the shower. "And it says we need to wear our boots."

"That's ominous," I say, peeking around the bathroom door. "But I'm all for more Lovelace. I'll be out soon."

I close the door and duck into the shower, letting the hot water beat down on my face. I must've been asleep when Tanya came back, but I stayed up pretty late, reading through the notebook. After the first dated entry, there were a lot of sketches of Brachiosauruses, and then pages and pages of numbers that I puzzled over for at least an hour before I realized they were stats—Agnes's and Olive's stats. Heart rates, weights, pounds of food consumed, pounds of, um, waste . . . the owner of the notebook recorded it all in minute detail. I must've fallen asleep after that, because I didn't finish the whole thing.

I get out of the shower and dry off, doing my whole morning routine double-time because being late is never an option. Breakfast is set up in the same conference room as yesterday, and Amanda joins us like she did last night. Art's smiling at her as they immediately fall into conversation, just like they did over dinner.

"Love is in the air," Tanya says in an undertone so they don't hear and get embarrassed.

"Shhh," I say, but I agree with her; they'd make a cute couple.

Everyone's talking about going back to the valley as we head out after breakfast. We're allowed to drive ourselves to our assignment, and this time, I take the wheel while Justin navigates. The twins are riding with Ronnie, so it ends up being just the two of us.

"Does this thing have a radio?" He fiddles with the dials as we head out but finds nothing but static, so he turns to his tablet as Mr. DNA directs me to take a left in three miles. A minute ticks by, and then suddenly, a familiar tune fills the jeep. He's playing "The Lion Sleeps Tonight," and I'm laughing as they sing about being in the jungle, because Justin is a goof. A totally cute, utterly at-ease-in-his-own-skin, true-blue *dork*.

And I tell him that. Not the cute part. But the dork part.

"Unreservedly," he agrees. "I think you like it."

I bite the inside of my lip, and I don't fight my smile, but I don't confirm or deny it either. Whatever this is . . . I don't want to push or run. Go too fast or slow. I kind of just want to stay in this with him, and see, step by step, what might happen.

"Any other really old songs to play?" I ask as the song ends and we take the left at the sign that says VALLEY with an arrow.

He plays "Born to be Wild," and we don't stop laughing and singing along off-key until we reach our destination.

There's a whole group of people waiting for us outside the fence around the valley as we pull up and get out of the jeep. Bertie and her trainers are in regular khaki, and the rest of the adults—the veterinarians, I realize when I see their names embroidered on their tan shirts—are in light khaki pants. And then there are half a dozen men and women in black vests with guns unlike anything I've ever seen slung over their backs. These were the people in charge of security—the Asset Containment Unit. *Asset* seems a cold thing to call the dinosaurs, but maybe that removal is important when working this kind of job. You have to be a special kind of brave to face down a dinosaur in ways the ACU might have to. It's hard to even wrap my head around the kind of security protocols and plans that must in place now—and what's waiting in the future, once hundreds of guests are on the island. There are just so many variables to consider.

"Do I have all of you?" Bertie asks, counting us. "Yep! Okay, great. Gather round, everyone."

Bertie's wearing tall boots that go all the way up to her knees, and there's a knife sheathed in each of them. Her dark skin is shaded by a floppy khaki hat.

"Today we're doing fieldwork," she says. "As in, we're going in." She jerks her thumb behind her, to the valley sprawling below us.

There's a squealing noise behind me, and I look around to see Amanda turning red. "Sorry," she says.

But Bertie beams. "Never apologize for being excited. I'm excited too. Our dinosaurs are used to the trainers and the vets. But they must also get used to you. To young people, and to children . . . to all the guests who will soon be visiting us. Your presence on the island is an integral step forward in our animals' development, in their understanding of the world and of humans. And I'm grateful for your participation—and your excitement."

"I want to *be* her," Ronnie whispers to Tanya next to me, and I totally agree, though we might have different reasons.

The way I see it, Bertie's the boss of more than just her human team. She's the boss of the dinosaur team too. The *ultimate* boss. Who wouldn't want to be that?

"Let's go over the rules," Bertie says. "You stay within the security perimeter." She points to the three guys who are flanking our group on either side. "At all times. We're going to be doing a basic sweep through the valley to check on Lovelace. Her tracker shows that she hasn't moved in a few hours, and she's a little farther away from the herd than we'd like. She's in an area with a lot of tree cover, so cameras haven't caught her yet."

"Do you think she's okay?" Ronnie asks, sounding worried.

"Yes," Bertie says. "This is routine. We like to check in regularly with the newly integrated animals. Sometimes the first few days in a new habitat, they can get a little stressed," she explains. "It can lead to things like disorientation, excessive sleeping, or queasiness."

"Are we playing scut so you guys don't have to clean up dino vomit?" asks Wyatt, horrified. "I'm not a janitor. I go to Harvard!"

It's such a ridiculous thing to say that Justin and Eric burst out laughing. Tanya's trying hard not to join them, but Wyatt's serious. I roll my eyes.

"Collecting scientific samples is not scut, Wyatt," Bertie said, her expression going steely. "However, if the task's beneath you, you can return to the hotel."

He looks away, obviously fuming, and an awkward silence fills the space.

"I'll collect all the samples of poop and vomit you want," Amanda pipes up. "It doesn't gross me out."

Wyatt shoots her a disgusted look, and she shrugs at him.

Bertie chooses to ignore the drama and goes on. "As I said, stay within the security perimeter, and *always* listen to the adults—do not question them when you're given orders. Following them quickly could be a matter of life and death, just like it is working with any big animal.

"Tim is the head of our vet team." She points out a tall beanpole of a man with auburn hair, who raises his hand so we know who he is. "And Oscar is the head of the security unit," she adds, as a shorter, bald Latino man carrying a semiautomatic nods and waves from the group wearing black vests.

"Now, pull out your tablets and tap the Gyrosphere Valley on the map of the park," Bertie instructs. We obey, and the screen shifts to a terrain-style map showing the valley. "The blue markers that you see every half mile alongside the perimeter fence are stunner caches. This is not going to happen, because it hasn't happened in the entire time we've been here, but if there's a stampede, you need to run to the gate. If you can't get to the gate, head for one of the weapons caches and arm yourself with the stunners, then get to the gate. The code to get out is 5438. Do you understand?"

I gulp. How often do the dinosaurs stampede? Surely only when they're afraid of something or there's a fire or danger, right? So we'll be safe.

We nod. Some of us look nervous. Others excited. And a few just look sick.

But as Bertie gives the signal for the gates to open, we all move forward, no matter how we're really feeling. Because how could you walk away from such a chance?

Even if it does involve dinosaur vomit.

With the security guards flanking us, we walk through the gates, and they swing shut behind us with a clang.

"Keep the pace, kids," says one of the guards as we began to walk down the slope that leads to the lowlands of the valley. The terrain flattens out and grass swishes against my boots as we march. I'm scanning the hills and slopes ahead for any trace of them. I'm so focused on my surroundings ahead, I almost trip when the ground gives way suddenly underneath me. I look down, teetering on the rim of a giant footprint.

"Careful," Bertie warns, slowing down for a second until I regain my balance.

I look down at the print, how deep it's impressed into the dirt, how the grass is flattened . . . how incredibly huge it is. I could lie down inside it and do the snow angel thing, and I'd never touch the edges.

As we make our way through the valley, guided by the red blinking dot on Bertie's tablet that must be Lovelace, the herd still isn't visible, and I hear Art asking Bertie where they are.

"This time of day, they're near the lakes and river that lie beyond the tree line," Bertie says, pointing to the map on her tablet, where a bunch of red dots are blinking. "They like to sun themselves on the banks in the mornings."

"Is it just the Triceratops in the valley?" Justin asks.

Bertie grins and tilts her head to our right. "That probably answers your question," she says.

The ground under my boots shakes as we look to the tree line. We can't see her body, hidden by the trees, but her head, her neck . . . they tower far above the trees.

It's one of the Brachiosauruses. Surely not Pearl, since Pearl is the youngest of the Brachiosaurus quartet. If it is Pearl, and the older ones are even bigger . . . it's a staggering thought. Her long neck bends down and she grasps a hearty mouthful of treetop, munching away as she looks down in our direction. She's at least a quarter of a mile away, so high up, we must look like tiny specks to her.

"Which one is that?" Ronnie asks.

"That's Olive," Tim answers as he catches up with Bertie, adjusting the strap of his medical bag on his shoulder.

"Can you tell them apart even without their trackers?" I ask.

"Absolutely," he says. "There are big and little differences in the dinosaurs. And just like us, they all have different personalities. But Olive's got a scar on her neck, which makes IDing her extra easy."

"Is she gonna come out of the trees?" Eric asks. His camera is firmly fixed on Olive, who seems more interested in eating than seeing where we're going.

"Probably not," Tim says. "Olive is one of our older dinosaurs. She's very used to humans in her space, so we aren't really a novelty. Now, the younger dinosaurs, they can be a little more excitable."

"I need a higher place to get a better shot, then," Eric mutters, looking around. "Can I go up there?"

Tim looks at Bertie, who nods and gestures for a security guard to follow Eric as he scrambles up the tall hill to our left.

"Let's keep going, kids. They'll catch up," Bertie says. "Lovelace should be just a little north of here."

"She still not moving?" Tim asks, looking at Bertie's tablet. Am I reading into it, or does he sound worried?

"Heart rate's elevated," Bertie says in an undertone, and Tim frowns.

"Let's hurry, then," he says, looking concerned. "Pick up the pace, interns!"

Eric catches up with us just as we hit the tree line. The trees here are different, and don't grow thick and twined together with vines, like in the jungle. Tanya could probably explain the differences, but there's a lot of space between them; the branches just reach out, wide and free, so the sun filters through the leaves in a mosaic of light, painting everything golden and green. The crunch of our footsteps adds to the clicks and chirps of the birds that make the branches overhead their home. I'm surprised birds are still living in the trees here. I'd think maybe they'd migrate to the parts of the island that *don't* have dinosaurs, but then again, maybe they've adapted. Maybe it's actually safer here, because the huge herbivores must certainly dissuade any of the birds' smaller predators from hanging around.

A new circle of evolution, of prey and predator and adaptation, is already beginning . . . and I'm here near the start of it all, walking in its footsteps. Literally.

"Be mindful of the terrain," Bertie says. "There are a few steep gullies running through this part. I don't want any of you falling."

But as we approach the first one, a lowing noise fills the air, and I realize we *really* don't want to fall into it.

Because Lovelace is already there. And she's trapped.

12

Birds scatter as Lovelace bellows, the flapping of their wings blending with her cries.

"Set up a perimeter," Bertie says—more like *barks*. Her voice has turned authoritative, and the security team scurries to obey, radiating outward with their stunners at the ready.

The interns exchange nervous looks, and we all crowd together, try to make ourselves smaller and less obtrusive as the adults begin to gather around the gully—and Lovelace. She keeps thrashing back and forth, and her tail's bent at the end, like maybe she landed on it wrong when she slid down the embankment.

"She's hurt," Tanya says, a catch in her voice.

At first I think she means Lovelace's tail, but when I look where she's looking, my stomach clenches, and so do my fists. There's a big gash on Lovelace's side and a dark wash of dried blood down her flank. I look up at her face, where her eyes are partly closed, and she lets out a half sigh, half moan, like it hurts.

"Stay calm, kids," Bertie says, authority in her voice. "We want to keep her as calm as possible. It looks like she took a spill and might've hurt her tail."

"What about the wound on her side?" Art asks. "Did one of the other Triceratops do that to her?"

But the head trainer shakes her head. "That's not a horn wound," she says. "It would be less jagged if she'd gotten it in a fight with another dinosaur."

"More likely she snagged her side on a branch," says Tim. "The valley and grasslands have a wider variety of vegetation and terrain than she's used to. She could've cut herself, panicked from the pain, and run off and fallen into the gully." He rocks back on his heels, stroking his beard as he thinks. "I don't have fusion bandages in my kit," he tells Bertie. "I thought this would be a routine check-in, so I need to head back to my jeep and get bandages, antibiotics, and a large-bore needle."

"We'll hold down the fort here until you get back," Bertie says.

"Layla, Turner, come with me. I'll need your help to carry everything," Tim says, and he and two of the other vets head out.

Lovelace moans again, her beaklike mouth opening wide enough for us to see rows and rows of teeth. I shiver at the reminder that she could do some real damage if she weren't stuck.

"Sarah, we need to make a plan to get her out," Bertie says to the woman who must be her second-in-command. "I think a ramp is our best bet. Using a crane to pull her out would be the last resort, as it would cause more stress."

"I'll arrange for a ramp to be brought over," Sarah says. "And Oscar wants to talk to you." She hands Bertie a radio.

"This is Bertie," she says into it.

"Bertie, the herd's gathering around the thicket," says Oscar over the radio. "I've called in reinforcements, but your baby dinosaur's noise is making them nervous."

"Got it," Bertie says. "Go help them," she tells her team. And then it's just Bertie and us here with Lovelace. Bertie smiles. "You don't need to worry," she assures us. "As soon as Tim's back, we'll get Lovelace fixed up and her wound numbed, so she won't feel a thing."

She bends down on one knee, looking at the dinosaur below her. Lovelace moves her head back and forth, her frill rippling as she lows right in Bertie's face, dinosaur spit flying everywhere.

Bertie, obviously used to this, flips her sunglasses on at the best possible second. "Silly girl," she says, wiping at her cheeks and flicking the spittle to the ground. "It's okay, Lovelace. I know it hurts, but we'll get you fixed up."

The radio in her hand crackles. "Bertie, the Triceratops are getting very antsy from the noise. I sent two guys to grab the sonic barriers to prevent any charging, so I need a hand over here. I've got a gap in the perimeter," says Oscar curtly.

Bertie's mouth flattens. "Keep your distance from her," she tells us.

"You're leaving us alone?" Eric asks. He doesn't sound alarmed, more like eager. He's probably getting great footage of all this.

"I'll be right back," Bertie promises as her radio crackles again with Oscar's voice. "Lovelace isn't going anywhere, but respect her space. Tim will be back in a few minutes. I'll be just on the other side of the trees, if there's a problem. I can hear you if you shout. Take these. Use them if you need to."

She tosses the radio to Art, who catches it, and then hands me a stunner from the holster at her waist. "Green button is stun, red button is off. Got it?"

"Got it," I say, my fingers curling around it. It's like a giant baton, and I'm not gonna press the green button to see how far the charge reaches, but I bet it packs a wallop, considering it's supposed to put down a dinosaur.

Bertie jogs off.

For a second, we all just look at each other, and I wonder if everyone else is feeling like I am. Half excited that we're being given such freedom, and half terrified because we're *alone*. Some people pull out their tablets to take pictures of Lovelace, and I know I'm scowling, but I can't help it. She's hurt.

I walk over to Art, who has joined Amanda at the top of the gully where they can face Lovelace. Art's on his knees about five feet away from her, talking in a low, soothing voice. Lovelace seems to like him, because her tail starts moving back and forth, but the movement jabs the damaged tip against the rocks, and she cries out again.

"It's okay," Amanda tries to reassure her, but it must have really hurt, because Lovelace is backing up, unable to turn around, and she throws her body angrily against the sloping side of the gully, bellowing.

Dirt spills down the sides of the gully, and when she pulls away, I see that a big branch with thick, sharp thorns has dug into her wound.

"Art, do you see that?" I ask.

"Oh, that's not good," he says. Amanda continues to try to calm

Lovelace down, and half of the interns kind of back away farther, while our friends group around us.

"We need to calm her down and get those thorns out of her wound," I say.

"We need to wait for the vets to come back," Wyatt says over Justin's shoulder.

"It's hurting her!" I protest. Every time she moves, the thorns dig deeper into the already-raw wound and a fresh wash of blood trickles down her bristly hide. "Who knows how long the adults are going to be gone? She could tear her wound open even worse, and those bandages Tim went to get might not be big enough."

He just looks at me like I'm being silly.

"Fine. You don't have to do anything, but I'm going to," I say.

He shrugs. "Your funeral."

"What do we do?" Amanda asks, looking at me and then Art.

"There's gotta be some nonmedical way to calm her," Art says. "We've got to keep talking to her. Someone needs to distract her into staying still so the rest of us can get the thorns out."

"I don't think us talking to her is going to help," Tanya says. "It's not like we're familiar. She needs something familiar right now. She's freaking out because *everything's* new."

Tanya's comment triggers something in my brain. I clap my hands together. "Singing!" I say. The rest of them look at me like I just said the sky was purple.

"Singing?" Ronnie asks, her dark brows knit together.

"When we were coming over on the ferry, I overheard one of the scientists talking about how she played music to the dinosaur eggs and then later on to the younger dinosaurs. She said the Triceratops like jazz. What if music helps?"

"You want to sing to the dinosaur to calm her down?" Wyatt asks.

"Well, not me," I say, trying not to snap at him because I don't want Lovelace to get more upset. "Does anyone have jazz music on their tablet?"

There's silence. I pull mine out, but I see we have no signal out here, so I can't download or play anything.

"Okay, someone's going to need to sing," I say. "I have a terrible singing voice. So Tanya should do it. She's got a great voice."

Now we're all looking at Tanya.

"I only sing in the shower!" Tanya protests, turning bright red under her green- and blue-streaked bangs.

Lovelace's lowing gets louder, and I can feel the ground vibrate just slightly—not from her thrashing, but from the dinosaurs waiting outside the thicket, worried about their newest addition. Nervousness wrapped in fear rises inside me. What if the security guards and trainers can't hold the herd back? What if they come running, thinking Lovelace is being hurt by *us*?

We've got to calm her down and reduce her pain. Immediately.

"Just try," I plead with Tanya.

She lets out a deep breath. "Okay. Fine." She looks over at her brother, who's still recording everything. "You are conveniently and 'accidentally' erasing this footage, Eric, do you hear me? It will not exist after today! I do not want it being played for tourists for eternity when I haven't even had a chance to warm up."

"Sure, sure," he says.

She licks her lips and then starts to sing under her breath, so softly at first that I can barely make out the words. A few bars in, her voice strengthens, and I recognize the song. It's one my grandma used to play, Nina Simone's "Feeling Good." By the time she hits the lyrics about new life, Lovelace's head is tilting and her breathing eases as she watches Tanya with rapt attention.

"It's working," Amanda hisses excitedly. Art begins to hum along with Tanya, and I join in, because I remember the music, but don't know the words.

"Keep going," Ronnie urges as she and I circle around our friends to get a better view of the branch stuck in Lovelace's wound. Ronnie scoots toward the ledge of the gully, but when she reaches out, her arms aren't long enough.

"Let me try." I hand the stunner over to Ronnie and she backs up to give me room. The loose dirt shifts under my boots as I gingerly make my way to the ledge. I bend down, my knees pressing into the dirt, sending little rocks skittering down into the gully. If I flatten myself down I can *almost* reach it . . . but then my hand barely brushes up against the branch and one of the thorns slices through my fingertip.

"Crap." I pull my hand back, wiping it on my cargo shorts before getting up.

"Let me help," Justin says, and I turn to see him holding out his hand. "I won't let you fall."

I grasp his hand with my noninjured one, and with him bracing me, I scoot out farther over the ledge of the gully and then wiggle down into the embankment until I find a spot where my boots can dig in. Now I'm almost at eye level with Lovelace's wound. I can easily reach the branch, and my fingers close around it.

"I've got it!" I call over my shoulder.

"Okay, I'm gonna pull you up and back really fast," Justin warns. "Just in case she starts thrashing."

Sweat trickles down my forehead, and my fingers tighten around his. He squeezes back, his hold strong and sure. He's got me.

"I'm ready," I confirm.

"One. Two. Three."

I yank with all my might on the branch, and Justin pulls me back up and out of the gully at the same time. Lovelace lets out a confused bellow, her head whipping away from Tanya's singing like she's surprised at the sudden pain. Justin stumbles backward at the shift in weight and we tumble to the ground safely, a few feet away from the ledge.

For a second, I just try to catch my breath. Then I realize I'm basically sprawled over Justin and his arm is slung around my waist, and it's a *really* nice feeling. Like when a cat curls up on your stomach . . . a warm, kind of comforting weight.

I scramble to my feet, rubbing my hands against my shorts again. I feel more than a little dirty.

Wait. No, not that kind of dirty! Like, grubby dirty. I'm covered in mud and splashes of blood from the thorns—some of it mine and some of it Lovelace's.

Lovelace grumbles at us, her frill ruffling in a way that reminds me of a slobbery dog shaking off drool. Then her attention shifts back to Tanya, who's started singing some love song I don't recognize.

"Sorry, I think I jabbed you in the stomach with my elbow," I say to Justin.

I toss the bloody branch to the side, wiping my fingers on my shorts before I hold my hand out to Justin, who's still flat on his back, having taken the brunt of the fall. He lets me pull him up, dropping my hand only when he bends down to grab his glasses, which were knocked off.

"I think it worked," he says.

I look over my shoulder at Lovelace. He's right. Now that the thorns aren't digging into her wound with every breath and she's got music, she's much calmer.

It's kind of incredible, the difference. But the scientist on the ferry did say her theory is that music operates like a kind of heartbeat. At the very least, it's reminding Lovelace of a time when she was safe and comfortable. I take a deep breath and relax a little myself, hoping to hear Tim or Bertie driving up with their teams, but the only sounds are Lovelace's heavy breathing and Tanya's soothing alto belting out "Ain't Misbehavin.'"

About fifteen minutes into Lovelace's personal concert, Tanya's voice starts to crack, and Art takes over while Justin offers her some water. I pull my own bottle out of my bag, eager to rinse my hands off. I'm just uncapping it when Art stops singing abruptly, and everyone goes quiet.

I look up and gulp.

It's not Bertie or Tim, but Oscar, the head of the security team. He's staring right at me, and I look down at my clothes covered with dirt and my hands streaked with blood, and I swallow hard. This does not look good. I should have waited for Bertie or Tim to come back. They're trained to deal with this, and I . . . am not. I probably just broke about a dozen rules.

But I couldn't just let her *suffer*. Not when I could do something about it.

Oscar's frown deepens as he looks me up and down.

"What exactly is going on here?" he demands.

13

I swallow hard, not knowing what to say. He's *glowering* at me.

"Were you antagonizing her?" he demands, looking at my bloody hands.

"What? No!" I say, horrified.

"Claire was *helping* her," Justin rushes to explain. "Lovelace was thrashing around and got this"—he bends down and grabs the thorn branch carefully, holding it up—"stuck right in her wound."

"The thorns were causing more damage," Art adds. "She was bleeding all over."

"We needed to get it out," I say, but Oscar's expression is still the definition of glowering.

"And you didn't think to call one of the highly qualified medical professionals less than half a mile away?" he asks.

"You left us alone," Tanya points out, coming to stand next to me. Lovelace backs up in the gully, trying to track her music source.

"That's beside the point," Oscar says. "You—"

"What's up?" Bertie comes jogging over to us, followed by Tim and the rest of the vets. They have enormous duffel bags slung over their shoulders, and Tim's pulling a large wagon filled with a huge stack of silver foil packages—the fusion bandages for Lovelace's wound.

"The interns decided to play vet," Oscar says, pointing to the branch in Justin's hand. "That one"—he points to me—"seems to be the ringleader."

"We *weren't* playing vet," I protest, looking pleadingly at Birdie. "She was in *pain,* and *bleeding*! Was I supposed to just sit back and let that continue when I could do something about it?"

Bertie looks at me and then at Lovelace.

"You pulled that out of her?" she asks, sounding skeptical. "And she didn't stampede or lash out? No biting or bellowing or panic?"

"Tanya's singing calmed her down enough for Claire to get the branch," Eric pipes up. "Lovelace barely noticed. She was grooving to the jazz."

A few titters erupt in our group.

"Singing," Bertie echoes. She looks down at Lovelace, who is positively chilled out, still watching Tanya hopefully. She shrugs. "Okay, then. Go ahead and sing, everyone, if it makes her happy."

"Bertie—" Oscar protests.

"They're fine, Oscar," Bertie interrupts him. "They problem-solved a tricky situation. Isn't that what we want from them? No one's hurt. Claire, are you hurt?"

I shake my head quickly.

"And Lovelace isn't in distress either. So we're fine," Bertie says firmly to Oscar. "Just . . . next time, everyone, call us on the radio first, okay? That's why I gave it to you."

"We promise," Justin says.

Oscar sighs. "I'm going to go back to perimeter patrol," he says. "Radio me when you're ready to transport out."

When he's gone, Tim and the vets get to work. They clear us out of the way, and we end up a good ten feet back from the gully, watching them. Tanya gets to stand closer, because her singing is really helping. I hear Bertie tell Eric to be sure to forward her the footage for future training ideas, and I try not to smile, because Tanya is *so* not going to like that.

The fusion bandages are this weird, jellylike material that Tim loads into this thing that looks like an old-fashioned cookie press, but ten times bigger. Using this gel gun, Tim spreads the goo over Lovelace's wound, and we watch as the substance activates in the air, expanding to a firm, foamy white seal on her skin. Instantly, the trickle of blood slows and then stops completely.

"Don't you need to clean the wound first?" Art asks.

"The compound we use is an antiseptic and propellant— sterilizes the wound as it lifts all the dirt and debris, which will come out in the foam—see?" Tim points to specks of dirt and splinters of branches already popping up to the top of the high-tech bandage.

Art's eyes widen, and he leans forward to examine this amazing new tech.

"That's so cool. When is something like that going to be available to us non-dino vets?"

Tim grins. "Soon, I hope. The military is also interested, but we haven't gotten it to adhere to anything other than dinosaur skin yet."

He straightens up and hands the gun to one of his teammates. "I want to get her out of there before we start any fluids or antibiotics," Tim says to Bertie. "What's the plan?"

"Sarah's team's bringing the ramp," Bertie says, nodding to the group of trainers carrying large, flat steel segments toward us to assemble. "We back Lovelace up about ten feet, place the ramp, and then use her favorite snack to lure her out."

"You think we've got enough strawberries for that?" Tim asks, sounding skeptical.

"It's less stressful than using a winch and dragging her out," Bertie points out.

He nods decisively. "Okay. We'll get out of your way. All you interns, move over here with us. We need to give the trainers room to do their thing."

We scramble to obey as a team member hands Bertie a large basket of strawberries. She walks to the ledge and waves a particularly juicy-looking one in Lovelace's line of sight, and the dinosaur's frill ruffles excitedly when she detects the scent.

"Come on, Lovelace," Bertie coaxes, backing up so the berry's about to disappear out of the Triceratops's field of vision. She lures the dinosaur down the gully a few feet and then tosses it to her. Lovelace catches it neatly in her beaklike mouth, exactly like a giant, fifteen-thousand-pound horned dog grabbing a treat.

"Good girl. Just a few more steps."

It takes five minutes to get Lovelace backed up enough from the front of the gully to install the ramp securely across it, and another twenty to convince her that really, stepping on the ramp is okay and not scary. But with patience and a lot of strawberries, they finally get her across the gully up over the ledge to safety. We're all rejoicing inside as the vets hurry to administer her medications. She makes a noise of protest when she gets jabbed with a big needle, but I'm surprised at how docile she is, standing there and letting Tim and his team check her over.

"All done," Tim announces. "The wound doesn't look too bad. We'll need to monitor her more closely the next week, and the bandage will come off then."

"Should we send her off, then?" Bertie asks, and Tim nods.

She looks over her shoulder at us, flashing a wide smile. "Watch," she says. She cups her hands around her mouth and lets out a trilling call. Almost instantly, her call is answered, followed by a rumbling sound—the Triceratops in the valley stomping their feet in anticipation.

Lovelace trots off toward the sounds. Full of strawberries, with her wound no longer bothering her, she doesn't even look back at us.

It's such a relief that the whole group breaks into a spontaneous cheer. After we dismantle the ramp, we follow the trainers out of the thicket, carrying the parts with us. There are jeeps and trucks parked along the tree line, and beyond that, the rest of the Triceratops have gathered, surrounding Lovelace, who is totally going to be the drama queen of the herd, I can tell. Always getting into trouble—and getting all the strawberries as a result.

"Load up, everyone," Bertie calls. "We're running a little behind, and Beverly won't like it if you're late for your afternoon assignments."

We hop into the jeeps, and I turn around as we drive away, staring out the back window, keeping them in sight for as long as I can.

Next to me, Tanya hums, a smile on her face.

After our first few days on the island, we begin to settle into our routines. Two weeks in, and it's like we've always been here. Like I belong in a way I never have before.

The roads to the Gyrosphere Valley are familiar now—and so are some of the dinosaurs. I can identify a few of them by sight, and even more by behavior. You haven't lived until you see a pair of Brachiosauruses tussle over a particular tasty patch of monkey puzzle tree. Agnes and Olive, the old ladies of the bunch, live up to their names: they are *crotchety*. We've also been able to observe the Gallimimuses, herbivores that remind me a little of ostriches with their powerful legs, and sleek heads. They do this thing where they like to race against the jeeps. Not that Bertie and her team are, you know, trying to outdrive a dinosaur, because that's a terrible idea. They're the most birdlike of the dinosaurs so far. It's in their heads and how they tilt them sometimes, like, *Hey, you, time to run!*

While we've caught brief glimpses of the Parasaurolophuses with their huge crested heads, we haven't gotten a good look at them, which is a disappointment. I want to hear them, because there are all sorts of theories about how their crests might actually function as a resonating chamber for low-frequency sounds. But we haven't gotten close enough to them yet.

We've spent the last two weeks mainly with the trainers and the vets—apparently Dr. Wu is dragging his heels about letting us into his lab, if the conversation I overheard with Beverly and Jessica was right. Not that any of us are complaining. Well, except Wyatt, who seems to think it's beneath him to catalog dino droppings and review drone footage of the herd's behavior around the watering hole.

The trainers haven't integrated the Ankylosauruses into the valley with the rest of the herbivores. The armored dinosaurs are still very little, all hatched from the same cloning round, and Bertie told us that picking the right moment in their development to integrate them is crucial—choose too early and the Triceratops might get territorial; choose too late and the Ankylosauruses' tails might cause some major damage.

Choose wrong, and they'll have a dinosaur war on their hands instead of a peaceful coexistence.

"Hey, Claire, are you sure you don't want me to stay and help?" Tanya asks.

I look up from my notebook. "No, it's fine. Go ahead."

"You sure?"

"Totally. I could use some quiet time anyway."

Tanya smiles. "Introverts," she says, shaking her head as her eyes shine with an affectionate acceptance.

"That's me!"

"Okay, well, I'm going to drive with Eric, so there's still a jeep for you to get back," Tanya says, tossing me the keys.

I catch them and slide them into my pocket.

"See you at dinner!"

"I'll be there." I turn my attention back to my notebook as I hear the door swing shut behind her and the muffled sound of Eric greeting her outside. I tap on my tablet, turning up the music to work up some motivation.

We've spent the afternoon in one of the trainers' supply sheds, taking inventory. I chose one of the hardest, nitpickiest jobs: counting and cataloging all the tranquilizer darts. About two hours ago, just as I finished the second row of boxes, Wyatt stumbled into the remaining stack, scattering the darts *everywhere.* The look he shot me afterward told me it was anything but an accident, but I bit my tongue as my friends hurried to help me get them back into the boxes. Of course, I had to recount them after that. Everyone offered to help, but I wasn't about to keep them from dinner, so I insisted I was fine.

And now I have the supply shed to myself. I have to admit, it's kind of neat to be in here alone. They call it a shed, but it's really a two-room building that opens onto a dirt training yard with a larger, wooded habitat area beyond. The two spaces are divided by a sturdy, welded fence, and the thick walls enclosing the entire habitat and the supply building tower are so high I wonder if this is where they kept the Brachiosauruses before moving them to the valley. I'll have to ask Bertie next time I see her.

The supply area itself is sectioned off, with the normal training tools hanging and boxed, and the more dangerous stuff like the stunners and the tranquilizers locked in a large steel cage that takes up most of the room. It reminds me of those evidence lockers in TV police shows. I prop the door to the cage open with a box, since the trainers didn't leave us a key, and I check the box from time to time because I don't want to get caught inside—or locked out.

It takes another hour and a half, but I work through most of the boxes till there's finally an end in sight—just five to go. Thank goodness—my neck is killing me from hunching over. My music stops playing, and I glance down to see that my tablet's gone dark. The battery's dead.

There's a socket on the other side of the wall, so I get up and plug it in. It flashes back on, but before I can get the music going again, a scuffling noise behind me makes me whirl around, and the tablet falls from my hands.

It crashes to the floor, but I'm not paying attention.

"Hello?" I call out, leaving the tablet on the ground and stepping over the box and out of the supply cage. "Tanya?" Has she come back for me?

I walk into the supply building's second room—the trainers' break room. There are some tables and chairs, a coffeemaker, and a stainless-steel fridge, which is open just a crack.

My frown deepens. I grabbed a soda out of there less than an hour ago. I'm *sure* I closed it.

Is someone messing with me? The twins wouldn't . . . and anyway, I heard them drive off.

Wyatt, maybe? Has he come back to annoy me further? That'd be more than a little likely . . . and creepy.

Determined not to act scared in case it is Wyatt—that's what the jerk would want—I square my shoulders and walk briskly toward the break room door that leads to the outside training area. I may not be *acting* scared, but my heart's thundering in my ears and that prickly sensation of being watched fills me as I step outside. I remember Wyatt's talk of the phantom intern and shiver as I scan the horizon, searching. If this were a horror movie, I'd be seconds away from getting attacked by a guy wielding a comically huge knife.

I hesitate once I step into the dirt training area—I didn't realize darkness had already fallen. It's late. I breathe in the oppressive, moist heat, the night reverberating with the sounds of the jungle, its insect, bird, and amphibian inhabitants singing their symphony.

I peer into the darkness, at the thick twist of trees and vines that spreads beyond the training area, past the fence that bisects the training yard and the larger habitat. Is there something out there? My instinct is to call out, but I stop myself. What if something got loose? Even if it isn't a dinosaur, surely other kinds of predators roam this island. Removing them would be too much of a hassle—especially when you can just let nature take its course.

Clang. The sound of metal on metal, like a door swinging shut, fills the air.

My stomach tightens and I turn on my heel, racing back to the door.

The closet! Crap, I just left it open!

I rush inside, through the break room and into the supply areas, my blood pounding under my skin, but there's no one in sight.

But the box—the one holding the metal door open—is hanging askew, almost off one corner. That's *not* how I left it.

Someone was in here. My stomach sinks as I hurry over to the stacks of boxes of tranquilizer darts and frantically count, then recount them. A hundred thirty-four . . . is that right? I grab my notebook where I set it and I flip through the pages, breathing a huge sigh of relief when I see I've written *134 boxes.*

But then I feel sick as I look around at all the other equipment in the cage. I don't have counts for any of it. I have no way of knowing if something's missing.

I swallow hard. What am I going to do? I should never have gone outside. That was so stupid. If someone sneaked in and stole something . . .

"Claire?"

I'm so on edge that the sound of my name in the quiet room makes me jump, my hand knocks against the boxes, and to my horror, the stack closest to me begins to teeter. Not again!

I grab the top few boxes just before they fall, and manage to pin the stack up against the wall. I look over my shoulder and realize it's Beverly who called my name. She's standing right in front of the door that leads to the break room, and she does *not* look happy.

"Um, hi," I say, pushing the boxes back into position before I turn to face her.

"What are you doing in here so late?" she asks, looking down at the watch on her wrist. "You've missed dinner."

"I'm sorry. The boxes of tranquilizers I was cataloging got knocked over halfway through my count, so I had to start over again," I explain. "I didn't want to make my friends wait for me and miss dinner, so I stayed behind to finish up. I didn't realize how late it was."

I'm not sure if I should tell her that I think someone might have been sneaking around the supply room. I'm not sure if that's what happened. What do I have as proof? A scuffling noise, an open fridge door, and a box that might have been moved a little? I'm already starting to doubt myself. Ever since I discovered that notebook under my bed, I've been thinking about Wyatt's tall tale of the phantom interns. Maybe it's making me paranoid. He has to be making it up. I know big corporations like Mr. Masrani's always have a lot to lose, but a cover-up like the one Wyatt described . . . it seems absurd.

And I didn't see anyone. I guess I might have left the fridge open a bit and not realized it. And maybe I bumped the box with my foot when I stepped over it and didn't notice?

But then what about the clanging noise? I didn't make *that* up.

"Claire?" Beverly's frowning at me, her strong brows knit together.

"I'm sorry; what did you say?" I ask, trying to figure out what to do.

"I asked if you've finished with your inventory count," Beverly says.

"No, I have those last boxes right there." I point to the stack next to the stool.

"Okay, I'll take care of them," Beverly says. "You should get back to the hotel. Go to the kitchens and get some dinner, since you missed it. Your new rotation in the labs will start day after tomorrow, and I want you in tip-top shape for Dr. Wu."

When I don't move, she shoots me a puzzled look. I'm torn. I don't want to get in trouble, but I also don't know if I'm making a big deal out of nothing.

"Beverly, have you found it—" Jessica comes barging through the break room door, into the supply room and Beverly turns, shooting her a look that could only be described as *quelling*. Jessica's eyes go wide as a porcelain doll's when she sees me. "Oh," she says, coming to a halt.

Something is not right. I can feel it, but I can't do anything about it. The two women are having a silent conversation with their eyes, and I want to be out of here.

"I didn't realize you were still around, Claire," Jessica says, trying to smooth out the awkward moment with a smile. "We're just here to lock up."

I'm pretty sure that's a lie. When she let us in this morning, Sarah, Bertie's second-in-command, mentioned that only she and Bertie have the key cards to this supply cage. But maybe she just meant on her team? Maybe all the senior staffers have access cards?

"I was just going," I say, grabbing my tablet and charger and shoving them and my notebook into my bag. "Sorry I took so long."

"It's fine, Claire," Beverly says with a tight smile. "Just get back to the hotel. We'll finish up here and make certain everything's secure."

"Okay," I say, but I worry that I sound skeptical or suspicious. And as I walk out of the supply rooms and the building into the parking lot, I'm wincing internally, knowing they're watching me.

I'm feeling even more worried after I jump into the jeep and start it. I can't stop myself from staring at the building in the rearview as I drive away, wondering why Beverly and Jessica are really there.

My headlights cut through the darkness ahead, the beams glancing off the trees and winding cliffs. Shadows stretch ahead of me, and I try hard to shake the creepy feeling I've had ever since I heard that scuffling sound.

Something darts in front of my jeep on the road—something *big*.

It's pure instinct, the shriek that comes out of my mouth. My feet slam on the brakes, and it's like I lift out of my entire body as the jeep spins across the asphalt.

14

For a sickening moment, I think I'm going to hit something—whatever jumped out in front of me, a tree, a piece of electrified fence. But the jeep slows halfway into the third spin across the road, the momentum dying as it comes to a shuddering halt.

My stomach flips, and I have to grit my teeth to keep from throwing up. I straighten, my ribs aching from where they slammed against the seat belt. I unbuckle it, and I want so badly to get out, but I don't dare leave the shelter of the vehicle. Not in the middle of the jungle, in the dark—talk about horror movie material!

What *was* that? I peer out the back window—the final spin left the jeep facing in the opposite direction from where I was heading—but nothing's there.

This time, I'm sure I'm not imagining anything.

It was big. Not like *dinosaur* big—at least, I don't think so. But still big. Shadowy. And *fast*.

A primate, maybe? Gorillas, baboons, orangutans, and chimps

aren't native to these islands, though. And this isn't some tiny tree monkey.

I lick my lips, trying to breathe in deep but feeling like I can't get enough air. My head's pounding and my fingers, still clenching the steering wheel, are white. I loosen my grip and crack my knuckles nervously.

I need to get going. If whatever almost caused me to crash comes back, I'm a sitting duck. I quickly turn the jeep around and drive out of there, squinting at suddenly scary shapes in the dark, my heart hammering in my sore chest all the way back to the hotel.

When I get there, I don't go straight up to my room. Instead, I walk over to the kitchens. The workers there give me a sandwich and salad and chips, and I eat at one of the empty prep tables, keeping out of the staff's way. I'm not ready to go up to my room and deal with Tanya. She's great, but she likes to talk. A lot.

After the crazy thump in the jungle, I need some peace and quiet—or rather, the background hum of the kitchen. My heart's still beating too fast.

I pull the notebook I found under my bed out of my bag, where I've been keeping it. I've been sneaking bits and pieces of it whenever I can. Whoever Iz was, they were meticulous. Reading their notes is like taking a master class in Brachiosauruses. I've impressed Bertie once already with stuff I pulled from Iz's notebook, and I want to learn everything I can from it. And *about* it . . . but how?

I munch on my turkey and Swiss while I read Iz's journal entry from three weeks into their stay on the island.

2./1

Yesterday I noticed a slight swelling on Olive's neck. When I reported it, Savannah dismissed me, because ever since she found out I go to Yale, she's got it in her head I'm resting on my Ivy League laurels. Ha—I wish. I got into Yale by the skin of my teeth, and if it weren't for that scholarship, I would never have made it there ... or here.

So today, when I measured the swelling and saw that it was bigger, I went to Tim, her assistant. I didn't know what else to do—she wasn't going to listen to me. Luckily, Tim did. I showed him the measurements of Olive's neck from last week and today, and he immediately ordered an ultrasound.

It's not good. They're not sure, but it looks like a tumor. If we're lucky, it's just an abscess, but either way, they have to operate.

That's a first: dinosaur surgery. The vets are freaking out, trying to prep, running theory after theory by each other; the entire staff is humming about it, and Savannah is pissed. She tried to corner me to "discuss my behavior," but Mr. Masrani showed up before she could really light into me. I spent the rest of the day with Agnes, kind of hiding out.

Olive's surgery is tomorrow. I'm sitting outside her paddock right now, and she's all sorts of sulky because she hasn't been allowed to drink or eat anything for the past day.

Poor thing. It'll be better soon.

I hope.

Is that where Olive got the scar on her neck? I flip through a few more pages of scientific notes and drawings to find another entry, dated two days later.

2/3

Olive pulled through surgery! It was just an abscess, and all the infected tissue has been removed, but it was touch-and-go there for a while. The vets are developing the techniques as they're doing them, so all surgeries are experimental.

I was so relieved—I thought this was all behind us. But this morning, we discovered Agnes has a similar swelling on her neck. We caught it earlier this time, but now we're worried it might be something more than an injury. Is it a virus? Environmental? A genetic anomaly? Maybe a version of dinosaur distemper? Side effects from the cloning process? Or just a couple of playful nips that went a little too deep?

Everyone seems to have a theory, but no answers! If we don't figure it out soon and the oral antibiotics don't work, Agnes is going to need surgery too. What if she doesn't pull through? What if the infection is something serious ... and recurring? We can't just keep cutting them open!

I'm worried. Is this infectious?
And how do we stop it?

"Yikes," I mutter to myself. Even though I know Agnes and Olive are fine now, I can feel the anxiety and worry coming off these pages, which makes my own anxiety start to spike again. Rolling my shoulders back, I wince at how sore they are. I shove the notebook back into my bag and stand up. Ouch. I should get up to my room before curfew.

I throw my garbage away and wash the plate I used, setting it back on the drying rack. "Thanks again," I call, waving to the kitchen staff before I head out.

My eyes are drooping by the time I get up to our floor, and I stumble down the hallway, dying for a shower and my soft bed. It's dark when I open the door to our room, but I flip the lights on when I realize Tanya's not here. She's probably off hanging out with her brother or maybe Ronnie, and I'm too tired to wait up for her.

I collapse on the bed, all thoughts of a shower fleeing my head as soon as it makes contact with the pillow. I drag the blanket over my shoulders and fall asleep.

"Hey, I was looking for you," Justin says, jogging to catch up to me as I wait for the elevator to take me down to breakfast.

"What's up?" I ask, my voice sounding rough even to my own ears.

I slept terribly last night, my dreams full of car crashes and dinosaurs waking up midsurgery, confused and in pain. When I woke up and saw Tanya, who had gotten in sometime in the night, she took one look at me and offered to make me a cup of tea from her special blend before we went downstairs. So I know I look exhausted.

"I'm taking a Gyrosphere out in the valley for terrain mapping today," he says. "Art was supposed to partner with me, but Tim offered him a chance to observe some medical procedure on one of the Ankylosauruses, so he ditched me. Beverly said I could ask anyone, so what do you think?"

"Okay," I say, feeling a little apprehensive, considering I almost got into a car crash last night. But surely the Gyrospheres are different. They aren't really like driving. They're like . . . rolling. They practically drive themselves.

"I promise to have your back if Pearl finds us and decides to play whack-a-Gyrosphere," Justin says, his eyes twinkling behind his glasses.

"You'd better!" I say as the elevator dings and we step in.

"How did your inventory day go yesterday?" he asks as we ride down and get off into the lobby. We head toward the conference room–turned–intern dining hall, our footsteps muffled by the dark red carpet emblazoned with the Jurassic World insignia every ten feet or so.

"It was fine until Wyatt knocked over all the boxes of tranquilizer darts I was counting. I had to start over," I complain. "I'm pretty sure he did it on purpose."

Justin makes a disgusted noise. "That guy," he says.

"Tell me about it," I sigh as we line up to get our breakfast. For a second, I consider telling him about wondering if someone had broken into the supply room, but I decide not to. It would just make me sound paranoid.

We sit down with the rest of our friends and get caught up in a debate between Amanda and Art about gene splicing. By the time our group breaks apart for our daily assignments, yesterday's stress has almost faded.

It's just Justin and me going down to the valley today, so we have a jeep to ourselves. The twins and Ronnie are headed to the command center, and Amanda's managed to get an invitation to the Ankylosaurus medical thing too, so she and Art set off together.

Justin's tablet beeps several times as I drive us to the valley, and I glance down to see a bunch of email alerts on his screen.

"My mom," he explains with a grimace. "I haven't emailed her as much as I promised."

"Oh God," I groan. "I got some postcards from my sister last week and I still haven't written back. And I was supposed to call my mom last night and I didn't."

"We're both bad children, then." We share a rueful smile.

"I'm trying to be careful about what I say," I explain as I take a right off the main road, and the jungle starts to fade into the flatter, savannah area of the park. "I may have kind of misled her about exactly what I'd be doing as an intern here."

"'May have kind of,'" he echoes skeptically.

"Okay, I totally lied. I told my family there's no way we'll have any contact with the dinosaurs and I'll probably just be getting coffee for the lab techs the whole time and barely see any dinosaurs. And then only from far away."

He laughs. "Claire!"

"I know, I know," I say as the road turns from asphalt to gravel. The crunch of rubber against rock fills the air. "But my mom's head would've exploded if she knew I'd actually be up close and personal with dinosaurs."

"That's *all* my mom's emails are about," he says, shaking his head. It makes me laugh, but it also makes me a little envious that they have the kind of relationship where they can talk about stuff.

"You two are close," I say, and it's not really a question. I can tell by the way he talks about her.

"For a long time, we were all the other really had," he says, and it's such an honest, open admission. "We didn't have a lot when I was little, but she made sure things were good and fun, and that I was always learning. Like, I look back sometimes, and I just . . . well, we were *really* poor." His voice thickens a bit. "There were times before her company took off when we would've been homeless if it weren't for my grandma. So going through that . . . I think it changes you. I don't ever want to be one of those guys who takes things for granted. Whatever I had growing up was because of her hard work. And she's the kind of person who pays it forward."

"Like with the Ivy Rose House," I say, remembering that on each Ivy Rose product, there's a little note that says ten percent of proceeds go to the women's shelter his mother established in Portland.

"Yep," Justin says.

"Was that . . ." I pause, not knowing if I'm allowed to ask this. "Did she deal with something like that?" I ask.

There's a long silence. His mouth's tight, and I worry that I've crossed a line.

"Yeah," he says finally, a faraway look in his eyes. He doesn't elaborate, and I don't press. But I have even more admiration for this woman I've never met. Who created an entire makeup empire for herself, who raised a really excellent son who makes my heart twist, and who put her riches toward helping other women.

We pull up to the makeshift parking lot in front of the valley's main gate, and I see that Oscar and some of the security team are already there. Several Gyrospheres are set near the gate, and when Justin and I get out of the jeep, the security team waves us over.

"I thought you were bringing Art" is the first thing Oscar says, and I cringe. He's still mad at me for taking the branch out of Lovelace's wound instead of waiting for the vets and trainers. It makes me feel small for a second, but then I remember the way Lovelace bellowed in pain, and my resolve hardens.

If I were faced with the same choice, I'd do it again, even knowing it's made the head of security think I'm an out-of-control ringleader.

"Tim asked Art to observe some medical thing today," Justin says. "So I brought Claire instead."

Oscar's lips press together. "Are you going to follow the rules this time?" he asks.

"Yes," I say.

"And not perform any heroics, even if there's an animal hurt?"

I hesitate. Just a little too long, because he's raising his eyebrows like he cannot believe me.

"We'll call if there are any problems or hurt animals," Justin says hurriedly.

"Hmm," Oscar says, but he steps back and gestures at one of the Gyrospheres.

"How do they work?" I ask as he presses a button on the side and the doors on the clear sphere pop open. There are blue seats inside, the only color other than the silver metal framework where the doors fit. It's totally futuristic, something that wouldn't look out of place in one of those sci-fi shows my parents grew up with. "Does the sphere spin around the seats?"

"Yes, you'll be steady and sailing along. The Gyrosphere moves around you, carrying you through the terrain. They're self-guided, to an extent," Oscar explains. "You can drive them—that's where this"—he points to the joystick set between the seats—"comes in. It's how you steer. There are safety guards in place—you can't drive right into a dinosaur, for instance."

Justin frowns. "Why would you want to do that?"

"Panic. Surprise. Idiocy," Oscar ticks off dispassionately. "When the Gyrospheres go off-track, a special alert will blare. But for our guests' safety, we can't just stop them remotely whenever they get off-track. Sitting ducks and all that. Which is where your assignment comes in. We've calibrated the various routes the Gyrospheres will typically take, but we need to take them on an off-road trip, basically. Then their sensors will get acquainted with all the terrain and learn to problem-solve around any similar new environments and obstacles they encounter."

"Like the gully Lovelace got trapped in," I say.

"Yes," Oscar says. "A Gyrosphere falls into a gully like that, and the guests won't be able to get out unless they leave the safety of the sphere. We don't want that. So we put these gyros through every kind of test and terrain and situation imaginable so the sensors get smarter and the Gyrosphere gains enhanced functionality."

"So what happens if *we* get stuck?" I ask.

"You radio us, and whoever's closest will come assist," Oscar says. "Screen is here. Controls are here." He points to the screen affixed at eye level in the front of the sphere and the joystick controls. "Brake is the red button." He walks us through the process twice, and then we're climbing inside and the doors are encircling us.

It's an odd feeling, the sphere moving around us as we descend into the valley, the guards in their own spheres following us and branching out.

The seats are comfortable, and I check three times that my buckle is secure—and then I check again, remembering the other night in the jeep. Crashing in a Gyrosphere would be extra horrible, even though the aluminum oxynitride glass is supposed to be stronger than any steel.

It's like gliding across the grass rather than driving . . . almost floating along. Once I get the hang of the joystick steering wheel—what a weird throwback for such a modern invention—it's fun. And the view it provides . . .

"You couldn't get this in a jeep or on the monorail," Justin says as we whiz through the valley, following the map on the screen. It's exhilarating. Oscar's sketched out a route for us to follow, and for a few miles, it's like the Gyrosphere knows exactly where to go. But as we reach the trees and a deep dip in the terrain, it begins to slow, and the words *Scanning the Area* replace the map on the screen. The sphere hovers, and a red light appears in front of us, blinking as it takes in the foliage.

We inch forward and then, almost as if the sphere is gaining confidence, speed up again. Which is . . . not exactly reassuring. I'm already gripping the edge of my seat hard when we hit a patch of rocks and sway back and forth.

"You good?" Justin asks, grabbing the joystick and urging the sphere over a fallen tree. We land with a teeth-rattling *thump* on the other side.

"Yeah," I say, but then I realize we're not moving.

"Are we stuck?" I twist in my seat, looking behind us. Justin pushes the navigator forward, but all the Gyrosphere does is knock back and forth against the fallen tree at our back.

"I think we're caught on something," Justin says, looking down. He fiddles with the navigator again, doing the equivalent of the gunning-the-engine thing, but Gyrosphere-style. We rock back and forth harder against the tree, but we've got no momentum. Something's gumming up the works.

"We should call for help," I say. "If I get out and try to push and Oscar finds us, he'll ban me from the valley."

"He's not so bad," Justin says. "He just likes rules."

"So do I!" And it makes him laugh. "What? I do!"

"For a girl who likes rules so much, you're pretty willing to break them when it comes to certain things," he teases. "Especially dinosaurs."

"You're the one who helped me with Lovelace."

"And I'd do it again," he says firmly. "You were right. We needed to help her." He pushes at the navigator again, and the screen flickers alarmingly. I gasp as it suddenly goes dark.

"Um," Justin says, eyes wide. "That's not good."

"Leave it to us to get the faulty Gyrosphere," I say, tapping on the screen. "Can we restart it or something? We can radio them without the screen, can't we?"

"I don't think so," Justin says.

"Okay. What do we do now?" I look around. We're in a wooded area, but through the trees, I think I see a glimpse of blue. One of the dinosaurs' watering holes? We could get out and try to dig the Gyrosphere out of whatever it's stuck on. . . . Oscar will be livid, but it's not like we can call him.

I bite my lip. I don't want to get in trouble, but we also can't just stay stuck. Oscar's warning about "sitting ducks and all that" is playing and replaying in my mind right now.

"I think we need to get out and see if we can unstick ourselves," Justin says. "You okay with that?"

"I don't see what else we can do," I say reluctantly, hitting the blue button near my seat. Our doors pop open, and a wailing alarm sound fills the air.

"Crap!" I yell over the din. It's a disorienting sound, and even when Justin and I leap out and slam the doors shut, it keeps on going.

"Well, I guess we don't have to worry about security not finding us," Justin shouts over the noise.

I'm about to make some wisecrack when something stops me. A vibration in the ground. At first, I think it's the blare of the alarm, but as it grows to a rumble, the branches of the trees begin to shake, leaves raining down on our heads.

I look up, and everything inside me flips over.

Because Pearl the Brachiosaurus is moving toward us at a startling speed.

And her eyes are on the prize: the Gyrosphere, aka Pearl's favorite toy.

15

I'm frozen, unable to move as Pearl barrels up, birds scattering as her long neck bends toward us. She's aiming for the Gyrosphere, but I'm *right there, in her path,* and oh my God, she's going to bop me with her giant dinosaur nose and flatten me like a pancake.

My heart feels like it's about to jump out of my chest and do a tap dance there on the jungle floor and I'm just . . . stuck. Like my feet have decided not to work. The fear is that swift, it blots *everything* else out. Even my motor functions.

"Claire!"

And then I'm not right there anymore: Justin grabs my arm and yanks me out of the way just a second before her head whips around to where I was and makes contact with the Gyrosphere. Our shoulders knock together and I almost sag against him in relief. But there's no relief coming yet—she's still in play mode. And an herbivore in a playful mood can be just as deadly as a carnivore in a hunting mood.

At first she noses at it, a croaky sound burbling from her throat as it pops up out of the hollow it was stuck in and bounces on the tree trunk.

We scramble out of her way, crouching against a turned-up stump that's almost big enough to shield us, but she's stomping all over and tapping the Gyrosphere with her nose, and every time it bounces off a tree like she's playing a giant pinball game, she makes this satisfied crowing noise, like *best thing ever!*

We dodge as her foot lands *right next* to the stump we've just been crouching behind. I dive out of the way, Justin right behind me as she steps back, her foot crushing the stump, wood flying everywhere. My hands fly up to shield my eyes, and sharp bits spray against my skin, luckily not hard enough to cut me. It's more like someone's thrown a handful of splinters at me.

"Oh my God, we're gonna die," I mutter, scrambling to my feet and helping Justin up. Bits of wood scatter off our clothes as we sidestep Pearl's tail whipping toward us.

"Oscar and the guys will show up in a minute," Justin assures me, but he doesn't look one hundred percent convinced. One tap of Pearl's nose to the Gyrosphere and the alarm has stopped blaring. Who knows if they even heard our distress signal?

They've gotta have extra trackers on these things, right?

I gulp, my throat dry and my heartbeat still so loud in my ears I'm afraid I won't even hear Oscar and his guys coming if they do come. Justin's sweating next to me, his glasses hanging off his nose like they don't have a prayer.

I look around, trying to find some sturdier cover than the stump as Pearl bops the Gyrosphere particularly hard and it slams against a rock, causing the lights to go a bit wonky. But it's pretty tough to hide from a dinosaur as tall as Pearl. Climbing a tree is no use, running is risky, and hiding behind anything is just an invitation to be squished.

I clench my fists, trying to think it through. But it's hard to think clearly when every molecule in your body is screaming at you. I feel like I'm going haywire, like any second my head's just going to pop off from the adrenaline.

I look at Justin, who looks back, just as torn as I am. Do we leave a hugely expensive piece of equipment in the hands—or rather maw—of a dinosaur that thinks it's a soccer ball—or do we stay and try to distract her?

Pearl chooses this moment to kick the Gyrosphere with her hind legs, donkey-style.

We look back at each other—yeah, there is no distracting her. She has what she wants. If we try to take it from her, it might not be pretty.

"Bail?" I ask Justin.

"Bail," he agrees.

"Okay." I scan the area again, trying to figure out the best way around Pearl without getting knocked off our feet by her frolicking. Trees. Rocks. Clear open space beyond them. We need to get out of the trees. She seems to like knocking the Gyrosphere against them.

Sweat trickles down the small of my back, which aches from all the running and falling.

"We need to get to clearer ground. It'll be easier to avoid her away from the trees. She doesn't want us. If we head that way"—I jerk my thumb behind me—"we'll run into whoever's hanging out at the watering hole, and they might not like us interrupting their relaxation time. We go *that* way"—I point ahead of us, toward the valley—"and we've got a dino-Gyrosphere dodgeball match to get through."

Slam. The Gyrosphere slams the tree so hard it knocks off the bark. Pearl leaps forward, pouncing like it's going to get away from her.

I see an opening: her back's to us, and she's got the Gyrosphere pinned against the tree. Even with the glass's reputation for strength, I'm kind of surprised it's held up so well.

It's now or never. A risk, but one we need to take.

"Let's go!" I grab Justin's hand, and we run across the small clearing, leaping over Pearl's tail in the process and making it to the other side of the trees before she starts rolling the sphere across the ground again. I let out a huge sigh of relief as we gallop through the trees that thin into valley after about a half mile, and then I promptly start coughing because I'm so out of breath.

Justin pulls off his glasses. The frames are bent badly, and when he tries to bend them back, they snap in two.

He lets out a short laugh. "That about sums it up," he says.

"That was . . . I don't even know," I say. It was terrifying, sure. But now that we're far enough away from getting squished . . .

It was also kind of amazing.

I scan the horizon, looking for any sign of Oscar and his guys. Sure enough, I see the sun glinting off something in the distance that's fast approaching. The ACU's Gyrospheres.

"Look, they're coming," I say. "Do you think they're gonna be mad we got out?"

Justin shakes his head. "Are you kidding me? If we'd stayed in that thing when Pearl charged toward us, we'd be concussed or squished by now."

"Bertie did say she only chased the empty ones," I say.

"Do you believe that?" he asks. "Did you *see* the look on her face?"

"I was a little distracted by mind-numbing fear," I admit.

Oscar and his guys are getting closer. I hold up my arm and wave so I'm sure they'll see us.

"They've *got* to get that dinosaur some toys or she's gonna be chasing tourists," Justin says, shaking his head. "Talk about a legal nightmare."

"But if the toys look like the Gyrosphere, she's still gonna associate them with play," I point out.

"You're right," he says. "So she needs something that gives her the same satisfaction but looks nothing like the spheres."

"That's gonna be hard, considering how happy she was to make it roll all over," I say as the security guard's Gyrospheres draw close enough for us to see Oscar's thunderous expression. He gets out of his sphere and looks expectantly at us.

"We got stuck," Justin explains. "And then Pearl happened by."

Oscar's grouchy expression melts away to worry. "Are you two okay?" he asks immediately.

"We're fine," Justin says. "The Gyrosphere, however . . ."

"Don't worry about that." Oscar waves off Justin's concern. "She charged at you? While you were in the sphere?"

"No," I say. "We got stuck, then got out of the sphere to unstick ourselves, and she came running when she saw the empty one."

The grouchy expression is back. Did he *want* Pearl to play with a human-occupied Gyrosphere?

"That animal," he mutters. "They need to put her away."

"She wasn't being vicious," I say, compelled to defend Pearl. "She just wanted to play. The other Brachiosauruses are older than she is, right? So she probably doesn't get to expend her energy."

"Expending her energy by attacking our guests is not acceptable," Oscar says shortly. "I've told Bertie time and time again that Pearl needs to be in isolation." He lets out a sigh. "She'll have to listen to me now," he says.

Irritation prickles inside me. "She just needs a different kind of toy to distract her."

Oscar shoots me a look. *That* look. The "you're a silly girl" look that only guys seem to give. It's condescending and tinged with frustration. I think about Pearl. Yeah, it was scary when she came running toward us, but she wasn't interested in us at all. She wasn't targeting us—she just wanted to play with a ball. That's a problem, sure, but it's a *fixable* problem.

My chin tilts up. "You can't tell Bertie she needs to be isolated. It's months before the park opens. There's plenty of time to redirect her attention and give her better outlets for her energy. She's not malicious—she's playful. You can't expect dinosaurs to behave perfectly. They're not robots."

"Get in the Gyrosphere and get back to the parking area," Oscar says, like I haven't said a word. "You're both off for the rest of the day. Go to the nurse at the hotel to make sure you're not injured."

"We aren't hurt—she barely even noticed us," I go on, worried he'll use the nurse as another way to convince Bertie to lock Pearl away.

My lips press together, and Justin glances at me nervously.

"Claire . . ."

"Fine," I say, because I don't want him to get in trouble. Plus, if we leave now, I can talk to Bertie before Oscar does. With a plan forming in my mind, I walk away and get into the Gyrosphere Oscar drove over.

"I thought you were going to yell at him or something," Justin says as he guides us up the rolling hills toward the gate.

"They just can't lock her up somewhere," I insist. "That's not fair."

"I agree that they have time to train her into better habits," Justin says. "But also . . . Oscar's job is to keep everyone safe around enormous wild animals that are dangerous. They could be as docile as a cat—"

"Have you *met* a feral cat?" I ask skeptically.

"Okay, docile as a bunny, then," Justin says. "My point is, no matter how sweet or slow the herbivores are, they still pose a significant risk just because of their size. I don't even know how Mr. Masrani managed to get whoever's insuring the island to agree to let him build an attraction like this valley."

"Maybe he bought an insurance company," I say.

"This park can't exist if the dinosaurs hurt someone," Justin says softly.

"I know," I say. "I just . . ." I look up at the sky through the Gyrosphere, trying to gather my thoughts. "It's the Bone Wars argument again, I guess," I say. "Knowledge and advancement versus consequences. The consequence here is if Pearl is her normal self, she gets isolated. And that's not fair."

"So what's the solution?" Justin asks.

"I don't know," I say. How do you teach a creature who never existed around humans to exist around them? How much is nature? How much is nurture? How much instinct is written in those precious DNA strands? Can you undo it?

Should you?

I think about the owner of the journal. About how Iz wrote about the dinosaurs. The care. The concern. The connection.

"I don't know," I say again. "But I'm going to figure it out."

The gate comes into view. It's closed, but as the Gyrosphere approaches, it triggers a sensor and the gate swings open. It closes behind us as we clear it, and we get out of the sphere, the fresh air hitting our faces. I take a deep breath, the tightness in my shoulders beginning to ease, and adrenaline drains out of me.

"You want to head back to the hotel?" Justin asks. "You're gonna have to drive, though. I don't have a spare pair of glasses on me."

I shake my head.

He shades his eyes from the sun, looking at me. "No, you won't drive?"

"No, I don't want to go back to the hotel," I say. "I want to go find Bertie before Oscar gets a chance to talk to her."

Bertie isn't at the first training center, but I get Mr. DNA on my tablet to give us directions to the one on the north side of the island. It's a little out of the way, and the jungle is denser over here. We pass several groves with gigantic cranes towering next to the trees, where they're assembling enormous walls.

"Those are the carnivore habitats," I say, rolling down the window and peering out.

"Look, that one's complete," Justin says, pointing ahead to the paddock. The walls look solid, but there's a part of me that still can't wrap my head around the fact that we've contained something so powerful. That cement and steel and whatever reinforcements Masrani's scientists have whipped up are enough to keep that kind of strength, that kind of predator, in check. I slow down a little as we approach the paddock. "I wonder if it's occupied," Justin says.

Before I can answer, a roar splits through the air. Birds go flying from the trees all around us and I jerk in my seat, practically rising off the cushion. My foot taps the brake and we stop in the middle of the road, and for a second, we just sit there, frozen in shock.

The sound . . . her sound, her *call* . . . I can feel it in my bones. A primal sort of feeling that's written in my DNA, into my species, one that says *danger* and *run*.

But there's another feeling underneath it. A hunger. A need.

To see her. To know. To witness that fierce glory.

"You think . . . you think she heard me?" His voice cracks a little, and he lets out a nervous laugh, and I join him, because *oh my God.*

That's her. The T. rex. I know it. She's right on the other side of that wall. She probably heard the jeep's engine. I wonder if she thinks it's someone bringing her dinner. *How* do they feed her? Bertie mentioned being on shift to do it once a week, and I want to ask her more about it now. They can't possibly go inside the paddock with her. That seems way too risky.

"We should go," Justin says, and I almost protest, even though it's silly.

It's not like I can go inside.

"Yeah," I say, my eyes still fixed on the wall, half hoping she'll roar again. But as I press on the gas and we continue, there's just the normal rustle of the jungle and the wind whipping my cheeks.

When we get to the training center where the herbivore trainers hang out, I look over at Justin after we park. "You don't have to come inside with me," I say, but Justin shakes his head.

"I get where you're coming from," he says. "And Bertie should have all the details so she can make an informed decision. It's not fair to Pearl otherwise, and Oscar doesn't like her, clearly."

So we knock on the door lightly and a voice shouts, "Come on in!"

This building is set up much like the one we did inventory in. Sarah's sitting at the break table, a sandwich in front of her. When she sees us, she wipes a smear of mustard off her cheek.

"Hey," she says. "I . . . don't have interns assigned to me today, do I?"

"No, we were assigned to the valley today," Justin says.

"We're looking for Bertie."

"She's off for lunch too," Sarah says. "Anything I can help you with?"

"It really needs to be Bertie," I say. She has the most authority here. She'll listen to me.

"Okay, well, I think she was going over to Main Street. Her girlfriend runs one of the construction crews working over there. You'll probably be able to find her if it's urgent."

"Thanks," I say. "We'll go do that." Hopefully, Oscar hasn't beaten us there.

It feels like every time we visit Main Street, it looks different . . . more put together. We park the jeep at the construction cordons and head down the street on foot. The buzz of a saw fills my ears as we pass an empty building that looks like it'll be a restaurant eventually, and we stop to give a wider path to some workers carrying barstools topped with scaly faux dinosaur hide before we move on.

"There she is," Justin says, nodding across the street, where Bertie's talking to a shorter woman with explosively curly hair. Bertie bends down and kisses her on the cheek, then plucks the hard hat out of her hand and places it on her head. She turns to leave and catches sight of us. I wave, and she says one last thing to her girlfriend before heading toward us.

"Claire, Justin, what are you doing here?" she asks.

"We wanted to talk to you," I say. "There was an . . ." I pause. I don't want to call it an *incident* because that sounds bad. "Something happened today when we were testing the Gyrospheres with Oscar and his team. Everything's fine," I hasten to add. "It's just . . . we had to get out of the sphere, and Pearl saw it sitting there, empty."

Bertie's eyes widen. "Oh no," she says.

"Yeah," Justin says. "She was pretty excited."

Bertie rubs her temples, closing her eyes. "And Oscar saw all this?"

"No, he wasn't there," I say. "We're fine. Obviously. She just wanted to bat it around."

"I don't even know if she noticed we were there," Justin adds. "But she got the Gyrosphere pretty good. We had to get away, so we ditched it."

"That was smart," Bertie says. "I'm really glad you two are okay. Pearl isn't vicious, but her size and her energy can make her scary. I understand if you're feeling shaken."

"Oscar and his team had to pick us up, so he does know," Justin says.

"He wasn't happy," I say. "But it wasn't her fault, Bertie. I promise. She wasn't going for us."

"I know she wasn't," Bertie assures me, reaching out and clasping my shoulder for a second, giving me a warm smile. "I appreciate how concerned you are about her."

"Oscar said he was going to talk to you," I tell her. "That's why we came over. I wanted to tell you about it from our perspective too. So you have the whole story."

"Thank you, both of you," Bertie says.

"He said . . ." I bite my lip. "He was talking about isolating her."

"It's a subject that's been discussed," Bertie says, gesturing for us to follow her down Main Street, out of the way of a crew carrying a large window down the sidewalk. She leads us to a little picnic area overlooking the water, and we sit down across from her at a table.

"You won't let that happen, will you?" I ask.

"It's not fully up to me," Bertie says solemnly. "It's not what I want. But Pearl is very energetic for a Brachiosaurus. She's like a Saint Bernard that thinks it's a lapdog. And while she's highly trainable, I admit, it's been difficult to find distractions and stimuli for her that she enjoys as much as batting the Gyrospheres around."

"Could you try another kind of ball?" Justin asks.

Bertie sighs. "None of them held up for more than a minute."

I look out at the water, racking my brain. There has to be some way to help Pearl.

"We're going to continue to work on it, I promise," Bertie says. "I will listen to Oscar's concerns and bring all this to management, of course. But there is still time to find a happy solution for Pearl that doesn't involve taking her out of her home or away from her family. We just need to get creative."

"We can help," I offer. "I know it's probably not much, but we'd be happy to. All of our friends too. I know they'd be happy to brainstorm stuff."

Bertie smiles at me. It's not an indulgent smile, but a grateful one. "Thank you, Claire. That's a very kind offer. And I'll take you up on it. If you or any of your friends think of any ideas that might help, come and find me."

The radio in her pocket crackles. "I should get going," she says. "Oscar will be looking for me. Thank you for giving me the heads-up about Pearl. And I'm glad you're both okay and think quick on your feet."

She heads off, disappearing in the hustle and bustle of the construction workers, and I get up and walk toward the water, feeling restless and disappointed.

"They'll figure out a solution," Justin says, catching up with me. "Masrani has the greatest minds of several generations working here."

"I hope so," I say, wishing I could be more of an optimist. I just hate the idea of Pearl being punished for being herself. It's not fair.

We walk down the path near the water until we come across a flagged area and a sign warning WET CEMENT. The newly poured sidewalk stretches in front of us, shining in the sunlight.

"I guess we should get back," I say, and I'm about to turn when I catch the mischievous glint in Justin's eye.

"Or," he says, "I could cheer you up."

He kneels down, ducking underneath the tape that blocks off the area.

"Justin!" I step forward, but it's too late. He's dipping his finger in the wet cement, writing something. For a second, I can't quite see what it is, but after about a minute, he pulls back, and he's right. It completely cheers me up. It makes me laugh and it makes me like him so much and it makes me want to . . . I dunno. It makes me want to do a lot of things. Most of all, lean over and kiss him, I think.

But I am not that brave. I do kneel down next to him, though, and smile.

He's written *Pearl Was Here* in a corner of the square of sidewalk and sketched the outline of a Brachiosaurus footprint. It's sweet and it's forever and it's definitely the nicest thing a guy's ever done for me.

"Can I?" he asks, and I nod before he takes my hand and presses it into the cement, and then does the same with his own, next to mine, our pinkies almost touching.

When we pull our hands out, leaving our little mark on Jurassic World, there for future guests to see and wonder about and walk over, I look at him.

"You took my side," I say. "Even though you see Oscar's point."

"I told you I have your back," he replies. "I mean it. And your approach makes more sense."

"All about logic, huh?"

His smiles and shakes his head. Without his glasses, his eyes shine brighter. His hair falls right into them, and I want to push it back, but I'm wise enough not to do it with a hand coated in wet cement.

"You're smart, Claire," he says. "Not just book smart. We're all book smart here. But you think about things differently. You come at stuff from angles other people don't consider. That's . . . I guess it should be intimidating, but I've been too busy thinking it's cool."

I lick my lips. They feel very dry all of a sudden. My fingers curl in the grass, and blood rushes to my cheeks.

"That's possibly the nicest thing anyone's ever said to me," I say. Because it is. Because I'm sitting here with him, and it's comfortable in ways I never thought something like this could be.

"I like the way you think too," I say. "I may come at stuff from different angles, but you pull back to see the whole picture. How the different sides and goals of this place intersect and feed into each other. You see how everything's connected. And I'm over here focused on the dinosaurs."

"They *are* kind of attention grabbing," he deadpans.

I laugh, almost pressing my hand against my lips before realizing that's a bad idea at the last second. I fish around in my bag with my dry hand and come up with a package of wet wipes and a bottle of hand sanitizer. We wash the cement residue from our hands and stand up, examining our work.

Pearl Was Here. A dino print and two handprints.

I look up at Justin, only to find him already looking at me. It's one of those moments when everything teeters and then stills. Then he speaks.

"You know I like you, right?" The way he says it is so easy and the way it makes me feel is so fluttery, as if I'm going to rise off the ground at any second.

"I like you too," I say, because I can be brave sometimes and I can be truthful even more often.

His smile widens, and I smile back, and then we both kind of nervously start laughing, the confession out there, the tension dissipating with our laughter.

"Come on," he says, and when he holds out his hand, I take it, and he doesn't let go until we get back to the jeep.

16

"Claire? Hey, Claire!"

I startle, looking up from Iz's notebook. I've become absorbed in her story—I finally got a first name from one of the journal entries. Iz is short for Izzie, which is probably short for Isobel. Izzie had a hypothesis about the Brachiosauruses' throat infections. While the vets managed to catch Agnes's infection before it got bad enough to need surgery, both Brachiosauruses were on high levels of antibiotics in February. I wonder if they still are. But maybe they found the underlying reason and fixed it . . . I'll have to look ahead to Izzie's later entries. I haven't had a lot of time to read it, since the program has so much going on and I have to prioritize my own note-taking.

Today is my first day in the lab with Dr. Wu. I'm more nervous about going there than I was in that clearing with Pearl, I swear.

"Sorry," I tell Tanya, closing Izzie's notebook and putting it in my bag. "Are you ready to head over?"

"Yes and no," Tanya says with her usual cheerful honesty. "You think he's going to be as tough as they say?"

Everyone's who's spent any time doing an assignment in Dr. Wu's lab—even if it's just dropping off equipment or papers—seems to have a story about his dislike of the interns. It makes me even more worried about today. What if he's even tougher on me because I'm not a science student like Tanya? She has the definite advantage here.

"Probably worse," I say, and she lets out a short chuckle. "But maybe we'll impress him . . . somehow."

I grab my bag and get up, and we head toward the hotel lobby. We're almost at the lobby doors when a voice calls out.

"Hey, Claire, Tanya, wait up!"

We turn to see Eric loping toward us, his camera around his neck. "Mr. Masrani asked me to get lab footage today. Can I drive with you?"

"Dr. Wu's gonna *love* that," Tanya says.

Eric shrugs. "Gotta do what the boss says."

"Do not mess this up for me," Tanya warns her twin. "Dr. Wu's in charge of hiring all the science team. If I get a recommendation from him, I'll be able to get into any graduate school I want."

"I know," Eric says, and his voice softens. "I'm not gonna do anything to screw it up. You're gonna blow him away."

"Seriously, Tanya, you don't have anything to worry about—you were his first pick," I say.

Tanya looks at me. "What?" she asks.

"I overheard him talking to Mr. Masrani the first time we visited the lab, after you talked about habitats. You were the first person he said he wanted to work in the lab."

"Oh my God, really?" Her eyes widen at the thought. "That's incredible."

"He already thinks you're smart. You'll impress him."

"So will you," Tanya says as we get into our jeep.

"I don't think so," I say. "He didn't seem to like the fact that Justin was a business major, even though he's minoring in chem. He'll probably hate it when he finds out I'm in poli-sci."

"Well, that background gives you a different take on things," Tanya says helpfully, and I laugh, shaking my head.

"It's okay. I'm just gonna try my best. It's all I can do."

Even though I sound positive, I feel anything but as we pull up to the command center and take the elevator down to the labs. My palms are sweating as the door dings open. Dr. Wu is standing there, waiting for us.

"Ms. Dearing. Ms. Skye. Mr. Skye."

"Mr. Masrani sent me to record footage," Eric says.

"I've been informed," Dr. Wu says brusquely. "Come along."

He leads us through the labs, which are bustling with activity. I count at least thirty people on our way through the four main lab rooms. There's a whole group of them gathered around a centrifuge, staring at it like it holds the answers to the universe. Farther along, two women have a series of blood samples laid out on the table, and as we pass by, I can see they're labeled *Tyrannosaurus rex*. I think about the roar Justin and I heard yesterday and shiver just at the thought of it. It was like I could *taste* the roar at the back of my throat, and I didn't even see her. The power of one sound. I guess that's what helps make her the true ruler of Jurassic World. The top of the food chain. What must it be like to look into her eyes? To see all those teeth? I desperately want to know.

Dr. Wu leads us to the back of the lab floor down a corridor to a small room lined with long tables holding a series of beakers set on burners.

"I believe you've seen our fusion bandages in action?" Dr. Wu asks.

"Yes, when Lovelace was hurt," says Tanya.

"Ah, what name will they come up with next?" Dr. Wu says, shaking his head, but I think there's a smile in his eyes. "Anyway, the compound that makes up the bandage is quite complex and requires a number of steps to formulate. This is step one. These liquids need to be kept at seventy-five degrees Celsius for twenty-four hours. You will sit here"—he points to the stools—"and monitor them. I will be right over there, doing my own work." He settles down at the table opposite ours, facing us as he sets out his computer and tablet. "Any questions?" he asks.

"What's in them?" Eric asks.

"That's a secret," Dr. Wu says, steel in his voice. "Any other questions?"

Tanya and I shake our heads, but Eric doesn't seem to know when to stop, "So we're just going to be in this room watching liquid boil?"

"Boiling point is one hundred degrees Celsius, Eric," Tanya mutters, looking like she wants to jab her brother.

"I'm just saying it won't make the most interesting footage," Eric says, and Tanya flushes, mortified.

"I cannot let you wander around my lab unwatched, Mr. Skye," Dr. Wu says.

"Just for a little bit?" Eric asks. "I won't touch anything."

"No," Dr. Wu says firmly.

Eric sighs in defeat, sitting down on one of the stools.

Tanya and I take our places, our eyes glued to the beakers and the thermometers fixed to them.

It's boring work. Incredibly boring. But sometimes something tedious turns into something amazing. And those fusion bandages are amazing. I can't even imagine the difference they'll make in the medical field once they—*we*—figure out a way to get them to adhere to nondinosaur skin.

"Dr. Wu, is your team experimenting with getting the fusion bandages to work on other animals and people?" I ask.

He looks up from his tablet. "Not my team," he says. "But there is work being done on that particular project." He doesn't elaborate.

Eric fiddles with his camera, not bothering to record us, because why would he? He's reviewing old footage, I realize as I glance at him. Stuff from the Gyrosphere Valley. I can see the Triceratops from here.

Tanya and I exchange looks. I shrug, because I don't know what to do other than sit here and stare at the beakers, as ordered. Is Dr. Wu going to sit there? Does he just expect us to stay quiet the whole time?

"Can you tell us about any of the projects your team is working on?" Tanya asks, taking on the awkward silence for all of us.

"Much of our work is focused on preparing for the opening of the park," Dr. Wu replies—the vaguest possible answer. He must notice Tanya's disappointed look, because he sighs and relents a little. "Right now, my personal team is focused on building the necessary DNA strands to acclimate a Mosasaurus to the changes in the ocean since the Maastrichtian Age."

"You found *Mosasaurus DNA*?" Tanya squeaks with excitement. "Was it extracted from the mosquitoes in amber? I know the theory is they never dove very deep in the water, but were they surfacing enough to get fed on by the mosquitoes? Or did you find different DNA sources?"

"We are exploring many source options," Dr. Wu says, not quite answering her questions. I have a feeling that in his work, he has to sidestep so many questions that he's become a master at it. "We got extraordinarily lucky with the Mosasaurus DNA, I will admit. But we still have a way to go before we can create a viable specimen."

"That's so cool," Tanya says. "Amanda's gonna freak when she finds out."

"Definitely," I agree.

The silence envelops us again, and I keep one eye on the thermometer, the other on Dr. Wu. Tanya shifts in her seat as the minutes tick by, and then finally, she blurts out, "Dr. Wu, are we supposed to just be quiet the whole time?"

He pauses for a moment before looking up and meeting her questioning gaze. I can't tell if he's annoyed or impressed by her gumption. But that's Tanya for you.

"Feel free to talk among yourselves," he says. "As long as it doesn't distract you from the work at hand. I want temperatures confirmed every ninety seconds as protocol demands."

"Got it," Tanya says, relief in her eyes.

Eric doesn't even look up from his camera. He's moved on from footage of the valley to close-ups of some of the command center screens.

"I've been thinking about Pearl," Tanya says to me.

"What about her?" I ask. I told Tanya what happened with Pearl and the Gyrosphere, and she was just as horrified as I was at the idea of Pearl being kept isolated, away from the valley.

"I've been trying to come up with solutions," she says. "We've seen with Lovelace and music that the dinosaurs respond to different stimuli, right? So maybe the solution to Pearl's playfulness is to find what mellows her."

I think about it. "So we're looking for the dinosaur version of anti-catnip?" I ask, and is it my imagination, or does Dr. Wu let out a soft chuckle?

"Actually, that's not a bad idea," Tanya says. "There are probably some plants that could have calming effects on her."

"Like koalas, and how the eucalyptus leaves they eat make them sleep a lot?"

"That's actually a myth," Tanya says.

"Seriously?"

"Yeah. Turns out they're sleepy all the time because eucalyptus is kind of toxic and they use up so much energy just to digest it. There are a lot of other plants that have sedative effects. But I'm not sure how we'd identify which ones would work . . . or if we could get Pearl to eat enough so she'd be calm but not keel over."

She taps her capped pen against her mouth, frowning at the beaker in front of her as she goes over it in her head. "My gut says the medicinal approach is the wrong one. There are just too many variables that makes it unreliable in this situation."

"So we're back to behavioral modification and training," I say. "Redirecting her attention."

"The problem is that if an empty Gyrosphere is the trigger for her behavior, she needs a bunch of exposure therapy, basically, around it. But that might result in a bunch of smashed Gyrospheres before she gets the point. Those things can't be cheap."

"They are not," Dr. Wu says.

"What do you think, Dr. Wu?" Tanya asks. "Pearl the Brachiosaurus keeps wanting to play with them. How do we get her to stop?"

"I am not a behaviorist," Dr. Wu says.

"Well, neither are we," Tanya says.

"Why don't you take the question to your intern friends?" Dr. Wu asks, and for a second I wonder if he's being sarcastic, but he seems serious. Maybe even a little interested in the Pearl problem. "Bouncing ideas off your colleagues can lead to fresh perspectives."

"That's a good idea," Tanya says.

"For what it's worth, Bertie is very good at her job," Dr. Wu says. "And she is dedicated to the herbivores. It will take quite the fight to get her to make a choice that is wrong for them."

"But what if it's between what's best for them and what's best for the park?" I ask, and Dr. Wu's lips tighten at the corners.

"This is the endeavor of many people's life work, Claire," he says, his voice serious. "And nothing will stop it now."

I shiver, my mind flashing back to Wyatt's phantom intern story just for a second, but before I can even think about the repercussions, Eric leans against the counter, his eyes fixed on the camera instead of where he's putting his elbows. He bumps into a large stack of empty beakers and they teeter and tilt before crashing to the floor with a shattering sound that makes me jump.

Dr. Wu gets to his feet, a dangerous expression playing across his face. "All right. Time to go," he says, or more like orders. "It's almost lunch anyway. You two can return afterward. But you" —he points at Eric—"tell Mr. Masrani you've gotten enough footage."

Red crawls along Eric's cheeks. "Yes, Dr. Wu," he mutters. "I'm sorry. I can help clean it—"

"I'll have it taken care of," Dr. Wu interrupts. "Just go."

We skitter to obey, the three of us not breathing freely until we get through the maze of lab rooms and into the elevator.

"I thought he was going to explode," Eric confesses, leaning against the elevator wall, his shoulders slumping. "Do you think Mr. Masrani will be mad?"

"Things get knocked over," I assure him. "It happens. He knows that—that's why he didn't yell. He's just a control freak, and we control freaks don't like messes."

"I should've looked where I was leaning," Eric admits. "But I was thinking about how to edit together these long shots I got of Brachiosauruses at the watering hole last week, and the next thing I knew . . ."

"Don't beat yourself up," Tanya says gently. "The only person you need to impress is Mr. Masrani, and you know he'll love all the footage you've got. He wouldn't have chosen you for this job if he didn't like your work."

The elevator dings open and we walk out of the command center, joining Ronnie, who's been shadowing some of the security guys who work up in the monitoring center on the top floor. We've got lunches in our jeep, and we take them out and eat on the steps of the command center before Eric heads back to his room and we girls return to the lab.

Dr. Wu is waiting for us at the elevator doors again when we get back downstairs. "Come along," he says.

But instead of taking us back to our oh-so-scintillating assignment of temperature monitoring away from all the action, he makes a right at the end of the first group of labs. I raise my eyebrows at Tanya, who shrugs as we follow him down a narrow hallway. At the end, there's a windowless steel door with the word RESTRICTED stamped across it. Dr. Wu steps in front of the retina scanner set in the wall beside it. A line of red light passes down his face, and then he punches a code into the keypad under the scanner.

The door swings open as a disembodied voice says, "Welcome, Dr. Wu."

"Follow me," he says, walking briskly down the all-white hall. The walls here are solid, not the glass walls of the lab, and the silence makes everything feel just a little spooky.

Dr. Wu comes to a stop in front of a set of double doors and turns to face us.

"Before we go inside," he says, "I'm going to remind you two that you signed NDAs when you accepted your internships. What you see in the next room needs to be kept secret even from your fellow interns—including your brother, Ms. Skye—do you understand?" He fixes us both with a searing look.

My mouth's dry with anticipation—just what is inside that room?—as Tanya and I affirm our understanding to the doctor.

"Very well," Dr. Wu says. He presses his hand against the scanner, and the doors click open.

The room is cold. That's the first thing I register as we step inside. Cold enough that I can see my breath in front of me, and it's such a sudden change from the jungle's oppressive humidity that's filled our days. I close my eyes in relief for a moment.

And when I open them and see what's in the room, I can't look away.

"Is that . . . ?" I ask, unable to believe it as Tanya and I draw forward.

"Yes," Dr. Wu says, a proud smile spreading across his face. He walks over to the enormous nest, set on a low steel pedestal that has all sorts of wires and monitors hooked up to it. A glass dome is set over the nest—an incubator shield of some sort. I lean forward to peer inside, and it's an unbelievable feeling to see the dozen large eggs tucked away in the twig and straw bedding.

"These are the very first hatchlings of the new era," Dr. Wu says.

"I can't believe this," Tanya says. "These are Pteranodon eggs?"

Dr. Wu nods. He goes over to the lab table set in the back of the room and selects several bottles out of the cupboards set above it.

"What's their gestation period?" Tanya asks, pushing her bangs out of her eyes as she leans forward to stare at the eggs in the incubator.

"Several months," Dr. Wu says. "I've decided to give you an assignment."

Those words are both exciting and kind of terrifying, because impressing this man is *hard* . . . and I know we're both determined to do it.

"Today, I will be performing a procedure that involves using a microneedle to pierce the shell and the sac within." He holds up a silver syringe with a long needle so fine I have to squint to make it out, even though he's only a few feet away. "We do this in order to inject a cocktail of antibiotics and steroids directly into the developing embryo."

I frown. In Izzie's journal, she talked about a special mix of antibiotics and steroids that the Brachiosauruses were put on after their throat problems started. Is this the same thing? Does that mean other dinosaurs are getting sick too?

"Why risk the eggs so early?" Tanya asks. "Even with a microneedle, there's a chance you might compromise the sac, right?"

"Correct," Dr. Wu says.

"Okay, then why not wait until they're hatched to administer the steroids and antibiotics?"

"It's because of the throat infections, isn't it?" I ask, and Dr. Wu looks at me, eyebrows raised.

"How did you know that?" he asks.

I flush. "One of the vets," I lie, because I don't want to show anyone Izzie's notebook. "I asked how Olive got her scar. She said it was because of a surgery on her throat. Some sort of infection, right? Did any dinosaurs other than the Brachiosauruses have it?"

"It was a recurring problem in both the Brachiosauruses and the Triceratops after they were transported here," Dr. Wu says. "Which is why we take these precautions now, even though they can be risky."

"Did you figure out what was causing the infections?" I ask.

"No," Dr. Wu says. "It doesn't occur in all the dinosaurs, and we've been able to keep it at bay with medications in the ones who are vulnerable. And now, we treat it prenatally as a preemptive measure. But the cause of the infections is one of the many mysteries we have yet to solve about these creatures. There will always be more."

"Did this ever happen during the original park's time? Or at Isla Sorna?"

Dr. Wu's eyes flicker. "No," he says.

"So that suggests it's environmental, specific to this region and time," Tanya says, cluing in on my thinking.

"That would be my hypothesis," I say.

"It's not a bad one," Dr. Wu says, and my mouth almost drops open because that's a huge compliment from him. "But we've done extensive testing and can't find any environmental source. Nor does it seem to be infectious or airborne."

"That's frustrating," Tanya says.

"It is," Dr. Wu acknowledges. "But a temporary solution has been found in the meantime. And the science will persist until a permanent one is discovered."

There's something so balanced about Dr. Wu's words . . . and his world. He is in control, ruler of this tremendous domain of science and steel, keeper of the kind of knowledge and talent and brilliance most people can't even dream of.

"Now, after the drugs have been administered to the embryos, they will need to be carefully monitored," Dr. Wu explains. "That's where you come in. Every morning, at seven a.m. sharp, you'll report here for an hour to monitor the eggs. The scanners here do most of the work." He gestures at the row of screens that take up most of back wall of the room. Each one displays a 3-D rendering of the egg and Pteranodon embryo. "But sometimes there are minute changes in sac pressure and weight that the scanners can't catch, but dedicated interns can. Do you think you can be that dedicated?"

"Of course," Tanya and I say at the same time.

"You can count on us," Tanya assures him.

"And we're very appreciative of the opportunity," I add.

"Very well," Dr. Wu says with a brisk nod. "Then be on time tomorrow morning, and we will go through the protocol and your duties. You're dismissed for the day."

Tanya and I manage to contain our glee as Dr. Wu escorts us back through the lab and to the elevator. But as soon as the doors close, my mouth drops open.

"Oh my God!" I say.

Tanya jumps up and down. "Pteranodon eggs!" she says—well, more like *shrieks*.

"Did you see how big they were?"

"Did you see the totally vivid, by-the-minute renderings on the monitors?"

"I can't believe this," I say. "He actually picked us! I thought we were pissing him off!"

"Me too!" Tanya says. "Way to go with the bronchial infection thing. That's crazy. Which vet told you that?"

"Um, you know, I can't remember. One of the guys. Dark hair? I'm bad with names." I feel bad about lying, but I'm not ready to let anyone in on my secret weapon. Izzie, whoever she is, left her work behind for some reason. On purpose? Accidentally? The farther I read through her maze of a journal, the more questions I have about her and the mysterious infections she dealt with during her time here.

"Anyway, I didn't impress him as much as you did," I tell Tanya as the elevator opens into the lobby. The sun's still high in the sky as we get in the jeep and begin the drive back to the hotel. "I wish I were as bold as you. You just kept asking him questions!"

We glide past Main Street and across the bridge, the water shimmering below us. In just the few weeks since we've arrived, the monorail track across the water has almost been completed. I wouldn't be surprised if it was running before our time here is up. My stomach twinges at the thought of leaving, and I frown, trying to drive the feeling away.

"You're bold," Tanya says as she takes a right toward the hotel. "Justin told me how you faced down Oscar about Pearl."

"I guess it's easier when I'm angry," I admit, and Tanya laughs.

"Well, they do say redheads are supposed to have tempers," she teases.

17

After dinner the next night, I'm sitting on my bed, finishing up my postcards to Karen and trying for the twentieth time to understand the map in Izzie's notebook that has all the X's on it, while Tanya video-chats with her family at the desk.

I can hear her little sister ask all sorts of questions about the dinosaurs, and I laugh when Tanya pretends to be a T. rex in front of the screen.

"Who's that?"

"That's Claire, my roommate!" Tanya says, tilting the screen toward me. Victory, Tanya and Eric's little sister, looks like she's about eight. Her hair is dark like the twins', but it's cropped close to her head in a pixie cut, a contrast to her pale skin. She's super cute . . . like a frail little elf.

I wave at her. "Hi, Victory! You have a really cool name."

Victory giggles. "Thank you. You have pretty hair."

"So do you. I was just thinking that you look like a magical pixie."

Tanya's eyes go bright, and I wonder if I've said something wrong, but instead she says, "Okay, sweetie, I've gotta go. Tell Mom and Dad I'll call them tomorrow to talk more. I love you! Mwuah, mwuah, mwuah!" She blows exaggerated kisses at the screen, which Victory imitates before signing off.

"You okay?" I ask, because Tanya's jaw is tight.

"Yeah," she says, in that way that tells me she totally isn't. I hesitate, wondering if I should push. Maybe she just misses her family. I decide not to say anything when Tanya pastes a determined smile on her face. "She's really sweet, isn't she?"

"The sweetest," I say. "I kind of always wanted a younger sibling. But I have my nephew. He's a ton of fun."

Tanya lies back against her mound of pillows. "I am really excited about tomorrow, but I'm not looking forward to waking up early," she confesses.

"You'll need all the tea and I'll need all the coffee," I say. "We'll make it work."

There's a knock on our door. I look at the clock on the bedside table. It's nearly nine.

"Are you having someone over?" I ask Tanya.

"Some*ones,* actually," she says with a grin.

I open the door to find Ronnie and Amanda standing there.

"I brought snacks," Ronnie says, holding up two canvas bags stuffed with food.

"And I brought the whiteboard and the face masks," Amanda says.

"We're going to help you figure out the Pearl Problem," Tanya says.

A smile breaks across my face. "Seriously?"

"We can at least come up with a few decent ideas to bring to Bertie," Amanda says. "There's no way Pearl should be isolated just because she's got a mischievous streak. Also, can you *imagine* the kind of draw a Brachiosaurus playing with a toy would be for the park?"

"Especially for the little kids," Tanya adds. "The carnivores are going to be *way* too scary for the little ones. My baby sister would probably faint if she saw a real T. rex. But if she saw Pearl? Especially if she's doing something a kid can relate to, like playing ball? She'd think it was so funny. It'd be a gold mine!"

I step aside to let the girls in. Amanda sets up the whiteboard, scattering a bunch of markers on Tanya's bed for us, and Ronnie sets out the array of chips, dips, and candy.

"How was your assignment with Dr. Wu?" Amanda asks as we pass back and forth the jars of mud masks and the selection of sheet masks she brought.

"Tanya and he bonded over potential Mosasaurus specimens," I say.

"There are Mosasaurus specimens?" Amanda's voice rises, her eyes turning feverish with delight. "Oh my God, I have *got* to get back into that lab."

"I don't think they have the actual specimens yet," Tanya says hastily. "He said something about working on certain strands to acclimatize it to these waters."

"Makes sense," Amanda says. "Wow. A Mosasaurus. That's like

the be-all and end-all. Their teeth alone . . ." She lets out a dreamy sigh that really shouldn't be associated with rows and rows of deadly dino teeth. "I think I'd die if I saw one."

"Don't say that! Especially because there's probably going to be one in the park in a few years!" Ronnie says. "Knock on wood right now!"

Amanda laughs, but raps her knuckles on the wooden headboard. "Okay, so, masks and then brainstorming, or brainstorming and then masks?"

"Why not masks while brainstorming?" Tanya suggests, picking up the jar containing a mint mask. "Multitasking."

"Sounds good to me," Amanda says. "That one's really good," she adds, nodding to the tube I'm holding, a cucumber gel mask from Ivy Rose.

"Did you know Justin's mom owns that company?" Tanya asks.

"What? No way!" Amanda's eyes light up. "I love Ivy Rose!"

"I'm gonna use this one," I say, and get up and walk into the bathroom to apply it. The girls follow me, and we spend a few minutes jostling each other in front of the mirror, applying our masks. When we're done, Amanda's got a gray charcoal mud mask on, Tanya's gone green with the mint mask, I can smell Ronnie's brown sugar scrub/mask combo from across the room, and my own cucumber mask feels silky and smooth against my skin.

"Okay, I've set a timer for the masks. Let's brainstorm until it goes off," Tanya announces, clapping her hands together.

We go back into our room, sitting on the edges of the beds and facing the whiteboard. I write *The Pearl Problem* at the top in big red letters, and Amanda adds a little Brachiosaurus chasing a Gyrosphere doodle at the bottom.

"Let's break it down," Ronnie says. "Pearl's energetic and clearly an independent thinker."

I add these things to the board.

"She's not even fully grown yet," Amanda adds. "I checked her stats with Bertie. She's only six. She won't reach full maturity for another four years or so. But the three other Brachiosauruses are approaching their twenties. They're from Dr. Hammond's original park."

"Do you think it could be as simple as giving her a friend her age?" Tanya questions.

"The problem is, even if that *was* the solution, it kind of can't be," Amanda says. "There *isn't* another Brachiosaurus her age. And they can't integrate any of the younger ones into the valley because the Triceratops might get territorial or mean. The reason the dinos coexist as well as they do in the valley now is because the Triceratops aren't going to mess with the mostly grown Brachiosauruses. Smaller ones might be another story. The scientists have decided it's just too big a risk."

"Okay, so a Brachiosaurus friend isn't an option." I divide the bottom of the board into three sections: *OPTIONS, NON-OPTIONS, LAST RESORTS.*

"I hate to say it," Ronnie says. "But medication might be a last-resort option. Maybe something to calm her?"

I start a list under the *LAST RESORTS* heading and write *Medication*, even though I hate the idea of sedating her so she's complacent and slow.

I look back at the *NON-OPTIONS* section, where I add *Friends her age*.

"What happens if Pearl gets a friend who *isn't* a Brachiosaurus?" I ask, thinking about how much Earhart loved Sally.

Amanda raises an eyebrow. "What do you mean?"

"What about Lovelace? She's the youngest in her herd. Could they become friends?"

"I mean, cross-species animal friendships exist. The Internet is full of cute videos of bears and tigers being best friends, and that domestic cat that nursed the bobcat cub that was rejected by her mom," Tanya says.

"I love those videos," Ronnie admits.

"It'd be cute," Amanda acknowledges. "But usually for those types of bonds to exist, the animals need to be raised together from a really young age. And with dinosaurs . . . who even knows? It'd be a big maybe. And it'd take a lot of time. Probably too much."

We continue to brainstorm, bouncing ideas off each other and going back and forth. After we wash off our masks, we settle down on various spots on the bed, dividing the chips and candy among us, examining our now-filled whiteboard.

"I'm still thinking that creating some sort of toy for her is the answer," Amanda says, crunching on a salt-and-vinegar potato chip.

"Combined with in-depth training to distract her and keep her away from the Gyrospheres?" Tanya asks.

Amanda nods. "But what kind of distraction is the question. It would need to be made out of the same material as the Gyrospheres. . . . What is it, again?"

"Aluminum oxynitride," Ronnie says. "It's strong enough to stop a fifty-caliber bullet. The military is making shields out of it."

"It'd need to be made out of that," Amanda continues.

"But if it's made out of the same material as the Gyrospheres, she's going to keep associating them with play," Tanya sighs. "And then we're back at square one."

I bite my lower lip, staring at the whiteboard, which is chock-full of ideas—from the really good to the positively ridiculous—trying to see a path through.

My eyes fall on the sketch Amanda did at the bottom of the board, a cartoony Pearl chasing a Gyrosphere. Something occurs to me, and I sit straight up.

"Amanda," I say. "How good is Pearl's eyesight, do you know? I mean, the Brachiosauruses in general—is their eyesight good?"

"I'm not sure . . . ," she says. "Why?"

"I remember reading about how surfers in Australia will sometimes paint black stripes on their surfboards because it's like an optical illusion. It makes them invisible to sharks."

"Oh, I remember that article!" Tanya says, sitting up. "The stripes resemble the markings of the striped pilot fish, which have a symbiotic relationship with them—they feed off the remains of their prey. Sharks don't have good eyesight. The theory is that they see a surfboard and associate the shape with prey, which is why they attack surfers. That's where the stripes on the board and even on wet suits come in—the sharks don't associate the stripes with prey. They assume the surfers are pilot fish and stay away most of the time."

"Exactly," I say. "So what if we take that theory and twist it to this situation?" I ask, gesturing to the drawing. "We could take a few Gyrospheres and paint them in patterns that would differentiate them from the Gyrospheres the guests will be using. If she's trained to see the painted Gyrospheres as *hers* and *toys,* then she won't be interested in the ones that aren't hers."

"Ooh, that's an excellent idea," Ronnie says, her eyes shining at the possibility.

"I agree," Amanda chimes in. "Especially because with the brain scanning technology they have here, the vets and trainers will be able to zero in *exactly* on what kind of patterns stimulate Pearl's pleasure centers."

"This is so cool! Do you think they'll listen to us if we bring this up to Bertie?" Ronnie asks.

"Bertie told me to come to her if we have any ideas," I say. "Maybe we could all go and pitch this to her at lunch tomorrow?"

"That sounds great," Amanda says. "And speaking of tomorrow, Ronnie and I have got to get back to our room before Beverly calls curfew on us."

I look over at the clock and am shocked to see it's almost eleven. "Go, you two. Tanya and I will clean up."

"We'll do this in our room next time," Amanda promises.

I smile at the thought of a next time.

They hurry out, on the alert for Beverly, and I close the door behind them, leaning against it for a second.

I love my friends from college, but a lot of them are English and poetry majors, like Regina, and our study gatherings were kind of a bore. This session was incredibly fun. *And* productive. So basically, my two favorite things.

"I can't wait to tell Dr. Wu he was right—brainstorming as a team is key," Tanya calls, picking up a few empty chip bags and dumping them in the trash next to the bed. I hurry over to collect the soda cans and bottles and put them in the recycling.

We get everything cleaned up and then get ready for bed. I pack my bag so I don't have to do it in the morning, and drop Izzie's notebook in the front pocket of my satchel.

I slip under the covers and Tanya turns the light off. I can hear her rustling around, and in the dark, I get the courage to say it.

"Hey, Tanya?"

"Yeah?"

"Thanks."

"For what?" she sounds bemused.

"For tonight. It was really fun."

"Of course," she says. "I know this is important to you. It's important to me, too. I'm just glad we were able to help. I mean, that's what friends are for."

She says it like it's so easy, and I'm grateful for the dark as I stare up at the ceiling, because it's never been easy like that for me.

I drift off, and I dream of the jungle, of great waxy leaves brushing the top of my head, my boots squelching in the rich soil, the chirp of insects in the air. And the farther I venture into the island's tangled embrace, the more I feel at home.

18

"You've got to be kidding me," Tanya says, when the elevator to the lab opens and we see Wyatt standing there.

He smirks. "Dr. Wu sent me to come get you," he says.

"Why are you here?" I ask.

"The same reason you are," he says. "Did you think I was going to miss a chance to monitor the first hatch? That's historic."

"Every time we're around the dinosaurs, you complain," I say. "Do you even know what monitoring like this will involve?" I ask.

"Claire," Tanya says, very seriously, placing her hand on my arm. "You know that doesn't matter. He goes to *Hahhh-vard*!" And she draws out the *ahh* to an absurd length.

I go bright red trying not to burst out laughing.

Wyatt goes bright red for an entirely different reason.

"Dr. Wu's waiting," he says icily.

"We know the way," I say.

"Do you have the key card?" He holds it up.

I grit my teeth, and Tanya and I follow him through the lab. We pass by the amber room, and I see that the scientists have moved on to a new area of the giant chunk we saw them working with on our first visit here. I wonder if they've identified any of the DNA draws yet . . . and then I wonder if I can get Tanya to ask Dr. Wu for me, because he's still pretty intimidating.

He's waiting right in front of the first scanner, and he leads us into the hatching room, where the eggs are gleaming white in their nest.

"All right, let's get started," Dr. Wu says, all business. "The microneedle treatments were performed at five o'clock yesterday evening. The eggs will be particularly prone to fracturing in the next week as the shell and the sac heal over the entrance points. If you look closely"—he directs our attention to the nest, where each egg is situated perfectly—"you'll see that each egg is set over a sensor that helps us scan growth, healing rate, and any potential problems. You will not touch the eggs or the incubator shield. You will sit and watch the monitors and record your observations every fifteen minutes. Any questions?"

"What kind of observations are you looking for?" Wyatt asks.

"Your own," Dr. Wu says. "Not the ones you think I want."

"Are we allowed to watch the nest as well as the monitors?" I ask. "I won't touch. I promise."

"Yes, feel free to observe the eggs themselves, though if all goes well, there will be no activity to speak of. The data will be more interesting."

"And we just have an hour?" Tanya asks.

"Unless you want to go back to monitoring the fusion bandage compounds," Dr. Wu says.

"No, no, this is great," Tanya says quickly.

"Press the call button here"—he points to the red button near the farthest monitor—"if you identify a problem or anomaly."

"How will we know?" I ask.

"You'll know," Dr. Wu says. "The tech knows what it's doing." He looks down at his watch. "And I am late for a meeting with Mr. Masrani. Behave, all of you. This is a great privilege I've decided to bestow on you. I'll come get you in an hour."

He sweeps out of the room, leaving us alone with the eggs.

Tanya and I cross the room to look at the monitors. There's one screen for each egg, the sensors in the nest helping the computer render a perfect image of the growing embryos. It's incredible to see how tightly folded the mini Pteranodons are within the eggs, which are pretty big, about three times the size of a chicken's egg.

On this one, I can see the little curl of her claw tucked against a tight spike of wing. I reach out and trace the claw on the screen, unable to stop myself.

"Look at the detail," I say.

"This is so neat," Tanya says, walking from monitor to monitor. "How do you want to do this?" she asks.

"Look, they all have letters." I point at the corner of the first monitor, labeled *EGG A*.

"Okay, good," Tanya says. "So we'll divide them up between—"

A red light suddenly starts flashing behind us, and a beeping sound blares. I whirl around and my mouth drops open when I catch Wyatt snatching his hand away from the incubator shield.

"What are you doing?" I demand, hurrying over to the nest and peering inside. "Are they okay?" I scan the eggs, searching for cracks or any sign of distress; then I look over to the monitors Tanya's checking, praying there are no alerts or alarms or anything wrong. Thankfully, everything seems normal, and she gives me a relieved nod.

"I just wanted to see," Wyatt says.

"He just *told* us not to touch it," Tanya snaps. "Can you maybe not piss off the scientist in charge of all of this? He'll kick us out! He doesn't want us here in the first place."

"He's just an employee," Wyatt says scornfully, like it's something dirty.

Tanya rolls her eyes. "Look, I don't care if you want to coast and have us girls do all the work. But don't screw up this opportunity for Claire and me, because we don't have a dad on Masrani's board of directors who will bail us out of every mess we get into."

Wyatt's eyes narrow. "You better shut your mouth."

"Or what?" Tanya asks. "Gonna run to Daddy?"

He doesn't say anything, because he doesn't have any ammunition other than that. Pitiful.

"Just leave us alone," I say. I join Tanya at the monitors, and we begin to divide up the eggs, her taking A through F and me taking G through L. We ignore Wyatt, who's just skulking around the lab, opening cupboards and snooping around.

We write down the eggs' initial stats, recording the time, and repeat that fifteen minutes later. That's when we start to compare before the next round.

"It looks like the calcium levels in egg G are a little higher than the others," I say, scanning our notes. "We should keep an eye out for that if it continues."

"Look at egg B," Tanya points out, staring at a monitor. "Is it me, or does she have an extra claw?" She traces her pen along a shadow on the monitor's view of egg B's embryo. She's right—it does look like there's another claw growing.

"Maybe it's a mutation. . . . Dinosaur polydactyly?" I suggest.

"I had a cat with extra toes when I was little," Tanya says. "I called her Thumbs because I was a very original five-year-old."

I laugh. "Let's make a note of it for Dr. Wu," I say.

"It might just be the way she's positioned, too," Tanya says, tilting her head as she looks at the monitor again. "But it really looks like a claw to me."

Wyatt snorts behind us. We just keep ignoring him.

Our hour is up faster than I expect. Even though it's kind of tedious work, being able to see the embryos on the monitor is fascinating. I could watch them all day, given the chance.

But Dr. Wu ushers us out of the incubation lab as soon as our final fifteen-minute round is up.

"But what about the rest of our day?" Tanya asks. "We can go back to watching the beakers; I don't mind."

"No, no, I have a better job for all you interns," Dr. Wu says, and his smile is positively wicked. "You'll be reporting to the greenhouses. It's processing day."

"You mean new plants are getting delivered?" Tanya asks, her face lighting up like sunlight across fresh snow.

Dr. Wu's smile grows wider. "Not exactly," he says.

"This may be our biggest challenge yet," Justin says, pulling on his work gloves and crossing his arms.

I lean against my shovel, trying to breathe through my mouth.

"This is *ridiculous*," Wyatt hisses.

"Oh my God, stop complaining," Amanda sighs. "It's just a little poop."

There's a beat of silence, and then a ripple of laughter reverberates through the entire group. Because "a little poop" is basically the understatement of the century, considering the gigantic pile of dinosaur manure that's been dumped behind the research greenhouse.

Our job is to shovel it into bags, label them, and then stack the bags. Very simple. Very tiring. And very smelly.

"The sooner we get started, the sooner we're done," Ronnie declares, grabbing one of the white bags labeled *Brachiosaurus Manure (Aged 6 months)* and marching toward the pile, which is about three times as tall as she is.

"I'm going in," I tell Justin.

"Do you want to be the shoveler or the bag holder?" he asks as we take the far corner of the pile, dragging over a wheelbarrow full of bags and two shovels.

"If we set up half a dozen bags at a time and add enough manure to hold the sides up, we can both shovel. It'll get done faster," I say, grabbing one of the shovels to gauge its heft. I look up to catch him staring at me. "My dad likes to garden," I explain. "He always roped me into digging stuff for him because I have the opposite of a green thumb."

After the first few bags, Justin and I fall into a rhythm. It's hard, sweaty, and stinky work, but with a dozen of us working—well, make that eleven, since Wyatt's doing more complaining than work—it takes only three hours with a few breaks to get it all done. After we finish stacking the last bag, I stumble over to the lawn that stretches along the front of the research greenhouse, and I collapse in the shade of a palm tree. Tanya and Ronnie join me and slouch up against the trunk, while Justin and Art sprawl on the other side.

"We stink," Ronnie observes.

"Getting clean requires getting up, though," Tanya says.

"That is a problem," Art agrees.

"I'm getting up," I say, but then I don't move, and it makes Justin laugh.

"Okay, someone's gotta be first," he says, pushing off the tree. He holds his hand out to help me up, and then looks down and realizes it's more than a little grubby, but I take it anyway. It's not as if I can get dirtier.

And it's not as if I don't like the butterflies.

"How about we all clean up and then meet at the falls to swim?" Art suggests. "We have a few hours before dinner."

"Ooh, yes!" Amanda says. "I haven't been yet."

"Me neither," I say.

"Why don't we meet in about an hour?" Justin suggests.

We agree, loading into the jeeps, whose seats are covered with towels in anticipation of today's dirty job. When we get back to our room, Tanya and I flip a coin to see who gets the shower first—and I win.

"I'll be as fast as I can," I promise. And I try to keep my word—but I do wash my hair twice, just to be sure there's no eau de dinosaur poop in it. And I slather myself with the peony lotion I have instead of my normal scentless aloe, just in case any of the stink might be lingering on my skin.

As Tanya showers, I rummage through the dresser, trying to remember where I put my bathing suit. I finally find it tucked away in one of the pockets of my suitcase with my extra socks. I'm just finishing pulling on a pair of denim shorts over it when Tanya comes in. She's already got her suit on, a blue and silver metallic bikini that reminds me of the Milky Way.

"Oh, that's so cute on you," she says when she sees my one-piece. "The gingham is very classic. You should put your hair in braids, like Dorothy in *The Wizard of Oz*."

I laugh and nod to her suit. "I love that material."

"Isn't it neat?" She dances back and forth, the bikini sparkling as the light catches it. "I wish I had a dress made out of this stuff. I love anything shiny." She pulls on a crocheted beach cover-up and shoves her feet into a pair of sandals. "After this morning, I am ready to do some relaxing," she sighs.

"The egg monitoring was awesome, though," I say. "I want to know more about how the sensors read everything. They must've designed the entire incubator system from scratch."

"If Wyatt messes up that chance for us . . . ," Tanya says, shaking her head, fire in her eyes.

"We'll make sure he doesn't," I assure her. "He's lazy, anyway. He just wants the prestige of being on the project, not any of the work. He'll probably stay out of our way and then try to take credit for everything afterward."

Tanya makes a disgusted noise. "It should be Amanda or Art in there with us, not him."

"Wyatt's stupid if he doesn't think there are cameras all over that room," I point out. "And with how afraid Dr. Wu is that we'll break something . . . what do you bet he's already watched the videos from our monitoring hour?"

Tanya's stormy expression clears. "Oh my God, you're right." She breaks into a wide smile. "Dr. Wu's going to be pissed," she singsongs.

"Maybe Wyatt won't even last the week," I say. "Anyway, let's get going so we can meet up with the others."

I grab a tube of sunscreen and my big black floppy hat, which makes Tanya laugh when she sees it.

"I am so glad I don't burn like you," she says as we leave our room and head toward the elevator. "But I wouldn't say no to having an excuse to wear a dramatic hat like that."

I grin, taking it off my head and tossing it to her as we walk. "Try it on."

She pops it on her head, posing. "How do I look?"

"Great," says Ronnie's voice behind us. Tanya beams at her as she and Amanda come out of their room.

"You two ready?" Tanya says.

"Yeah, we can walk over together. It's just across the bridge," Ronnie says.

Tanya hands me my hat as soon as we get outside, and I put it back on, grateful for the shade as the sun beats down on us.

"We have our weekly mentor dinner tonight," Amanda says. "I thought we could ask Beverly if we could sit with Bertie so we can tell her Claire's idea about painting patterns on the Gyrospheres and positive reinforcement for Pearl."

"It wasn't just my idea," I say. "We all worked on it. And you're the one who knows all about operant conditioning and brain scanning and pleasure centers."

"Shadowing Tim has been such an experience," Amanda says. "I came here thinking I wanted to go into research, but now I'm wondering if I want to do more fieldwork."

"Is there a way to do both?" Ronnie asks as we come to a stop in front of a large wrought-iron gate. She pulls the bar lock open and it swings open.

"Depends on where I put my focus," Amanda says. "Plus grad school."

"I don't know how you all do so many years in school," Ronnie says, shaking her head. "I'm excited about my four years at West Point, but I won't be able to take much longer."

"It is a lot," Tanya agrees. "And the expense . . ."

Amanda sighs in commiseration. "God, don't remind me. Every time I think about my student loan debt, I break out in a sweat."

"I'll be paying mine off from my grave," Tanya groans.

I wince, because I know that feeling. "Maybe we'll all luck out and get really great jobs," I say.

"I like your optimism, Claire," Amanda says.

"Maybe Mr. Masrani will hire all of us," Tanya jokes.

"I wish!" Amanda sighs. "Maybe by the time I graduate, I can get a Mosasaurus trainer job."

We take a brick path through the manicured landscape. To my eye—which is now accustomed to the wild and beautiful twining of chaos and order that is the jungle—it looks strange. The trees are set too far apart and the plants are trimmed just so, but when we turn the corner, I gasp, because the view of the rumbling falls crashing into a clear blue lagoon is the definition of wild and beautiful chaos. The rolling mountain range and deep rain forest that lie beyond the waterfalls lead to the roughest terrain on the island, the areas that are too hard for humans to navigate even on foot.

A dinosaur-free zone, by nature of topography. A terrain humans cannot traverse means a terrain dinosaurs would have too great an advantage on.

The boys are already there, sitting on some volcanic rocks near the shore, and they wave us over. The spray from the falls is a fine mist blowing in the wind, brushing across my skin like a chilly kiss as we pick our way across the rocky shore.

"Where's Eric?" I ask, when I see it's just Justin and Art.

"He said he wanted to chase the light," Art says. "I think he was going to hang out in the valley with the vets and get more footage."

"Yeah, the dinosaurs during golden hour would look great," Tanya says.

"Art was telling me we can jump off the top of the falls," Justin says. "There's a path carved into the side of the mountain over to the left." He points at the west side of the falls, and I squint, trying to make it out. Sure enough, there's a narrow brown line snaking up the wash of green algae and porous gray rock that make up the back of the falls.

"We did it last time we hung out here," Art says. "It's great. The water's really clear, and there are some cool rock formations you can see as you surface."

"I'm up for it," Tanya says.

"Me too," Amanda says.

"Ronnie?"

"Absolutely," she says with a cocky grin.

"Justin? Claire?"

I shake my head firmly. "I don't do tall things. And I *especially* do not do jumping from tall things."

"Fair enough," Art says.

"I'll stay down here with you, Claire," Justin says.

"You don't have to," I protest.

"It's fine," he says.

Tanya waggles her eyebrows at me, and I shoot her a quelling look that makes her grin wider before she trots off to join Ronnie.

"So the fear of flying, it's a height thing," he says as he pulls off his shirt, and it's just as distracting as I thought it would be. Not that I've been thinking about him shirtless.

Much.

"The flying part doesn't help, but yeah, mostly a heights thing," I say. I set my stuff down next to one of the huge boulders. I can hear my tablet beeping, and when I flip my bag open to grab it, my notebook falls out, and the pressed thistle flower from that day in the greenhouse slips from the pages.

He kneels down, scooping up the flower and the notebook, and my breath catches when his eyes meet mine.

"You kept it," he says.

"You gave it to me," I shoot back, and it makes him smile.

"I'll put it back," he offers. "I promise not to read any of your notes."

"Most of my notes are very boring," I say, scooting over to give him room to sit next to me on the rock. His foot knocks gently against my flip-flopped one, and I knock it back, watching him return the flower to its page in my notebook.

"Do you have tape?" he asks.

I lean over, grab my bag, and haul it up on the rock with us. He laughs when I unbuckle the front pouch and reveal the half-dozen carefully labeled bags of office supplies. "You were a Girl Scout, weren't you?" he asks.

"I got *all* the badges," I say seriously.

"I bet you sold all the cookies, too."

"I've never really liked half measures," I admit.

"I'm getting that," he says, taking the tape I offer him. He tapes the flower to the page, then holds out the roll. "Trade you for a pen?"

"What color?"

"Surprise me."

I choose purple, to match the thistle. I scoot a little closer to get a better view of what he's doing. Our thighs press together, his line of heat against mine. With sure, quick strokes, he sketches out a drawing of the flower next to the actual specimen, and then adds at the bottom: *Cirsium vulgare, common thistle flower* in handwriting that's even neater than mine—which is saying something.

"Hey, you're a good artist," I say.

"Oh, not really," he says dismissively. The tips of his ears turn red, and it's cute, because he's so confident most of the time.

"You are," I insist, because he is.

"It's not that hard when you've got an example right in front of you," he says.

I tap my foot with his. "Take the compliment," I say softly. "It's the truth, anyway."

He looks at me, and I look at him. The mist from the falls dances across my cheeks and his hand covers mine, our fingers weaving together. I can feel all of it: the twist of that *something* between us, the heat of his leg against mine, and the bone-deep understanding that in a moment, one of us is going to lean forward.

I know that if I look away, he won't push. He'll wait and he'll be honest and sweet and take little steps instead of big ones, because he keeps proving to me that's who he is.

And that's the reason I don't want to look away. That's the reason I lean forward instead.

19

Crash.

The sound startles me and I jerk back, away from Justin as Art makes his big jump and a huge swell of water breaks over the rocks near us. My pulse is thundering in my chest and my face goes hot all over when Justin gives my hand a quick squeeze before he pulls away.

"Hey, you guys, aren't you going to get in?" Art shouts when he surfaces.

Justin clears his throat. "Be right there!" he yells.

He shoots me an apologetic grin and we scramble off the rock, heading toward the water.

It's warm and so clear it almost doesn't seem real, the ground changing from rock to fine sand in one step. I'm about hip deep when Tanya jumps off the falls, shrieking the whole way down. When she bobs up in the pool below, she's beaming, and a big clump of algae is hanging off her head in two dripping strings, like green pigtails.

Ronnie laughs when she jumps off next and surfaces, plucking a few green globs off Tanya's head as they swim over to us.

"Are you sure you don't want to try, Claire?" Ronnie asks. "Even if you don't want to jump, the view from up there is stellar."

I glance over at the steep, twisting path that leads to the top of the falls. It looks wet and slippery and all kinds of dangerous.

"I'll stick to floating," I say firmly.

"Tanya, did you want to go up again and pick those flowers you saw?" Ronnie asks.

"Yeah!" Tanya says, paddling over to her, her green-and-blue-streaked hair floating in the water all around her. "I saw these aquatic flowers up there in the upper pool. I want to get a better look; I've never seen them before."

They head off, swimming across the pool and to the foot of the path to the falls. The rest of us continue to splash around, setting out to find out if the rumor Amanda heard is true—that there's a cave behind one of the waterfalls on the island. But each time we get near it, no matter what angle we approach the thundering spray from, the force of the water emptying into the pool is too powerful—there's no way through. Not unless you dare to dive very deep underneath.

"Maybe it's the waterfall in the valley that has the cave," Amanda suggests when we've finally given up and swum back to the shore.

I wrap myself in a towel, my hair dripping down my back.

"I hope not," I say. "Can you imagine if Pearl or Lovelace got it in their heads to go exploring? They'd get stuck."

Amanda giggles. "Is it weird that I kind of love how many problems the younger dinosaurs present?"

I shake my head. "I feel the same. I thought I knew what to expect here. And then here comes Pearl playing with the Gyrospheres and Lovelace getting herself all trapped. It makes them . . ."

"Vulnerable. Relatable," Amanda finished.

"Yeah," I say, a smile on my lips. "And I didn't expect that."

"Hey, we're gonna go to the top one more time, find Tanya and Ronnie, and then jump down," Art calls from the shore. "You up for it, Amanda?"

"Sure," she yells back.

"You okay here on your own?" Justin asks me.

"I think I'll survive," I laugh. "I've got some notes to take about my morning in the labs, anyway."

"We'll be twenty minutes, tops," Art says.

They splash back into the water, swimming off toward the falls path. I put my clothes back on and settle down on one of the big rocks farther from the shoreline and closer to the trees. I can see my friends reach the path and get out of the water, heading up into the distance, dark specks amid the green.

It's not as wet over here away from the shore, so I pull out Izzie's notebook, opening it once again to the map she drew of the island. While I can identify the landmarks, I don't get what the X's mean. They're scattered across the map in two different colors, red and blue. But they don't mark any place or landmark; it seems they were just drawn at random.

I don't get it. Izzie's notes are so meticulous, and several other maps in the notebook *don't* have X's. So what do they mean?

I flip past the map, searching for another diary entry among the endless Brachiosaurus statistics, but before I can find it, I hear a loud cracking noise behind me.

I turn, my heart knocking against my ribs as I peer into the thick maze of rain forest and mountain before me, trying to make out what made the noise.

There's something moving in there. Something big.

This whole side of the island is dinosaur free, which means it might be one of the native animals. I lick my lips, trying to decide. I want to look over my shoulder and see if Justin and the rest are within calling distance, but I know they won't hear me over the crash of the falls.

I edge forward until I've left the rocky shoreline for the wet press of leaves and soft branches under my feet. A yard ahead of me, I see it: a wet smear of blood dripping off a waxy leaf.

A pit begins to form in my stomach. I move forward, noticing that the sun's setting to my left as I venture deeper into the snarl of trees and vines. Ferns as tall as I am brush against my shoulders as I look for more signs of blood.

The light barely filters through the thick canopy of trees above me, and the green-tinged darkness that envelops the world makes everything look enchanted, unreal. But when I spot another smear of blood on a tree trunk, I frown.

Is that . . . a handprint?

I immediately dismiss it, even though shivers are trickling down my spine. It can't be. It's just the way it dried on the bark.

Crack.

I jump, my head whipping toward the sound to my left. I bite my lip to keep from crying out as I see a flash of purple, something fast and distinctly *human* streaking through the rich greens and browns of the rain forest. It's a blink-and-miss-it thing, and I'm doubting my eyes almost as soon as my brain catches up to what I *think* I may have seen.

I've just gotten myself convinced I was wrong—that there isn't another person here with me—when swift, unmistakable footsteps break through the jungle's hum, drip, and chirp.

I steel myself, my hands balling into fists, preparing to turn.

"Claire! There you are!"

Everything inside me turns over in relief when I hear Justin's voice. I turn and see him pushing through a bunch of vines just a few yards ahead of me. My knees almost buckle as all the energy that's been pumping through my body drains away.

His eyes narrow in concern when he gets a look at my face. "Hey," he says, reaching out and touching my shoulder gently. "Are you okay?"

I shake my head. "Sorry. It's just . . . I saw blood. Did you see it coming in?"

"No," he says. "But I wasn't looking for it, I was looking for you. I probably missed it. Do you think someone's hurt in here?"

"It was smeared on a leaf and then on a tree farther in. I thought there was a hurt animal. But I think . . ." I pause, turning back to look at the spot where I swear someone passed in front of me.

But no. It can't have been. Unless one of the park employees is playing tricks on me.

"It must've been an animal," I say. "Maybe one of the Compsognathuses snuck into this side? I know they like to bite. Maybe they got a bird or something."

"If it's a Compsognathus skittering around, we should get out of her way," Justin says. "They're small, but they can get chompy when they're in a mood. We can let the vets know so they'll be on the lookout. I'm sure they have trackers on them."

I smile shakily. I feel all wobbly as I put one foot in front of another, his arm still around me.

"I'm sorry I missed your jump," I say.

"Possibly injured animal is much more important," Justin says easily, and we begin to pick our way back to the shore through the forest. He's helping me over a huge fallen palm tree when my heel crunches against something.

I stop, bending down to look. Underneath a few soggy brown fern leaves is a memory card. The kind that goes into a video camera. It's got a spiderweb of cracks across the plastic.

"What's that?"

"Some sort of memory card," I say, wiping it off on my shorts. "Looks pretty new."

"Weird," Justin says. He waggles his eyebrows. "Maybe you've found some top-secret information. You'll have to ask Eric about it."

"Wouldn't it be wild to find something from the original park out here?" I ask, pocketing the memory card and ducking beneath a particularly tall fern bed. "Do you think they kept stuff from the original park? I mean, the gates are modeled after the original ones . . . and there's got to be existing infrastructure—at least underground what was part of the original park."

"I think the command center is in the same place Hammond's was," Justin says as we finally reach the edge of the rain forest, the foliage thinning. "Just rebuilt."

"Oh, see, I thought Hammond's original command center is where the Educational Center is now," I say, and wave as I spot our group in the distance.

"There you are! We thought you'd been lured away by some jungle cat!" Tanya declares when she catches sight of us emerging from the rain forest.

"There aren't any jungle cats," I scoff, though I can't help but think about whatever streaked in front of my jeep the other night, nearly causing me to crash. And whatever the heck that flash of purple was just now. Are my eyes playing tricks on me? Maybe it's just poor lighting and my own fear that made me think it looked like a human.

My rationalizations sound weak even to myself, but I try to put it all out of my mind as we gather our stuff and head back to our rooms before we eat. I have to take another shower to get some of the algae out of my hair, and I'm running late for dinner, so I tell Tanya to go ahead without me.

By the time I get to the dining room where the tables are set up with our mentors, the rest of the girls are already with Bertie and the food's already been served.

"There's Claire!" Amanda says, waving me over.

"I'm so sorry I'm late," I say. I see that there's a mound of lasagna and salad on my plate, and my stomach grumbles gratefully.

"It's okay—I heard it was manure processing day," Bertie says.

The table titters. "We got the job done," Ronnie says with a note of pride.

"I'm used to compost," Tanya says cheerfully. "Smells like home!"

"I like your attitude," Bertie says.

For a while, it's mostly just the clink of forks and glasses and *can you pass the garlic bread?* as we all attack our dinners. We definitely need the fuel after the day we've had. When our plates are clean, Bertie sets her fork down and says, "I believe Beverly said you requested this time with me because you had something to propose?"

"We do," Amanda says. "Claire, do you want to take it?"

I nod. We practiced our pitch together over lunch, just so we'd be prepared. "The four of us have been brainstorming ways to help Pearl," I say. "And we think we came up with a good one. We wanted to see if you think it would work or not."

"What do you propose?" Bertie asks, taking a sip of water.

"Stop trying to distract her completely from the Gyrospheres," Amanda says, taking the lead like we practiced. "And instead, start training her to differentiate the Gyrospheres by painting patterns on some that are visually appealing to her. That way, she'll be attracted to the patterned balls and not want to chase after the spheres that have people in them."

"We got the idea—well, Claire did—from the surfers who use striped boards to 'hide' from sharks," Tanya explains.

"This is just flipping the idea. The anti-camouflage," Ronnie adds.

For a long moment, Bertie just regards us, and then she smiles. "I must say, I'm impressed. That's a clever idea."

"Do you think it'd work?" I ask.

"I think it's definitely worth trying," Bertie says. "I'll have to consult with the vets about the best visual and color choices to make when creating patterns for the balls, but . . . this could be very helpful to Pearl's development. I will draft a proposal this week and get it sent in."

"Really?" Amanda squeaks.

"Really," Bertie says. "And I will make sure to credit all of you as the source of this idea."

I feel like laughing and hugging Bertie at the same time.

I settle on beaming at the rest of the girls, who look just as excited.

As dinner finishes and the adults get up to leave, Bertie bids us good night and thanks us again for sharing our idea.

I wait until she's walked halfway across the room before I stand up. "Be right back," I tell the girls.

"Hey, Bertie," I call, hurrying up to her through the press of tables and people. We're out of earshot of my friends, which is what I wanted.

"Yes?" she asks.

"Do you know an Izzie?" I ask—because how else am I going to find out what happened to her if I don't? "Her full name's Isobel, probably? She would've come here in January to work with the Brachiosauruses. Right around when Olive needed to have surgery on her throat."

"Hmm, no, I don't remember anyone by that name," Bertie says.

"But I'm not the best person to ask. I wasn't on the island during that ordeal. We were preparing for the Triceratops transport at that time, and there was a big storm. It delayed everything, so I ended up coming to Isla Nublar later in the spring."

"A storm?" I ask. That's what Wyatt mentioned in his phantom intern story. Odd . . . but that has to be him just making things up. The more real details you put in a lie, the harder it is to spot.

"It's an island; there are always storms," Bertie says. "Anyway, you might ask Tim," she continues. "He'd know old staff members better than me. He was part of the original team that came over with Olive and Agnes."

"I'll do that," I say. "And thanks for listening to our idea."

"Of course, Claire," Bertie says. "I'm glad you girls took the initiative and brought it to me."

Over her shoulder, I can see Tim talking to Mr. Masrani, who claps him on the back before Tim turns to leave the deck.

"If you'll excuse me, I'm gonna go ask Tim my question," I tell Bertie, who nods.

I hurry after the vet—he's already halfway down the hall before I catch up with him.

"Dr. O'Donnell!"

Tim turns, flashing a quick smile when he sees me. "Hi . . . which one are you?" he asks. "Forgive me. I don't think you've been on assignment with me yet."

"It's okay," I say. "I'm Claire. I just have a quick question for you."

"Sure," he says.

"I'm wondering if you could tell me where I could find Izzie," I say. "The Izzie who worked with the Brachiosauruses when Olive had her surgery."

When I mentioned the name to Bertie, there was no ripple of recognition in her face. No tension or worry. But Tim?

His thin lips twist and his ruddy face falls for a second; then he seems to realize it, and a cool mask falls over his features. "I'm afraid I can't recall an Izzie. And I was second surgeon on Olive's case, so I'd know." He shifts nervously from foot to foot.

His ruddy face reddens even further, his ears joining in on the crimson party. He's a bad liar, this guy.

"I'm . . . I'm wondering who told you an Izzie worked for us. Maybe she goes by another name?"

He's trying to cover now. I smile, hoping it doesn't look too fake as the corners of my mouth tremble. "You know what, that's probably it. I probably got the name wrong," I say. "My sister, she said one of her sorority sisters had gotten a job here in the early days and told me to look her up. But I'm *terrible* with names. I really need to start doing some mnemonic devices or something."

The tightness in his face begins to ease. "I've heard those are helpful," he says. "Anything else?"

"No, I'm sorry to have bothered you," I say. "I'll check with my sister for the right name."

"Not a problem," he says, but I can't tell if I've convinced him or if he's still suspicious of me.

"I'll let you go," I say.

He gives me a nod and walks away, leaving me teetering on an uncertain seesaw, wondering, wondering. . . .

And then, at the end of the hall, he turns, shooting me a curious look before he disappears through the door.

My stomach sinks.

Crap.

I've stumbled onto something. I just can't quite fit the pieces of it together, and now that Bertie's mentioned a storm . . . my mind's full of wild possibilities.

I need more information. Fast. Because I've just tipped off the adults that I know something. Tim isn't going to keep quiet.

I need to find out who Izzie is. *Where* she is. And I think I know how.

20

The next morning, as Tanya and I take the elevator down to the labs, I'm trying to figure out the best way to get the information I want from Wyatt. If there's some kernel of truth to his phantom intern story, maybe that's why bringing up Izzie's name seemed to spook Dr. O'Donnell so much. Was she an intern and not a staff scientist, as I assumed from her notes? She mentioned that she'd gone to Yale in one of the entries, but it didn't occur to me that she might have still been in school when she was writing in the notebook.

What part of Wyatt's story is true? Some of it? All? Or none? Am I making too much of a leap thinking Izzie was an intern?

But I can't shake Dr. O'Donnell's spooked look when I mentioned her name. *Something* is going on here, even if it isn't as nefarious as Wyatt's tall tale implies. And wherever Izzie went, she left her notebook behind. That's suspicious in itself. A person like that *never* leaves her notebook behind. Not someone who likes taking notes as much as she does. I know, because I'm the same way.

The elevator dings, and the doors slide open. But instead of Wyatt standing there, waiting for us as he has the last week—he seems to get some weird, perverse pleasure in getting here earlier than us, like it's a power play or something—an Asian woman with a pixie cut and houndstooth heels I'd covet forever is standing there.

"Which one of you is Claire?" she asks.

"Um, me," I say.

"Ms. Jamison would like to see you," she says. "She asked that I bring you to her."

"Okay," I say. "Tanya, can you tell Dr. Wu that I'll be late?"

"Why don't you tell Dr. Wu he'll have to do without Claire for today," the woman corrects me, a bland smile on her face that does *nothing* to make me feel better. Dread seeps through my stomach as Tanya shoots me a quizzical look.

"I'll see you at lunch, I guess," I tell her.

"See you then," she says.

"I'm Miranda," the woman says as she steps inside the elevator and hits the button for the very top floor of the command center. "I run Ms. Jamison's day-to-day."

"Nice to meet you," I say.

I want to ask her why Beverly wants to see me, but I'm pretty sure that's what she—and Beverly—want me to do. Because I know. Oh, I know.

I asked too many questions. And now I'm being brought in to figure out just what I know.

Will they kick me out? Are my bags packed and already waiting for me in Beverly's office?

The elevator ride is totally silent, and the higher we climb, the sicker I feel.

I'm a rule follower. I'll be the first to admit it.

But there's a streak in me that's part ruthless, part righteous—a twist of opposites, stronger together than apart. It's why I defied Oscar when it came to Pearl. It's why I asked about Izzie, even though I obviously shouldn't have.

The elevator doors slide open when we reach the top floor, and Miranda leads me down a long hall and gestures to the waiting area in front of the corner office. "She'll be with you shortly," she says before disappearing inside the office, her truly enviable heels clicking against the shiny bamboo floor.

I force myself to breathe normally even though my heart's knocking against my chest. This is part of the game: she wants me to sweat. To worry.

I admire Beverly. She's made her way to the top, and I'm just beginning at the bottom.

But she shouldn't underestimate me. I press my lips together and breathe deep, steeling myself, preparing myself for the next move. Like a chess game.

Finally, after what feels like forever, the door in front of me opens.

"Ms. Jamison will see you now," says Miranda.

I try to look calm as I walk through the door and into Beverly's office. It's all white—not in a soothing way, but cold and sterile. Her desk is white, her office chair is white, even the chair set in front of her desk—the chair I'm clearly supposed to sit in—is white. In contrast, she is a wash of blue silk in the pale sea.

"Claire, come in."

It's like being pulled into a high-tech dean's office. I know exactly why I'm here and so does she, but I'm guessing she's going to dance around it, which makes this even more panic-inducing. I don't want to be in trouble.

But I also want to do the right thing. And if I've accidentally stumbled onto some sort of conspiracy, if Izzie's journal is the key to something . . .

I don't know. There's a hypothesis forming in my mind that I don't quite want to voice, because it means all sorts of bad things. Not just for Izzie. But for me. For Jurassic World.

I shift the strap of my bag on my shoulder, resisting the urge to pat the place where Izzie's notebook is tucked.

"How are you enjoying your internship?" Beverly asks, folding her hands in front of her. She's wearing an enormous amber ring, which shines against all the white.

"I'm loving it," I say. "I'm learning so much."

"I'm glad," Beverly says. "I like to check in with everyone at about the four-week mark, which we've just passed. See how they're feeling."

"I'm feeling great," I say.

"And you're doing great," she assures me. "Every person you've worked with has reported how pleased they are with your performance."

"That's nice to hear."

I'm frustrating her, with my non-answers to her non-questions.

She wants me to reveal something. But I'm not going to. Not unless she reveals something first.

"You've been quite the standout from the start, Claire," she says, picking her words carefully. "Mr. Masrani himself was very taken with your personal essay, and I was pleased to see your goals. We need more women in politics. It's nice to see a young woman who knows what she wants so early."

"Thank you," I say.

"I'm sure you know that Masrani Corporation has a very far reach," Beverly goes on. "Jurassic World is just the tip of a very large iceberg. Mr. Masrani has interests in thousands of companies in hundreds of industries. And he has the ear of the men and women who run those companies and industries. The ones who do things like fund political campaigns and form super PACs."

"Mr. Masrani is a man of varied interests," I say, keeping my voice level.

"And he is a friend to many," Beverly says. "He could be a friend to you, Claire. A valuable friend, to someone with your political ambitions."

There it is: an oh-so-subtle dig and threat.

"But friends help each other," Beverly continues. "They protect each other."

I straighten, because Beverly's just confirmed something without realizing it: the Masrani Corporation *needs* protection from something.

"I'm sure you believe in protecting your friends," Beverly says, that snake-oil-salesman smile on her face. "And staying out of friends' private business. Because if you don't believe in that, opportunities—incredible, life-changing opportunities—could be lost. Do you understand?"

"I do," I say.

"Excellent," Beverly says, getting up smoothly, her amber ring catching the light. "I'm glad. We'll just forget all about this, won't we? No more questions about the past. The past should stay in the past. This place, this park, our people . . . we are all about the future."

It's such an obvious and dismissive sales line, it makes my skin crawl, like I've just flipped a log and revealed the slugs and bugs beneath it.

"I won't take up any more of your time," Beverly says. "I'm so glad we had this little talk about your future. With Mr. Masrani's help, it'll be a great one."

"I hope so," I say with a smile, and she escorts me out of her office and I walk numbly down the hall, struggling to keep the smile on my face, just in case. I don't let it fall from my lips until I get to the elevator and the doors shut.

Beverly thinks she's warned me off, but what she's actually done is give me the bread crumbs I need. Tim must have gone straight to her as soon as I asked him about Izzie. And for her to threaten my entire future . . . whatever I've stumbled on by finding Izzie's journal must be big. *Very* big. Does Mr. Masrani know Beverly brought me in? Did he tell her to talk to me . . . to threaten me?

Sickness churns in my stomach as the elevator climbs to the main lobby. There's a lot I don't know, and I have even more questions now than I did when I found the notebook. But there is one thing I do know: I can't let this go. Not until I find out what happened to her—and why everyone freaks out when I bring up her name.

The elevator doors open, and I adjust the strap of my bag as I step out, catching sight of a blond buzz-cut just ahead of me.

Wyatt.

"Hey!" I call out. I slip my hand inside my bag and turn on my tablet's recorder, leaving the flap open so the speaker can catch the sound.

When he sees it's me, he turns around and keeps walking. I hurry to catch up with him.

"Wait," I say. "I want to talk to you."

Wyatt's mouth twitches. "Going to lecture me about breathing wrong near the eggs, like Tanya did yesterday?" he asks.

"I want to know how you found out about the first round of interns," I say, because beating around the bush has never been a talent of mine.

He shrugs nonchalantly. "Like I said, there have always been rumors."

"Please," I say. "You've done nothing but brag about your con-nections since you got on the island. So where did you hear the *real* dirt from . . . not the stuff from the conspiracy websites?"

He doesn't say anything for a moment, then jerks his chin toward a corner of the lobby with chairs grouped around a small table. I take a seat across from him, setting my bag on the floor, close enough to keep recording our conversation. I don't know if Tanya has come up from lab duty yet, so I've got to make him spill fast.

"Come on, Wyatt," I say. "I know you've got inside information. Is it from your dad? Did you overhear something?"

"Why are you so curious all of a sudden?" he asks. "You totally dismissed me the last time I brought it up."

"Maybe I found something that confirms your story has some truth to it," I say.

His eyes widen and he leans forward in his seat, startling me a little. I flinch backward, and luckily, he doesn't get any closer to invading my space. "What did you find?" he asks, his voice suddenly urgent and interested.

"That's my business," I say. "Or at least, it is until you tell me what *you* know."

"That's completely unfair," he complains.

I shrug. "You've got info, I've got info. Someone has to share first. And it's not going to be me."

He presses his lips together, and I can practically see the wheels in his head turning, wondering if he can outwait me in what boils down to a game of chicken.

"Fine," he says, caving just as I hoped he would. "Last year, around Christmas, my dad was taking a lot of meetings. One day I was in his office and I saw a list of names—names of interns for Jurassic World. I asked him about it because I wanted to apply, and he got all pissed and told me I was imagining stuff. I hate it when he does things like that, so I waited until he was out of the country on a business trip and I broke into his office and took photos of the list," he says, and I can't stop my eyebrows from rising.

"You have their names?" I ask.

"Yep," he says with pride. "I contacted a few of them when the rumors about the storm and the evacuation hit online."

"What did they say when you asked about the internship?" I ask.

"Every one of them gave me similar lines," Wyatt says, smiling in that superior way of his. "'I've never been to Isla Nublar. During that time I was interning at . . . ,' and then they'd give me a company name. Well, I kept track of all the companies they supposedly interned at. You trace the money, and they're all under the Masrani Global umbrella."

A cover-up. I look at Wyatt. "You really don't like your dad, do you?" I ask. Does this guy like *anybody*? Everyone seems to just be a means to an end with him.

Wyatt snorts. "What tipped you off?"

I shake my head and change the subject. "So where's the list?" I ask. "Were you able to track them all down?"

"Nah, I lost interest after a while," Wyatt says. "I got on the crew team and didn't think about it much until I applied to Bright Minds."

Typical. Or is Wyatt just leaning into his lazy image to throw me off the scent of something bigger? He seemed *very* interested when I mentioned having information of my own. Sure enough, he leans back in his chair, going for casual as he says, "So, I showed you mine, time to show me yours."

My lip curls at the innuendo. "Cut out the misogynistic grossness," I say.

"I see someone's taken a women's studies class." Wyatt grins meanly. "Come on, we had a deal."

"Yeah, about that," I say. "I think I'm going to keep my information to myself. My women's studies class taught me the worth of my own work—and how guys like to take credit for it." I smile, and I put a sharp edge to it, just like he did. "And you're going to show me that list of intern names."

His eyes narrow to slits. "Why would I do that?"

"Oh, because I recorded you," I say, gesturing to the tablet in my bag between us. He lunges for it, but it's too late. It's automatically uploaded to my personal databank, and I tell him so. His fingers curl around the tablet, his eyes glowing furiously at me, but I hold my ground.

"I don't think your dad or Mr. Masrani would appreciate your admission that you took photos of private company documents," I say. "Why don't we find out for sure?"

"You're blackmailing me?" he demands, incredulous.

"That's not the nicest way of putting it, but I guess so," I say. "I mean, *you're* not doing anything with the list . . . are you?"

He's fuming. He leans forward menacingly, trying to use his size to psych me out. "You'll regret this," he says.

"List, please," I say, trying to look bored.

"Fine," he snarls. He grabs his own tablet from his bag, pulls up a file, and thrusts it at me.

I take a screenshot with my tablet and back it up instantly. I don't have time to glance at the dozen or so names, not when his nostrils are flaring with anger like that. People don't get the better of him often, I take it. He'd better get used to it.

"Happy?" he demands.

"Now I am," I say. "Don't worry, I got what I wanted. Your

dad doesn't have to know you're a snoop and plotting—probably badly—against him, for whatever reason."

"You underhanded little—"

"Careful," I warn, just before the elevator doors open, and Dr. Wu comes sweeping out—followed by Mr. Masrani.

Instantly, Wyatt's entire demeanor changes. His cheeks lose their red flush as a smile replaces his glare. "Mr. Masrani—hello, sir!" He doesn't even bother to greet Dr. Wu.

"Hi, Dr. Wu, Mr. Masrani," I say.

"Wyatt, Claire." Mr. Masrani smiles. I feel a flash of nervousness because I don't know how much Mr. Masrani knows. Was Beverly acting on her own steam when she pulled me into her office, or under his orders? Can I trust him, or is he part of all this?

"Where were you today, Claire?" Dr. Wu demands.

"I'm sorry, Dr. Wu," I say. "Ms. Jamison needed to talk to me." I watch Mr. Masrani carefully as I say this, but there's no ripple of recognition in his face at my words.

Dr. Wu sighs, shooting a disapproving look at Mr. Masrani. "Tell your intern director to stop taking my interns!" he says.

"Oh, so now you *like* having the interns around," Mr. Masrani says, needling Dr. Wu. I get the idea he likes to do that.

"They have performed adequately," Dr. Wu acknowledges, and Mr. Masrani chuckles.

"You're too hard on them, Doctor!"

"It gives them something to strive for," Dr. Wu says dryly. "You want to be the best, don't you, Claire?"

"I do," I say. And I mean it.

"See? My way of teaching works better than yours," Dr. Wu says triumphantly. "It fosters ambition."

"And mine fosters inspiration," Mr. Masrani shoots back, amused. "Come now, Doctor, let's not argue. We have a lot to prepare for in the next week."

My ears prick up, and I can see Wyatt standing to attention as well.

"Is a new dinosaur finally getting delivered?" Wyatt asks. For the last week, the rumor has been flying around the island.

"It's a little more complicated than that," Mr. Masrani says, which is not really a *no* or a *yes*. With about eight months before the park opens, they need to be moving the rest of the Sorna dinosaurs in pretty soon if they follow the same adjustment time line the transported herbivores do. But maybe it's a carnivore, and most of the carnivores aren't herd animals, so the protocol could be different. I want desperately to ask, but will I be crossing a line?

I'll never know if I don't try.

"Are there many dinosaurs left on Isla Sorna?" I ask.

"There are enough," Mr. Masrani says. "Sadly, one of the greatest threats posed to the dinosaurs on Nublar and Sorna after Dr. Hammond's death weren't each other, but the poachers who might be bold enough to seek the islands out now that their existence is known. After the islands were purchased, we of course put measures into place to prevent this. And once the park opens and the public sees all the park has to offer, there will be no question of the importance of the dinosaurs' place in the world."

"And the dinosaur you're bringing over, is it another herbivore?"

Mr. Masrani smiles and shakes his head, and a frisson of electricity goes through me.

"So it's a carnivore?" Wyatt asks. "Which one?"

Dr. Wu rolls his eyes when Mr. Masrani doesn't answer. "Why be so mysterious, Simon?" he asks. "They'll be asked to stay in their rooms the night we transport the asset into the quarantine habitat anyway. You keep telling me how smart they are—surely they'll figure it out."

"It's happening soon?" Wyatt asks eagerly—a little *too* eagerly. What is he up to? I'm on to him now. Beneath the lazy jerk act, there's someone calculating, someone who holds grudges and makes plans.

"Next week," Mr. Masrani says, his eyes sparkling like he can't stand to keep the secret either. Considering how much enjoyment he takes in our awe over the park, it's kind of amazing he's kept his plans for Jurassic World under wraps for so long. He likes to share his joy. "The first Velociraptor will be transported from Sorna to Nublar."

"There's more than one Raptor?" I ask.

"There are," Mr. Masrani says. "But transporting them together . . . would not be wise." He chooses his words carefully, like there might be a story behind them. "Moving the Sorna carnivores to their permanent habitats on the island here can be a slow, challenging process. There are territories established by our Nublar carnivores, and while for obvious reasons the carnivores aren't in the Gyrosphere Valley, the herbivores' presence still affects things."

"The smell," Wyatt says. "The carnivores can smell them."

"When the wind's right," Mr. Masrani says. "A hungry Raptor who's disoriented from a boat trip gets a whiff of a Gallimimus and they'll spend the night trying to find a way through their quarantine paddock to get to it."

"There isn't a way out, right?" I ask, and Mr. Masrani laughs.

"Of course not," he says. "The concern here isn't so much that the carnivores will break through all the safeguards keeping them from the herbivores, it's more about the Velociraptors adjusting well to their new habitat and not harming themselves by trying to claw through or scale a wall they haven't yet learned is impossible to breach. Transport from Sorna is stressful on the dinosaurs. The vets have found that it's best to keep them very quiet and isolated the first few days in the quarantine habitat so they can adjust in peace. That means that after transport and delivery, they're left alone for a few days, but monitored via sensors and cameras."

Dr. Wu's pocket beeps, and he takes his phone out. "I will answer your Raptor questions tomorrow," he says. "I really must get back to my work, which is why I was escorting Mr. Masrani out."

"He's always kicking me out before the fun stuff happens," Mr. Masrani complains with an exaggerated sigh.

"Yes, making the fusion bandages is *so* much fun," Dr. Wu drawls. "Go! All of you! I have delicate chemicals to combine."

Dismissed, we follow Mr. Masrani out of the lobby, the blue-and-gray jeep I drove over this morning sitting there in the parking lot like a temptation.

Everything in me is screaming impatiently that I need to get somewhere alone so I can start going through the intern list. Is

Izzie on it? If I have her full name, I can at least search for her on-line, figure out where she went—and what happened to her after she left the island.

"Sir, I'd love to talk to you about some future plans," Wyatt says. "Would you mind if I drive with you?"

"Not at all," Mr. Masrani says. "Claire?"

"I promised Bertie I'd come help paint the first set of play Gy-rospheres for Pearl," I say, which is true, but I still have a good two hours before she expects me.

"I heard about your project," Mr. Masrani says. "Well done for taking the initiative."

My cheeks redden. "Thank you, sir," I say. "I'll leave you and Wyatt to your discussion."

"Good luck with the spheres," Mr. Masrani calls as he walks away. "I look forward to watching the trainers try them out on Pearl."

I gulp, praying that our idea will actually work. Otherwise we've wasted a bunch of other people's time.

Wyatt hangs behind while Mr. Masrani gets in his SUV. "I'll be right there, sir," he says in that cheerful voice that's all kinds of fake. Then he turns back to me, his volume lowering to a hiss. "You think you can threaten me?"

"Well, I don't *think* I can. I know I can. Because I just did," I say, refusing to be cowed. That's how guys like him work. They steamroll over everyone by using their connections or their size or the fact that older men in charge might see them as their younger selves. But when a guy like this meets someone who plays the game even better? And it's a *woman*? He can't handle it.

"You think that list is all I've got on the interns?" Wyatt sneers. "You're an idiot if you believe that."

I shrug. "Whatever else you know, I can find out on my own," I say. "Unlike you, I won't get distracted from research because of the crew team."

A muscle tic jerks in his jaw, and I meet his eyes, projecting an icy disinterest that makes it jerk again.

"You better get back to your sucking up," I say, nodding toward Mr. Masrani's car.

"This isn't over," Wyatt says, a threatening note in his voice.

"It really is," I reply. "Even if you insist on talking like a movie villain." My little joke makes me smile, which seems to be the last straw—he whirls around, stalks to Mr. Masrani's car, and gets in.

I wait for them to drive away; then I wave at Mr. Masrani, just because I know it'll piss Wyatt off. I'm about to grab my tablet to go through the list of names I got out of Wyatt, when a truck pulls up next to mine. I look over and smile when I see that Bertie's inside.

"Hey, Claire," she says. "Are you on assignment today?"

"I got excused early," I say.

"You're free, then?"

"Yeah."

"Want to help me out? I've got some heavy lifting to do, and Sarah tweaked her back, so I'm down a woman."

As eager as I am to get to the list, helping Bertie is just as intriguing. Plus, I definitely owe her since she's taking our Gyrosphere idea seriously. The list will have to wait.

"I'd love to." I grab my bag and get out of my jeep and into her truck. She backs away from the command center, and instead of heading toward the herbivore habitats, she takes the other way— toward the carnivore paddocks.

I don't want to hope. They've kept us away from the carnivores our whole internship so far. I get it, I do, but . . .

"Where are we going?" I ask as we drive down the road, the landscape thickening from manicured jungle to wildness in a blink of the eye.

Bertie grins. "We're going to see Rexy."

21

"Seriously?" I almost squeak the word. "The T. rex?"

"Yep. It's my turn to feed her."

Every single hair on my arms rises at the thought of her. Rexy. I didn't realize that's what they call her. I've heard her roar, but seeing her is another story. How close will we get to be to her? Is it safe?

Does it even matter, if I get to see her?

I mean, of course it does. My mom will freak if a T. rex bites a chunk out of me. But Bertie wouldn't let me come if there were even a sliver of a chance of that happening.

"It's lunchtime for her," Bertie explains. "Today is a little special, because it's the day we'll be giving her the treated meat. We add a mix of amino acids and other nutrients monthly to make sure we're keeping her healthy and strong."

"And she eats it fine, not bothered by the change in taste? Or does that matter?"

"Taste definitely matters. She has her preferences, just like any animal. But our scientists have done a great job at masking any difference in taste," Bertie says. "Now if they could only figure out how to make a cough syrup that doesn't taste gross . . ."

I laugh. "That would be *quite* the scientific achievement."

Bertie takes a right, the light around us darkening as the jungle deepens and the road becomes the only spot of civilization in the wild. We're getting farther and farther away from the populated— well, the human-populated—part of the park.

"We'll stop at the quarantine paddock first. That's where her meat is prepped. We can take a little tour, if you want, before we go to her paddock."

"Is the quarantine paddock where the Raptor will be held when she's transported from Sorna?" I ask.

"Where did you hear about the Raptor?" Bertie asks. "Is the island rumor mill already spinning?"

"I ran into Mr. Masrani after my lab assignment," I say. "He was hyped up about it."

Bertie smiles indulgently. "He always is," she says. "Every single time a dinosaur is transported from Sorna to Nublar, after they're settled in and left alone to adjust, he holds a champagne toast up at the very top of the educational center. Everyone is required to go."

"That sounds fancy."

"It's a nice little tradition," Bertie says. "A time for all of us invested in these animals to come together and celebrate."

"Have you ever worked with the Raptors on Sorna?" I ask as she steers around a clump of vines that haven't been trimmed back from the road. This part of the park is so dense and thick—and isolated. Which makes sense. You don't want dinosaurs in quarantine getting all excited by people smells or noise from Main Street.

Bertie shook her head. "The Raptors are part of a special program within the park. I've done some observing and brainstorming with the trainers, but a lot of what they're doing right now is classified—and even I don't have the clearance to know."

"There are a lot of secrets here," I say, thinking about Izzie and the throat infections.

"With discovery come secrets," Bertie says. "As well as the threat of them getting exposed to the wrong people. People who might want to exploit or harm our dinosaurs."

We pull up to the paddock, which has a large sign that says QUARANTINE in front.

The quarantine paddock also has a two-story building in front of the towering cement walls that close off the space from the rest of the jungle. The walls are so high it seems like the clouds might brush the tops of them on a stormy day. It's imposing, this paddock. It's all about security and reinforced cement and steel, and it's such a contrast to the wide, open spaces and beauty of the Gyrosphere Valley. There's no nature here, no sense of wildness merged with science.

This is human engineering at its finest—and maybe at its most protective. This is a place designed to keep people from getting in—and dinosaurs from getting out.

"There are herbivore quarantine paddocks too, but this place was made specially for the carnivores," Bertie explains as we get out and go inside. The building is like the other training centers, with a break room to hang out in and a room full of supplies on the ground floor.

"What's on the top floor?" I ask.

"Sleeping quarters," Bertie says. "Once there are regular hatches on Nublar, the caretakers will need to be with the baby dinosaurs from their first moments so that they'll associate us and our scents with *home* and *friend*. It's a round-the-clock job when you're working with the young ones—helping mold them. Though sometimes I think working with the herbivores . . . it's changed me more than it's changed them."

"They put things into perspective, don't they?" I ask.

"They do," Bertie says. "Come on, I'll show you the yard before we load up the meat."

She leads me out of the supply room and through a long tunnel with spooky yellow light. There's a wheelbarrow full of what looks like aloe leaves in the middle of the tunnel, blocking the way, and Bertie sighs, rolling her eyes. "The vets are always leaving a mess," she said, grabbing the cart and wheeling it toward the end of the tunnel.

"Will you get the code for me?" she asked. "Seven zero three one."

I punch it into the keypad next to the door for her and the reinforced door clicks open. I hold it so she can get the wheelbarrow out of the tunnel and then follow her into the yard, which is slightly shadowed by the huge walls. Here, the ground has been leveled and stripped of all plants. It's just dirt and enormous metal walkways that crisscross the yard above our heads.

I tilt my head up to look at them. They look almost like cages—to protect the humans from the dinosaurs.

Bertie catches my gaze. "Obviously, we do most of our work with the herbivores in their habitats, but with conditioning and treating the carnivores, there have to be some very strict precautions. The walkways protect the caretakers and vets and allow them to move freely above the yard to observe and direct when the smaller carnivores are running around. There are two holding pens that are connected to this yard, there and there." She points to the end of the training yard, where two steel doors—the kind that slide up, not out—lead to the pens. "That's where our Raptor will be spending her first night on the island."

"You don't let her run around?"

"It's best to keep any animal that's undergone sedation and a boat trip quiet for the first twenty-four hours on land," Bertie says. "Otherwise, you're dealing with a lot of dinosaur vomit."

"I'm not sure I can think of anything grosser—or scarier—than a dinosaur with motion sickness," I say.

"There's not enough ginger pills in the world," Bertie joked. "So there's also an emergency hatch over there." She nods to the indentation in the cement on the wall opposite us. "It rises when triggered."

"But what if the dinosaur gets out?" I ask, alarmed.

"There are layers and layers of protection and protocol to prevent that. The engineers are finishing up construction on a mini-paddock next to ours now. So if the hatch is ever opened when there are guests in the park, the dinosaur will just end up in another controlled environment. No threat to anyone. The emergency hatch is just in case of a natural disaster—bad weather out here can be deadly. And so can fires."

"And what about over there, across the yard?" I point. "That's definitely not an escape hatch." On three sides of the yard, there are large, thick cement walls closing us in, protecting us, but the north wall is a fence. A really sturdy-looking fence, with a big gate at the center, but still a fence that bisects the space. I can see walls on the far side too. Another controlled environment. But beyond the fence is thick jungle, not carefully flattened dirt like in the training yard.

"That leads to the paddock itself," Bertie says. "We've got about twenty hectares of space, divided between the training yard and the attached paddock. We're in the training and treatment yard. It's where the trainers and vets do their work with the dinosaurs. The paddock is where the dinosaurs who are in quarantine live and recover. They heal and adjust faster if they're in familiar surroundings."

"So the whole setup is dual purpose," I say.

"Yes. The trainers use the yard to get the dinosaur adjusted and to keep recovering dinosaurs from getting bored. You can hit a button, the gate to the paddock rises, and they're rewarded with a controlled run through the jungle. You drop meat at the very end of the habitat, which is a good chunk of space, and you see how long it takes them to sniff it out. It's like a game."

"A dinosaur gold star for a job well done," I say.

"That's a good comparison," Bertie says. "I'd raise the gate and let you look into the paddock, but it's going to take the two of us to get all of Rexy's lunch loaded into the truck, and we shouldn't make her wait."

"That's okay," I say. "Maybe another time."

We go back through the tunnel that leads to the supply house, and we spend the next twenty minutes using a wheelbarrow to cart Rexy's special lunch from the big fridge out to the truck. It's a heavy, bloody load of goat parts. I have to grit my teeth and swallow a few times while we load it because, well, *gross.* By the time we're on the road again, I'm feeling kind of grubby, but all that fades when we head to the area where Justin and I heard the roar and arrive in front of her paddock. It's bigger than the quarantine paddock. The walls are even higher.

Number Nine. It's there in white on the walls, and just looking at it sends adrenaline shooting through me like a firecracker. Bertie gets out of the truck and goes to the left side of the paddock, where a keypad is. She punches in a number and the door slides open to reveal a freight elevator—and a huge cart with brown stains on the bottom.

Blood from Rexy's last meal. The shiver that goes through me is part fear, part anticipation, and all deep, thrilling excitement.

The first live dinosaur most people ever saw was a T. rex. When it got loose in San Diego, it changed the world.

It changed me. And now I'm minutes away from seeing one live. Seeing *her.* One of the oldest dinosaurs on Isla Nublar. One of the originals.

Bertie and I load the goat meat into the cart, push it into the freight elevator, and close the door.

"Okay, one last thing before we go inside," Bertie says, pulling a small aerosol bottle out of her pocket.

I frown. "Hair spray?" I ask.

"It's a scent masker," she explains. "We'll be safe where we are, but it's an extra precaution I like to take. Not only do you smell like a human, which means *food*, but you've been helping me load goat meat, which is her favorite. Dr. Wu's team whipped this up for the trainers and vets a while back. It makes your scent blend into the other scents of the jungle so it's harder for them to pinpoint it. It's not perfect, but it's a useful tool."

"That's amazing," I say, watching as she sprays her face and her clothes and the rest of her exposed skin. Then she hands the bottle to me and I do the same.

The mist has no odor, and it's absorbed almost as soon as it hits my skin.

"Great. We're good to go now. We go up this way," she says, jerking her head to the door next to the freight elevator.

I follow her up the stairs, our footsteps echoing hollowly against the solid walls around us. The stairs lead up to what I can only describe as a viewing booth. The wall that overlooks Rexy's paddock is transparent, and there's a clearing right below us within the labyrinth of a jungle that makes up her habitat. I'm surprised at how dense the jungle growth is for as far as I can see. I would think she'd need more room—but maybe she just knocks trees down at her pleasure.

"How does the meat get down there?" I ask, stepping toward the polymer. I don't dare put my hand on it, but I want to. I want to press my nose against it and search for her until my eyes bug out.

"We have a drop system," Bertie says. "When she's not getting her meds, she gets live, whole meat."

I wince at the thought. Poor little goats.

Bertie goes over to the screen on the other wall of the viewing booth. She presses a few buttons and I watch as an automated crane dumps the contents of our cart into the clearing. Bertie walks over to a box set in the corner, pulls out a red stick flare, and walks over to stand next to me.

I barely glance at it. My eyes are glued to the pile of meat in the clearing—and the jungle that borders it. I wait to hear a rustle.

"What's the flare for?" I ask.

"Visual aid. She associates the flare with food, so lighting one makes it easier to get her to come out of the jungle."

"Does she hide?" I ask.

"It's not exactly hiding," Bertie says. "You have to understand, Rexy is one of our oldest dinosaurs. She's seen a lot. Experienced even more. And for several years, she had free rein of this island."

"Do you think she feels trapped?" I ask, feeling wistful for her.

"I don't think it's that," Bertie says. "She has her space. Her behavior is more . . . withholding. Like she's decided we need to earn her respect."

"So she's pulling rank," I say.

"Well, if there is a queen of dinosaurs," Bertie says, "it's probably her." She holds out the flare. "Want to do the honors?"

I take the flare from her, my hand closing around it. "What do I do?"

Bertie guides me to the very end of the wall, where she presses her hand into the bioscanner. There's a beep, and then right above the scanner, a metal shutter no bigger than a paperback book rolls up. A breeze hits my face and I let out a shaky breath, looking out at the paddock through the hole Bertie has exposed in the wall.

I pull the cap off the flare and toss it through the opening. As soon as my hand is clear, before the flare's even fallen to the ground next to the meat, the shutter rolls down again and locks with a beep.

I dash back to the window, and this time, I do press my hands against the glass, peering out into the jungle, and with every breath, I feel my chest get tighter and tighter.

I start to count in my head to make it easier. *One Mississippi. Two Mississippi. Three . . .*

Thump.

I flinch.

Thump. Thump.

I can hear her coming before the trees even begin to move. Her heavy footfalls, crushing whatever gets in her way.

I breathe in, my hands still pressed against the glass. The trees shake, but no birds fly away.

Did she eat them all? Or do they just know better not to encroach on her empire?

I think I know what to expect when the trees part and bend as she tromps through them. When she emerges into the clearing, I think I'm ready. But those fuzzy pictures from San Diego . . . they did nothing to prepare me.

She's enormous. The ground shakes with each step she takes, lured by the red light of the flare. She bends, swinging her head down, saliva dripping off her jaws and onto the meat. She noses at it, like she expects it to start running, and when it doesn't, instead of chowing down, she swings her head back up.

And suddenly, she's looking right at me.

My breath stutters in my lungs as she moves toward the window. My knees lock, and I've never felt smaller in my life. This is different from being around the herbivores. There's a benevolence to the ones who live in the valley, a slow sweetness that makes me feel comforted, even if their size is intimidating.

Rexy isn't sweet or slow. Rexy is *queen*. And she knows it.

In her face, I see wisdom. Calculation. Curiosity.

And so many *teeth*. Her lip curls in a snarl, exposing them further as she rumbles the noise out, and she's so close her breath fogs up the window between us where my hands are pressed. I can feel the heat of it through the glass. It sends a wash of terror through me, but I still can't move. I won't. She's too close. I can see every marking. Every scar. Every single thing that makes her unique and special is right there, just a foot away.

One Mississippi. Two Mississippi. Three . . .

Her head whips back to the meat—she's decided I'm not interesting enough, I think—and she stomps forward, her tail swaying back and forth as she bends down, grasping a mouthful of goat in her jaws. Without another look at us, she disappears into her jungle.

"What do you think?" Bertie asks next to me.

I sound breathless even to my own ears when I speak. "You were right, what you said about her when we first met," I say. "She's beautiful."

I still feel shaky after Bertie drops me off at the hotel, with strict instructions not to tell my fellow interns that I got to see Rexy already. Apparently Mr. Masrani has a whole reveal planned for our eight-week anniversary here.

When I get up to my room, it takes me two tries to open the door. I can hear voices inside, and when I finally get the door open, I see Eric and Tanya on her bed, looking at a video on her laptop together.

"Claire!" Tanya snaps the laptop shut fast. "Where've you been?"

"I was just helping Bertie with some inventory," I say. "What's up with you two?"

"Not much," Eric says, getting up, taking the laptop from Tanya, and shoving it into his bag quickly. "I was just getting Tanya's opinion on some cuts I did of our first few weeks. We're gonna head down early for dinner. You want to come?"

"I'll catch up," I say. "I want to take a shower."

"I wasn't going to say anything, but you kind of smell like . . ." Tanya leans forward, her nose wrinkling. "Is that *goat*?"

"Yeah, that's what I was helping Bertie inventory. Goat meat. So not glamorous." I feel kind of bad about lying, especially because I really want to share with someone the glory of what I just saw, but I'll save it for my journal until all of us interns get to share in the same experience.

"Ew," Tanya says. "We'll save you a seat at dinner, okay?"

"I'll be there," I say.

But instead of jumping in the shower immediately after they

leave, I grab my bag and pull out my tablet. Even in my T. rex–induced excitement, I haven't forgotten about the list I got from Wyatt. Is Izzie on it?

I pull up the screenshot of the list of names and scan it eagerly. There she is. Third from the bottom.

Isobel James, biochem major.

I plug her name into a search engine, my heart hammering as the page takes a second to load. There are a quite few Isobel Jameses. So I add her major and *Yale* to the search terms, waiting again as sweat crawls down my back.

When the page loads and I see the second link, my stomach sinks.

It's an obituary.

Izzie's obituary.

22

I grab Izzie's notebook and set it next to my tablet on the thick comforter spread across the mattress. Taking a deep breath, I read through her obituary.

> Isobel James, age nineteen, passed away Sunday morning at the home of her parents. A promising student at Yale and a member of the Yale chapter of the American Institute of Chemical Engineers, she is survived by her loving family: her parents, Bill and Kathy, and her brother, Donnelly. There will be a private, closed service, and the family asks for donations to the Mighty Girl Initiative in lieu of flowers.

I check the date on the obituary again, just to be sure. March 5. Which would put Izzie in Boston at her parents' house on March 4.

Except she wasn't *in* Boston on March 4. I flip through Izzie's notebook until I find the rows and rows of food and waste stats for Olive and Agnes, and sure enough, there it is:

3/4

Olive (still recovering from surgery): 100 lb. consumed, 20 lb. waste (bring up fluid retention w/ Tim)

Agnes: 130 lb. consumed, 30 lb. waste.

My heart hammering, I sit back against my pillows, trying not to freak out too much.

Because all the clues are telling me that the most unbelievable parts of Wyatt's story about the intern who got left behind maybe—even probably—happened.

Izzie wasn't in Boston on March 4. Did she die that day? Was *that* the day of the big storm?

Next, I pull up weather data, because I'm going to need all the details to figure this out. I type in the weeks before and after the fourth, and there it is: more confirmation. A giant storm front moving right toward the island and then enveloping it—on the night of March 4.

Sickness churns inside me as I trace the inked words in Izzie's journal. Did she leave this behind that morning as she headed out on her rounds, not knowing she wouldn't be coming back? Not knowing that her thoughts, her notes, her valuable research would just be lost . . . until I found it?

What happened that day? Was it human error? A mistake in the chaos of the storm?

Or was it something more sinister?

Or did the *sinister* happen later . . . after . . . when they realized they'd left someone behind? I shudder. *When* had they realized she'd died, scared and alone on this island, with only the creatures of the jungle—dinosaur and other—as company? Did they already know as they headed away? Or did they hear after they arrived safely in Costa Rica? Is that when they started their cover-up? And how did they get Izzie's parents to go along with it?

That last question is what keeps snagging me, like a thorny branch. Wyatt's right—the company could have easily bought off the other interns' silence: Money, jobs, prestige—Mr. Masrani could deliver all that without blinking an eye. And people are craven. They want to get ahead.

But Izzie's parents—this obituary, probably written by them . . . the lie about her dying at home . . . *that's* what keeps hanging me up. Because my parents would never let that happen. They'd never let themselves get bought off. And I want to think that all parents are like that. But they aren't, are they?

Some parents are not good. Some people are downright evil, so that means some parents are too. It's just a logical conclusion, even if the idea is strange to me.

Or . . . an even worse idea strikes me, making me shiver. What if Izzie's parents *did* hold strong? What if whoever covered this up threatened them?

I page through the notebook, searching for the final entry. They grow sparse right around the time Olive got sick—Izzie was probably working around the clock monitoring her. Finally, I spot it, near the very back, next to a sketch of a waterfall. Dated just three days before her death, if the obituary date is correct.

3/1

Did some work in Sector C. I'm still not sure what I'm looking for, but I had to dodge Oscar and his cronies. They're test-driving those sphere things all over the valley and would've freaked if they knew I'd snuck in.

I got what I needed and snuck out undetected, though. I'll start testing tomorrow. I know it's a long shot, but what else am I supposed to do?

What if they keep getting sick?

"Way to be vague, Izzie," I mutter, flipping through the rest of the notebook, hoping to see another entry I somehow missed during my first skim-through. In the empty final twenty pages or so, my thumb brushes against a page that feels a little too thick. I frown and look closer.

The pages are stuck together.

I peel them apart.

"What the . . ."

A scrap of paper is tucked between the pages. It looks like it was torn from a yellow legal pad. In big black letters, it says *Watch your back.*

It's definitely not Izzie's handwriting.

A threat? Or a warning? A shiver goes through me as my eyes

fall on the pages that I unstuck, and my curiosity grows as I set the yellow paper aside.

It's a list, with rows and rows of plant and animal species followed by the letters *AC/AK,* one set of those letters circled each time. There are X's next to each entry.

I trace my finger down the page . . . What do the X's mean? Are they related to the ones on the map Izzie drew in her second month here?

There's a knock on my door, and I'm so deep in thought, I jump what feels like a foot off the bed.

"Claire?"

That's Justin. I look at the clock on the bedside table and realize I'm late for dinner. I want to keep looking through Izzie's notebook and putting the pieces together, but I need to eat.

I haven't even showered yet, though. Ew.

"Just a second," I call. I scramble to shove Izzie's notebook and my tablet back into my bag, swing it over my shoulder, and hurry to the door.

"Hey." He smiles when he sees me. "Tanya sent me up here to find you. She and the rest of the girls want to talk about painting the Gyrospheres with Bertie tomorrow."

"I totally lost track of time," I say. "Thanks for coming and getting me."

He smiles. "Any time."

The next day, Justin and I drive over together to the valley, where Bertie's asked to meet us for our Gyrosphere painting session.

"So, are you ever going to tell me what you're doing in Dr. Wu's labs every morning?" he asks as I take a right away from the hotel and toward the valley.

"I can't," I say. "I promised not to."

He sighs. "So unfair," he says.

"Would you really risk the wrath of Dr. Wu if you were in the same position?" I ask, slowing down as we get stuck behind a truck full of bricks heading to Main Street.

"He really is intimidating," Justin admits. "I read this great profile about him; it must've been a few years ago."

"The one in the *New York Times*?" I ask.

"Yeah, that one," he says. "What he said about life's work, how if you have a calling, it shapes you just as much as you shape it—it stuck with me."

"Do you think that's true?" I ask.

"Don't you?" he asks. "Do you feel like politics is your calling?"

I concentrate on the road, the question hanging between us. A few months ago, I could have answered that with a surety I'd felt for ages. Changing the laws that needed to be changed was the quickest way to reach my goal of protecting animals. But now . . .

Politics is a ruthless game. That's what Mr. Masrani said at dinner that first night at Jurassic World. And I had told him that maybe I'm a ruthless girl.

But I think about Izzie. About the mystery surrounding her death. Without power, without ruthlessness, that cover-up would never have happened.

To reveal it would be righteous, wouldn't it?

But the righteous hardly ever win. And the ruthless do.

"What about you?" I ask, still avoiding Justin's question. "What's *your* calling?"

"Not sure yet," he says as we pull up to the training center.

"Not business?" I ask.

"That's such a vague term," he complains good-naturedly, unbuckling his seat belt. I slide out of the jeep.

"I do have some other news, other than what's going on in the labs," I tell him as we walk up the dirt road that leads to the training center.

"Oh yeah?"

"Next week they're transporting a Raptor from Sorna back to the island."

His eyes widen, like he's a kid in a candy store. "Really?"

"Apparently we're going to be asked to stay in our rooms," I say—or more like complain—and it makes him smile.

"You want to observe, I take it?"

"Don't you?" I ask.

"From a healthy distance," he says.

"But a close-up view means you get to see all the teeth!" I grin, and he shakes his head as we reach the training center's main building.

Bertie has stuff set up out back, in the unused—for now, at least—training area. I wonder if this is where they'll keep the Raptor for quarantine, or if they have a special, more secure place tucked away.

There are two Gyrospheres—empty of seats and tech, just the shells—set in the dirt training area, the steel fence separating it from the jungle beyond.

"There you are!" Amanda says when she spots us.

"I'm sorry, I lost track of time."

"It's okay," she says. "We're just sorting out the paint."

"Are these the patterns?" I ask.

"Yeah—come look!" She waves us over.

Bertie is standing in front of two hologram projectors, each beaming a patterned sphere: one with a dozen or so large red dots placed strategically on a white background; the other with an intricate hexagon pattern of red and an eye-popping neon yellow.

"So, simple versus complex?" Justin asks Bertie. "Or round versus angular?"

"She responded best to circles and hexagons when we did her neuro-scan," Bertie explains. "So we figured this would be our baseline."

"And the bright colors?" Ronnie asks from behind me, where she's standing with Tanya. "I thought they might be green, so she'd associate them with food?"

"Actually, they're red and orange, to do the opposite," Bertie says. "She registers certain colors, from what we can surmise. But I thought making them a color she doesn't typically associate with the terrain or food or other dinosaur stuff might be more of an attraction."

"Like a bee's attracted to bright things," Tanya pipes up.

"Yes," Bertie says. "So what we'll do is project the holograms onto the Gyrosphere shells as an outline for us to paint. Like so." She hits a button on the remote in her hand, the head of one projector swivels, and the holograms soar across us to light up the actual

Gyrospheres with patterns. It's a neat trick, and way easier than the old-school blue painter's tape.

We get to work, Justin, Tanya, and I, painting the hexagon patterns on one sphere while Amanda and Ronnie paint circles on the other. Bertie's on her tablet, and when she passes by, I see that she's watching video footage of Pearl. From the crashing and crowing sounds I hear, it's likely one of her earlier escapades.

My heart shrivels in my chest at the thought of her being taken away from the valley—what kind of a life would she have in isolation? Or worse . . . would they euthanize her as a failed specimen? The idea horrifies me. Our science brought the dinosaurs here, which means we owe it to them to give them good lives. They are our responsibility.

If these toy spheres can prevent that, I suddenly realize, even with all the other problems swirling around me, then my presence here will be worth it. And that's what matters, isn't it?

I turn back to filling in the hexagons while Justin traces them with sure, precise strokes of his paintbrush. We work well as a team, though every few minutes, Bertie makes us duck out of the spheres because of the paint fumes.

"Are you afraid we're going to get the giggles or something, Bertie?" Tanya asks, grinning.

"I'm afraid you'll get headaches," Bertie says. "This paint is safe for humans and dinosaurs, but it's smelly. We opened the cans this morning to mix them, and Tim got a migraine."

Tanya winces in sympathy. "No headaches here so far," she says.

It takes about two hours to finish the hexagon Gyrosphere as well as the doors that will be fused shut to create a seamless ball for

Pearl to play with. My shoulders are aching by the time we finally stand back to survey our work.

"Well done," Bertie says. "We'll hoist them up so they dry evenly tonight. In the morning, we'll fuse the doors on, and we'll do a test run in the afternoon with Pearl."

"Can we come?" Amanda asks.

"Of course," Bertie says. "This was you girls' idea. You deserve to be there. The boys can come too," she adds, when Justin and Art look disappointed. "I'll let Beverly know that I need you tomorrow afternoon . . . say, one o'clock?"

"We'll be there," Ronnie promises.

"We'll be early," Tanya adds eagerly.

"Good job today." Bertie smiles. "Go back to your rooms. Clean up. Get your dinner and your rest. Big day tomorrow!"

We shower her with thanks and goodbyes, leaving her to her videos and Pearl's new toys.

Tanya tilts her head back and forth, her neck popping at the movement. "Ow," she groans. "I should've stretched before I spent two hours with my arms in the air."

"I told you so," Ronnie scolds, making me smile as we load into the jeep.

"I hope she likes ours the best," Justin says in a low voice as Ronnie pulls away from the training center and heads back to the hotel.

"No way—Pearl's a polka-dot girl," Ronnie says, overhearing him. "Bet you ten bucks."

"I'll take that bet," Justin says. "She's all about the six-sided life."

Tanya laughs. "I don't care which—let's just hope she likes at least one of them!"

When we get to the hotel, I tell Tanya to go on to dinner without me. "I've got to make a quick call to my parents," I say.

But when she leaves to join Ronnie in the hall, I don't make any calls. Instead, I go right back to Izzie's journal and the plant lists.

Ceiba pentandra AC/AK X
Heliconia collinsiana AC/AK X
Gunnera insignis AC/AK X

"*AC/AK*," I say to myself, tapping the letters, trying to think. Ac in the periodic table is Actinium, but there isn't an Ak. So it has to be some other sort of abbreviation. I trace my finger down the rows of circled *AC*s and *AK*s. They're always together—no *AC/AC*s or *AK/AK*s in any one entry. So it's something that has to be one or the other . . . *A* and *A* . . . *acidic* and *alkaline*!

Izzie was testing different plants' acidity levels! And the X's? Suddenly it hits me, and I flip back to her map of the valley, where seemingly random spots bear X's.

She must have decided that whatever was making the Brachiosauruses sick was environmental. The most logical cause was something they were eating. So Izzie was using one of the basic scientific methods: the process of elimination.

"Allergy testing for dinosaurs," I say to myself, because it's clever. It's a huge undertaking, especially with as many plant species as the valley holds. Did she find the source? I scan the lists of plants with fresh eyes, searching for any difference, anything to make one stand out. My gaze falls on one near the middle of the third column.

Cyanobacteria AC/AK XX

The *AC* is circled, but the double X is what catches my eye. *Cyanobacteria* is algae, so I flip back to Izzie's detailed map of the valley, and sure enough, there it is: a double X positioned on the rocks behind the falls.

It's the only double X. That has to mean something, right?

I try to put it together. It's hard, because I'm no biology major. I know I should ask Tanya, but she'll want all the details. And I'm not ready to spill about Izzie's notebook yet. Especially with that *Watch your back* note. When did she receive that? Before her last diary entry? After?

Did someone kill her? Did Mr. Masrani cover it up? Surely he wouldn't cover up *murder*. Even Wyatt's left-in-the-storm story is way more likely than that . . . right?

My stomach churns as I close the notebook and tuck it under my pillow. I have to get to dinner.

And I have to make a plan. I'm not sure what it involves yet, but I need to get my hands on that algae.

23

The next afternoon, as we're all getting ready to go to the valley for Pearl's big introduction, I chase Eric down in the hall, calling his name.

"What's up?" he asks.

"When I emptied my bag last night, I found something I totally forgot to ask you about," I say, fishing out the smashed memory card I picked up in the jungle.

"Where'd you find that?" he asks.

"In the jungle a few weeks ago," I say. "It's a memory card that goes in a camera, right?"

"Yeah," he says. "Not my brand. I use NuTech cards because they've got more data and the resolution is way sharper. . . ." He trails off, catching my glazed eyes, and smiles. "These are a little on the lower end. Cheaper. I think Wyatt has a few for his camera, actually, because he kept trying to steal mine, saying they were better, and I had to tell him to quit it."

"Wait, Wyatt has memory cards like this?" I ask.

"Yeah—I mean, I think so," Eric says, frowning at my sudden interest. "I kind of try to avoid the guy, I admit. He's a crappy person and a crappier roommate."

"I'm sorry," I say, my mind whirring. Was Wyatt the figure I swear I saw in the jungle that day when everybody was jumping off the waterfall? Was he *filming* us? That's so creepy. And weird. Why would he do that?

"Eric, could you pull the images or recordings off this?" I ask.

He takes it from me, examining it. "No," he says. "It's pretty smashed, and you say you found it in the jungle? The moisture is a big factor too. Any data would be really corrupted. Sorry."

"It's okay," I say as he hands it back and I slip it into the front pocket of my bag. "Long shot."

"You excited for today?" he asks as we join the rest of our group at the elevator.

"And nervous," I say. "I hope it works."

"I think it will," he says. "It's a neat idea. With enough positive reinforcement, the trainers can work wonders."

"We'll have to stock up on strawberries," Tanya jokes.

"Let's hope she likes them as much as Lovelace did when she was trapped in the gully," Amanda adds.

It's wild to think that was over a month ago, and that in a few days, a new dinosaur will be on Isla Nublar.

"Have you seen how Lovelace keeps scratching her head against stuff in the valley?" Ronnie asks. "It's so cute."

"Her horns are growing," Art says as the elevator finally arrives, and we all crowd inside. "She broke a bunch of saplings the other day. And then ate the tops. You got footage of that, didn't you, Eric?"

"I'm gonna edit it soon," Eric promises. The elevator dings open into the lobby, where Justin is waiting for us.

"Do you think they'll let us do, like, an intern video yearbook?" Amanda asks. It's hot already as we step outside and walk to the fleet of blue and silver jeeps parked in the lot nearby. She hops into the driver's seat of the nearest one, and Art takes shotgun as Justin, Eric, and I pile into the back.

"I'll ask Mr. Masrani," Eric says. "But probably not. At least not until after the park opens. He won't want the footage leaked online."

Amanda purses her lips. "Aw, you're right," she says. "That sucks. I'd love to have something to remember this summer by. It's been so amazing."

"And we're not even half done," Justin adds.

"Just think of the trouble the dinosaurs will get into in the next month and a half," Art says, shaking his head.

"Well, let's hope Pearl doesn't," Amanda answers firmly, taking a right turn off the main road toward the valley. We all ride in silence for a moment, thinking of the day ahead. Pearl's future—and the future of many dinosaurs like her—could count on it.

"I think it's going to work," I say, almost like it's a magic wish and if I speak it, it'll come true.

"It'll be great," Amanda says firmly, but she sounds as nervous as I feel.

We pull up to the valley fence, where Bertie and Sarah are waiting for us.

"Hi, everyone," Bertie says when we all group around her. "The rest of the team's already setting up at the watering hole. We're going to head in. Load on up." She jerks her thumb behind her at the large truck. We climb up into the bed, and she and Sarah jump into the cab. "Hang on," Bertie calls out the window, and off we go. Justin's hand presses against mine as I grip the truck railing for support, and he winks at me when I catch his eye.

It's a whole different experience, riding in the valley in the open air. The wind's in my hair, and my friends' laughter rings in my ears. About halfway there, we pass three Gallimimuses sunning themselves, and they perk up as we whiz by, leaping to their feet and running after us, flanking the jeep, almost close enough to touch, though I don't dare reach out. Their heads are so small and sleek, their long necks powerful, and I can see the muscle definition under their skin, the way the tendons move together, giving them such power. Their bodies and footfalls make the ground under the truck wheels vibrate, and I have to grab the railing to keep steady.

The trio of Gallimimuses races ahead—we're going too slow for them, I guess—and their powerful back legs propel them to speeds that make my head spin as they disappear ahead of us.

We pass a group of Triceratops that don't even look up, so I assume it must be a group of the older ones—definitely no Lovelace, who has been excited to see any human every time I'm in this valley. I keep my eyes peeled for one of the Parasaurolophuses, but I'm starting to think they prefer to keep to the other side of the valley. Maybe there's more flat space to run over there.

Pulling up to the enormous watering hole, we come to a stop in front of a circle of large pillars set strategically around it. I can see Pearl in the distance, splashing in the shallows on the far shore. She's the only dinosaur in sight.

"Sound barriers," Bertie explains when we hop out of the truck and Eric asks what they are. "These allow us to do one-on-one in-habitat work with the dinosaurs without the other ones butting in or distracting us."

"Does it hurt their ears?" I ask.

"It emits a sound at a frequency they dislike if they pass through it," Bertie says. "But they don't. We've done a lot of training when-ever we put them up, so now they avoid them. They know they get treats if they do."

"The lure of strawberries is strong," Justin laughs.

"Pearl actually prefers watermelon," Bertie says. "Big surprise, since it's round, like her favorite toy."

We all laugh at that.

Our ears can't hear the frequencies the sound towers emit, so we just walk past them toward where the group of trainers are stand-ing with Pearl, who's stomping her feet in the water, bending down from time to time to select a proffered treat from a trainer's hand.

"I've got security over here." Bertie points to the clump of trees across the watering hole from us. "And we're going to roll the Gyrosphere in. We'll start with the hexagon one."

"So it's just . . . click and treat?" Eric asks. "Like a dog?"

"Positive reinforcement is something that works across a lot of species," Bertie says. "Even dinosaurs. It's more complicated with the carnivores, of course, because they see a person and their natu-ral instinct is to think *food* first and *friend* second. The caretakers conditioning the carnivores are still in the very beginning stages of how to even properly approach them so the vets can treat them regularly. Each species is so different, which makes it tricky business."

"Some of them operate like a pack, don't they?" Ronnie asks.

"That is one theory the caretakers are researching through in-depth observation," Bertie says. "The next few years will teach us so much, and the more everyone learns, the more we can help and establish trust. Because dominance can work, but trust? Enough trust will get an animal to follow you anywhere."

"Do you think it's easier to build trust with the herbivores because they don't want to immediately eat you?" Tanya asks.

Bertie laughs. "The herbivores do seem to be more responsive to working with humans so far. That's why we're able to create features like this valley and use vehicles like the Gyrospheres. Lots of positive reinforcement. Lots of praise. Lots and *lots* of work to cement the behavior."

"How can we help?" I ask.

"I'm going to have the girls come with me to the other side of the water, where the Gyrosphere will be introduced," Bertie says. "This is your project. You should be able to send it on its maiden voyage, so to speak. Justin, Art, Eric—I want you with the trainers. Your job will be to help them distract Pearl until we get the Gyrosphere in position. We don't want her to charge if she decides it's of interest, even if she's across the water. I want this to go as smoothly as possible. Positive experience for everyone, especially Pearl. Okay?"

"We get it," Eric says. "Come on, guys."

The boys head off with Sarah, and the girls and I follow Bertie to loop around the watering hole. We hike along the bank, our boots squelching in the mud and tall reeds and grasses. When we reach the opposite shore, I look across the water. The trainers and the guys have moved Pearl so she's facing away from us, thoroughly engrossed in whatever they're doing to distract her.

"Is Justin . . . dancing?" Tanya asks next to me, shading her eyes as she stares across the water.

"Eric too!" Amanda laughs.

They're right. Both of them are doing what looks like an awkward two-step as Pearl watches with interest while Art and the trainers clap out a rhythm.

Bertie looks over her shoulder. "Whatever distraction works!" she says. "Look, girls!"

We turn our attention to the clump of trees, where the security guards are rolling the hexagon-patterned Gyrosphere out. I glance back over my shoulder, but Pearl's totally distracted by the guys swirling around in front of her.

"We'll be right here," calls the guard, who rolls it over to us on the bank.

"It looks great," Bertie says, inspecting it closely. "So this is the plan: We'll stay here on the bank with the sphere while Sarah and the team turn Pearl around so she spots it. We'll see how she reacts. If she comes toward it slowly, we'll wait until she's about three-quarters of the way across the water before we push it to her. Then I want you up on the outer bank there." She points to where the shoreline fades up to sloping grass. "And if she charges, you girls run and get on the other side of the towers, okay?"

We all nod.

"I'm hoping she'll be curious and approach it slowly," Bertie says. "We want to see how she reacts to the toy at first, with no treats, no clickers, no trainers influencing her. After this first session, we can start reinforcing in the next one. Everyone ready?"

The four of us exchange excited glances. "Yep," I say.

Bertie pulls her radio out of her pocket. "Let's go," she says into it.

We watch as the boys end their dance and Sarah steps forward. Pearl's attention turns to her, and she stretches out her long neck as Sarah offers her a treat. Sarah clicks and treats, clicks and treats, slowly moving with each click so Pearl moves with her. It takes about two minutes to get her turned around, so that Sarah is standing hip-deep in the water and Pearl is facing us.

"She's in place," Sarah's voice crackles over Bertie's radio.

"Okay, Pearl," Bertie says under her breath. "Be my good girl."

We wait for Pearl to notice the big red ball on the other side of the water. I'm holding my breath the whole time, and I can tell the minute it happens. Her body suddenly goes rigid, and her head tilts to the side. Sarah moves out of the way when Pearl steps into the water, and the dinosaur makes waves—literally—as she wades into the depths.

"Good so far," Bertie says, all her focus on Pearl. "Hold steady, girls. We'll push the Gyrosphere forward on my signal."

Pearl's about halfway across the watering hole. In the middle, it's deep enough that she's paddling with her big feet and holding her head high above the water. It's more than amazing to see in real life something I've only seen paintings of in paleontology texts and museum dioramas: a Brachiosaurus swimming.

"Steady," Bertie repeats as Pearl gets closer. She's making that burbling sound I've become familiar with. It's not a purr or a low-ing like the Triceratops—there's probably something unique in her throat anatomy that creates it. My body tenses as she draws near, remembering how hard she slammed that other Gyrosphere against the tree in the clearing when it was only Justin and me.

"Now!" Bertie says.

We push with all our might, five pairs of hands shoving the Gyrosphere forward. It lands in the water with a splash, bobbing along the current created by Pearl's movements, and she follows it, like an enormous moth drawn to a porch light.

My friends and I scramble up the bank, out of the way, like Bertie told us to, but the head trainer stays there right at the edge of the water, ever watchful of her charge.

When Pearl's almost reached the Gyrosphere, she stretches her neck out and—*bop!*—bumps it with her nose. It skids across the water, lighter than the real Gyrospheres because it's empty. Pearl tosses her head, burbling louder as she paddles after her new toy. Bertie follows her along the bank, and we girls follow her too—at a safe distance.

"It's working!" Amanda says as Pearl hooks her neck around the sphere, pressing it down under the surface. When she releases it and it pops up out of the water, the splash seems to delight and surprise her, because she rears back a little and then jabs forward, attempting the move again.

"This is *so* cool," Ronnie says, her eyes glowing.

The boys—minus Eric, who is glued to the shore, recording Pearl's antics—come hurrying toward us, beaming.

"You four did it!" Art says. "She's completely into it."

"I told you hexagons were the way to go," Justin says to Ronnie, who laughs.

"I owe you ten bucks, it seems." She grins. "But she might like the polka dots too! You never know. Then it's a tie."

"Look, she's got it out of the water and onto the bank now!" Tanya squeals.

Justin and I exchange a nervous look. This is the real test.

We watch as Pearl lumbers back and forth on the sandy bank, nosing the painted Gyrosphere back and forth along the mud. When it gets stuck in a tangle of tall grass, she pauses, looking expectantly at Bertie, like she wants her to fix the problem.

But Bertie waits for her to solve it herself. Pearl spends a good minute munching on the grasses—probably thinking her way through it—and then delivers a mighty kick to the ball. The Gyrosphere goes flying, spinning over the bank and landing right between two of the sound-barrier towers.

The mournful sound that fills the air sets my teeth on edge. It's no happy burbling—she's upset. Pearl moves back and forth, clearly agitated that her new toy isn't accessible.

"Hey, Bertie, we can push it back for her," I call down.

Bertie nods. "Go ahead," she shouts.

"Come on," I say to my friends. We scramble up the slope and pass the towers, jogging the distance over to the Gyrosphere. Pearl's come right up to the space between the towers, watching us raptly. She looks torn, if that's possible. Like she wants to come forward, but she knows if she does, the bad sound will hurt her ears.

"It's okay, Pearl," I say.

"We'll get you back your toy," Amanda coos. "Just give us a second."

It takes all of us to roll it up the slope. I'm panting and my palms are sweaty as we reach the top, but then momentum is our friend, and we let it go. It rolls down through the space between the towers and right past Pearl, who lumbers after it in glee. She smacks it into the water again, and off she goes, splashing and trying to dunk it—and never succeeding for long because of the sphere's buoyancy.

I watch, amazed by the unrestrained joy of her, this giant creature who all the books told us was stately and magnificent—and she is. She's a miracle.

But she's a playful, curious, and funny miracle. And as I stand there, watching her skim the Gyrosphere across the water, I know, with a certainty I've never felt about anything before, that this is where I belong. For good.

Which makes me even more determined to see if my theory about Izzie's notes is right. What if Pearl gets sick next? Or Lovelace? What if the antibiotics stop working for Olive or Agnes? They have to build up a certain degree of immunity. It can't be good for all the dinosaurs to be on so many medications just as a precaution.

My mind's made up.

I have to get my hands on that algae.

I just have no idea how to do it.

24

It takes me two days to gather everything I need. And then, on our afternoon off, Tanya hangs out with Ronnie and I stay back in my room, waiting. At breakfast I asked Justin to come up, and just a few minutes after I finish packing my bag with everything I need, he knocks on the door.

I'm nervous, but I get right to the point.

"Will you do something for me even if sounds really risky?" I ask when I let him into my room.

"The question every person loves to be asked," Justin says. "Are you going to tell me what it is?"

I take a deep breath. "I need to break into the Gyrosphere Valley. I have to collect a specimen near the waterfall."

"And you don't want to just ask one of the trainers if you can go get it?" He raises an eyebrow. "Or Dr. Wu?"

"It's complicated," I say. "I think . . . I think I may have stumbled upon something. But I'm not totally sure. And I have to be before I tell anyone."

"Even me? Because I know you well enough now to realize you aren't telling me the whole story here."

I flush and look up at him. Ever since I met him, he's proven over and over again who he is: someone good and kind and willing to help. Someone who cares about me in a way that I didn't know I could be cared about. And I want to trust him. I *do* trust him.

But I don't know if I should trust *anyone* with this. With Izzie. With her words and her thoughts and her drawings, which are so personal but resonate with me so deeply.

And if something happened to her here—if this place is the reason she's dead—that needs to be found out. Her work needs to be finished. Especially if it helps the dinosaurs.

"I'm not ready to tell the whole story yet," I say. "Is that . . . is that okay?"

"Yeah," he says.

"Even if I want you to break the rules?"

"Claire, you've been getting me to break the rules ever since we met," he says. "Brilliant women are clearly a weakness of mine." He grins, pushing his glasses up his nose. "When do you want to go?"

"The security guards do a shift change at six," I say. "The trainers usually head back from feeding time around then too. There's a little window of time when it's just trainers in the valley. If we tell them we're doing a night-vision Gyrosphere test for security like before, they'll probably believe it."

"And just slip in before the next security shift takes over?" Justin asks.

I nod.

"How do we get out, though?"

"We use Bertie's code to open the gate from the inside," I say. "She gave it to us during the test run with Pearl. It's not the code to get in, but it's the code to get out."

"You've got this all figured out," he says, looking impressed.

"This is really important," I say. "I wouldn't ask you to do it if it weren't. I promise."

"I know," he says, with the kind of faith I hope I'm worthy of. "Okay. Let's do it."

"Seriously?"

He smiles. "Joyride among the dinosaurs? Mysterious specimen collecting? Playing sidekick to cute, smart girl? It's a science geek's dream. Kind of can't say no."

He's always coaxing this laughter out of me. The kind that makes me bite my lip, trying to suppress it, but it comes out anyway.

"You are just . . ." I don't even know how to finish my thought. He's a lot of things. Really good things. Exciting things. "Thank you," I finally say. "It would've been a little too irresponsible, even for me, to go out there alone."

"I agree. Especially when you're dealing with a waterfall. We won't be jumping off, I take it?"

I shake my head. "Kind of the opposite," I say. "We'll be going behind it."

My plan to avoid the security guards works perfectly. The spare Gyrospheres are kept up on the bluff, and we wait until the guards leave before sneaking up and activating one. We roll down just as the trainers appear, finishing the afternoon feeding, and we wait until one of them catches sight of us.

"Hey, you two," Sarah, Bertie's second-in-command, calls through the gate.

"We're doing some tests in the Gyrosphere at dusk," Justin calls. "Ryan said you'd let us in. He had to go deal with something for Oscar. Prepping for the Raptor delivery, I think."

"Cool," Sarah says, accepting the lie. She goes over to the keypad and punches in a code. After the gate swings open, we roll right in. "Good luck."

"Thanks!" I call out as we zoom past them, Justin gunning the Gyrosphere a little. We only have so much time before the security guards start their night patrols.

"Well," Justin says. "That was kind of easy, actually."

"I've noticed how the brains of the park don't exactly associate with the brawn," I say. "When the guards show up, it probably won't even occur to Sarah to ask about our test run."

"I noticed that too," Justin says. "First thing I'd change if I were in charge."

"Really?" I ask.

He nods. "Teamwork and camaraderie across specialties is key to harmony and rooting out problems in a place like this. When you don't just go to work, you live and breathe and love and lose all in the same place, with no respite? It can wear on you if you don't have a support system."

"A family," I say.

"Yeah. A park like this, it's a living, breathing thing, every aspect of it. Sometimes you've got to nurture it. Sometimes you've got to be hard on it."

"I like that," I say.

"Yeah?"

"Yeah."

We zip along the valley, up and down the hills. There are no dinosaurs in sight—but that makes sense. After feeding time, it's snoozing time. They're likely all lolling near the watering hole, taking advantage of the last bit of sun before it sets. I hope we come across a few of them. I want to see how Pearl is getting on with her new toy.

Once we reach the tree line, I have to take Izzie's map out of my pocket. Justin glances at it when I do, but he doesn't ask any questions. He probably thinks I made it, not some mysterious dead girl.

"We're going to want to head right, which is north," I say. "If we keep going in that direction, we should hit the base of the waterfall instead of coming at it from the top."

Justin shudders. "Oh God, can you imagine? Going over a waterfall in this thing?"

My skin crawls at the thought. "Nightmare," I agree. "Do they float?" I look around at the Gyrosphere's door seals. "They're definitely not airtight."

"Lucky we're going to roll up to the waterfall, not over it, then," he says. "Do you know how deep the water is? Or how we're going to get behind the falls?"

"I'll have a better idea when I see it," I say.

"So you haven't seen it—yet you have a detailed map. Interesting."

"I'm a girl of many secrets," I say, because he's not the only one who can play the rogue.

"That's for sure."

We dip and curve through the trees, the late-afternoon sunlight filtered through the lush leaves. We bump against a tangle of vines and over a few rocks, and my stomach twists as I remember what happened the last time we were in a Gyrosphere.

The farther we venture away from the open valley into the cool, wet embrace of the rain forest that edges this part of the habitat, the darker and closer it gets around us. And then I hear it: a rushing noise. Water.

"Oh my gosh," I say as the Gyrosphere pushes through a long curtain of vines, revealing the waterfall and the dazzling blue pool beneath it.

"That's even prettier than the one at the resort," Justin says.

The dark stone cliff the waterfall spills over is covered in an explosion of plants growing from the rushing waters, wild and undisturbed. Birds flit in and out of the streams of water springing from the rocks, where they've built their nests. The waterfall is on the small side, so it should be easy to access the rocks behind it, where the algae grows.

We come to a stop before the ground gets too rocky, and then Justin's eyes widen.

"Claire, what about the alarm?" he asks.

"Eric showed me a trick," I say. I reach forward and tap in the code he's given me.

Manual Override, the screen flashes.

"Where did he learn that?" Justin asks.

"Apparently one of the security guards showed him. He's been driving around with them a lot, getting footage, and they got tired of him setting off the alarm whenever he stopped to find a better shot."

Justin shakes his head, looking torn between frustration and amusement. He presses the button to open the doors, and they spring open. We climb out and I grab my bag, swinging it over my shoulder.

"Look," I say, pointing to the large footprint in the sand near the banks of the waterfall. "One of the Brachiosauruses was here."

"Maybe they take the dinosaur version of a shower," Justin suggests.

"That I would like to see," I laugh. But maybe, in a way, he's right. If the algae is making the dinosaurs sick, maybe it affects only the ones who hang out here, munching on it while they bathe. It's a small lagoon, the smallest body of water in the valley, in fact, so the Triceratops herd might not be as drawn to it—unless they're independent minded, like Lovelace.

I set my bag on one of the bigger volcanic stones that Mount Sibo spit out hundreds of years ago, and I pull out the sealed plastic bag I've filled with everything I need: specimen tubes, rubber stoppers, petri dishes, gloves, stickers for labeling, and tweezers.

Justin eyes them. "So what are we collecting?" he asks.

"The algae that grows behind the waterfall," I say.

He glances over his shoulder. "We're going to have to swim."

"Thus the plastic bag."

"Forever the Girl Scout." He grins, doing that one-handed

yank-off-the-shirt move that guys always seem to pull off effort-lessly. It's like their version of hair flip, I swear.

"I brought towels and everything," I say, patting my bag.

"My heroine," he says, taking off his glasses and placing them carefully on the rock.

I pull off my own shirt, my bathing suit underneath it. I place my folded clothes neatly on the rock and grab my plastic bag of supplies.

"Ready?" I'm feeling a little nervous about jumping into water full of algae that could be poisonous. Why didn't Izzie write more about it?

Because she probably died before she could.

The thought is constantly lurking in the back of my head now. It makes me even more nervous.

We wade into the water together—it's warm and bubbly and *so* clear, I can see strings of algae tumbling through the water with every move we make. The rocky floor drops off deep after a few steps in, and I swim across the pond one-handed, holding the bag of supplies over my head as Justin follows me. He hefts himself up onto the ledge next to the falls, then holds out his hand to pull me up.

"Careful, it's slippery," he shouts over the tumult of falling water beside us. The spray drenches my hair and body, but there's some-thing incredibly exhilarating about being so close to the falls. It's so powerful, the might of nature herself, carving through stone and mountain to create something beautiful . . . and possibly deadly, if the algae is the source of the infection.

There's a massive stone ledge behind the falls, and walking

behind the water is like entering a portal to another world. The roar of the water blocks out every other sound, and the jagged stone walls behind the falls are a wash of green, algae growing on every available surface, glistening like fuzzy emeralds against the dark volcanic rock.

"Don't touch it," I tell Justin quickly, grabbing his hand as he reaches out.

He raises an eyebrow at me. "Do you think it's going to eat me?"

"Possibly," I admit, opening my bag of tricks and pulling out the specimen tubes, handing them to him. He opens them as I snap on a pair of gloves. Next come the tweezers and petri dish. I use the tweezers to delicately scrape the algae off the rock and into the petri dish, and then I transfer the algae into the collection tubes. I label the stoppers with different-colored dots: red, blue, yellow, and green to indicate where I collected the specimens: the right side of the falls, the left, the central, the upper, and the lower. You want *all* the information you can get when you're testing multiple variables.

Before I seal the specimen tubes, I bend down and let water trickling from fissures in the stone half-fill each tube so the algae stays hydrated until I can test it. I want it in as close to its home environment as possible.

I fill one final tube chock-full of algae with no water for the field test I plan on doing, pop the stopper in, and add it to the plastic bag full of specimens. Now I have the whole range—enough to test in the field, enough to test in the lab, and hopefully, enough to find out exactly what is so harmful about this plant.

After our collecting is done, we swim back to shore, and those towels I packed come in handy. My hair is dripping down my neck as I dry off. I set the specimens carefully down on the rock, feeling a flash of triumph—I'm one step closer to finding out what Izzie discovered.

"So what's next?" Justin asks as he puts his shirt back on. His hair is still damp and it's falling into his eyes in this totally fairy-tale-prince way that is *distracting,* even with this possibly amazing scientific discovery spread out in front of me.

"Acid versus alkaline test," I say. "I couldn't find the pH test strips in the greenhouse, so I thought I'd do it the old-fashioned way." I pull a second bag from my satchel; it holds bottles of vinegar and distilled water, along with a box of baking soda.

A slow smile spreads across his face as he reaches over and grabs his glasses. "You know, Claire," he says as he puts them on, his voice serious, "I already told you I liked you. You don't have to woo me with fun, off-the-cuff chemistry experiments."

I burst out laughing, and he grins, pleased.

"You even have a garlic press to extract liquid from the plant matter to test it more accurately," he sighs. "Be still, my heart."

"It's stainless steel too," I say, plucking it out of the bag.

He clutches his chest exaggeratedly, making me laugh more. I like how I get to play along with him. I'm not the most jokey person, but he always makes me feel clever—almost witty.

"I'm not so sure how it'll work on algae, though," I admit.

"Let's find out," he says. He grabs the unlabeled specimen tube and the tweezers off the rock and hands them to me. "This your test group?"

I nod, taking them from him. I slide on another pair of gloves as Justin sets out two fresh petri dishes on the rock. I feed the algae into the garlic press, filling the chamber with the silty green stuff and then squeezing it through the fine holes. Green liquid drips into the dish, and I repeat the process for the second dish until both are full with a wash of gooey algae juice.

I press a red sticker onto the bottom of one of the petri dishes, because you never want to be asking yourself "Wait, which dish did I add which solution to?" when you're doing an experiment. And then I pour the bottle of vinegar into the dish. Justin and I both lean forward with bated breath.

Absolutely nothing happens.

"Okay . . . so not alkaline," Justin says.

My stomach leaps, because this is further confirmation that Izzie's hypothesis is right: the algae is acidic.

I turn my attention to the unmarked dish, pour in a measure of distilled water, wait a minute, and then add the baking soda.

"Claire!"

Justin grabs my shoulders, pulling me back as the solution in the petri dish doesn't just start to bubble—it smokes and spits, spraying all over the rock.

My eyes widen as the liquid continues to bubble fitfully over the rim of the petri dish. I grab the bottle of distilled water, pouring it over the solution and the rock, praying that I didn't just do some ecosystem damage. I mean, it was just baking soda—it shouldn't have reacted like that . . . right?

As if he's reading my mind, Justin says, "That shouldn't have happened," his eyes almost as wide as mine. He looks down at the other specimen tubes, his eyes alight with interest. "That was a way extreme reaction. What's *in* this algae?"

"I don't know," I say. "But this just confirms it's the plant I was looking for."

"Ah, yes, your mysterious map," Justin says. "Gonna fill me in?"

"Soon," I promise. "But we need to head back. It's getting dark."

He looks up at the sky. "Yeah, let's get going. We wouldn't want to come across Pearl in the dark. She might decide the lights on the Gyrosphere are fun to chase."

"Oh God, I hope not," I say. "Bertie says she's doing really well with her sphere."

"Did I ever tell you how cool it was that you figured that out?" Justin asks as we trek back to the Gyrosphere. My shirt is sticking damply to me, my suit still wet enough underneath to be uncomfortable.

"The rest of the girls and I did it together," I say. "Dr. Wu said we should team up, and it turned out to be a really good idea."

"See, teamwork does improve things," he says as he pops the Gyrosphere's doors open and we climb inside, packing the specimens and equipment carefully behind the seats.

"If some company doesn't hire you out of college to, like, boost worker morale, they'll be missing out," I say, and his eyes crinkle at the thought.

"That'd be a fun job, actually," he says, his eyes fixed on the screen as we back the Gyrosphere through the vines and head toward the open valley. We have to flip the lights on in the thicket because the trees are blocking the rapidly fading sun. As we turn a corner, the lights illuminate the clearing—and Lovelace, who is enthusiastically rubbing her horns against a tree. Branches and leaves rain down on our Gyrosphere as we maneuver carefully around her, and she barely glances at us as she gets her itchies out.

"Wouldn't it be cool if they just ditched their horns each season like deer shed their antlers?" Justin asks.

"But then people would start hanging them on the walls," I protest.

"Not a fan of deer heads and antlers?" he asks, and I wrinkle my nose, shaking my head.

"Responsible hunting? Absolutely. My dad hunts. That's how I learned how to shoot a rifle. But trophy hunting is awful. It's not respectful to the animal or to nature or to life and death."

"I agree," he says. "You really know how to shoot a rifle?"

I nod. "I've never gone hunting with my dad, though. He's asked me a few times, but I can't do it. I'm a wimp."

"You're not a wimp, you just know your limits," he says as the trees grow sparser and the landscape opens up to the valley. We roll through the hills, and when we reach the gate, I punch in the manual override code again, hop out, and then enter Bertie's code at the gate. It swings open, and we return the Gyrosphere to its spot, get in the jeep, and drive off. On the road, we see a team of security guards heading toward the valley—the night shift, who are none the wiser about our little trip. I let out a relieved sigh as their taillights recede in the rearview.

"And we're home free," Justin declares when we pull up to the hotel and park. I grab my bag with the precious specimens—I need to get them into a fridge as soon as possible—and we head into the lobby and step into the elevator.

"So have you devised some plan to sneak into Dr. Wu's labs for further algae testing?" Justin asks. "Because I think facing down a whole herd of Triceratops might be preferable to getting caught by him."

"I've gotta think about it first," I say.

His head tilts as the elevator continues to climb. "Why all the mystery, Claire?"

I bite my lip. He's been so nice to help me, and I've been pretty cagey about my reasons for all this. I want to tell him—I do. But there's some small part of me worrying that if I discover the park had some part in Izzie's death, Justin will side with the business, not the person. It makes me hesitate, and I don't even know if that's fair to him, because he keeps showing me over and over that he's worthy of my trust.

But this . . . this isn't just about trust. This is life and death. This is a cover-up. This is possibly *murder*.

And it holds me back. Just enough.

"I promise, I have a good reason," I say.

"I know you do," he says. "You wouldn't go to all this trouble if you didn't."

The certainty in his voice makes me look up. The smile in his eyes makes me move forward.

I've never initiated a first before. I've never wanted to, except maybe earlier at the falls. But here, in this elevator, I finally do.

So I take his hand, and our fingers entwine, our hands still a little pruney from our swim. I stand on my toes, and when my lips brush his, his other hand comes to rest on the small of my back, drawing me closer. It's like all the thrilling things about discovering something—someone—wrapped in a simple touch, in his breath against my cheek, and his hand warm through my T-shirt.

When the elevator doors slide open, neither of us notices for a long time.

25

Now that I have the algae specimens—and know something weird is going on with the acidity of the plants—I feel impatient. Two lab days have passed, and I still haven't figured out a way to get Dr. Wu's help in evaluating the specimens further without tipping him off. And this morning, our third in the lab this week, Dr. Wu isn't even here. One of his scientists takes us back to the incubator lab to do our work.

"I bet he's preparing for the Raptor coming," Tanya says excitedly as soon as the scientist leaves us alone. Wyatt, as he typically does, goes and sits in the corner with his tablet, leaving us to do all the monitoring work.

"At breakfast, Beverly said they'll be showing movies tonight," Tanya continues. "They're trying to keep us distracted so we don't go sneaking out to watch them delivering the Raptor."

"How long do they get put in quarantine?" I ask. Even though I've seen how luxurious the quarantine paddock is, I don't like the idea of any of the dinosaurs being kept away from their own habitat for long.

"A few weeks, Amanda said. But it's not like they're in a cage," she adds quickly, like she knows what I'm thinking. "And the quarantine paddock is huge, like forty acres or something, so hopefully she won't be cranky."

"Can you imagine if she got cranky during transport?" I ask.

Tanya shudders. "She might tear a ship apart! Or jump into the water!"

"Can they swim?" I ask. Even as a kid, other than my desire to see and/or be a T. rex—because, well, come on, the San Diego footage blew everyone's minds—I was always more focused on the herbivores than the carnivores, especially when it came to reading about them, so I'm not as well informed about Raptors as I should be. I'm kind of kicking myself now for not studying up enough before I came to the island.

Wyatt snorts from his spot at the lab table, like my question is *so* stupid. I shoot a glare at him.

"You know, I'm not sure," she says. "They've got those little arms." She makes a funny paddling movement with her hands as if she's thinking through the logistics. "Maybe? We'll have to ask Amanda or Art."

The eggs are doing great—being able to watch them grow centimeter by centimeter over the last few weeks has been fascinating—and when Dr. Wu's scientist shows up to escort us out after our monitoring hour is done, I hate to leave.

"Where are you assigned today, Claire?" Tanya asks. She's been in the research greenhouses all week so far.

I pull up my schedule on my tablet. "Oh, I guess it's my day off," I say. I didn't realize. I've been too wrapped up in gathering the algae and then trying to figure out how to test it. "I might go and see if Bertie needs any help."

"Why don't you drop me off at the greenhouses, then?" Tanya asks. "I can get a ride back with whoever's working with me today."

"Sounds good."

After I drop Tanya off, I go back to our room. I take a long shower, thinking through my options when it comes to the algae and Izzie, but I'm still at a loss. I need more information, and the only person I know who has it is Wyatt. He's been avoiding me ever since I beat him at his own game, so where does that leave me?

My tablet starts buzzing as soon as I finish getting dressed, and I see that it's my sister video-calling. I set the tablet on its stand on the desk and sit down before accepting the call.

"Well, at least I know you haven't been eaten by a dinosaur!" Karen says when the video loads and we're seeing each other on our screens. "Your postcards have been great, but you've been sending all my calls to voice mail!"

"I know, I'm sorry. I've loved your postcards and all the pictures you sent of Sally and Earhart. Things have just been *so* busy," I say. It's good to see Karen, her pretty face smiling at me. There's a pile of books behind her, and a stack of quilts that are obviously Mom's handiwork. Uh-oh. Has Mom been stress-quilting?

"How are Mom and Dad?" I ask nervously. I've been dodging their calls too.

"You know, I think they're good," Karen says. "I got them this apple-picking package upstate where they stayed in this farmhouse-turned-B-and-B and they had a lot of fun. I think they're really reconnecting."

A happy glow lights inside me. "That's *great*," I say.

Karen beams at me. "Now tell me about you! What's going on? How are the dinosaurs? How's the cutie with the glasses you mentioned last time?"

I turn scarlet, and Karen's smile widens. "Oh, I see how it is," she teases.

"I'm actually having kind of a problem," I say.

Karen frowns. "He's not pressuring you, is he?"

"What? God! No!" I say. "Justin's, like, the most respectful guy ever. It's not about anything like that." I bite my lip, trying to think of a way to put it into words. I can't tell Karen I think I stumbled on a possible murder because she'd *freak* and get on the next plane to Costa Rica to come get me. "I have something. This big idea. Justin's been helping me with it, but to move forward, I have to tell him the whole story."

Karen tilts her head. "Why don't you want to?"

"It's not that I don't trust him," I say. "I do. It's just . . . there might be consequences. To my idea."

"You're being really vague," Karen says, raising an eyebrow. "Are you being this vague with him?"

"Yes," I admit.

"And he's been helping you this whole time—total faith in you?"

"Yes," I repeat.

Karen sighs. "Oh, Claire-bear. Sweetie, I love you. You're a wonderful girl. But you've always had a way easier time letting animals in than people. Even the people who deserve it."

She's right. Sometimes I feel like I have armored skin like an Ankylosaurus.

"You build walls," Karen says. "And it's really hard for you to knock them completely down. But when you do, aren't you better off?"

I don't say anything.

"Do you think you'd be better off if you tell him the whole story?" Karen asks. "If you let him in on it?"

"Probably," I say, and Karen rolls her eyes at my indecision in typical big-sister fashion.

"Maybe make a pros and cons list?" she suggests, and I know she kind of means it as a joke, but it's not the *worst* idea. "At least think about it. If he's as nice and respectful as you say, then you don't want to miss out on a guy like that. It's okay to let someone who cares about you in sometimes."

I know, intellectually, that she's right. But it's scary.

"I'm gonna be late for lunch if I don't head out," I say.

"Do you have your bear spray?" Karen asks.

I blink, not even remembering for a second. Bear spray? And then it hits me: the bear spray she insisted I get when we went shopping for my trip. It's stashed in my top drawer with my socks.

"Yeah," I say, and she shoots me a look that's *pure* mom, so I get up and grab it out of the dresser, holding it up to the screen and dropping it into one of the side pockets of my cargo shorts. "Satisfied?" I ask.

"Very," Karen says. "I love you. Be safe." She blows a kiss at the screen, and I wave, ending the call.

And then, true to my nature, I go and make a pros and cons list.

After dinner, as everyone heads to the conference room where they're showing the movie, I pull Justin aside. "Can we talk?" I ask.

"Sure," he says.

We go back up to my room. Tanya's already off with Ronnie and the rest of the girls at the movie, so I pull Izzie's notebook out from under my pillow.

"Finally going to let me in on the mystery, huh?" he asks, sitting down on the bed across from me.

"Yes, but you've gotta promise you'll listen with an open mind," I say.

"Deal," he says easily, but I wonder how easy it will actually be. The story seems kind of far-fetched, even now that I have some evidence.

"Remember how in our first week, Wyatt was running his mouth about phantom interns and one getting left behind?" I ask.

He chuckles. "Yeah."

"So . . . there was truth to that story," I say.

"Really," he says, and he sounds skeptical.

"I found this notebook." I push Izzie's journal across the bedspread. "It was tucked in the box springs under the bed. It's dated from the beginning of this year, and it details months of time spent on the island when the herbivores from Isla Sorna first arrived."

He flips open the notebook, his puzzled expression deepening as he leafs through it.

"How do you know it's the journal of the intern who supposedly got left behind in the storm, though?" he asks, finally looking up.

"Wyatt has a list of the first group of interns—he found it in his dad's office. I got him to give it to me."

"Got him to?" Justin echoes.

"He admitted to me he snuck into his dad's office and took photos of the documents—and I recorded him. So he decided it was in his best interests to give me the list. That's how I found out Izzie's last name and was able to search for her online."

"What did you find?"

"Her obituary," I say, and his eyes widen beneath his glasses.

"Seriously?"

"It says that she died at her parents' house in Boston on March fourth. But here"—I flip through the pages of the notebook and point to the March 4 entry in the Brachiosauruses' feeding schedule—"the notebook tells us she was still on the island on the fourth. That's the day before the storm hit, according to the weather data I pulled up. And then there's the threat."

"What threat?"

"I found this pressed between the pages," I say, showing him the yellow scrap of paper that says *Watch your back* on it.

"That's not reassuring," he says. "Okay. So what's your theory? She got left behind because of human error and the company covered it up?"

"I don't know," I say. "But I do know she didn't die on March fourth in Boston."

"Wow." He stares at the floor for a second, absorbing it. "What does this have to do with the algae?" he asks.

"When Izzie was an intern, Olive and Agnes started getting these throat infections. Olive's got so bad she needed surgery to remove the abscess. I asked Dr. Wu about the infections, because the dinosaurs—all of them—are on antibiotics. Apparently the throat infections cropped up across the species, and they couldn't figure out what was causing it, so they've been dosing all the dinosaurs as a precautionary measure—some even in utero."

"The algae's causing the infections," Justin says.

"Izzie was in the process of testing the plants in the Gyrosphere Valley for acidity. She believed that something the herbivores were eating was causing the infections. She narrowed it down to the algae."

"Which is weirdly, highly acidic," Justin muses.

"Could it, like, burn their throats?" I ask. "And maybe that's what caused the infections?"

"It's possible," Justin says. "You'd have to get it tested. But the reaction we saw at the waterfall is *not* typically how algae reacts to a simple baking soda test. There's obviously something going on with the plant. You should really ask Tanya. But . . . you don't want to tell her about this." He taps the notebook.

"I don't know what to say," I admit. "If Izzie did die on the island . . . if the company covered it up . . ."

"That's unacceptable," Justin finishes for me. "It's not right on any level."

"But what if I'm jumping to conclusions?" I ask. "Maybe there was an accident or something, and her parents wanted to keep it private and I'm just spinning stuff. The things I know for sure are that she didn't die in Boston when her obituary says she did, and that the first batch of interns on Isla Nublar won't talk about being interns. It's like that period never happened. I feel like I don't have enough information, and Wyatt . . ." I trail off. "He knows more than he was letting on during our first conversation," I say. "I should've pressed him, but I was excited about actually getting Izzie's full name, and I played my hand too fast."

Justin glances down at the notebook again, thinking. "So then I guess we need more information," he says.

Now I'm doing the eyebrow raising. "What do you suggest?"

"How do you feel about breaking and entering?"

26

The hotel hall is empty—all the interns are watching the movie and all the adults are probably dealing with whatever they have to do when a new dinosaur comes to the island. My heart's beating fast—not only at the thought of a Raptor on the island, but because Justin is currently kneeling on the ground in front of Wyatt and Eric's room with a bobby pin and one of my copper hair sticks, picking the lock.

"And you said *I* was the rule breaker," I whisper, and he grins as he uses the hair stick as a tension wrench and the bobby pin to push up the lock's pins. "Where did you learn how to do this?" I ask.

"Online," he says. "My mom has this incredibly annoying automatic lock on our back door. I kept locking myself out. Then I learned how to do . . . this." He twists the knob, I hear a *click,* and the door unlocks.

"I'm still a little surprised they don't have key-card scanners," Justin says.

"Maybe they wanted to do dinosaur-engraved keys," I suggest as we slip into Wyatt and Eric's room.

It's the same as mine and Tanya's, though one side is incredibly messy, the bed unmade, dirty socks at the foot.

"Look, camera equipment," Justin points to the neater side of the room. "That's Eric's side."

"Eww," I say, looking back at Wyatt's side. "I should've brought gloves."

"I'll go through his drawers," Justin offers. "Do you see his tablet anywhere?"

I look around. "No luck. He probably brought it with him. I'm going to check the bathroom. Maybe he hid stuff in the cupboards."

There's just your normal stuff in the medicine cabinet—hotel shampoo with different dinosaur species stamped on the wrappers, an electric razor, Q-tips. I bend down to look in the cupboard under the sink, but there's nothing but pipes and extra toilet paper. I dig carefully through the cabinet holding the neatly rolled towels, but there's nothing there either. I'm about to turn around when something hits me: the towels in my room weren't rolled by housekeeping—they were folded.

I turn back to the cupboard, take the stack of neat terry-cloth cylinders, and set them on the bath mat on the ground, unrolling them one by one.

They're empty. Except for one.

Something falls out of the last towel I unroll, and I have to reach forward to grab it before it rolls away.

It's a tranquilizer dart. The same kind I spent all that time cataloging—the kind Wyatt knocked over. And I thought he was just being a jerk . . .

"Justin," I call.

He pokes his head into the bathroom. "Did you find something?" he asks.

I hold up the tranquilizer dart. "This was rolled up in one of the towels."

"What's he doing with something like that?"

"I don't know," I say, rerolling the towels and shoving them back into the cupboard. "Where else would he hide stuff?"

Justin looks around the bathroom. "You try the shower curtain rod? Sometimes they're hollow." He walks over and tests it, trying to pull it down. But it's screwed to the wall. "Hmmm." His glance falls on the toilet. "The tank," he says.

We lift off the lid, and I gasp. There are two waterproof bags taped to the sides of the half-filled toilet tank. Justin pulls off the tape, grabs the bags out of the water, and lays them on the bath mat.

I open one, and my stomach sinks.

Inside are the same kind of memory cards as the crunched one I found in the jungle—but in better shape—plus four cylindrical glass containers full of a clear gel.

"That's the fusion bandage compound," Justin breathes. "He stole it. What the hell?"

"What's in the other bag?"

"A bunch of security specs. Look, they're all stamped *INTERNAL ONLY*." He passes me a thick wad of folded papers, and I leaf through them as quickly as I can. They're layouts for the paddocks and training areas, even a few fuzzy gray pictures that look like they were taken by aerial drones. Some of the papers have notes about the location of fuse boxes, and even a few number sequences that look like key codes for places like the training area and the valley.

"He must've stolen this from his dad too. Like the intern list," I say. "What is he up to?"

"I don't know, but we need to take this to Mr. Masrani," Justin says, gathering it all up and dropping it back into the plastic bags. "What if he's planning to steal more stuff tonight, when everyone's distracted?"

My stomach sinks. "Let's go check to see if he's watching the movie with everyone else," I say.

"And if he isn't?"

"Then we need to find Mr. Masrani—fast—before Wyatt does anything," I say. "He's had access to the Pteranodon eggs for weeks now. That's what Tanya and I have been doing in Dr. Wu's lab every morning. We're monitoring the first hatch. Wyatt somehow weaseled his way into the job too."

"A Pteranodon egg would be easier to smuggle out than a live dinosaur," Justin says, looking disturbed. "But if he's already stealing tranquilizers and fusion bandages . . . he's stealing them for *something*."

"Maybe he's got a buyer," I say as we hurry out of Wyatt and Eric's room with Wyatt's stash. "The fusion bandage will revolutionize trauma medicine once they figure out a way to get it to stick to nondinosaur skin. And I'm sure the tranquilizer is some special megapowerful kind. They'd need it to knock out a dinosaur."

Justin closes the door behind us, and we walk down the hall, no one the wiser.

"Let's hope he's got a buyer," Justin says.

"Why?" I ask. The elevator dings open and we get in.

"Because if he doesn't, it means he's got something else planned," Justin says. "Tranquilizers? Bandages? Security specs of the paddocks and valley? What if his aim isn't the Pteranodon eggs? What if he's after one of the dinosaurs?"

A cold snap of shock sweeps through my brain. It didn't even occur to me that Wyatt might try his hand at dino-napping. He isn't that stupid, right? No one's that foolish. He'd be caught. And the logistics and the sizes of the dinosaurs, even the young ones . . .

But then I think about the Compsognathuses. They aren't very big. They might be vicious little biting and eating machines, but if Wyatt manages to get his hands on a sedative, he might be able to smuggle one out.

The elevator doors ding open, disturbing my thoughts.

"Come on. Let's go," Justin says. "The movie's playing in the second-floor conference room."

We jog down the hall, both of us too impatient to walk. The conference room is dark, with couches grouped around a projection screen. I can see the top of Beverly's head in the front, so I stay low as I creep up to the couch in the back, where Amanda is sitting with Art, his arm around her shoulders.

"Hey," I whisper.

She turns, shooting me an expectant look.

"Is Wyatt here?"

She shakes her head. "He told Beverly he had a headache and was gonna lie down in his room," she says softly. "He made a whole deal out of it."

Of course he did. He's up to something.

"Thanks. Sorry to bother you."

I creep back to Justin, who's standing in the doorway, and shake my head to indicate he isn't there. We slip out before Beverly notices us.

"He made some excuse up about having a headache," I say.

"Typical," Justin says.

We take the stairs instead of the elevator down to the main floor. Rather than going through the lobby, we make a left at the bottom of the stairs and end up in the service hallway that leads to the kitchens. I don't want to risk running into any security guards in the lobby.

The kitchens are hot and bustling with activity. When we pass by the short-order cook, he shoots us a look. "Sneaking out?" he asks.

"We're just trying to avoid someone," I say.

"You and everyone else," he says, and I raise an eyebrow.

"Someone else came through here?"

"Sneaky interns are always coming down here and bothering me," he says. "Now shoo!" He waves his spatula at us, and we turn around before he decides to rat us out.

We take the exit out of the kitchen, and the muggy night air envelops us like an oppressive hug. The intern jeeps are parked in the back lot as always, and the keys are in the lockbox, so Justin grabs one and we jump in.

"Where's Mr. Masrani this time of night?" Justin asks as he starts the engine.

"He's got to be at the quarantine paddock. It's west of here." I say.

"You sure that's where he'll be?"

"Yeah. Bertie said they did a toast at the command center after a new dinosaur was brought to Nublar, but they would've locked us down earlier if the Raptor was arriving before dark. They probably wait until nightfall because of light sensitivity or something. Masrani being at the paddock's the smartest bet."

"Let's go, then," Justin says, pulling out of the parking lot with a screech and heading down the road. He keeps flexing his fingers around the wheel, and I feel as nervous as he looks as we speed through the jungle, the glow of our headlights the only thing breaking the darkness as we head deeper into the thickly forested, mountainous part of the park.

When we pull up to the quarantine paddock, it's totally dark. I frown as we get out of the jeep. I expected the kind of setup we saw when Lovelace was released into the valley our first week: huge trucks, tons of trainers, floodlights, armed guards.

But there's nothing. The outside light isn't even on.

"Has she not arrived yet?"

"They could be still on the docks, waiting to transport her," Justin suggests.

"That's a good idea," I say. "Let's go down there."

I'm about to turn back to the jeep when all the lights in the training center suddenly flash on, then off. Like a power overload.

"Claire, smoke!" Justin points, and then I see it too. A wisp of smoke rising from behind the training center—from the training yard.

"We need an extinguisher," I say immediately. I dash to the door and grab the knob tentatively, worried it'll be hot. But it's not—and it's unlocked. Justin's right behind me as I run inside, and he grabs the fire extinguisher fixed to the wall and we hurry to the back door that leads to the security tunnel that opens into the training yard.

When Bertie brought me in here before I got to see Rexy, I saw her punch in the key code. I do it now from memory and the big steel door clicks open. All I'm thinking about is what she said about how deadly fires could be on the island. What if sparks fly into an occupied paddock? We need to get it out—fast!

I cough as we hurry into the dirt training yard. There's not a ton of smoke, but it smells terrible—not like plant matter burning, but like plastic and metal. The taste of it coats my tongue and I want to gag.

"Where is it coming from?" I ask Justin, squinting in the darkness. The training yard is big, at least a few hectares, and the cement walls and steel walkways crisscrossing overhead cast huge shadows, making it even darker with all the smoke.

"It's thicker over there," Justin says, pointing through the haze. We forge ahead. My boot kicks something—I think it's a feeding trough—and I stumble into Justin, who makes sure I don't fall.

"Steady," he says. He reaches out, and his hand makes contact with the fence that divides the training yard from the paddock. We use it as our guide moving forward.

And then I hear it, just before I see the shadowy figures ahead. A voice.

"Hurry up!"

As I squint in the darkness, a cloud shifts in the sky and moonlight spills across the yard, slicing through the smoke . . . and I see.

But it's not Wyatt, as I expected.

It's Eric and Tanya.

My mind stalls like a broken truck. The world flips, and it's cold and it's hard and so confusing.

"What are you doing?" Justin shouts, his voice booming across the yard.

Tanya shrieks, jumping from her spot behind her brother's shoulder. Eric's crouched down in front of a giant steel box, wires spilling out of it, a soldering iron on the ground next to him, along with a burnt-off padlock. Tanya's shriek startles him, and I watch in horror as his hand jerks and the clippers he's holding slice through the red wire he's clutching between two fingers.

Neither twin has any time to answer. Because a metallic screeching sound fills the air and I whirl around as holding pens and paddock gates begin to open—and the emergency hatch that leads to the unguarded, unwalled jungle rattles starts to rise.

"Oh my God, Eric, what did you do, what did you *do*?" Tanya says, her voice shaking.

"The main power port—I didn't mean—" he stammers. "I can fix it. I promise. I just need to access the backup generator. Just give me—"

Justin's hand clamps around mine, his entire body going rigid, and I turn to look where he's looking.

There's something moving toward us through the smoke, something big and curious, and when I see the glow of her yellow reptilian eyes through the haze, it's not like Rexy. There's no control. There's no safety. There are no adults. There's no food to distract her with. And in this moment, I truly understand what Bertie said about carnivores and how they look at you and think *food* first and *friend* second.

There's no friendliness in her eyes.

Just hunger.

I do the only thing I can do.

I open my mouth. And I scream.

"Run!"

27

There is no fight *or* flight when a dinosaur is involved. There's only flight.

We run. It's not mindless, but it might as well be. There's no way we'd make it across the training yard and into the security tunnel. She's blocking our way. There's only one choice: into the paddock.

Into the jungle.

"Go, go, go!" Justin chants as we pelt toward the paddock's gate. We dash through, and the three of them keep running toward the trees, but I hesitate, looking around frantically. Where is it? The emergency button . . .

"Claire!" Justin shouts, glancing over his shoulder.

But I've spotted it. Six feet away, shining like a beacon. I bolt toward it, even as I see the Raptor out of the corner of my eye, circling, getting ready to dive for the opening the gate provides.

I slam my palm down on the button and run toward the trees.

Behind me I hear a metallic whine as the gate scrapes across the road, and *Please let it close fast enough, please, please . . .*

I glance over my shoulder and the Raptor's diving for the gate as it closes, her speed and her strength giving her all the advantage, but her tail . . .

Slam. The gate pins her down by the tail. The Raptor screeches, an inhuman sound of pain that makes my stomach cramp with sympathy, even though I'm so, so scared of her. She jerks forward, but she can't move. Not without really hurting herself.

I keep running, vines whipping my face, branches cracking under my boots as I scan the jungle ahead, trying to find Justin.

"Claire!"

He runs toward me out of the dark, grabbing my hand.

"The gate's got her pinned, but she'll be after us soon," I pant, bending down, my hands pressing into my thighs as I try to catch my breath.

"You locked us in here with her!" Eric hisses.

"You idiot, the emergency hatch opened with the gates! What if she got out?" Justin snaps. "She'd kill someone if she got into the more populated areas."

"So now she'll just kill us!"

"You're the one who was breaking into the security power grid!" Justin says. "What the hell are you up to? That stuff Claire and I found in Wyatt's and your room—that was your stuff. You two have been stealing things."

"You guys," I say firmly. "We have to move."

"Claire's right," Tanya says, and I want to glare at her, because what was she *thinking*? But we have way more pressing matters now.

"We need to get out of here," Tanya says firmly. "The walls aren't climbable, but the trees . . ."

Justin's anger seems to fade as he scans the canopy. "We need to get to the wall. Find a tree that we can use to jump it."

"What if the tops are electrified?" I ask.

"They're not," Eric says. "They have sonic barriers like the portable ones they use in the valley for training."

"Let's move, then," I say.

We've gotten all turned around in our dash through the jungle, and I have no idea what direction we're actually facing . . . whether the gate and the training center—and the Raptor—are behind us or in front of us, or if she'll come at us from the side this time.

Run, run, run! It's like a heartbeat inside me; each step I take might be my last. I'm poised for it, my shoulders tight, my body a rush of adrenaline and fear, waiting.

Justin's hand squeezes mine before dropping away as he climbs over a huge fallen tree. I scramble up next. We're on higher ground here, more ferns, fewer vines, and I think I hear the rush of water in the distance—or is it the rustle of Raptor feet swishing through the thick fern underbrush?

We move through the darkness for I don't know how long. At some point, I realize that there's blood dripping down my cheek. I wipe it away the best I can, but I worry. Will the Raptor be able to smell it?

Does it matter? She'll find us in the end anyway. She's bigger and she's stronger and she's way faster.

"There," Tanya hisses. "It's the wall."

I press my palms against the thick cement, relief flooding me.

"Okay, we need to find a tree tall enough," Eric says. "Hurry."

We begin to jog along the wall, trying to find a climbable tree with overhanging branches. But the farther we run, the less likely it seems. It looks like the landscapers trimmed all the trees.

Eric swears rapidly under his breath, sweat trickling down his face in the moonlight. "What do we do?" he mutters, mostly to himself.

"We'll find a tree. We'll get out," Tanya says, or more like begs, like she needs him to believe it. For the first time, I look at her, and I see how scared she is. I bite the inside of my lip, refusing to feel bad. She and Eric are the reason this is happening.

"We need another plan, just in case," I say. I have to stop for a second, and everyone else slows too, sagging against the wall with me. My lungs feel like they're on fire.

"We could hide," Tanya says. "You hit the emergency gate alarm. That has to have sent out an alert to the command center, right? Maybe they're already here. They'll get the Raptor contained."

"The alert might not go out, considering Eric messed up the power," Justin growls.

"We need to get to the armory," I say, remembering the security protocol Bertie ran us through when we were assigned to the training center. "There's a cache of stunners and tranquilizer guns in every habitat. If we're armed, we're safer."

"Wait, look," Tanya says. The moonlight's shifted again, and I see it too. Ahead of us is a large tree with a few thick branches almost brushing the wall.

We run toward it, and Tanya scrambles up first. I keep watch on her while the boys keep an eye on the horizon for any danger. My stomach twists as Tanya crawls belly down along the branch, and it wobbles furiously when she straightens up and then *jumps.*

"*Oof!*" She lets out a pained grunt as her hip hits the wall, and she has to pull herself up to the top and over; then she drops to the ground on the other side. Shakily, she gets to her feet. "Come on, you guys," she hisses as loudly as she dares.

Eric follows her up and over, making a jump neater than his sister's, and the twins clutch each other when they're both safe on the other side. Justin's next. When he gets to the first V in the tree, where it splits into two thick branches, he turns back and holds out his hand to pull me up.

I'm just reaching for him when Tanya's voice cuts through the silence.

"*CLAIRE! TO YOUR LEFT!*"

I don't look. I know I can't waste that kind of time. I just react. I dive to my right, away from Justin and the tree and safety.

I roll down an embankment, and for a moment, it's just a blur of green and brown and panic and *Get up, Claire, get up get up get up!* Dizzy, I force myself to my feet as soon as my free fall stops, and I look up to see a thick press of eucalyptus trees grown tightly together, just ahead. I run toward it, sliding through the narrow spaces between the trees, my stomach scraping against rough bark as I do.

I'm whimpering, and I have to stop. I press my lips together, trying to stifle the sound. I have to be quiet. I have to stop shaking. I need to run. I need to survive. I need . . .

Click. Click. Click.

All the hairs on the back of my neck rise as I see the glow of amber in the darkness. The Raptor has caught my scent and is coming near. My heart's beating so loud, surely she must hear it. She cranes her neck, trying to squeeze her head between the trees, but she can't quite fit. She gnashes her teeth at me, and I scramble back as she rears away, trying to jam herself between another clump of trees.

She's already learning. Adapting.

The trees sway back and forth, and I freeze, terrified.

If I run, will it spur her on, now that she's got the fix on me? Will it spur her hunting instinct? They hunt in packs. I know that. And if she's confused and scared and hungry and alone . . .

"Hey!"

A rock comes sailing through the air, striking the Raptor on the flank. Her head jerks to the side, all her attention leaving me.

But instead of feeling relieved, all I can feel is terror.

Because it's Justin running toward me, darting through the trees as the Raptor tries to chase him. He hasn't made the leap to the wall. He's come back for me. Oh God, he's come back for me. *Why* has he come back for me?

"Claire, go, *run!*" he shouts, and I follow him, I have no choice. Running full tilt through the eucalyptus grove, the trees our only protection, I'm terrified to see them thin out ahead. I can hear her behind us, her frustration audible in the air between us, her angry roars pulsing through me like electricity.

At the edge of the eucalyptus grove, she has some trouble

navigating through the trees, which gives us a head start—not much, but we'll have to make it work.

"We need the weapons," Justin gasps as we leave the shelter of the trees for vulnerable open space.

"There's a cache in each corner of the habitat," I say, stopping for a second to catch my breath. I look around, trying to see if I can identify anything familiar from our sprint before the grove. But it's too dark, the moonlight's too weak, and we don't have time. We need to run.

"So we just run until we hit wall again," Justin says, and the way he says it makes tears well up in my eyes. It's not a question. It's a statement. Like he's sure. Like we can do it.

Like it isn't the last thing he might ever say to me.

"Yeah," I say, gaining strength from his faith. "Let's go."

We run.

My existence narrows down to my pounding feet and the air cutting through my ragged lungs, and the creeping, terrible knowledge that comes with each step: *I am prey.* The jungle is merciless. My body aches as I squelch through ankle-deep mud and get tangled up in vines, the flies relentlessly swooping at my face. Just a few more steps, I keep telling myself. A few more steps, and it will clear. And the weapons will be in reach.

Surely someone is coming to help us. Even if the cameras aren't working because of Eric's wire blunder, surely the twins would go get help.

But I'm not sure at all. Not with what I know now about them. Thieves. Liars. I feel so naive. So stupid.

I push it out of my mind as Justin and I trek on, our footsteps and the buzz of the insects the only sounds. Has the Raptor lost interest already?

I know that's wishful thinking. The kind of thinking that will get us killed.

"Hey," I say, my hand closing on Justin's arm. "Look."

A glimpse of gray through the trees. The wall. Hope sparks in me as we draw closer, and I see a red box just fifty feet ahead, tucked into the corner next to some ferns.

The weapons cache. It's so close. We just need to get to it and open it, and then maybe we'll be okay. We'll at least have a fighting chance.

I'm about to rush forward when Justin flings his arm backward across my chest and presses his finger against his lips. He drags me behind a tree, we flatten ourselves against it . . . and then I see her. She's moving along the perimeter, striking the wall with her nose every few feet.

She's testing it for weaknesses. She's smart. It makes her even more terrifying.

We watch, frozen against the tree trunk, and I try so hard to not even *breathe*, because what if she hears? What if she smells us?

And just as that thought is going through my mind, she arches her neck, her head tipping back to the sky, her mouth open wide—and God, those *teeth*—as she inhales.

It's now or never, and Justin and I both know it. We don't need to speak. We need to run. It's either run toward the weapons—and the Raptor—or run away and she'll chase us.

I look at him, and when he smiles, I think it's to reassure me.

But then he straightens and turns, not to run away into the jungle, but to run toward the wall, and I realize it's not reassurance.

It's goodbye.

"No—" I start to say, but before it's even out of my mouth, before I can do anything to stop him, he's yelling, running out of the tree line and away from the weapons cache, drawing her attention.

I have to move. I force myself to, my heart *screaming* inside me like my mouth wants to. The Raptor chases Justin, leaving the weapons and me behind. He disappears into the jungle and so does she, and I want to scream, I want to yell and run after them, but I force myself to be quiet, and I run toward the weapons cache. With shaky, bloody fingers, I punch in the key code Bertie gave us as a precaution, and I flip open the box. Inside are stunners and tranquilizers. I grab a stunner and one of the tranquilizers. It's close enough to a rifle; it'll work. I shove the stunner in a pocket, swing the rifle strap over my shoulder, and turn back to the trees.

The jungle is silent. I have no idea where Justin is. Where the Raptor chased or—my stomach lurches—*dragged* him. Is he alive? Is he dead?

Is it hopeless?

I take a deep breath. *One Mississippi. Two Mississippi. Three Mississippi.*

It may be hopeless. And I may be human.

But it's time to be the kind of prey that fights back.

28

It doesn't take long to find the blood.

My heart sinks and my resolve hardens with each smear I find on the jungle floor. He's hurt. But that doesn't mean he's dead.

Fingers tight around the stunner, I prowl through the jungle. I wish I could say I'm some stone-cold badass who feels no fear, but I'm not. I'm just a girl, but I'm strong and I'm smart—which means I've never been so scared in my life. I shouldn't be doing this.

But I have to do this.

He came back for me. I won't leave him behind.

You don't leave people behind.

My parents . . . Karen . . . they'll understand if . . .

I lick my dry lips, my boot pressing down too hard on a branch, and the *crack* that fills the air makes me reach for the button on the stunner. Something rustles in the vines behind me, and I barely turn my head as I try to catch sight of her out of the corner of my eye.

But if it's her, she doesn't attack.

If it's her, she's still out there, watching, waiting.

Learning. Adapting.

It's time I do some adapting of my own.

I don't have the special scent-masking spray Bertie and I used before we entered Rexy's paddock, but there have to be other ways to disguise my scent. I keep moving, scanning the area ahead of me. Using a plant would be risky—some of them are stinky enough, but what if it's poisonous or something? I'm not good enough at identifying plants in the daytime, let alone right now, when I'm so scared I can barely think.

But I need to think. How do I blend in? How do I smell like the jungle, not like me?

My foot squelches loudly as I step forward and I look down.

Mud. Mud could work! *Please,* let mud work.

I bend down and scoop up as much as I can and keep moving as I rub it over my arms, my chest, my legs. I've gone a quarter of a mile by the time I'm covered, praying my scent has changed enough. That it'll be enough. I've gone off course, heading away from the last smear of blood I found, passing by the exact kind of cover I need: a group of big rocks with enough space below to hide in. But I keep going, focusing on a spot about twenty feet ahead. I can hear the scraping sound of claws against bark in the distance.

She's getting impatient.

I need to make my move.

I take an abrupt left, duck through the trees, and creep behind the rocks, where the ground dips into a hollow area just big enough for me to tuck myself into. I lie there, flat, the rifle digging into my back, the stunner clutched to my front, trying not to breathe as the rustling of the jungle grows louder.

Click. Click. Click. Those claws against the ground. I never want to hear that sound again. It'll haunt me forever.

The sound grows closer—so loud I'm sure she's right next to me, and when I turn my head to the side, peering through a crack in the rocks, I see her feet right there, standing next to the pile.

My entire body shakes. I try to tense my muscles, terrified I'll make noise, but I can't stop.

Please, please don't smell me. Please let it work.

Her feet stop.

One Mississippi. Two Mississippi. Three . . .

She moves away, her talons disappearing from my view, and I wait for silence, counting in my head and trying to calm my breathing until I'm sure I can stand on my feet, steady.

Then I crawl out of my hiding place and circle around, back toward the trail of blood. Running full speed away from where she's going—and hopefully toward Justin. I get to the last place I saw blood, a fern bed, and hurry in that direction, peering into the darkness, every sense on alert.

There, up ahead, is that another smear? I run forward, and my hand presses against the tree trunk. I can feel the rough scrape of clawed-up bark—and the wetness of something that's not water or tree sap. I'm on the right path.

I run forward, the rifle slapping the back of my legs with each step. I lose the path twice, but each time, I manage to circle back and find it again. There's still no sign of him.

Did she drag him somewhere I won't be able to find him? Did he get away from her and crawl to safety?

I step forward in the darkness and something crunches under my boot, the sound of glass breaking unmistakable.

His glasses. Oh no . . .

"Justin," I hiss into the night. I dart forward, all my focus ahead, and I don't see it coming.

I don't see *her* coming.

All of a sudden, my feet are swept out from under me. I slam down onto the jungle floor and my head strikes the rifle stock hard, dazing me. The stunner flies out of my hand, and I'm reeling, bewildered by what just happened, trying to catch the breath that was just knocked out of me. I cough and sputter, and then I hear it.

Click. Click. Click.

She steps right in front of me, shifting from foot to foot, gaze intent on me.

She doesn't want me to interrupt her meal.

I sit up, looking around frantically for the stunner, but it's out of reach. I grab the rifle on my back, but when I rest it against my shoulder, I see that my fall has broken the tranquilizer darts inside the chamber. It's useless.

I'm useless.

Oh God.

I scramble backward, but my shoulders hit the trunk of a tree, and then I'm stuck, pinned there by her predatory gaze. I stare at her long, sharp claws gleaming in the moonlight. She's tensing. Her muscles bunching, her talons curling.

She's going to pounce.

This can't be the end. I can't . . . I won't . . .

Think, Claire. Breathe.

Adapt.

Something's pressing into my leg. A cylinder.

The bear spray Karen made me buy and bring to the island. The bear spray I put into my pocket to appease her this morning. The stupid, silly, *miraculous* bear spray.

I yank it out of my side pocket just as the Raptor makes her move toward me. I leap to my feet, raise it in the air as high as I can, and press the button. The peppery spray bursts from the spout, and the Raptor gets it right in the eyes. She rears back, shrieking in pain.

I dive for the stunner, flip it on, and press it against her flank, sending shocks through her. She shrieks again, and I hate the sound; it's horrifying. I hate that I'm the cause of it. But just the one poke puts her down, totally unconscious. I prod her a few times, just in case.

As soon as I'm sure she's out, I run.

I find Justin in a clearing about thirty feet from the spot I found his glasses. He's dragged himself over to a tree and is propped up against the trunk, his eyes half closed, his hands loose in his lap.

"Justin!"

I run to him and kneel by his side, looking up and down frantically.

"You're here," he says. His voice wobbles. There's a dark wash of blood across his chest, and when I press my hands on it, he groans and bats them away.

"Of course I am," I say. "She's knocked out. I got her. It's gonna be okay now."

His head lolls to the side, and for a horrible second I think this is it, but then he slowly raises it. I place my hands over his, and he tries to turn his own to clasp mine but can't quite find the strength. My thumb presses against the inside of his wrist, and his pulse is so shallow I can barely feel it.

"I think—" he says. "I think I've got an answer."

"An answer?"

He licks his lips, his chest rising and falling in stuttered, painful movements. "If the progress is worth the consequence," he says. "Remember. When we . . ."

"When we met," I finish for him.

"You were right," he gasps out. "The cost . . . it's too much."

I cup his face, swallowing back the tears. "It's okay," I tell him. "They'll be here soon."

"Don't cry," he says. "It's . . ." He shudders. "It doesn't hurt any-more."

"That's good," I say. "They'll fix you up as soon as they get here."

"You're a bad liar," he chokes out.

I wipe the trickle of blood away from the corner of his mouth. I know what that means. He's bleeding internally. My fingers clench his. I can't breathe. I can't think. I can't do anything.

I can't fix him.

I can't save him.

All I can do is be here with him.

"You came back for me," he says.

"I couldn't let you be the only hero," I say, and he coughs when he tries to laugh. "Don't," I say gently. "Justin . . ."

More blood trickles down his neck, this time from his ear. His eyes flutter close and then snap open.

"I'm . . . I'm glad you're here," he forces out, his words so soft it's hard to catch them. "Wouldn't want to do this alone."

"I'm here," I say. "I'm here."

And I am.

Until his very last breath.

29

I don't know how long it takes for them to find me. Oscar and his security guards. Minutes? Hours?

When they do, it's all bright lights and concerned shouting. Guards swarming Justin, and then me, and then people in lab coats, and finally Mr. Masrani, running forward, shouting my name, looking more shaken than I've ever seen him.

It's like everything's on mute. I let them help me up. I'm guided into a jeep, and they drive me back to the training center, where doctors shine more lights in my eyes and ask a million questions and say things like *shock* and *trauma*.

"Where are Tanya and Eric?" I ask.

"Who?" asks the doctor who's stitching the cut on my arm. When did I even get that?

"Tanya and Eric," I repeat. I look around the room. There are at least a dozen people in the training center: people on radios, people on phones. Mr. Masrani is in a corner in deep conversation with a guy who looks like a lawyer. "You need to find them. They're stealing. They let the Raptor out. They didn't mean to, but they did."

The doctor frowns and calls Mr. Masrani over, and I repeat what I said to him.

"I know," he says. "Don't worry. They're being taken care of. I just want you to think about yourself, Claire." He reaches out to clasp my arm and I flinch, unable to stand the contact.

All I can think about is Justin. Justin dying out there. Justin dying because he came back for me.

I don't know what to do with any of this. There's no pros and cons list for this. No way to control this.

This is life. This is death.

This is the cost of progress.

I do what they tell me. I let them stitch me up and shine lights in my eyes and carefully ask me questions I don't really want to answer. I don't let them give me any shots, though. I don't trust them that much.

Finally, they let me go back to the hotel. Beverly is waiting for me in the lobby, and her face is a mask of sorrow.

"Claire," she says, and then she doesn't say anything else. Like she doesn't know how.

I guess that's okay, because I don't know what to say either.

My entire body feels slow and bruised and not like my own. Beverly hovers over me as she takes me up to my room.

"I've informed the other interns," she says softly. "Your friends . . . they wanted to be with you. But I told them you might need some time alone."

Alone. The word echoes inside me. His words echo inside me. *Wouldn't want to do this alone.*

I don't want to do this alone. I can't.

But as the elevator doors open and I see Amanda and Ronnie standing there, tears in their eyes, I realize that I don't have to.

"Claire," Amanda says, hurrying forward. "Oh my God. This is awful. Are you okay?"

I shake my head.

Ronnie sniffs, wiping away tears. "I'm so sorry, Claire," she says. "Justin was such a nice guy."

"Do you want a hug?" Amanda asks, pausing in front of me.

I nod, and she holds me gently, and Ronnie comes forward, taking the other side, and we hold on to each other and it makes it a little better, just for a moment. It's a brief respite, but it's something.

And right now, I'll take anything.

"We can stay with you tonight," Amanda says, keeping her arm around my shoulders as we walk down the hall. "We'll get you cleaned up and you can rest."

"You deserve to rest," Ronnie says, taking the key from Beverly and opening my room.

The girls take over, and I let them. I trust them. Amanda starts the shower for me, and Ronnie puts on some instrumental music I don't recognize. I go where I'm directed, feeling so numb and so tired, all the adrenaline, all the fear, all the fight circling through me like water down a drain. I stand under the spray, letting everything wash off me, knowing that it's not just dirt and blood that's washing away.

It's so much more.

When I finally lie down, Amanda and Ronnie quiet next to me, I start to cry, and I tell myself it'll be the last time.

Two days later, Mr. Masrani asks to see me. He has someone drive me over to his offices, like they're afraid to leave me alone.

What do they think is going to happen? Something even worse?

That bitter twist in my chest just keeps growing as I take the elevator to Mr. Masrani's top-floor office. He's waiting for me inside, but instead of taking a seat at his desk, he sits down in the antique leather chair next to the one I choose, so we're next to each other.

I almost wish he'd sat behind the desk.

"How are you feeling, Claire?" he asks.

"I'm fine," I answer, because what else am I going to say? I'm furious? I'm heartbroken? I'm someone different now, someone who was born anew in that jungle, when blood and survival were my only concerns?

When you narrow yourself down to base instincts, strip everything else away—family, love, loyalty, intelligence—you discover who you truly are.

I'm not sure I like it. But I guess that doesn't matter. This is where . . . and who I am now.

There is before, and there is after. Before Isla Nublar. Before finally feeling like I belong. Before Justin.

And now there is after. It's all grief and anger, this fearful knowledge that I can't control *anything*. I'm falling and there's no ground to hit, no branch to hold on to, no one waiting to catch me.

I have to catch myself.

"I want you to feel like you can come to me," Mr. Masrani says. "Anything you wish for, you will have. If you want to go home, we can arrange that. If you want to stay, we very much want you to."

"His mom," I say, because it's the thing that's been circling in my head. "Where is she? Has she . . . did you . . . ?"

"Ms. Hendricks has been informed," Mr. Masrani says. "This morning, his . . ." He pauses, his lips pressing together tightly. "This morning, he was taken off the island so that she could make arrangements."

So there is nothing left of him in this place anymore. He'll get to go home. To his mom. And then . . .

Then he'll go in the ground. That's not comforting, to think of him returning to the earth, because nature is what helped steal him. A stone marker, a handful of words carved on them, and that will be it.

His mark on the world. No calling. No great, bright life. Just a headstone and grief in the hearts of those who loved him.

The unfairness of it makes my fingers curl, my nails imprinting half circles in the flesh of my palm.

Will they lie, like they lied with Izzie? Everything Justin told me about his mother . . . the idea of them being able to buy or scare her off seems impossible. So did they tell *her* the truth?

What *is* the truth? I don't even know. What were Tanya and Eric thinking, stealing from the park? Why would they do it? Risk their entire futures for . . . what? Money? Did they think they'd get away with it?

The questions spin in my mind like a lopsided top, wobbling more with each one.

"Is there anything I can do for you?" Mr. Masrani asks.

I shake my head automatically, hoping that we're done. That I can go back to my room and hide under my blankets and the world. But of course, it's never that easy.

"Then I have something to ask you," Mr. Masrani says, his voice careful and gentle, like he thinks the wrong word or inflection will make me shatter like glass. "And I am sorry I have to ask it of you, but Tanya Skye refuses to speak to Oscar until she speaks to you. And Eric is following his twin's lead."

I swallow hard, a piercing stab of anger lighting inside me. "You want me to talk to her?"

"I know it is a lot to ask—" Mr. Masrani starts to say.

"No," I say, and I don't even have the grace to be embarrassed at interrupting him. I don't think I have any kind of grace anymore. Not when I feel this—this raw wound that is my heart. Resolve hardens me. "I'd be happy to talk to her."

Mr. Masrani shoots me a skeptical glance—does my voice betray me? But then he nods. "I appreciate that, Claire. We very much need to get to the bottom of this."

I can't help but think there's more than just *this* to get to the bottom of, but my discoveries about Izzie . . . they seem so far away now. Like another life. Another girl.

Can you change in a handful of breaths? Because I am changed. I feel so different, like my very molecular structure has been altered.

I think I know what it is. This is what it feels like to survive.

I survived, and Justin didn't. And I can't quite figure out what I did to deserve that. I want to know why. I want to apply some sort of logic to the situation, run the statistics and probabilities of both of us living versus one of us versus none of us, and then my head spins and my heart hurts and I lose myself in the moments that came before, because I don't know what to do with this new identity settling over me. Should I run from it . . . or embrace it?

"Shall we go now?" I ask, but my voice doesn't sound like mine. So formal. So steely.

It must show on my face too, because Mr. Masrani's head tilts. "If you think you'll be all right."

"I'll be fine," I say again. I wonder whether, if I say it enough—a hundred times? A thousand?—it'll become true. I can only hope. Or wish. Or pray. Maybe all three.

But as I follow Mr. Masrani out of his office and down to a floor that only he can access, I'm not fine. He presses his hand against the scan pad on the elevator doors; the screen flashes *Good afternoon, Mr. Masrani* and they slide open.

I follow him out of the elevator, but unlike the other floors, I don't see any windows here. The lack of natural light makes everything look stark under the fluorescent tubes recessed in the ceiling, the shadows stretching artificially, the dark walls oppressive.

Now I realize where I am: the security floor. The one where they hold people.

Prickles of nerves wash over my shoulders as Mr. Masrani leads me down the hall, where Oscar is waiting, standing outside a locked door, his hands clasped behind him.

His eyebrow arches when he sees us. "Do you think it's wise to cater to her like this?" he asks in a low voice, and at first I think he's talking about me. And then I realize no, he's talking about Tanya.

I clench my fingers, lock my arms, trying so hard to keep from shaking. I want answers. I *need* them. But seeing Tanya again, after that night, after Justin . . .

It's like I'm running and running and I know there's a cliff coming, but I can't stop.

"I've decided this is the best course of action," Mr. Masrani says firmly. He turns to me. "Claire, we'll be on the other side of the frosted glass. We can see through it, but you won't be able to see us."

"Like a one-way mirror," I say. "Just more high-tech."

"Yes," he says. "Everything will be recorded. You'll be in no danger."

"I'm not worried about that," I say.

Mr. Masrani folds his arms across his sleek suit. "Do *I* have to worry about Tanya's well-being?"

I shake my head. "I fight my battles with words," I say. "Not fists."

There's a flash of emotion across his face—almost a smile in his kind eyes. I wonder if he's a liar. Is everyone? I used to not think so, but now I don't know. Everything's topsy-turvy. Will it ever be right again?

"Are you ready?"

I nod. Oscar reaches forward and grabs the doorknob, unlocks it, and swings it open for me.

Tanya's sitting at a table. There's a cot in one corner and a bottle of water on the table in front of her, an empty chair on the other side. She looks up as I enter the room, and even as angry as I am, I still feel a twinge when I see the dark, puffy circles under her eyes. She's been crying. Maybe for hours.

I should be glad. But I'm not.

Taking the chair across the table from her, I sit down. I fold my hands and lean forward, the stainless steel cool on my forearms, because I'm afraid if I don't keep them there, I might go back on my word about not using my fists.

Tanya doesn't say anything, but a tear slips down her cheek as our eyes meet.

"You're really going to make me start this?" I ask. I let out a harsh breath as more tears well up in her eyes. "Okay. Fine. What do you want to tell me?"

"I want to apologize," Tanya says—more like croaks. Her voice sounds like mine did that night as I screamed myself hoarse. Has she done the same, trapped in here like one of the Raptors? "I'm so sorry, Claire. Eric is too. Both of us . . . we never meant for this to happen."

"What did you *expect*?" I bite out. "You're a thief and you're a liar, and I still cannot figure out why you would do this . . . why you would risk it."

There's a long pause. Then Tanya whispers, "I have my reasons."

"If you were actually sorry, you would tell me," I say. "You would tell me what Justin died for. Money? Did someone promise you a job?"

"God, no!" Tanya says, visibly horrified.

"Then *what*?" I ask. "His blood is on your hands." My voice shakes. "He died in my arms. He was scared and he was so hurt and he was trying so hard to hold on and he couldn't and . . ." I can't continue for a moment; it's too much, the memory of it, that shaky smile he tried to summon up right before . . .

"His mom is somewhere in Portland right now, waiting for her son's body to come home," I finally go on, my voice gaining strength. "You . . . *Why* would you do this? I looked up to you. I admired you. I thought we were friends."

"We are," Tanya insists, her eyes swimming with tears. "You *are* my friend, Claire. But I . . . I came here on a mission. I had no choice."

"There is always a choice," I say.

"Not when it comes to my little sister's life," Tanya says, and for the first time, she doesn't look guilty. She looks determined. Sure of herself.

My mind trips over her words, trying to make sense of them. "What are you talking about?"

"After Eric and I got accepted into the program, we were contacted by Mosby Health."

"That pharmaceutical company?"

"Yes. They have a groundbreaking medical trial that's helping kids who have the same heart problems as Victory," Tanya says. "Not just helping them—*healing* them. But it's impossible to get in—there's a waiting list years long. So Mosby made us an offer: spy for them, get as many samples and as much information on the medical technology and treatments as possible, and Victory doesn't just get into the trial, they'll pay for all her future treatment."

It's like shards of ice in my veins are being melted by a terrible, consuming heat. She isn't lying now.

I *understand* now.

This is Tanya and Eric's sister. If I were in the same position, if Karen were sick and someone came to me with the solution? I would pay any price. I would lie to anyone and everyone. I would do *anything*.

I would be the sister she deserves.

Tanya has decided to be the sister Victory deserves, no matter the cost. But I don't think, even in her deepest nightmares, she knew the cost would be this great.

Tears slip down my cheeks, and I want more than anything to reach out and squeeze Tanya's hand, but I don't. Because it hurts too much. Because I feel like my skin's been peeled raw by this lesson in grief I never wanted to learn.

"It was you that night in the training center when I stayed behind to count the tranquilizer darts," I say in a flat voice.

Tanya nods. "I needed at least six vials of the tranquilizer. They gave us a list of things they wanted. The fusion bandages and the tranquilizers were at the top, plus all the security details we could get for future infiltrations."

"Did you give them any of this stuff already?"

Her eyes sweep down—a confirmation, if I've ever seen one.

"I sent the tranquilizer darts out on the first mail day after I got them," Tanya admits. "And I don't regret it," she adds, but her voice is unsteady. "The very next day, Victory started treatment. She's already starting to respond. But now . . ." Her face crumples, emotion brimming over. "I didn't think anyone would ever get hurt. I never thought Justin would die. I'm so sorry, Claire."

"I'm not the one you should be apologizing to," I say. "How about his mom? You should be apologizing to her. You should be apologizing to him, but that can't happen, can it? I'm no one, Tanya. I was just a girl he liked . . . who liked him back."

"You *aren't* no one," Tanya says. "He loved you. And you were my friend. And I'm sorry . . . I *had* to. And now Justin's gone and they'll stop Victory's treatments as soon as they find out we got caught, and . . ." She begins to cry in earnest, and I wish I could join her. I wish I could fix this.

But I've gotten the information that Mr. Masrani needs. And if I stay in this room any longer, I'm going to break. There is no cold, icy core to the old me—or the new one.

"I'm sorry about Victory," I say, getting up. "I have to go."

"Claire—" Tanya starts, but I don't listen.

I just leave.

Mr. Masrani and Oscar are waiting as I close the door behind me. Oscar locks it again, sighing deeply.

"I told you this kind of old-school espionage was going to happen," Oscar says, looking back at Mr. Masrani. "And you were more worried about hacking."

"Yes, Oscar, you were right," Mr. Masrani sighs. "I was wrong. I am man enough to admit it. We will put together a plan to address it, all right?"

"And the twins?" Oscar asks. "Mosby Health?"

"I will be making some phone calls," Mr. Masrani says, and the words are benign, but the way he says them . . . they're anything but. Heads are about to roll. I gulp as he turns his attention to me.

"Thank you, Claire," Mr. Masrani says soberly. "I know how difficult that was."

"Can I go now?" I ask.

He nods. "I will have someone drive you."

I almost protest, but then I decide it's not worth it. I let him call a driver, and they take me back to the hotel. When I go back up to my room, all of Tanya's things have been stripped from it—they're probably going through everything for evidence. It makes the room look strange. One half lived-in, the other half empty.

Sitting on the edge of my bed, I uncurl my fists. My fingers feel cramped and numb, the bones protesting as I straighten them. I lie back and close my eyes, and finally, finally, I sleep.

When I wake, it's morning, and bright light is shining across my bed. I know what I need to do.

So I get up, and I do the thing I should have done all along.

I call my sister.

30

"Sweetie, come home," Karen says, when I'm finally done telling her everything, sobbing through half of it. "No one will be mad at you for leaving. Everyone will understand. I can book you a ticket right now. You can be home by Wednesday. Home with me and Mom and Dad, and you can snuggle Earhart on the couch and not have to worry about any of this anymore."

Trembling, I wipe the tears off my cheeks. It sounds so appealing, what she says, the picture she conjures. I can almost feel my dog's fur under my hands. I want to be there so badly. My eyes are swollen, my nose running and chapped, but Karen's voice, wrapping around me, oh, it is the comfort I need.

The reminder I need.

"I don't know," I say.

"Okay," Karen replies, in that careful way I recognize. It's the voice she uses when she doesn't want to push because it'll make me dig in my heels. She knows me too well.

She knew the old me.

I'm not sure anyone knows me now. Even myself.

I came here to be part of something great. To learn, and to bond with the dinosaurs before anyone else had the chance. I planned to take what I learned and the connections I made and sail off to my bright future. I was going to rise in DC and make my mark and change things for the better. I wanted a better world for the animals who trust us, who love us, who are part of a healthy ecosystem.

But now, what I loved has taken something from me. Not just Justin, though he's the biggest part, the most important part. But I've also lost my hope. My safety. And I don't know what to do about that. Do I kill the instinct inside me, the one that tells me to reach out, to help, to shelter? Will it hurt less if I do?

If I go home, I'll be wrapped in love and hugs and normalcy. I'll spend the rest of the summer helping Dad in his garden, Mom watching from the porch because after she finds out about this, she won't want me out of her sight. I'll go back to school in a few months and . . . then what?

Go to class and pretend everything is like it was?

I don't know if I can do that.

I wipe away more tears, sniffling. "I need some time to think," I say. "That doesn't mean I'm staying," I add.

"But it doesn't mean you're coming home, either," Karen says softly. "Oh, Claire . . ." I can hear just breathing on the line for a moment. I try to picture her, probably standing in her office, counting in her head.

One Mississippi. Two Mississippi. Three Mississippi.

"I'll be okay," I say, because I can't use my canned *I'll be fine* excuse with her. I don't know why *okay* is different, but it is. "I can deal with this."

"You shouldn't have to," Karen says, and the words are so small, but they mean so much. I choke back another sob.

"I'm gonna go rest," I say. "I'm so tired."

"Of course," my sister says. I know that as soon as we get off the phone, she'll call our parents, even though she promises me she won't. Some things override promises. I understand, I guess.

Tomorrow will come, and with it my mom and dad's fear and worry and begging for me to come home. I don't want to have to think that through or prepare for it, so instead, I just say, "I love you. Bye," and I hang up before she can say it back.

I lie on my bed, staring at the ceiling. I try not to think about anything, but my sister's voice fresh in my mind makes me think of Victory, of what Tanya and Eric did for her and what might happen if she's pulled out of that medical trial. She smiled so brightly when I saw her on the video call with Tanya. The thought of another mother losing a child to this mess makes something stir inside me. Something that isn't grief or pain.

It's anger.

Suddenly, fiercely, I cannot be in this room any longer. I keep half expecting Tanya to come bursting in, talking a mile a minute, and I can't stand it. It feels like the walls are pressing in closer with each passing second.

I try to calm down. I count in my head, breathing in and out, deep and slow. But it's not working. So I get up, grab my bag, and take the back way out. The security guard in the lobby who's supposed to follow me never even sees me.

Unfortunately, as I get out of the service elevator, I run straight into Wyatt.

I've barely seen anyone but my friends since that night in the paddock. Seeing Wyatt . . . well, I want to be anywhere else even *more* now.

"Hi," he says.

"I've got to go," I say, walking past him.

"Hey, I'm sorry about Justin," he says, and for a second, I wonder if he's actually going to redeem a sliver of himself. And then he continues, "But now do you see what I mean about this place? The secrets? The conspiracies?" The smugness on his face is enraging.

Red flares along my vision and my fingers curl. I think about everything my dad ever taught me about throwing a punch and then I think about risking it, being *that* person. I want to be. Just for a moment.

And then I breathe and my fists uncurl and I think of Justin's tilted smile, of thistle flowers and wet cement on fingers. Of his trust in me, of what the world lost when it lost him.

When I'm sure my voice won't shake, I say, "You always have to be right, don't you, Wyatt? No matter what."

He smirks. "What can I say. Some people are just winners."

It's really hard not to sneer at that. "Well, I solved the mystery of the phantom intern, not you. So I guess that means I'm the winner."

His gaze shifts from smug to curious. "You're messing with me."

"You think after everything I've been through the last few days, I'd waste my time messing with you?" I ask.

He believes me now, the curiosity burning in his pale eyes and cheeks. "I want to know what you found out," he says.

"Too bad we can't always get what we want," I say. And then I walk away, leaving him behind.

He's not worth any more of my time.

"Claire," Dr. Wu says, and he's the first person who isn't using that soft, cautious tone with me; an unexpected relief. "You're not assigned to me today."

"No," I say.

It's hot this morning. I drove over here with the jeep windows rolled down and I'm sweaty and miserable, but I'm determined. I couldn't save Justin, and that might break me still. But I might be able to finish Izzie's work—and figure out if her theory about the algae is right. If it is, I can save the dinosaurs a lot of pain, and the risky surgery will be unnecessary.

I took the elevator down to the labs and waved to get the attention of one of the techs through the glass. She looked startled to see me, then disappeared down the rows of tables and returned a few minutes later with Dr. Wu in tow.

"Did you want to work?" Dr. Wu asks, and again, there's that sweet, sweet relief of being treated like I'm capable. Like I'm not broken. It's a balm to my soul.

"I actually need your help," I say, pulling the algae specimens from my bag. "I need to test these, and I don't have the equipment."

Dr. Wu's gaze zeroes in on the specimen. "May I?" he asks.

I hand it over, and he holds it up to the light. "Algae?" he asks.

"From the waterfall in the valley," I say. "It grows behind the falls."

"And what do you want to test it for?" he asks.

"Acidity," I say. "I did a basic pH test, but I want more details."

"And I assume you have a good reason for this?" Dr. Wu asks.

"Yes," I say, but I don't tell it to him.

Any other time, I think he would push to know more. But maybe . . . just maybe . . . he just trusts me to have a good reason.

"Very well, come along," he says.

The scientists' eyes are all on me as I follow Dr. Wu past the main labs. Whispers surround us—they think they're being subtle, but they really aren't.

Dr. Wu takes me to his personal office, the one I've never seen, the one where no one is usually allowed. Large pieces of amber are arranged on shelves above his desk, glowing gold in the overhead light.

"Come over here," he directs, and I walk to the small lab table tucked in the corner. It has the basics spread across it: microscope, test tubes, a Bunsen burner. He rummages in the cabinet above for a moment and pulls out a set of slides, a pair of long tweezers, and a stack of petri dishes.

"You kept the algae hydrated?" he asks as he pops open the tube, using the tweezers to grasp a bit of the green plant.

"Yes."

"From the source or from the tap in your hotel room?"

"From the source," I say. "Just in case it was the water causing a reaction."

"The water here has been extensively tested, I assure you," Dr. Wu says. He drops a piece of algae into the petri dish and then adds a few drops from a bottle he plucks from the cabinet. I lean forward eagerly, but nothing happens.

He picks up the dish, tilting it from side to side, and all of a sudden, the clear solution he added turns bright red.

"Hmm." He frowns. "That shouldn't happen. Claire, fetch me that apple on my desk."

I go over and grab it, handing the fruit over. He takes a scalpel and with clean, precise movements carves a thin strip of peel off and drops it into the petri dish with the algae.

My eyes widen as I watch it happen. The apple peel begins to disintegrate before our eyes—whatever's in the algae is eating away at the organic matter.

"Where did you say you collected this specimen?" Dr. Wu asks, crossing his arms as he regards the rapidly disappearing apple peel.

"In the Gyrosphere Valley," I say.

"But what body of water?" he asks. "The lake? The pond?"

"The waterfall," I say.

"The waterfall," he echoes, his eyebrows knitting together. "Of course," he breathes, his extraordinary mind putting it all together. "When we moved the herbivores back into the Gyrosphere Valley at the beginning of this year, we expanded it to include more natural water sources, and while we were at it, we began adding a chemical compound to the bodies of water monthly."

"You're drugging the dinosaurs through their water?" I ask.

He shakes his head. "It was a health measure. It's a compound to help strengthen their bones and teeth," he explains. "So the vets don't have to administer it via needle."

"Like putting fluoride in water systems?" I ask.

He nods. "The compound itself is absolutely harmless. But it seems that when it combines with the deposits left on the stones from the last volcanic eruption, five hundred years ago, and is mixed with the cells of the plant, it creates a highly acidic new strain of algae. Interesting . . . very interesting. I could not have predicted this."

He finally looks up from the petri dish. "How did you come across this?" he asks.

"Some of my friends, we snuck in to swim at the waterfall," I lie. "I got the algae on my leg, and the next morning, my skin was all red and raw. Not like a rash, but more like a burn. It made me curious."

"Well, thank you for bringing it to my attention," Dr. Wu says. "Naturally occurring acidic compounds like this have many possibilities and uses. This will be very interesting to investigate."

I watch him carefully, wondering if he's going to make the connection between the apparently flesh-eating algae and the Brachiosauruses' bronchial infections. But he doesn't seem to make the leap, and I don't fill him in.

I'm starting to put together a plan. I'm going to need all the power I can get to make my next move. And right now, information is power.

"How are you doing, Claire?" Dr. Wu asks, and the question startles me. I thought that he'd be the one person who wouldn't force me to answer that.

But when I look into his eyes, I don't see pity. I see understanding. Recognition.

Dr. Wu was there when it all started with Dr. Hammond. He

was there that night everything went wrong. He must have lost colleagues.

This place has taken from him, too.

But he has stayed. And suddenly, all I can do is ask why. I blurt it out in a rush, and he looks at me for a moment, quietly, with a patience he's never shown before.

"The island takes, yes. But it gives, too. That is nature, Claire. That is life."

"So you just . . . deal?" I ask.

His mouth twitches into a smile. "You move forward. Step by step. Some days it is hard. But the more days you put behind you, the easier it gets. The more you learn about what it is to have a calling. To do work that is *more* than just you or your colleagues."

"And it's worth it? The loss? The consequences?"

"There's always risk in working with predators," Dr. Wu says. "Not only dinosaurs. Think of the big cats that have attacked trainers. They are always only so tame. But part of this island operates like a wildlife refuge. And certain dangers come with that. We take precautions. We have protocols and weaponry and drills. But sometimes mistakes happen. That is what it means to be human."

"These kinds of mistakes shouldn't happen," I say, feeling as small as my voice sounds.

"Mistakes will always happen," Dr. Wu says, his usual bluntness still there, but his eyes are soft as he looks at me with sympathy. "It is what we choose to learn from them that makes a difference."

"I don't know what I've learned from this," I say dully.

"I think you do," Dr. Wu says. "You've learned which kind of mistakes are unacceptable. What you do with that knowledge . . . well, that's up to you, isn't it?"

"What would you do with it?" I ask.

"Knowledge is power, Claire. It's not just a quaint adage. It's the truth. You have been given a unique perspective on this place. So will you take advantage of that? Or will you run from it?"

"You make it sound like it's an opportunity," I say.

"It is," Dr. Wu says. "An opportunity born out of a tragic mistake. Ask yourself, what would it be like to be the person making the decisions? Making sure the mistakes made this first summer you spent here never happen again? You could leave, live a boring little life, or you could stay and be part of something truly revolutionary. And someday, if you work hard enough, you might climb high enough to be in charge of it all."

My breath hitches; the idea soars inside me, and it's like finding a key to something I didn't know was locked up. Me . . . in charge of the park. Making sure everyone is safe. Making sure tragedies like Izzie's and Justin's deaths never happen again. Being in complete control.

It's a dazzling thought . . . a great gift Dr. Wu has given me. Something to distract me, something for me to fix, and a solution— all in one neat ambition.

There's a knock on Dr. Wu's office door, and he calls "Enter!" over my shoulder.

"Dr. Wu, we need you," says the scientist who pokes her head in.

"Can you find your way out?" Dr. Wu asks me.

I nod, still stunned by the prospects he's laid out.

He hesitates before going, his gaze meeting mine. "Be well, Claire," he says. "Think about what I said. It gives and it takes."

The sun's rising high in the sky—it must be close to noon—as I drive back to the hotel. I visit my room briefly, just long enough to grab Izzie's notebook. This time, instead of taking the back way, I make sure the security guard—a woman with hair almost as red as mine—sees me. She follows at a discreet distance as I make my way to the valley, and keeps going past the turnoff that I take. I ignore it, park and get out of the jeep, then climb the bluff overlooking the valley. I sit down on a bench made of a couple of sawhorses and a sturdy board and watch the Triceratops in the distance below. A Brachiosaurus is grazing on the tops of trees, her head bobbing along through the thicket.

I take Izzie's map out from where I've slipped it between the pages of the notebook and tuck it into my pocket for safekeeping. And then I wait.

It doesn't take him long. His spy would've told him that this is where I wandered off to. As I hear the car door shut, I force myself to keep looking out at the valley, instead of toward Mr. Masrani, who strides up the hill, looking at home in the wild, even in his ten-thousand-dollar suit.

"I hope I am not interrupting your solitude," he says, coming to sit next to me.

"I was waiting for you," I say, because there's no point in dancing around this. He's got more power than most people could even dream of. And I'm about to try to meet him step for step, power to power. It scares me. It thrills me. It ignites me, burning away whatever was left of the girl who first stepped on this island, leaving the one who stepped into the jungle, a stunner in her hands and nothing but fight in her heart.

"You want to talk?" Mr. Masrani asks.

"What did you do with the Raptor?" I ask, and it almost surprises me, the question that comes from my lips. It isn't how I wanted to start this conversation.

But looking out at the valley, it's one of the first things that springs into my head.

There's a weighty, unsure silence. "Euthanasia is required if a carnivore is the cause of human harm in my park," he said.

"So she's already gone too." Am I supposed to be glad? Feel like justice was done?

I don't know. The world—the park—is safer because of Mr. Masrani's choice. But there's a voice inside me that tells me it's wrong. That the people who created her shouldn't be ending her.

Maybe some creatures just can't be tamed. Maybe we shouldn't even try.

"It was necessary, Claire," Mr. Masrani said. "And painless."

"I understand," I say, like maybe if I say it, it'll be true.

"I know this all has been very hard on you," he said. "If there's anything I can do . . ."

"You said . . . that night . . . you said you owed me a debt." I wish my voice were stronger. I can't look at him. I keep my focus on the valley below, where Lovelace is rubbing her growing horns against the grass. They're probably itchy.

"I owe you quite the debt," Mr. Masrani says. "You hit the alarm."

"I trapped us in there with the Raptor," I say.

"It was an unselfish act," Mr. Masrani says. "You acted for the well-being of the whole rather than for yourself."

"I made a split-second decision," I say. "I don't know if it was the right one."

"You saved many lives, Claire," Mr. Masrani says. "If the Raptor had gotten loose, the destruction she could've caused . . ." He lets out a long breath, and out of the corner of my eye, I can see him staring at his clasped hands. "I owe you a tremendous debt. You didn't just save lives—human and dinosaur—you saved my park."

And it only cost Justin's life.

I'm determined that Justin's death will be the last.

"The Mosby Health medical trial . . . the one for the kids with heart conditions . . . what's going to happen with it when you take the company down?"

"The FDA will yank their approval for the trial," Mr. Masrani says.

"So all that progress will just stop? The kids won't get the treatments?"

"Without the money or approval to back it, no, they won't." He doesn't sound too concerned.

I don't steel myself, I just say it: "That's what I want. For my favor. I want you to make sure that trial continues. I want Victory Skye to continue her treatment. And I want her education paid for, after the trial saves her. I want to make sure that little girl goes on to live the long, happy, healthy life she deserves."

Mr. Masrani raises an eyebrow. Just one. A delicate arch that's both amused and shocked at my hubris.

"You want me to fund a costly medical trial? And an education? That's a bold ask."

"She deserves a fighting chance," I say.

"And if I say no?" Mr. Masrani asks.

"You won't," I say, and he laughs. "You said I saved your park. So you'll do this for me."

"You are a singular person, Claire," he says. "Many people twice your age would never dare to speak to me so. But you could ask me for anything. Money. Introductions. Power. A job. Instead, you want me to help someone else?"

"No one else is going to die because of this," I answer. "The choices Tanya and Eric made, the choices I made, the sacrifice Justin made . . . they led us here. And an eight-year-old girl's life depends on that treatment. So you're going to make sure she keeps getting it—all those other kids too. Consider it a charitable contribution."

"And you want nothing for yourself?"

"This is for me, too," I say. "This is for my soul. So some part of it can be at peace."

"Very well," he replies. "I will make arrangements by tomorrow."

"Good," I say.

I keep my eyes on the valley, but I can feel him watching me. I've thrown him off balance. Did he expect to find some sobbing girl watching the creatures she used to love but now fears? I refuse to do that. I refuse to be that. I will be strong. For Justin. For Izzie.

For myself.

"There's something else," Mr. Masrani says, almost tentatively.

"More that you want to talk about? The consequences for the twins?"

"You won't get them in trouble," I say. "It would be a bad look for Bright Minds. And you certainly don't want a scandal, do you?"

His eyes widen. "Claire," he says. Is it a warning? A scolding? An indictment?

It doesn't matter.

I smile, and it is not soft and it is not sweet. It is sharp. Honed by what came before all this, shaped by every step I've taken to get here, stained with the bitterness of a loss I still don't know how to bear.

I am not the same as I was. I am different. I am *more* than I was in some ways. Less in others. I'm still learning . . . but I've always been a quick study.

"I figured something out," I tell him. "A solution to a problem no one's been able to fix."

His eyes sparkle. "Really?"

"I know why some of your dinosaurs keep getting bronchial infections," I say, and the sparkle fades from his dark eyes, a sudden shift to seriousness falling over his face as he straightens.

"I'm listening," he say intently.

"It's a recurring, cross-species infection," I say. "I understand why nobody could pin down the cause—it's a hard one."

"But you've figured it out," Mr. Masrani says.

"It's the algae," I say.

"The algae?" he echoes.

"The algae that grows behind the waterfall in Sector C of the

Gyrosphere Valley, if this map is accurate." I pull the copy of Izzie's map out of my bag and hand it to him.

"The chemicals you're using to treat the water have combined with the deposits on the volcanic stones that make up the falls. The resulting algae produces a highly acidic effect when introduced to organic matter," I explain as he unfolds the map and stares at the double X's over the waterfall. "Total freak occurrence. Dr. Wu says it wasn't something that could be predicted. But it's burning holes in the dinosaurs' throats, which lead to infections that disguise the original cause. But only some of them seem to like to eat the algae at all. They need a taste for it, I guess. That's why it was only showing up across the herbivore species, not in every dinosaur. If you change the compound you add to the water or take steps to kill off the algae, it won't be a problem anymore. Dr. Wu has a specimen of it. He'll be able to tell you the best direction to take. You won't have to keep medicating the dinosaurs as a precaution."

"How did you discover this?" Mr. Masrani asks, looking up from the map.

"I didn't," I answer. At any other time, I'd feel scared about what I'm about to say. But everything feels so inconsequential now. I am numb and I am angry . . . and I am *ready*.

His eyebrows draw together. "Then who did?"

"Isobel James."

31

Mr. Masrani's gaze doesn't break from mine as I say Izzie's name. And I see no guilt or terror in his eyes—just sadness. A deep kind of sadness that I recognize, because it's the same thing I saw in my own eyes when I looked in the mirror this morning.

He finally breaks our staring contest to look again at the map in his hand. "This is hers?" he asks.

"I found one of her notebooks," I say, nodding. "Stuffed in the box springs of my bed."

"Ah," he says, understanding flitting across his face. "She must've had your room."

"Who was she?" I ask. "What happened to her here? The same thing that happened to Justin? Are you going to cover up his death like you did hers?"

Mr. Masrani's fingers clench around the map. "You have the wrong idea, Claire," he says, a note of steel in his voice.

"Do I? Because something tells me she didn't die quietly in

her parents' home like her obituary says. Especially because there are stats in her notebook dated the day she apparently died in Boston."

I should quake, standing up to this man. But it's like I'm beyond that, the ruthless outweighing the righteous. Forever? I don't know. I don't think I care. Not now. Not when it makes me feel better. Not when it might help me find out the truth.

"Izzie James was an intern," Mr. Masrani says. "One of the select few chosen personally by me to assist my experts as we began to bring some of the dinosaurs from Isla Sorna to Isla Nublar."

"She figured out the algae problem," I say. "I'm guessing she died before she got a chance to tell anyone."

"Yes," Mr. Masrani says hoarsely.

I wait, half sick, wondering if he'll tell me the truth, and if I can even tell between his truths and his lies.

"Izzie was quite gifted," Mr. Masrani says. "Not just intellectually. She had this way with the dinosaurs. The kind of energy that all great trainers have. It's . . . I don't know. There's not a scientific explanation for it. Perhaps a spiritual one? She had that touch. They trusted her, the Brachiosauruses. She bonded with them faster and in ways I'd never seen in all my . . ." He trails off, that sadness in his eyes deepening. "After her surgery, Olive had a rough time. And then Agnes started getting sick. Everyone was working around the clock. And then . . . the storm hit."

A chill goes through me.

"We had very little warning. It covered the island fast and hard, and we had a very small window during which to evacuate. But Izzie . . . she didn't want to leave them."

My eyes narrow. "Are you telling me that she just refused to evacuate?"

"No." He shakes his head. "She was headed to the evacuation point when an overloaded fuse box started a fire in the paddock Olive was being kept in for recovery. There was no way to open the paddock to free Olive remotely, with the power so unreliable. She would've likely survived the fire with bad burns, but the smoke inhalation . . . with her surgical wounds still healing . . . She would've died. There was no way to give her a fighting chance."

"Izzie went back to free Olive," I say, and Mr. Masrani nods.

"We held the boat for as long as we could, but . . . she never returned. The captain had to leave, and I couldn't fight him. I had to get my people out of there."

He's quiet for a long time, staring out at the valley, rubbing a hand over his mouth. "Her jeep crashed into a fallen tree heading back to the evacuation point," he says finally. "It was fast, the doctors said. She didn't suffer. A small, pitiful consolation to those who knew her."

"You covered it up," I say. "If it really happened like that, why all the secrecy? Why not just say she died in an auto accident?"

"Our insurance would have been revoked for an investigation," Mr. Masrani says. "Work permits would stop being issued. Everything would be put on hold and we would be unable to build the rest of the park until it was resolved. And the PR would have been devastating. I made a choice. Perhaps it was not the best choice, but it was the one I made. I truly believe it's the choice Izzie would've wanted. To protect the dinosaurs she loved. To protect the park that is their home."

But Mr. Masrani failed to protect Izzie.

Just like I failed to save Justin.

My eyes burn as I stare hard at the dirt, knowing if I meet his eyes, tears will slip down my cheeks.

"So you bought everyone off," I say. "Bought their silence."

"It's a remarkably easy thing to do," Mr. Masrani says, and he sounds almost sad, which is kind of a trip.

"Will you buy Justin's mom off?"

Mr. Masrani shakes his head. "Ms. Hendricks has been told the truth about what happened. The contracts that you signed with the company have clauses for this type of incident."

"You learned your lesson from the first interns," I say venomously.

"I understand why you are angry, Claire," Mr. Masrani says.

"Do you also understand that I don't have a good reason to believe you?" I ask.

"Yes," he says simply. How does he do that? Why is it so easy for him to seem so honest, when he's covered up so much? "That is why I am going to make you an offer."

I wait, silent.

"I understand if you want to leave this island and never come back," Mr. Masrani says. "But I would like you to consider staying. Not just for the summer. I'd like you to stay until we open."

He's startled me, I'll admit it. But then my eyes narrow. "So you're bribing me with a job?" I ask.

"No," Mr. Masrani says. "I cannot bring Justin back. I cannot bring Izzie back. They are losses, Claire. Great losses. All I can do now is try to make sure losses like that never happen again. And you . . . you are a smart young woman."

"There are lots of smart young women," I say, looking back at him skeptically. "And none of them pose a risk to your company."

"You're dogged," Mr. Masrani goes on, ignoring my dig. "Figuring out Izzie's hypothesis from her notes must've been difficult. You kept at it. You solved a problem that has been plaguing us since we moved the herbivores back to the valley. That alone would make me want to hire you.

"Stay here, Claire. Work with us. Help me fix problems. Help me make this place as safe and as wondrous as it can possibly be."

I close my eyes, trying to tamp down my warring desires. Part of me just wants to yell at him; most of me flat-out doesn't trust him. But there's another part, one that wants control and power and possibility. . . .

That part is surging forward greedily, like a fire gobbling up the forest floor.

The island gives and the island takes. Science gives and it takes. Progress gives and progress destroys.

If I leave, will it just happen again?

If I stay, can I even hope to make any kind of change?

"You know, this is the first place where I've ever felt like I belonged," I say, looking out over the valley, the dip and roll of the hills. I can hear the lowing of the Triceratops in the distance. "A different kind of home. A whole new level of being understood."

"And now?" Mr. Masrani asks, instead of asking *And after?* because that's a little too cruel.

"And now I feel like I don't know anything," I say. "My place or myself."

"You know why I think you feel so at home here?" Mr. Masrani asks. He doesn't want me to answer. "This is a place of opposites. Human and dinosaur. Predator and prey. Technology and nature. Life . . . and death." He sighs, hanging his head. "There are costs for progress. Some we expect to pay. Others we do not."

"And the cost of this place of opposites is Izzie's and Justin's lives," I say—or maybe I ask . . . I can't even tell anymore. Should it be a question or a statement? Because it's a fact, isn't it? I'd be naive to think it wasn't. I'd be foolish to ask him that.

And I will not be naive or foolish, ever again. I have learned that lesson; Tanya's betrayal is still a fresh scab in my heart.

"Izzie gave her life for Olive's safety," Mr. Masrani says. "It shouldn't have happened. But it did. You may not like the way it was handled, Claire, but she saved Olive. And for someone like Izzie? That is a good death."

I look at him, horror and awe swirling inside me. A good death. Is there such a thing?

"And for Justin . . ."

"Don't you dare tell me that was a good death," I grit out, my voice so low it sounds almost deadly. All I can think about is Justin gasping in my arms, the effort it took to say those last few words before . . . "It was horrible and unfair and it will never, ever be *good* or even okay. It'll never be right, what happened."

"What happened was he sacrificed himself for you," Mr. Masrani says, and there it is. Another fact I don't want to face. "It's a small comfort, I'm sure."

"It's *no* comfort," I choke out. "He died because of me."

"*For* you," Mr. Masrani corrects me gently. His gentleness makes those long-held-back tears slip free. I bite my lip, taking quick and shuddering breaths, wiping the tears away as fast as they come. Gaining control on the next exhale. A there-and-gone moment that he witnesses, that I can't hide, even though I so desperately want to.

"You may not call it a good death," Mr. Masrani says. "It was unfair. It was horribly premature. And the loss is immeasurable. But what Justin did was what any person hopes they are brave enough to do, if that terrible moment ever comes. He protected the person he loved with his life."

I can't say anything to that. Because it's a burden I'm going to live with forever: He died for me. He's gone, and I'm here.

"I hope you consider my offer," Mr. Masrani says. "If you want to go home, I can have a private plane waiting for you within the hour. But I very much hope you will stay. That you'll be here, working with us, when the park opens."

He turns and leaves me looking down into the valley, watching Lovelace and her friends.

I don't know if I believe him about Izzie. I think about that little scrap of paper tucked in the notebook pocket. *Watch your back.*

It wasn't her handwriting. What does it mean? Was someone trying to warn her? Threaten her? Does it have something to do with her car accident? Did someone stop her from getting to the evacuation point in time, or was it just a tragic accident?

There were so many people on the island—if someone had targeted Izzie, Mr. Masrani might not realize that her accident wasn't an accident at all. That, maybe, is the scariest thought. That the man in charge isn't diabolical—he just doesn't have total control, and yet he thinks he does.

You'll never find out if you leave.

It's a tiny voice inside me, but it's there. Lurking. Piping up at the most annoying moment.

Do I owe it to her to find out for sure? I can't do anything for Justin. But for Izzie . . .

Maybe I can do some good to outweigh the bad that has happened.

The sun's setting behind the valley now, and I watch the Triceratops gather and head toward the watering hole for dinner. I get up myself and walk down the bluff, tilting my face to the fading sun.

If I stay, I've made a decision: I will not allow anyone or anything to take from me again. Not the wildness that permeates every inch of this place. Not the creatures that are more awe-inspiring than anything in existence. And not the people in power, who make choices that play with dinosaur and human alike.

Instead, *I* will be doing the taking. Of power. Of influence. Of control.

The ground flattens out as I get to the bottom of the bluff. I pass the gate, heading toward my jeep, when *bang*.

I jump, my arms flying over my head, but then I realize it's not an attack.

It's Pearl. Pearl and her hexagon Gyrosphere. She knocks it against the gate with her nose a second time, burbling when it makes the crashing noise she likes so much.

Now she bumps it with her foot, sauntering forward to hang her neck over the fence, waggling her head at me, like she wants a treat for playing so well.

And my resolve ... oh, it was so strong before. No more giving—only taking. But Pearl's looking at me like she remembers me from the first time I nudged the Gyrosphere toward her, like she knows I gave her a gift, and it's so hard to turn away.

It's impossible not to move forward.

She bends her neck down to me until her head is almost level with mine.

I reach out, scared and grieving, and as her eyes meet mine and my fingers stroke the rough skin of her snout, I feel it—the thing I thought I'd lost.

That spark. That wonder. That miracle. It's small, but it's steady.

It's her and it's me and there's nothing else. Dinosaur and human, both reaching across the eons, desperate for some kind of connection.

"Hey, funny girl."

ACKNOWLEDGMENTS

A book always takes a village, or in this case, a very clever Raptor pack. Writing this book was a dream come true, and I owe many people thanks for their hard work, attention, and care.

My most grateful thanks must go to:

My agent, Jim McCarthy, who had no idea what a gift he was giving me with this project when he asked, "Hey, do you write sci-fi?" Thank you for always seeing the potential in me.

This book's inimitable editor, Rachel Poloski, who encouraged me every step of the way and helped me add such richness to the characters.

The wonderful Kurt Estes, whose extensive insight and spot-on instincts were so valuable to this entire process.

The whole team at Universal, for all their notes and support.

Bryce Dallas Howard, who embodies Claire on-screen with power, grace, and smarts and whose performance was hugely inspirational in creating teen Claire's voice and viewpoint.

The cover artist, Shane Rebenschied, and the cover designer, Megan McLaughlin, whose combined talents created an absolutely perfect cover.

Most grateful thanks to the eagle eyes of copy editors Colleen Fellingham and Alison Kolani.

Elizabeth May, who always pushes me to be my best and boldest.

My mother, Laurie, whose long game of naming me after a scientist finally paid off with this book and the Tesla/Edison joke.

Thank you for indulging my preteen archaeology obsession so much.

My dear friends who put up with me being very mysterious about this project for several months before I could tell anyone: Charlee Hoffman, Paul Krueger, Dahlia Adler, Sharon Morse, Jess Capelle, Kelly Edgeington Stultz, EK Johnston.

Special thanks to the friends who I grew up with in various fandoms, especially Franny Gaede and Mercedes Marks. Sometimes, all the fanfic you wrote as a teenager *does* pay off.

My husband, who luckily finds me charming when I run around our homestead pretending to be a dinosaur. I love you and thank you for building endless fires as I wrote this book through the winter.

And finally, so many thanks to the Jurassic fandom and all the fans of Claire Dearing, who love her just as much as I do, and whose enthusiasm had a hand in this book's creation.